PRAISE FOR
## Steven L. Kent

## THE CLONE ELITE

"If you enjoy military science fiction, then this is the book for you . . . fast paced and hard-hitting. Punches, bullets, and nuclear bombs are not held back. The characters face hard choices and don't regret them after they are made."     —*SFRevu*

## THE CLONE ALLIANCE

"Offers up stunning battle sequences, intriguing moral quandaries, and plenty of unexpected revelations . . . [a] fast-paced military SF book with plenty of well-scripted action and adventure, [and] a sympathetic narrator."     —*SF Site*

## ROGUE CLONE

"Exciting space battles [and] haunting, quiet moments after war has taken its toll . . . Military SF fans looking for stories that combine mystery, action, espionage, politics, and some thoughtful doses of humanism in exploring their not entirely human characters would do well to add Steven L. Kent to their reading lists."     —SF Reviews.net

## THE CLONE REPUBLIC

"A solid debut. Harris is an honest, engaging protagonist and thoughtful narrator, and Kent's clean, transparent prose fits well with both the main character and the story's themes . . . Kent is a skillful storyteller, and the book entertains throughout."     —*Sci Fi Weekly*

"The first sentence gets you immediately . . . From there, the action begins fast and furious, with dark musings, lavish battle scenes, and complex characterizations . . . *The Clone Republic* feature[s] taut writing and a truly imaginative plot full of introspection and philosophizing." —*The Village Voice*

"A character-driven epic that understands that the best war stories are really antiwar stories . . . a smartly conceived adventure."     —SF Reviews.net

# THE CLONE EMPIRE

## STEVEN L. KENT

ACE BOOKS, NEW YORK

**THE BERKLEY PUBLISHING GROUP**
**Published by the Penguin Group**
**Penguin Group (USA) Inc.**
**375 Hudson Street, New York, New York 10014, USA**
Penguin Group (Canada), 90 Eglinton Avenue East, Suite 700, Toronto, Ontario M4P 2Y3, Canada
(a division of Pearson Penguin Canada Inc.)
Penguin Books Ltd., 80 Strand, London WC2R 0RL, England
Penguin Group Ireland, 25 St. Stephen's Green, Dublin 2, Ireland (a division of Penguin Books Ltd.)
Penguin Group (Australia), 250 Camberwell Road, Camberwell, Victoria 3124, Australia
(a division of Pearson Australia Group Pty. Ltd.)
Penguin Books India Pvt. Ltd., 11 Community Centre, Panchsheel Park, New Delhi—110 017, India
Penguin Group (NZ), 67 Apollo Drive, Rosedale, North Shore 0632, New Zealand
(a division of Pearson New Zealand Ltd.)
Penguin Books (South Africa) (Pty.) Ltd., 24 Sturdee Avenue, Rosebank, Johannesburg 2196,
South Africa

Penguin Books Ltd., Registered Offices: 80 Strand, London WC2R 0RL, England

This is a work of fiction. Names, characters, places, and incidents either are the product of the author's imagination or are used fictitiously, and any resemblance to actual persons, living or dead, business establishments, events, or locales is entirely coincidental. The publisher does not have any control over and does not assume any responsibility for author or third-party websites or their content.

THE CLONE EMPIRE

An Ace Book / published by arrangement with the author

PRINTING HISTORY
Ace mass-market edition / November 2010

Copyright © 2010 by Steven L. Kent.
Cover art by Christian McGrath.
Cover design by Judith Lagerman.
Interior text design by Kristin del Rosario.

ISBN: 978-0-441-01958-8

ACE
Ace Books are published by The Berkley Publishing Group,
a division of Penguin Group (USA) Inc.,
375 Hudson Street, New York, New York 10014.
ACE and the "A" design are trademarks of Penguin Group (USA) Inc.

PRINTED IN THE UNITED STATES OF AMERICA

10  9  8  7  6  5  4  3  2  1

*This book is dedicated to Steve Baxter,*
*who is an excellent friend.*

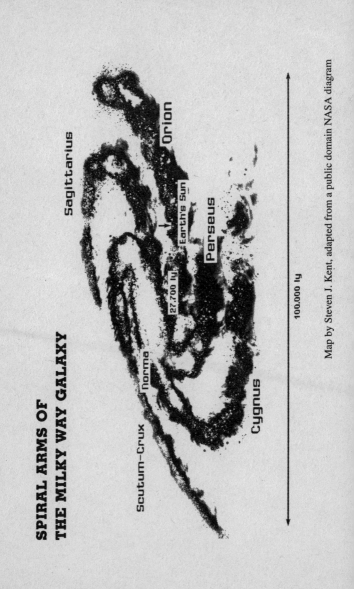

## SPIRAL ARMS OF
## THE MILKY WAY GALAXY

Sagittarius

Orion

Earth's Sun

27,700 ly

Perseus

Scutum–Crux

Norma

Cygnus

100,000 ly

Map by Steven J. Kent, adapted from a public domain NASA diagram

# SIX EVENTS THAT SHAPED HISTORY:
## A Unified Authority Time Line

### 2010 TO 2018
### DECLINE OF THE U.S. ECONOMY

Following the examples of Chevrolet, Oracle, IBM, and ConAgra Foods, Microsoft moves its headquarters from the United States to Shanghai. Referring to their company as a "global corporation," Microsoft executives remain committed to U.S. prosperity, but with its burgeoning economy, China has become the company's most important market.

Even with Toyota and Hyundai increasing their manufacturing activities in the United States—spurred on by the favorable cheap labor conditions—the U.S. economy becomes dependent on the shipping of raw materials and farm goods.

Bottoming out as the world's twelfth largest economy behind China, Korea, India, Cuba, the European Economic Community, Brazil, Mexico, Canada, Japan, South Africa, Israel, and Unincorporated France, the United States government focuses on maintaining its position as the world's last military superpower.

### JANUARY 3, 2026
### INTRODUCTION OF BROADCAST PHYSICS

Armadillo Aerospace announces the discovery of broadcast physics, a new technology capable of translating matter into data waves that can be transmitted to any location instantaneously. This opens the way for pangalactic exploration without time dilation or the dangers of light-speed travel.

The United States creates the first-ever fleet of self-broadcasting ships, a scientific fleet designed to locate planets for colonization. When initial scouting reports suggest that the rest of the galaxy is uninhabited, politicians fire up public sentiment with talk about "manifest destiny" and spreading humanity across space.

The discovery of broadcast physics leads to the creation of the Broadcast Network—a galactic superhighway consisting of satellites that send and receive ships across the galaxy. The Broadcast Network ushers in the age of galactic expansion.

### JULY 4, 2110
### RUSSIA AND KOREA SIGN A PACT
### WITH THE UNITED STATES

With the growth of its space-based economy, the United States reclaims its spot as the wealthiest nation on Earth. Russia and Korea become the first nations to sign the IGTA (Intergalactic Trade Accord), a treaty opening the way for other nations to become self-governing American territories and enjoy full partnership in the space-based economy.

In an effort to create a competing alliance, France unveils its Cousteau Oceanic Exploration program and announces plans to create undersea colonies. Only Tahiti signs on.

After the other nations of the European Economic Union, Japan, and all of Africa become members of the IGTA, France discontinues its undersea colonization and joins the IGTA. Several nations, most notably China and Afghanistan, refuse to sign, leading to a minor world war in which the final holdouts are coerced into signing the treaty.

More than 80 percent of the world's population is eventually sent to establish colonies throughout the galaxy.

### JULY 4, 2250
### TRANSMOGRIFICATION OF THE UNITED STATES

With most of its citizens living off Earth, the IGTA is renamed "The Unified Authority" and restructured to serve as a government rather than an economic union.

The government of the Unified Authority bases its rule on a new manifesto that merges principles from the U.S. Constitution with concepts from Plato's *Republic*. In accordance with Plato's ideals, society is broken into three strata—citizenry, defense, and governance.

With forty self-sustaining colonies across the galaxy, Earth becomes the political center of a new republic. The eastern seaboard of the former United States develops into an ever-growing capital city populated by the political class, families appointed to run the government in perpetuity.

Earth also becomes home to the military class. After some experimentation, the Unified Authority adopts an all-clone conscription model to fulfill its growing need for soldiers. Clone farms euphemistically known as "orphanages" are established around Earth. These orphanages produce more than a million cloned recruits per year.

The military does not commission clone officers. The officer corps is drafted from the ruling class. When the children of politicians are drummed out of school or deemed unsuitable for politics, they are sent to officer-candidate school in Australia.

### 2452 TO 2512
### UPRISING IN THE GALACTIC EYE

On October 29, 2452, a date later known as "the new Black Tuesday," a fleet of scientific exploration ships vanishes in the "galactic eye" region of the Norma Arm.

Fearing an alien attack, the U.A. Senate calls for the creation of the Galactic Central Fleet, a self-broadcasting armada. Work on the Galactic Central Fleet is completed in 2455. The newly christened fleet travels to the Inner Curve, where it vanishes as well.

Having authorized the development of a top secret line of cloned soldiers called "Liberators," the Linear Committee—the executive branch of the U.A. government—approves sending an invasion force into the Galactic Eye to attack all hostile threats. The Liberators discover a human colony led by Morgan Atkins, a powerful senator who disappeared with the Galactic Central Fleet. The Liberators overthrow the colony, but Atkins and many of his followers escape in G.C. Fleet ships.

Over the next fifty years, a religious cult known as the Morgan Atkins Believers—"Mogats"—spreads across the 180 colonized planets, preaching independence from the Unified Authority government.

Spurred on by the growing Morgan Atkins movement, four of the six galactic arms declare independence from Unified Authority governance in 2510. Two years later, on March

28, the combined forces of the Confederate Arms Treaty Organization and the Morgan Atkins Believers defeat the Earth Fleet and destroy the Broadcast Network, effectively cutting the Earth government off from its loyal colonies and Navy.

Believing they have crippled the Unified Authority, the Mogats turn on their Confederate Arms allies and attempt to take control of the renovated G.C. Fleet. The Confederates escape with fifty self-broadcasting ships and join forces with the Unified Authority, leaving the Mogats with a fleet of over four hundred self-broadcasting ships, the most powerful attack force in the galaxy.

The Unified Authority and the Confederate Arms end the war by attacking the Mogat home world, leaving no survivors on the planet.

## 2514 TO 2515
## AVATARI INVASION

In 2514, an alien force enters the outer region of the Scutum-Crux Arm, conquering U.A. colonies. As they attack, the aliens wrap their "ion curtain" around the outer atmosphere of the planet, creating a barrier cutting off escape and communications.

In a matter of two years, the aliens spread throughout the galaxy, occupying only planets deemed habitable by U.A. scientists. The Unified Authority loses 178 of its 180 populated planets before making a final stand on New Copenhagen.

During this battle, U.A. scientists unravel the secrets of the aliens' tachyon-based technology, enabling U.A. Marines to win the war. In the aftermath of the invasion, the Unified Authority sends the four self-broadcasting ships of the Japanese Fleet along with twelve thousand Navy SEAL clones to locate and destroy the Avatari home world.

When the Unified Authority Congress holds hearings investigating the war, military leaders blame their losses on lack of discipline in the enlisted ranks. Synthetic conscription is abolished, and all remaining clones are transferred to man the outer fleets—fleets that were stranded in deep space when the Mogats destroyed the Broadcast Network. The Navy plans to use these fleets as live targets in a series of war games designed to test newer and more powerful ships.

# PROLOGUE

Earthdate: July 16, A.D. 2517
Location: Terraneau
Galactic Position: Scutum-Crux Arm

"You can't possibly be serious about attacking Earth."

"Why not?" I asked.

The rising sun might have been a molten copper penny and the sky around it made of gold. The financial district of Norristown no longer bristled with business. War had turned the city into a wasteland. Only three skyscrapers remained in what once had been the most significant financial district on this side of the galaxy. Surrounded by debris and desolation, the buildings looked like gigantic gravestones.

Colonel Philo Hollingsworth and I stood on a hill overlooking the ruins of what once had been the government center for an entire galactic arm . . . the Scutum-Crux Arm. His laugh was bitter and derisive. Hate resonated in that laugh.

"You are eighty thousand light-years from Earth, you only have twenty-two hundred Marines under your command, and every last specking one of them blames you for starting the war in the first place. No, let's just be honest, they hate you."

"My engineers don't hate me," I said. I had a thousand-man corps of naval engineers on the planet along with my Marines.

"Don't tell me you think they like you," Hollingsworth said.

"I didn't mean they liked me. I just wanted to keep our census accurate," I said.

Hollingsworth went back to counting the reasons I could

not attack Earth. "You don't even have any ships left in your fleet. Face it, Harris, the war is over. You lost."

I saw no reason to argue the facts: the distance to Earth; the number of men I had under my command; how much they despised me.

"I might have some ships left," I said.

Hollingsworth rolled his eyes and said nothing. In the two months since the Earth Fleet had attacked Terraneau, there had been no word from our fleet. Dozens of broken ships floated in the space outside our atmosphere, but they only accounted for a portion of the missing four hundred ships that once made up the Scutum-Crux Fleet.

Morning light spread slowly over the city as the cranes moved into place. Today, they would excavate the misshapen mound that had once been the Treasury building.

Three cranes struggled as they pulled slabs and columns from the wreckage, the ground below them visibly shifting under the stress. The arm of one of the cranes bent and shook like a rod bringing in a big fish.

Keeping an eye on that crane, I walked over to Lieutenant Scott Mars, my chief engineer, and asked, "Are you sure your cranes can handle that much weight?" I had to shout for him to hear me above the din of his equipment.

Mars shrugged, and answered, "It's fine, sir."

"That column isn't too heavy?" I asked.

He gave me a sardonic smile, and said, "Look, General, you worry about the tanks, and I'll take care of the cranes and bulldozers."

He did not come across as hostile, but that did not mean he respected me. Since landing on Terraneau, Scott Mars had adopted an evangelical lifestyle. He testified about being "born again," a claim that the rest of us did not take seriously. He was a clone, just like the rest of us. He could not be born again because he wasn't really born the first time.

Mars was universally perky and ready to please, and we got used to him saying "praise this" and "praise that." Everybody liked Mars. The hallelujah chorus was just part of having him around.

I was glad to have a friend, even if he wasn't so much a friend as a nonhostile acquaintance. In his version of the gospel, smiling at people drew him closer to God. What was the harm in that?

One of the cranes struggled to pull a thirty-foot section of wall out of the ground. The wreckage looked heavier than the crane, but that did not seem to make a difference. After a short fight, the wall broke free, and the crane pulled it out like a fisherman reeling in a trophy bass.

Seeing that Lieutenant Mars had everything under control, I returned to Hollingsworth to restart our conversation. "There are fifteen fighter carriers floating up there. What happened to the other twenty-one?" The Scutum-Crux Fleet had had thirty-six fighter carriers when the Earth Fleet attacked. Searching with telescopes and radars, we had located twelve of our carriers. We located three more when we started searching the area with transports.

"Even if they got away, they wouldn't have gotten very far," Hollingsworth said. "Not with those new U.A. ships chasing after them."

He was right. The ships that the Unified Authority sent were stronger, faster, and better shielded than our ships.

Hollingsworth continued his assault. "Just for the sake of argument, let's say you have twenty-one carriers waiting for you. What are you going to do with them? The Unifieds smashed us when we had thirty-six carriers. They'll just smash us again."

"They didn't smash us down here," I said. It was a weak argument, but it was true. "We beat their Marines."

As far as the Unified Authority was concerned, the battle had been nothing more than a war game, but not all of the game went as expected. They sent three thousand Marines in shielded armor to attack my five thousand men in old-fashioned unshielded armor. We had the numbers, they had the impenetrable armor that rendered our bullets and particle beams useless. We won by way of a battlefield miracle.

Of course, what one side labels a miracle, the other sees as murder.

"You dropped a building on them," Hollingsworth said. "You buried them. Next time, they won't be so quick to chase you into an underground garage."

Below us, two of the cranes worked in tandem to hoist a

long stretch of outer wall from the ruins of that underground garage. With cables pulling at it from two different directions, the concrete crumbled like a giant cracker, and the cranes fished out nothing but shreds.

"It doesn't look stable," Hollingsworth said.

"You better be grateful for that. We buried three thousand Unified Authority Marines down there; if it were stable, they might have dug themselves out," I said.

Mars jogged over to join us. "We've dug an entrance, sir," he said, his fingers covering the microphone on his headset. "I've got a team ready. Is there anything you want to tell them before I send them in?"

I shook my head.

Down along the wreckage, five men in soft-shelled armor ventured into the gap that the cranes had opened.

"If you don't mind my asking, sir, do we really need to do this?" Mars asked, his new born-again values leaving him uncomfortable about excavating graves.

"I want a better look at their armor," I said.

"We're pulling them out to look at their armor?"

"You worry about the engineering, I'll worry about the ethics," I said.

"The general wants to examine their armor for weaknesses," Hollingsworth volunteered.

"Why does he care about that?" asked Mars

"He wants to know how to get through their armor before his return engagement," Hollingsworth answered. He and Mars carried on their conversation around me as if I weren't there.

"Are they coming back?" Mars asked.

"Nope; Harris wants to invade Earth," Hollingsworth said.

For a moment, Mars looked stunned, then he laughed. "You're joking, right?"

I started to say something, but Lieutenant Mars's expression suddenly shifted. Something he'd heard over his headset caught his attention. He took a step toward the wreckage, then turned to me, and said, "They've got one, sir."

"Are they certain it's one of theirs?" I asked. We had lost nearly as many men as the Unified Authority in that battle.

Most of ours were killed on the top level of the underground garage. Most of theirs were killed on the lower levels. They found this stiff so quickly, I thought it might be one of ours.

"It's a U.A. Marine," Mars confirmed.

"Are his shields still up?" I asked. Six weeks had passed since we brought the garage down on the bastards; the power in their suits should have gone out long ago.

"No, sir. The suit's gone dark."

"Is the armor in one piece?" I asked.

Mars relayed the question, then told me, "Good as new."

*Of course it was good as new. What's a little thing like a twenty-thousand-ton avalanche to a suit of shielded armor?* I asked myself. "Let's have a look at it."

A few minutes later, two engineers came out of the ground, carrying the dead Marine. They brought the body over so I could examine it. Without the glowing skin of its shields, the dead man's armor looked very much like the combat armor my men wore. It was made of the same dark green alloy. Quarter-inch ridges traced seams along the shoulders, sleeves, legs, and sides of the helmet. The shielding must have been transmitted from those ridges.

Looking down at the body, I felt no regret for killing this man. The war was of their making, not mine. I was only twenty-eight years old, but I'd spent the last ten years of my life running from one battlefield to the next. Any compassion I had ever felt for the dead had long since burned out of me.

"The visor's cracked," I told Mars.

A hairline break ran vertically across the glass face of the visor. The crack was thin and shallow, so minor you might not even be able to trace it with a sharpened pencil.

"Where?" Mars asked as he bent down for a closer look. "That? That's not a crack, it's a scratch."

"I told you, perfect condition," I said.

"As long as the visor works—"

"You have your orders," I said.

"We're getting four more sets," he argued.

"Five more suits," I corrected him. If I'd left it at four, he might have taken it as tacit permission to keep this suit. "And those five suits had better be perfect, or I'll send them back."

"Five suits in perfect condition, aye," Lieutenant Mars

said, making no effort to hide his frustration. He relayed my orders down to his men, whispering something extra into his microphone so I would not hear.

Finding armor in working condition might take time. Once the shielding turned off, the armor would be crushed under the weight of rocks and concrete; but the garage was big and cavernous. With three thousand Unified Authority Marines buried in its depths, there had to be five undestroyed suits down there.

Nearly an hour passed before the engineers returned with their next specimen. I examined the armor. There was no dust on the seals around the shoulder plates. One of Mars's engineers had taken a helmet from one cadaver and added it to the body armor of another. Clever. I pretended not to notice the switch.

"Send it to the labs," I told Mars.

"Aye, aye, sir," he said, trying to hide a smile. He must have known about the switch and thought he had pulled one over on me.

As his commanding officer, I could not allow him to think he was smarter than me, so I added, "And, Lieutenant, tell your men to stop with the mix-and-match armor. Next time, I'll send it back."

"Yes, sir," he said.

Mars called down my orders as his men loaded the body onto a jeep and left for Fort Sebastian. As I watched the jeep bounce away, Colonel Hollingsworth said, "Looks like we've got us an audience."

"Damn." I sighed.

A small crowd of locals had gathered around the chain-link fence that we'd built around the area as a perimeter. Leaning on the fence and watching us, they reminded me of inmates staring out of a prison yard.

"Maybe you should have a word with them," Hollingsworth suggested.

"Don't tell them that you are planning to invade Earth," Mars added. "You wouldn't want to upset them."

"Just get me the specking armor," I muttered to Mars as I headed for the gate, hating what would come next. The locals had caught me with my hand in the cookie jar. By mutual agreement, the underground garage had become a designated no-man's-land forbidden to both us and the civilian government. Along with Unified Authority Marines, we had buried an armory filled with guns, grenades, mines, vehicles, and bombs when we blew up the garage. The locals didn't want us visiting the armory, and we didn't want them raiding it, either.

Throughout the morning, low clouds had floated in from the east, blocking out the sun and threatening to rain. Now the first drops of rain fell, splattering on shards of concrete, turning their gray surface to taupe.

I walked to the fence where the locals waited. Rain fell on them, but they did not seem to care.

"This is a flagrant violation of our agreement," the Right Reverend Colonel Ellery Doctorow said as I approached. He stood a few inches from the chain link, his arms folded across his chest, an angry scowl on his face.

"I'm not here for weapons," I explained.

"I don't care why you are here," Doctorow said. "Pull your men out and leave immediately."

Doctorow was at least halfway through his sixties. The highest-ranking chaplain in the Unified Authority Army in his former life, he had come to Terraneau five years ago as the Army prepared to fight off an alien invasion. After the aliens massacred the fighting men, Doctorow shrugged off both his uniform and his cassock and became a civilian leader. He hated the military, and he viewed God as some kind of cosmic voyeur instead of a supreme being.

"We're exhuming bodies, not weapons," I explained. "You can hang around and observe if you like. You won't see any weapons come out of that hole, just bodies and armor."

Lieutenant Mars trotted over to tell me that his men had located a suitable stiff.

"How's his armor?" I asked.

Mars repeated my question into his microphone, pressed his finger against his earpiece, then said, "The legs were crushed. The helmet is perfect."

Under different circumstances I would have given the order to throw it back, but I did not know how long I could hold Doctorow and his civilian posse at bay.

"Take the legs from the first guy you found, the one with the cracked visor," I said.

"Praise Jesus, God is good," Mars told the men in the hole. "He says we can keep it."

"Why are you digging up dead Marines?" Doctorow asked.

I started to answer, but Lieutenant Mars spoke first. "He's preparing for the invasion."

"Is the Earth Fleet coming back?" asked Doctorow.

"It's the other way around. He's planning on invading them," Mars said, the glimmer in his eyes revealing the lightness with which he regarded my ambition.

"That's not funny," Doctorow said.

"He's not joking," I said.

"You're planning to invade Earth?" Doctorow asked.

When I nodded, he smiled, and said, "Well, if that's the case, Harris, dig away. If it gets you off my planet, I'm all for it."

# PART I

# SECRETS AND COMBINATIONS

# CHAPTER
# ONE

Once Lieutenant Mars's engineers broke through to the third level of the underground garage, the work went quickly. They found hundreds of bodies, many of which were as neatly preserved as eggs in a carton. The engineers filled their body quota and radioed Mars to say they had found guns, jeeps, and ammunition.

"They've found a mother lode of munitions," Mars told me.

"Leave it," I said.

"Are you sure you want to do that, sir?" Mars asked.

I looked back at Ellery Doctorow and his militia lined up along the fence. The bastards didn't trust us, and I didn't blame them. "Leave it," I repeated. "I gave them my word."

Cheerful as ever, Mars said, "Yes, sir," and told his men to exit the underground garage and seal it behind them. "We don't want to tempt the locals," he said. The engineers said something, I could not hear what, and he said, "It's the golden rule. Yeah . . . You know, 'Arm thy neighbor as thyself.' We don't get the weapons, and neither do they."

Mars must have felt my eyes upon him. He looked at me and flashed an innocent smile.

It took the engineers about an hour to carry the last of the bodies out, set the charges, and clear the pit. They made sure no one lingered too close to the hole, then they sealed the tunnels they had dug, sending a thirty-foot plume of dust into the air.

Seeing that our work was done and that we had not exhumed any weapons, Doctorow and his militia returned to their homes.

Hollingsworth joined Mars and me as we watched Doctorow and company load into their trucks and cars. "Specking anti-synthetic pricks," Hollingsworth muttered. Colonel Philo Hollingsworth was a clone. Scott Mars was a clone. Every man under my command was cloned, and none of them knew it. They were programmed to think they were natural-born.

"He's not so bad," I told Hollingsworth. "Now his wife . . ."

Sarah Doctorow was an antisynthetic bitch; but Doctorow didn't share her prejudice. She saw no difference between clones and robots. He, on the other hand, did not care whether people came from a fallopian tube or a test tube.

Mars excused himself and went to help his engineers load the stiffs onto their truck. A few minutes later, Hollingsworth and I climbed into our jeep and headed back to Fort Sebastian, locking the security fence behind us. We did not electrify the fence, but we placed sensors around it to make sure no one climbed it or cut their way through.

"So what do you think they will call the war?" I asked Hollingsworth, as we pulled onto the street leading through the ruins of Norristown.

"Who are you talking about?" Hollingsworth asked.

"You know, a hundred years from now. What do you think people will call the war?"

"I don't think anyone will remember it ever happened," he said.

"Sure they will. Maybe they'll call it a revolutionary war," I said. "Isn't it a revolutionary war when you fight for independence?"

That was an exaggeration. In truth, we were already quasi-independent. Having decided to eliminate its clone military program, the Pentagon marooned us on its fifteen abandoned fleets. The goal was to use us for military exercises as they developed newer and more powerful ships.

"It wasn't a revolution," Hollingsworth said. "It's not a revolution unless you win."

"Well, okay, maybe we didn't win, but neither did they. I don't see any Unified Authority guard towers. Do you?" I asked, ignoring the obvious.

"We got crushed. We didn't win shit. They crushed us," Hollingsworth said, stating the obvious, which I had tried to ignore.

"Okay, so we didn't exactly win, but we didn't totally lose.

Maybe that makes it a civil war," I said. "Like the American Civil War."

Hollingsworth shook his head. "It wasn't a civil war, either, sir. It wasn't important enough to be a civil war. I bet the local media on Earth didn't even report the battle."

"They reported it. They lost a decorated war hero, they didn't have any choice," I said. "People notice when someone like Ted Mooreland goes missing." Mooreland was a general in the Unified Authority Marines. He had led the ground assault that ended in the underground garage.

"They'll just announce that he died in a training exercise," Hollingsworth said.

"You're probably right," I agreed.

"Damn right they'll say that," Hollingsworth went on. "That's all this was to them, just a training exercise. It wasn't a civil war, and it sure as hell wasn't a revolutionary war."

"Maybe it was a coup," I said, feeling a little brighter now that I had found a word to describe our insignificant revolt.

Hollingsworth shook his head, and said, "Don't flatter yourself. A year from now, no one remembers it."

"Oh, they'll remember it," I said. "The Unified Authority lost twenty-three ships. They lost three fighter carriers, five battleships, and three thousand Marines. Damn straight they'll remember it. Anytime the Navy loses three fighter carriers, it's a big deal."

Hollingsworth thought about this and gave ground. "A big battle, but a minor war."

"But it was a war," I said.

"Okay, so it was a war, and the war is over, sir. Unless they come back to finish us, your war is dead."

We drove across the newly restored viaduct that led along the southern outskirts of Norristown. Like seedlings springing up in the wake of a volcanic eruption, new buildings had begun to appear around the city.

"Maybe you're right," I said. "Only time will tell."

"Maybe I'm right about what?" Hollingsworth asked, sounding surprised.

"About the war being on hold," I said.

"I didn't say it was on hold; I said it was dead."

I could not fault Hollingsworth for his pessimistic attitude.

Based on the information he had at hand, our chances of winning a war with the Unified Authority seemed bleak. I had more information than he did, but now was not the time to discuss it. I needed to get back to Fort Sebastian to clean up. I had dinner plans that night, and I wanted to look my best.

# CHAPTER
# TWO

Ava, my significant other/girlfriend, and I ate dinner with Ellery Doctorow and his wife every month. It was never a friendly occasion. Doctorow considered me and my Marines a relic of Unified Authority intervention and wanted us to leave. As far as he and everyone else knew, we were landlocked on his planet. We couldn't very well fly off into space in a fleet of short-range transports, so he tolerated our settling into the Army base on the east side of town.

"Ellery tells me you want to attack Earth," said Sarah Doctorow, the Right Reverend's clone-hating wife.

"Wayson, are you planning attacks without telling me?" Ava pretended her feelings were hurt.

Sarah was Ellery Doctorow's common-law wife. Ava was more like my fiancée than my wife. I got the better deal.

Wearing an ivy-colored dress, Sarah Doctorow looked like a turtle—tiny flesh-colored limbs and head, massive green shell in the middle. Her breasts hung like watermelons, and her third chin sagged so far down her neck, it could have hidden an Adam's apple.

She looked over at Ava, gave her a warm smile, and said, "You need to keep a close eye on that man of yours. He's planning a war behind your back."

Ava answered Sarah in kind, smiling graciously, and saying, "That's my Wayson."

Ava had once been the hottest actress in Hollywood. She

was a dark-haired, green-eyed goddess who might have been remembered among Hollywood's greatest legends had word not gotten out that she had inherited her name and her DNA from an ancient actress.

U.A. society turned its back on Ava along with the rest of its synthetic progeny. About the same time that the gossip columnists began flogging Ava, the Joint Chiefs of Staff decided to jettison their clones. They sent us to the farthest reaches of the galaxy; and Ava Gardner, the fallen star, hitched a ride with us.

Sarah loathed Ava because she was a clone. Ava detested Sarah because Doctorow's wife was a bigot and a bitch. Both women put on a great show. The first time I saw them chatting, I thought they liked each other.

"What happened to your cane?" Doctorow asked, as our better halves conversed.

"I think I've outgrown it," I said.

"Congratulations on your remarkable recovery," Doctorow said. "Your doctor gave you even chances of survival two months ago, now you're walking around without a cane." He lifted his wineglass for a toast. "To what should we attribute your amazing recovery? Good genes, I suppose?"

Doctorow had a talent for delivering insults as backhanded compliments. I was a Liberator, a class of clone that had been discontinued because of a tendency toward uncontrollable violence. The reason I survived was because my Liberator physiology included a special gland that pumped testosterone and adrenaline into my system to help Liberators adjust to battle. They called that feat of anatomical engineering a "combat reflex."

The new Unified Authority Marines used fléchettes instead of bullets. The fléchettes were no larger than a sewing needle, but they were coated with a neurotoxin that would have killed me had my combat reflex not gone into overdrive. Strained but not destroyed, the gland went dormant during my recovery period. I was still weak but getting stronger.

Pretending not to notice the insult, I smiled and drank my wine.

Ellery Doctorow did not like me or my Marines, but that did not stop him from making a toast with wine we had provided him. The peas and the canned chicken his wife served for dinner all came compliments of the military he so despised.

The Avatari left Terraneau so battered that the people did not have enough food to feed themselves. Fortunately, the Unifieds lost a lot of ships when they attacked us; we might have starved if they hadn't come to kill us. Rummaging on the derelict warships floating above the atmosphere, my men found enough food to feed the planet while my Corps of Engineers built farms.

"I even went jogging this morning," I said. "Nothing too ambitious, just a couple of miles." Actually, I'd jogged a full ten miles, but Doctorow did not need to know that.

"Jogging? I'm glad to hear it," he said through a stiff grin that made him look anything but happy. "Now that you are up and around, have you put any thought into finding a new location for your base? I think it's high time you moved."

"A new location," I said. "Washington, D.C., comes to mind."

He laughed.

I leaned over the table, my eyes locked on Doctorow's, and said in a hushed voice as if confiding my deepest personal secrets, "I know what happened to my fleet."

Thinking that I meant I had found the wreckage of the missing ships, he asked, "How far did they get?"

"They made it," I said. "They survived."

The room had gone quiet. Ava and Sarah stared at me. I had not thought they would hear me, but I didn't mind.

"What do you mean they made it?" asked Doctorow.

"They escaped. They're fine," I said, both bluffing and telling the truth. I did not know whether or not they were "fine," but I did know how they had escaped.

# CHAPTER
# THREE

Ava saw through me. She always saw through me. Fortunately for me, she was an actress by trade. She knew when to hide her emotions, and how.

The tone of the evening changed after I made my announcement. Thrilled with the idea that my Marines might actually leave his planet, Ellery Doctorow wanted details. "Where did they go?"

"That's classified," I said.

"How soon will they return?"

"Classified."

"But you're in contact with them? You're making plans to leave?"

"Not in the foreseeable future," I said.

His silence was smothering. He shook his head to show disappointment.

Taking advantage of the silence, Sarah Doctorow butted into the conversation. "Oh, but, General, you can't possibly attack Earth from Terraneau, it's too far away. Wouldn't that weaken your attack?" She didn't care about my welfare, of course. That was just camouflage.

"Where do you suggest I launch from?" I asked her.

Her husband answered, "Anywhere but here."

"We don't have anyplace else," I said, though I did not know if that was accurate.

"Attack from wherever your fleet disappeared to. Where did you say they went?" he asked.

"I didn't," I said.

"You brought the Earth Fleet down on us once already. I won't allow you to do that again."

I wondered how he planned to stop me but did not ask. I also wondered why I tolerated the pontificating old windbag.

Hell, I didn't just put up with him, I kowtowed to him. I let him push me around. Somewhere in my mind, I accepted the notion that I was just a guest on Terraneau. This was not my home. Me and my Marines, we were here for a visit, and we could not wait to get away. Doctorow, he was here forever, and for that reason I gave him a little more authority than I normally would have.

Sarah took a different tack. "That is so brave," she raved. "They nearly annihilated you just two months ago, and you're already preparing to fight them again." She touched a hand to her voluminous bosoms as if genuinely moved.

Ava did not join in the discussion. She listened to Ellery and Sarah but kept her eyes on me. No emotion showed on her face.

And that was how the night ended—Doctorow angling to get my Marines off his planet, his wife praising me for my self-destructive spirit, and Ava watching in silence.

Seeing that I would not give out any more specifics, Doctorow finished his glass of wine, and announced, "It's getting late, perhaps we should call an end to the evening."

Sarah yawned, placing a hand as thick as a catcher's mitt before her mouth but making no effort to stifle the sound. Then she stood, started gathering dirty plates, paused to look at Ava, and said, "It's so nice to see you again."

"At least let me help clear the table," Ava offered.

As they went through the monthly ritual of Ava's offering to help with the dishes and Sarah's declining, Ellery Doctorow led me toward the door. "How much do you really know?" he asked in a whisper.

"I know they got away, and I know how," I said.

"Do you have any way of reaching them?"

"Maybe," was all I told him, then Ava came to join us, and it was time to leave. She kissed Doctorow on the cheek and thanked him for dinner. She and Sarah hugged as if they were sisters, then we said our final good-byes.

Had Ava and I held hands, hypothermia might have set in, her vibe was so cold. She did not speak. When I opened the door for her, she slid into her seat without a word.

"You're awfully quiet," I said as I slipped behind the wheel.

She did not respond.

I started the engine and pulled away. Both Ava and the Doctorows lived in a northern suburb of Norristown, a wealthy community that had somehow gone unscathed during the Avatari invasion. All of the houses still stood. Once my engineers had restored the power and water, the residents began taking care of their yards, and the streets returned to their prewar elegance.

We drove the short distance to Ava's house in silence. Then, as I parked, she finally asked, "When were you going to tell me?"

She climbed out of the car before I could answer.

Ava's house was not as big or nice as the Doctorows', but it wasn't bad—a single-story flat with a rock garden in the front and a backyard the size of a postage stamp. She also had two bedrooms, both of which would end up occupied for the rest of the night if I did not find a way to make amends.

"I was going to tell you," I said, as she unlocked the front door.

"Are they back?" she asked.

"Is who back?" I asked.

Ava was not the kind of gal who holds still for a fight. She removed her shoes and tucked them into the closet as she entered the house. Pulling off her right earring, she turned to me, and asked, "The ships. Your missing ships. Are they back?"

I stood motionless, watching her as she headed toward her master bedroom. "No," I said.

"But they're coming back?" she called from the bedroom.

Her clothes were coming off. Ava had no compunction about undressing in front of me, no matter what her mood. I, on the other hand, preferred not to watch her undress during fights. If I couldn't have it, I didn't want to see what I was missing. That way, I avoided nights spent in frustration.

"I don't know," I said.

"You don't know?"

"I haven't made contact," I confessed.

Her blouse unbuttoned, her bra exposed, she stepped into the doorway to take another shot at me. "Honey, from the way you were talking tonight, I would have thought you'd moved in with them."

*Oh shit,* I thought, *she's using the "H-word."* When Ava felt brassy, she began her sentences by calling me "Honey." Sometimes sentences that began with "Honey" were funny, sometimes they were brutal, but they were never nice.

"Yeah, well, Doctorow wants me out of here, and he'll be a lot easier to work with when he thinks that I'm planning to leave," I said.

She pulled off her blouse and disappeared into the bedroom. When she spoke again, her voice was softer. We had come to the heart of the argument. "Are you leaving?"

"Not without you," I said.

She came back into the doorway, this time dressed only in her bra and her panties. Giving me a snide smile, she said, "Who says you can't teach an old dog new tricks? Harris, you rang the right bell; now come and claim your reward."

## CHAPTER FOUR

The time had come to lay my cards out on the table.

Hollingsworth and I dressed in combat armor for this excursion. Lieutenant Mars came in a soft shell—that was Marine talk for the kind of armor worn by technicians and engineers. Unlike our hardened armor, Mars's shell was made of flexible rubber latex.

Mars, Hollingsworth, and I sat inside the kettle—the cargo and passenger section of a military transport ship—as our pilot prepped for takeoff. We talked, trying to make ourselves comfortable, but you were never really comfortable riding in the kettle. Everything was made of metal—metal floor, metal walls, metal ceiling, even the horseshoe seat in the head was made of metal. Everything was metal except for the wooden bench running the length of the walls and the restraining harnesses.

And the kettle was dark, too. It had a twenty-foot ceiling and a couple of red emergency lights, but most of the lighting came from the cockpit.

"You know, General, I could have had my men string lights in here," Mars said.

"Good thought," I said. "We'll take you up on that next time." I held up my helmet, which offered night-for-day vision that would allow me to see perfectly well. But although our helmets included interLink connectivity that let us hear each other, conversation flows more easily when you're not wearing an airtight helmet.

"General Harris, what exactly are we here for?" Hollingsworth asked. In the light that spilled out from the open cockpit door, I could see Hollingsworth's face. He was a young Marine. Like every other military clone, he had brown hair and brown eyes though like the others, what he saw when he looked in the mirror was a young man with blue eyes and blond hair.

"I'm going to show you how the fleet escaped," I said.

"No shit?" Hollingsworth asked. "How did they do it?"

"I'll demonstrate when we get there," I said. We sat in silence for a moment, then I asked Mars, "Were you able to get the shields running on that armor?"

Of the three of us, Mars was the one sitting in the most light; it illuminated a wedge of his face that started just above his chin and ended on his nose. He smiled, and said, "Yes, sir. All we had to do was recharge the batteries."

"And?" I asked.

"The shielding is worthless," Mars said.

"What do you mean by 'worthless'? Are you saying it's weak?" Hollingsworth asked. "It wasn't weak when we fought them; we hit those sons of bitches with rockets and grenades." Like me, Hollingsworth had seen that armor in battle.

"My particle-beam pistol didn't get through," I added. "I shot a man at point-blank range."

"You should have kept shooting," Mars said.

I might have kept shooting if the bastard hadn't drilled through my forearm with two fléchettes. After that, I was busy trying to breathe as the neurotoxins turned my body numb.

"Those shields are just for show," Mars continued. "Do

you want to know what they used as a power source? A battery pack about the size of my finger." He held up his little finger.

"Well, I suppose it's the age-old trade-off, power versus mobility," Mars began. Like every other engineer I knew, he got excited and started spouting jargon. He went on for a couple of minutes like that, babbling as if he had actually gone to engineering school. Clones did not go to officer training because they weren't supposed to rise beyond enlisted ranks. I was a general, Hollingsworth a colonel, and Mars a lieutenant, but those were temporary field ranks given to us by the Unified Authority. They made us officers so we could run our fleet, then they attacked. Bastards.

"In a perfect setting, they might have gotten forty-five minutes out of their shields," Mars went on. "Every time you hit them, it causes the power to spike. It doesn't matter if you hit them with a missile or a spit wad, the power in their shields spikes.

"Do you know how long those shields would hold up in a rainstorm? We tried it. We powered up a suit and splashed it with a hose. The battery died in eight minutes." He sounded disappointed by the armor's poor showing.

He dropped his voice and became a bit more reverent as he added, "Most of their shields failed three minutes after you brought that garage down on their heads."

"Wait," Hollingsworth said, sounding more than a little skeptical. "Some of those guys were alive for weeks. If their shields gave out, why weren't they crushed?"

"You only crushed the laggards, the ones who were still on the first and second levels of the garage," Mars explained. "The lower levels did not cave in, especially on the fourth and fifth. The men on those levels weren't buried, they were trapped. If they'd had food and oxygen, they'd still be alive today."

"Interesting," I said, interrupting Hollingsworth's next question in the hope of getting the conversation back on point. "So we can drain the battery by hitting them with a barrage."

"More or less," Mars agreed.

"Do you have any idea how long the armor would stand up to a particle beam?" I asked.

"Eight minutes," he said. "It doesn't matter what you hit it with, there's a power surge, and the battery goes dry after eight minutes."

"Good to know," I said.

"That's eight minutes of prolonged exposure," Mars said. "You would need to hit your target with a continuous wave."

"Does that include sound waves?" I asked.

Mars considered the idea. "That might do it. We didn't try that, but it probably would work."

"What might work?" Hollingsworth asked.

"Using sonic waves to deplete the batteries," Mars said.

"You sneaky bastard," Hollingsworth said, quickly adding "sir" to avoid the appearance of insubordination.

My pilot spoke to us over the intercom. "General, we're in position."

"How close?" I asked.

"Fifteen hundred miles, sir," he said.

"Give us a moment to suit up," I told the pilot. I turned to Hollingsworth and Mars, and said, "Helmets on, gentlemen. For today's demonstration, we will be opening the rear hatch."

After we pulled on our helmets, I contacted my pilot via the interLink. "Ready," I told him, giving him the signal to vent the air from the kettle. Once the oxygen had been evacuated, he opened the massive iron doors at the rear of the ship, revealing a wide field of stars and empty space.

"You brought us out here to see this?" Hollingsworth asked. "There's nothing here."

"It's what you don't see that counts," I told Hollingsworth as I picked up a handheld rocket launcher.

Speaking over the interLink on a direct frequency that only my pilot would hear, I said, "Lower the rear shields in ten, nine, eight . . ." I continued the count in my head.

"There's more going on out here than meets the eye," I told Hollingsworth. "Watch."

"What does this have to do with the fleet?" he asked.

*Five, four* . . . I continued counting silently to myself. Without answering, I aimed the rocket out the rear of the ship.

*Three, two, one* . . .

There was a barely visible blue-white flash as the rear shield of the transport came off-line. I fired the RPG.

Rifles, pistols, and rockets shoot perfectly well in space. If anything, projectiles fly faster and travel along a much more rigid trajectory without the distractions of friction and gravity. In a breathable atmosphere, the little rocket might never have broken the sound barrier. Here in space, it lit off at Mach 2 and would have kept at that rate forever, or at least until it bumped into a meteor or a ship or a planet. On this day, it found something else.

"Shield up," I told the pilot over a direct link.

"What is this about?" asked Mars, who clearly wanted more than a demonstration of physics in space.

The explosion took place about five hundred miles away, straight ahead of us, in the vast emptiness. Some of the shrapnel came back and struck our shields, creating sparks against the invisible pane of electrical energy.

"What was that?" asked Mars. "What just happened?"

"Gentlemen, we are at the edge of a battlefield. The area around us is crowded with broken ships and debris, and yet the space we are facing is almost entirely empty. Do either of you have any idea why no ships entered this zone?" I asked.

"You said 'almost empty,'" Hollingsworth observed. "What do you mean by 'almost'?"

"There's a broadcast station in the center of it," I said.

"A broadcast station?" asked Mars. "Are you saying Warshaw broadcasted the fleet?" Gary Warshaw was the clone sailor the Unifieds had promoted to command the Scutum-Crux Fleet.

"That can't be," said Hollingsworth. "The Broadcast Network was shut down during the Mogat Wars, that was years ago."

Hollingsworth missed the big picture, but Mars pieced it together. "The broadcast engines weren't broken, they just needed power. Warshaw must have installed generators on the station."

"That's my guess," I said.

"If he got the station running, he could have made it out with hundreds of ships," Hollingsworth said.

"Twenty-one carriers, seventy-two battleships, and who knows how many frigates and cruisers," I said.

The visor in my combat armor had equipment for surveillance, reconnaissance, and battle, such as lenses that could illuminate the darkness, see over long distances, and detect heat. Lieutenant Mars's soft-shelled armor had an entirely different set of lenses designed for engineers. When he whistled, and said, "The current out there is off the charts," I knew he had run some kind of test. "How far are we from the broadcast station?"

"Fifteen hundred miles," I said.

"And no ships got any closer than this?" Mars asked.

"Not much," I said.

There was a pause, then Mars asked, "Does the field go all the way around the station?"

"As far as I can tell, it forms a perfect sphere," I said.

"Warshaw must have supercharged the broadcast engines to create a hot zone," Mars said.

"If you say so," I said. I was a combat Marine. What did I know about supercharging broadcast engines?

"No. No, it doesn't make sense. Why didn't the Unifieds blast the station?" Hollingsworth asked. "They would have destroyed this station the same way the Mogats destroyed the Mars broadcast station."

"No, they couldn't," I said. "They couldn't hit it with a torpedo. You saw what just happened to that rocket."

"So they would have used a particle beam or a laser," Hollingsworth said.

I handed Hollingsworth a shoulder-held laser cannon, and said, "Be my guest."

"What about our shields?" Hollingsworth asked.

I had already asked the pilot to lower them. I told him, "They're already down."

Hollingsworth aimed the cannon out the back of the transport and fired. The silver-red beam disappeared only a few hundred feet from the ship.

"How did you do that?" Hollingsworth asked.

"The current from the broadcast station disassembled it," Mars said.

"It what?" asked Hollingsworth.

"Disassembled it. Pulled it apart," said Mars. "We used to communicate across the galaxy sending laser signals over the Broadcast Network. The current from the broadcast station must translate light waves."

"So what? We fire a laser at the station, and it comes out in another galactic arm?" Hollingsworth asked.

I shrugged my shoulders, an action made almost invisible by my combat armor.

"Not without an encoded address built into the signal to specify where it is supposed to go," Mars said. "Without an address, the waves stay broken apart."

"Have you tried contacting the people on the other side?" Hollingsworth asked.

"What do you suggest, shouting into it? Maybe we could float a tin cup on a really long string into the zone and see if someone picks up on the other side," I said.

# CHAPTER
# FIVE

"Why didn't the Unifieds send ships in after them?" Hollingsworth asked, as the transport doors closed.

The mood in the kettle had changed. Hollingsworth, who began the flight hostile, had suddenly become my pal. Lieutenant Mars, who'd boarded the transport confused about the fate of the Scutum-Crux Fleet, began dispensing answers about broadcast physics as if he had invented the technology.

"You wouldn't want to enter a hot zone unless you had a ship designed for network travel. The current from a zone like this would overload the engines in a self-broadcasting ship."

The Unified Authority Navy's new fleet was entirely composed of self-broadcasting warships.

"What would happen if one of their ships did go in?" Hollingsworth asked.

"It would cause a massive explosion," Mars explained.

"How massive?" asked Hollingsworth.

"Massive," Mars said, giving off the air of one who knows.

"You mean like a nuclear explosion?" asked Hollingsworth. Like any good Marine, he wanted things spelled out in combat terms.

Sounding more like a college professor than a boot-strapped engineer, Mars said, "Nuclear bombs come in all sizes, don't they? I suspect it would be the equivalent of a very small nuclear device."

That was bullshit, of course. Mars had no idea what he was talking about.

The pilot addressed me on an open interLink channel that Mars and Hollingsworth would hear as well. "General, the air and heat are online," he said. "You can remove your helmet."

I thanked him and removed my lid. Mars and Hollingsworth followed.

A dark emotion seemed to come over Hollingsworth. The excitement left his face. He sat in the shadows, quiet and sullen. Finally, he said, "I don't see how this changes anything. We know how they got away, but we can't go after them. I mean, what are we going to do, put a message in a bottle and toss it through the zone?"

"Not a message in a bottle," I said. "I'm going to fly a ship into the hot zone."

They greeted this statement with the kind of silence generally reserved for people discussing suicide. Hollingsworth broke the silence. "You're joking, right?" he asked, though he must have known I meant what I had said. "Unless you have a ship we don't know about, the only thing you have that flies is a transport."

"He's right," Mars said. "Only an idiot would enter a broadcast zone in a transport."

I wished he hadn't added that last line. Ray Freeman, my old business partner, and I once tried to modify a transport to self-broadcast. Freeman got electrocuted, and we ended up stranded in space.

I held up my hands, palms out, and said, "No working ships up my sleeves, but there's a whole fleet out there."

Hollingsworth shot me an incredulous look, and asked, "You mean the wrecks?"

"One man's wreckage may well be another man's pangalactic barge," I said.

Hollingsworth laughed, and said, "You're going to ride a wreck into a broadcast zone? That's suicide."

"Do you have any better ideas?" I asked.

He thought it over and shook his head, then admitted, "No, sir, I don't."

Still sounding enthusiastic, Mars offered, "I'll work out the details."

# CHAPTER SIX

It took Mars and his engineers more than a month to work out the kinks. That meant that a month had passed since the night I promised Ava I would take her with me when I left Terraneau. I meant what I said when I made the promise; but now that I knew the gory details, I needed to renege.

In truth, I was not sure she cared either way. An indefinable coldness had entered our relationship. We did not argue, but the passion was gone. We ate meals together and we had sex, but we didn't talk much. In her past life, she'd lived with generals and movie stars and billionaires. Was this how she ended relationships, by allowing them to dry up and blow away?

I did not want that to happen with us. Maybe the passion was gone, but she had become an important part of my world. I did not feel passionately about my right hand, but I could not imagine living without it.

I arrived at Ava's house just after sunset; the last fibers of sunlight streaked across the sky, making the clouds look like the embers of a dying fire. Above the clouds, the sky dithered from paper white to a blue so dark it qualified as black. Her house was in the Norristown foothills, overlooking the city in all of its stages of repair. In the dark world below, streetlights shimmered like tracer fire. Cars crowded onto newly opened streets. From her backyard, it looked like Norristown had more cars than people.

On this evening, I came bearing an offering for my Hollywood goddess—beer rescued from a derelict ship. She would have preferred wine, but the only way to get wine would have been through Ellery Doctorow, and sacrifice has its limits.

I didn't believe in fortune-telling, but I sensed negative energy in the air. I had the same feeling I got playing blackjack when I had twelve on the table and knew the next card off the deck would be worth ten.

I went to the front door and knocked. Ava opened the door. She looked beautiful. Her hair, which she frequently wore in an organized tangle of locks and tresses, hung down over her back. She wore a red dress that left her shoulders bare and showed just the right preview of cleavage.

"Hi, there," she said as she let me in. Her gaze met mine for half a second, but I thought I saw sadness in her eyes.

"I come bearing gifts," I said, brandishing the beers. "They're even cold."

She smiled, and said, "You know how to make a girl feel special," but her voice sounded distracted, and her eyes did not quite hold with mine.

"Is everything okay?" I asked, feeling nervous.

Ava sighed. She thought for a moment, then finally said, "We'd better eat while the food is hot and your beers are cold."

Her home was small but stylish. The dining table was about the right size for an end table. She had spread a white linen cloth across the top and wedged a candle between our plates. Her china was bone white, her utensils were silver and gleamed in the candlelight.

As we reached the table, she excused herself to get glasses for the beers. I waited for her to return before sitting down. I pulled her chair out for her, though I was not sure she wanted me to. There was something in the air, something cold and distancing.

Ava handed me a glass, and said, "There's a rumor going around about you leaving Terraneau."

"Really? Who's spreading it?" I asked, trying to outmaneuver the truth. "I hope you're not listening to Sarah."

"I didn't hear it from Sarah. I heard about it from Julie Neberker."

"Who is that?" I asked. I had never heard the name.

"She lives a few doors down," Ava said.

"Is she dating one of my Marines?" I asked, trying to figure out if she might have access to anything more than gossip.

"No."

"You can't take anything she says very seriously, she doesn't know what she's talking about."

"She heard about it from Rachel Johnson. Rachel heard Sarah and Ellery joking about you leaving at a bridge party," Ava said.

I always knew Sarah Doctorow had a big mouth. By that time, I had confided the information about the broadcast zone to Doctorow.

"I see," I said. "Did they happen to give any specifics?"

"No. All she knew was that you found a working broadcast station."

"I see."

"Are you going after the missing ships?" Ava asked.

"I think so," I said.

I expected her to ask if I planned to take her with me, but she surprised me. Instead of asking about going with me, she said, "Julie says they're not going to let you back on Terraneau once you leave."

"Who's not going to let me back on?"

She thought about that, and said, "Ellery, I guess."

"Don't worry about it," I said. "He'd need an air force to stop me. All he has is a civilian militia armed with popguns."

She studied my face, her olivine green eyes boring into me and seeing through my bluster. Did I see hurt in her eyes or anger? Maybe I was fooling myself, and all that was there was indifference. "I don't think it's just Ellery. I think Hollingsworth is with him. "

"Hollingsworth?" I asked. I did not know what to say. I knew he didn't like me, but he was a Marine. Marines did not turn on each other. I sat motionless, my head reeling. Our meal sat before us ignored—her food and my beers.

"Wayson, if you come back, they might shoot you down," she said.

"Not likely." I shook my head. Hollingsworth was a good Marine. He wouldn't do that, it was not in his programming. "Not Hollingsworth. He might ignore me, but he wouldn't shoot at me."

"What if he and Doctorow want to take over the planet?" she asked.

"Now there's an unholy alliance." I said it as a joke. "Ellery Doctorow doesn't want to conquer Terraneau, he wants to be elected king. He's an idealist, not a dictator, and he's not going to tag team with Philo Hollingsworth. It's not just me. Doctorow thinks every Marine is a serpent in his garden of Eden."

"That doesn't scare you?" she asked.

"No," I said.

"Wayson, tell me the truth. Are you leaving soon?" Ava asked.

That seemed pretty obvious at this point. I nodded.

"How are you going to do it?"

"It's just like Doctorow said, there's a working broadcast station. I'm going to ride a busted ship through it."

"What do you mean by 'busted'?" Ava asked.

"That's classified," I said, hoping to avoid telling her the details.

"How busted is it, Wayson?" Ava repeated.

"It was destroyed during the battle with the Earth Fleet," I said. I still had no idea which ship I would ride, but whichever one it was, it would be a victim of that battle.

"But you have it running now?" Ava asked.

"Not exactly," I said.

"Not exactly?" she asked.

I didn't say anything. I was divulging classified information. That made me worse than Doctorow. At least he was a civilian.

"If you haven't repaired the ship, how are you going to fly it?"

"Ava, that's classified information." I hoped the term would put her off.

"Classified? We're not at war, who are you trying to hide it from?" She pursed her lips and stared at me angrily, and I felt my resolve turn to mush.

"Scott Mars is going to seal me in a derelict ship and launch it toward the station," I said.

"Have you even tested to see if it's safe?" she asked.

"Why don't we have this out after dinner?" I suggested. I pulled the bowl of MRE beef stew she had heated and ladled some on my plate. As the highest-ranking officer on Terraneau, I made sure Ava's pantry was stocked with Meals Ready to Eat.

Her voice more stern, Ava repeated herself. "Have you flown anything else into the station?"

"A couple of grenades," I said as I took a bite of cold stew.

"How about something with people in it?" she asked, her voice as cold as ice and as hard as steel. "You have to send another ship through before you go yourself," she said.

"How will we know if it made it through?" I asked. I took another bite of stew; it needed reheating.

"Maybe you should send a guinea pig first to see if it's safe," she said.

"I suppose that's me," I said. *Commanding officer and head guinea pig Wayson Harris. Give me enough rope, and I'll hang myself.*

# CHAPTER
# SEVEN

Launching a derelict ship into the broadcast zone required more planning than I had anticipated.

The first problem was finding a ship that was solid enough to stand the stresses of the electrical current. It had to be one of ours. The Unified Authority's ships were closer to the zone; but they were all self-broadcasting, which meant they lacked the kind of insulation needed to keep me safe.

As we mapped the battlefield, a pattern quickly emerged. While we had lost almost three times as many ships as the

Unified Authority in the battle, all of the wrecks around the broadcast zone were from the Earth Fleet. They had all been destroyed from the inside out. Apparently they had entered the outer reaches of the broadcast zone and exploded when exposed to the current flowing from the broadcast station.

Mars held a briefing to explain the situation. Using a three-dimensional holographic map to show the area, he said, "These ships marked in blue are U.A. ships. Our job would be a whole lot easier if we could send you in one of these ships, but it wouldn't be safe."

"What if you sealed me in?" I asked.

"What do you mean?"

"What if you took tiles off the hull of an SC Fleet ship and sealed them around one of these ships?" I asked. "Would that be enough to protect me?"

"If it were that easy, we could just weld some armor to a working transport, and you'd have flight controls," Mars said. "The inadequacy goes deeper. It's structural."

Listening to him speak, I realized that Mars genuinely wanted me to survive the mission. Hollingsworth and Doctorow might have seen me as an obstacle, but maybe Mars did not.

"Since we can't launch you in a U.A. ship, we need to clear them out from between your ship and the zone."

Inspecting the display, I saw what he meant. The battle had apparently taken place on an almost two-dimensional plane, with the Unified Authority ships forming a solid wall between the battlefield and the hot zone. "Can you drag my ship around them?" I asked.

"And Jesus wept." Mars sighed. "No offense, General, but your grasp of physics never ceases to amaze me. We'll be lucky if we can get you moving at all; turns and course corrections are out of the question.

"You are going to be in a great big ship being propelled by tiny ships. Just building inertia will be a feat. Newton's Second Law . . . mass, force, acceleration?

"You are familiar with Sir Isaac Newton, right, sir? 'An object in motion'? 'Equal and opposite reaction'? Once we build up enough velocity to drive your wreck toward the zone, you will be traveling in a straight line. If something is in your way, we need to move it out of the way or break it. Those are the only options—clear a path or scrap this mission."

Having grown up in Unified Authority Orphanage # 553, I took a "Survey of Science" class that introduced chemistry, physics, astronomy, biology, and anatomy all in a ten-week term. I had never studied any of the sciences since.

"Why can't you just haul the flotsam and jetsam out of the way?" I asked.

"It's a matter of size," Mars said. He fingered his remote device, and the holographic display zoomed in on the wrecks blocking the route to the broadcast zone. Originally shown as squiggles and dots, the images now resolved themselves into discrete shapes.

"These five ships here"—he pointed with his device, which made the hulls glow—"are U.A. fighter carriers. They are thirty-three hundred feet long and eight hundred feet wide. We can't exactly tie a rope to their gunnels and tow them into port."

He played with his remote again, and this time an orange light appeared around three ships. "These are U.A. battle-ships, the new ones," he said. "They're twenty-six hundred feet long and five hundred feet wide. Three of these ships rammed into each other and got tangled. We think we can clear a path for you by breaking these ships apart. If it doesn't work . . ."

"We'll need to scrub the mission," I guessed.

"Probably so, sir."

I'd made a tactical error when I told Ellery Doctorow about the broadcast zone so early in the game. With each passing week, Doctorow became more insistent that I leave and take my military with me. After six weeks, he acted up.

The buzz from my communications console woke me from a near sleep. Turning on my side, I saw it was 02:30, sat up, and said, "This better be good."

"General, someone is breaking into the armory," Hollings-worth said. That got my attention. The armory was the under-ground garage, the place with all of the buried weapons.

"Do we know who?" I asked.

"I sent a squad to investigate."

"What did they find?"

"I've lost contact with them, sir."

I turned on the light and slid off my rack. The only people who would go after those weapons were Doctorow and his militia. He had never struck me as a man who turned to violence; but he if he wanted us off Terraneau badly enough, who knew what he would do.

I told Hollingsworth to muster a single company. "I want them dressed in combat armor and loaded on trucks in five minutes."

"Won't we need more men?" Hollingsworth asked. "What if—"

"Put the rest of the base on alert," I said.

"But what if—"

"You have your orders," I said.

"Yes, sir," Hollingsworth said, and signed off. The call to arms sounded a few seconds later. By the time it did, I had my bodysuit on and was fastening my armor.

I thought about the armory. As a show of respect for Doctorow and his government, I had decided against posting guards around the site. Perhaps I had made a mistake. My show of respect, however, only went so far. I might not have posted guards around the caved-in armory, but I'd had my engineers install a discreet security system around the grounds.

I grabbed my M27, left my particle-beam pistol in my locker, and headed out the door.

Sirens wailed. Across the grounds, men in fatigues rushed out of lit barracks, but most of the barracks were dark. Originally built to house twenty-five thousand soldiers, Fort Sebastian was now home to a mere thirty-two hundred men: one thousand naval engineers and twenty-two hundred combat Marines.

Four troop carriers lined up near the gate, their engines purring. Hollingsworth waited beside the first truck, already in his armor. Moments after I arrived, two lines of men in dark green combat armor formed, and a pair of sergeants shepherded the men onto the trucks. Hollingsworth and I rode with the men in the back of the first carrier.

"Has your patrol reported in?" I asked Hollingsworth, as we settled onto the bench at the back of the truck. With twenty-five Marines in camouflaged armor around us, the back of the transport looked like a forest.

"No response, sir," Hollingsworth said. "The bastards must have hit them."

"Must have," I said, though I had my doubts. Doctorow's militia could not afford to go balls out with us, and they knew it. They outnumbered us, but they did not have the stomach for collateral damage.

I put on my helmet and tried to listen in on my men's conversations over the interLink, but heard nothing. For a moment I thought something might be wrong with my equipment. I removed my helmet and stared into it. I tapped on the visor, knowing that tapping on the glass would be no more effective at repairing microcircuitry than patting a man on the back would be at removing a brain tumor.

"I'm not Linking," Hollingsworth said. "It's like my helmet went deaf."

As I stared into my helmet, the truck slowed to a stop. A moment later, the sea of men in front of me parted as our driver called out to me from the back of the truck. As I pushed through the crowd, I noticed that all of the men had removed their helmets.

"What is it?" I asked.

"General, I tried to contact you over the interLink, sir, but I could not get a signal."

"Somebody is jamming the signal," I said, trying to sound as if I had known that all along.

"Yes, sir," said the driver. "There's an overturned jeep about a quarter mile up the road from here."

"One of ours?" I asked.

"Maybe we should send some men to have a look at it," Hollingsworth suggested.

"See to it," I said, deciding to play things safe even as my instincts told me not to worry.

Hollingsworth sent a fire team in to investigate. The team included a rifleman, an automatic rifleman, a grenadier, and a team leader. I watched them as they went up the road, knowing that the time had come to make a tactical decision. I needed to choose between communication and equipment. If we wore our helmets, we would not be able to communicate;

but we would have radar, sonar, and optical lenses to provide us a tactical edge. With our helmets off, we would be able to speak; but we would be blind to snipers and traps.

*Communications or security?* I asked myself. I opted for security.

Using the heat-vision lenses in my visor, I scanned the road ahead and saw no signs of people other than the men I had just sent out. I pulled off my helmet and barked out orders.

"We're hiking in from here," I told Hollingsworth and the noncoms who had gathered around me. "Tell your men to stay in a tight formation and keep their helmets on until we give the signal to remove them.

"There may be snipers out there," I said. "If there are, I want to see them before they hit us."

As we fanned out, the men we sent to investigate the jeep were already on their way back. We sent four men, but eight men returned.

"What happened?" I asked the patrol leader.

"They hit the jeep," the man said.

"Was anybody hurt?"

"The jeep's in bad shape," one of them said. With their jeep destroyed and the interLink down, the men in Hollingsworth's original patrol could neither proceed nor call for help. Their only option had been to dig in and wait for backup.

The terrain was mostly flat, though much of it was buried under mounds of debris. We secured the area quickly, then moved forward.

We reached the jeep. It lay on its side, all of its wheels shredded. Somebody had gouged a two-inch-deep trench across the road, then filled it with spikes.

I knelt beside the spikes and tried to pull one out. They were wedged in tightly. It took a little work, but I managed to pry one out of the ground.

"Bastards," Hollingsworth muttered.

*Whoever set this trap wanted to get his point across without starting a war,* I thought. Placing a mine would have been easier. It would also have been lethal.

"Do you think the militia did this?" asked Hollingsworth.

"Why don't you ask your pal Doctorow," I said. "I hear you two are tight."

Hollingsworth heard me, but he did not respond. He stood still and silent for a few seconds, then excused himself to go check on his men. The stupid son of a bitch should have known it would get back to me.

I stood and looked off across the landscape. If the militia had time to set these spikes, they'd had time to set up more surprises. None of the traps would be lethal, just something to get our attention.

The street leading to the government compound was clear, but the ground on either side of the road was knee-deep in the debris of buildings destroyed long ago. Two-thirds of a mile ahead of us, the abandoned government complex rose out of the ground like small buttes in a desert. In the middle of the buildings, a wide gap marked the target—the building we had knocked down during our battle with the Unified Authority.

There might be bombs ahead. There might be snipers.

"See if you can contact Fort Sebastian," I told Hollingsworth though I knew it was useless. "I want to know if they've seen anything."

A moment later, he said, "Nothing, sir."

"Maybe we should send a man back to tell them what's going on," Hollingsworth suggested.

It was a good idea but not necessary. "Not yet," I said. "Not until I know what's out here."

"Yes, sir."

It was just after 03:00. The sky was dark except for the stars and a crescent of moon so thin it looked like it had been made with a single stroke of a pen. I put on my helmet and searched the area using night-for-day lenses, then I switched to heat vision. On the off chance that the locals had snipers hiding along the side of the road, I hoped to spot their heat signatures. The lenses showed me nothing but a barren landscape giving off very little heat.

As I thought about it, I became more convinced that Doctorow would not sanction a firefight. He would not send snipers, but he might have had his demolitions experts set some traps. Doctorow had a couple of retired Navy SEALs among his troops. They had top-notch demolitions training and field experience.

While the rest of us waited by the overturned jeep, a team

went out to look for IEDs. None of my men had extensive demolitions training, and it showed. One of my dupes accidentally set off a trap. He might have stepped on a cap, or broken a laser stream, or possibly kicked a trip wire. Whatever he did, he triggered fireworks, sending a fifty-foot phosphorous geyser of red-and-white sparks into the air. The man closest to the fireworks fell on his ass as if he'd been shot, but he'd only been startled. They hadn't set off a specking mine, after all, just a flare display.

Once we knew the only traps were for show, we pushed ahead. We moved slowly, spreading out over a rolling field of rubble and debris. Bits of glass reflected the dark sky along the ground. I stepped on small shards, grinding them into the dust under my armored boots. Larger blades only shattered. We did not worry about making noise as we covered the silent landscape. After the fireworks, we were pretty sure that any hostiles in the area would know we arrived.

Using the telescopic lenses in my visor, I located the remains of the fence we'd erected around the armory as a perimeter. They might have used trucks or tractors; someone had torn the chain link aside, leaving only the skeleton of a badly twisted frame standing.

I allowed my men to approach the edge of the grounds, then had them stop. I searched for heat, then holes, then radiation. The area came up clean.

"Have your men secure the area," I ordered the platoon leaders. "No one gets in or out."

"Aye, aye, sir," he said.

"The rest of you, spread out and look for holes, traps, bombs, tunnels, cameras, anything. I want to know if anyone has been digging or if this is a wild-goose chase."

"What about snipers?" Hollingsworth asked.

"If you find one, shoot him."

"Yes, sir," said Hollingsworth.

I looked across the area. Somebody had planted a row of six flagpoles along the far end of the field, just beyond the wreckage of the underground garage. Oddly shaped black flags hung from each of the poles.

I went for a closer look, putting on my helmet as I walked, skirting around the wreckage. As I stepped closer, I saw that it was not flags that hung from the poles but antique gas masks. The masks were not so much a warning as a message.

At the base of the poles sat a small silver box, no larger than a beer bottle. I approached the box for a closer look, already afraid that I would not like whatever I found. It might have been a small canister filled with any one of a million deadly gases or germs. It could also have been a bomb. It wasn't. It was a device for jamming communications, and my interLink gear came back to life the moment I fired my M27 into it.

I contacted Hollingsworth using the interLink. "Contact the fort, tell them to call off the alert," I said.

"You got the Link working," Hollingsworth said, sounding surprised.

I suspected we would find a bomb or some other weapon back at the base, but it would be disarmed or maybe just an empty shell. The locals were letting me know that it was high time for the Marines to leave their town. I only hoped Hollingsworth realized that the message was meant for him as much as me.

# CHAPTER
# EIGHT

Ellery Doctorow dropped by Fort Sebastian at my request later that morning.

I had the guards hold him at the front gate as I drove out to meet him. Doctorow left his car in an outside parking lot, and we rode together in my jeep.

"Someone left us a special delivery last night," I said, as we passed through the gate.

"Anything in particular?" asked Doctorow, not even pretending to sound surprised.

He was better dressed than usual. Instead of his customary combination of fatigues and civilian clothes, he wore slacks, a light button-up blue shirt, and a necktie. His long hair was pulled back into a ponytail. On this visit, Doctorow behaved more like a politician than a soldier or a chaplain.

I slowed as we approached a large truck bearing a fifteen-foot-long aluminum canister. NOXIUM was stenciled across the side of the canister in turkey red paint. Six antique gas masks hung from a rack at the back of the truck.

I stopped beside the truck and pulled one of the gas masks from the rack. Draping it over my left hand, I held it out so that Doctorow could get a better look at it. "Know what this is?" I asked.

"It looks like an old-fashioned breathing apparatus." He barely gave the mask a glance before answering.

"Yes it is. I'd never seen one of these before, so I looked it up on the mediaLink," I said as I spun it and studied it from different angles. "This one isn't for soldiers. It was made for firefighters. Marines don't use them at all, of course. We have airtight armor with a built-in rebreather."

The longer we hovered around the gas canister, the more uncomfortable Doctorow seemed to become. He did not look at me directly; nor did he seem to want to look at the mask or the canister. Instead, he stared at the road ahead.

"Firefighters don't use these masks anymore, either. Did you know that?"

"I wasn't aware of that," he said, still not meeting my gaze.

"Nope. They use combat armor . . . Marine combat armor. At least they used to. See, most Marines come in one size, being clones, so the armor comes in one size as well. They custom-make armor for officers, but that's expensive . . . really expensive; so firefighters had to use standard-issue enlisted gear. You know how they got around the single-size issue? They hired retired servicemen, you know, clones. Makes sense, doesn't it?

"They can't do that now, though, because they're out of clones. Now they probably use natural-borns. I suppose they could make robots, but that's even more expensive than custom-fitted gear. It's so specking—"

"All very fascinating, General, but there's no call for profanity," Doctorow said, interrupting me just as I was closing in on the punch line.

"Oh, sorry about that," I said. "I got carried away." I laughed. "Do you know what this is?" I pointed to the canister as I slung the gas mask back on the rack.

Doctorow barely glanced at the back of the truck before saying, "I'd say somebody was trying to send you a message."

"Yes indeed, it would appear so," I agreed. "Some of the boys and I went out on the town last night. We found this waiting for us when we returned home. Fortunately, the canister was empty."

"That is fortunate. As I understand it, Noxium gas makes quite a mess," Doctorow said.

"Quite a mess. Quite a mess, indeed. In fact, it's so messy that these gas masks would have done nothing to protect us. Even combat armor is useless against this kind of gas. Did you know that?"

"I think I have heard something along that line," Doctorow admitted.

I thought of an old memory and laughed. "One of my old platoon sergeants had some men who were killed by Noxium. Do you know how he got their bodies out of the armor? He washed them out with a fire hose. No joke. He said the Noxium ate their bodies until all that was left was this flesh-colored jelly, sort of a coagulated goo that washed out in clumps."

"This is all very fascinating, but—" Doctorow began.

I cut him off. "Now a canister this size, if it had been full, it would have held enough gas to wipe out half of Norristown. You'd have been cleaning out Fort Sebastian with a fire hose, but you'd also have needed to hose out every apartment, house, and car from Ford Street to West Angle, almost half of town."

"Is that so?" asked Doctorow. "I heard Noxium gas evaporates so quickly that it doesn't spread."

"Oh, you see now, that's just a myth. The truth is, Noxium doesn't evaporate at all. It dies," I said, stating information that any schoolkid would know. I was patronizing the bastard, and he knew it. "It's not really a gas, it's a cloud of microscopic organisms, voracious little bastards that will bore through anything they can sink their teeth into."

"There's no cause to use—"

I ignored him and went on. "The little bastards die quickly when you release them in small concentrations. Unleash a pint or two, and they die in a matter of seconds. That's why Noxium is such an effective tool for capturing enemy strongholds. You just shoot a few Noxium shells over the wall, and the gas turns the occupants into goo, then you capture their base and wash the enemy out with a hose.

"But that's with a small amount . . . maybe the amount of gas you'd get from a half-gallon shell. With a big batch like this, the microbes insulate each other from the atmosphere, and the cloud doesn't go away. If this much had spilled, the cloud would have spread all the way over to your part of town. My Marines wouldn't have been the only ones receiving the message; Sarah and Ava would have gotten it as well."

"How very fortunate for all of us that the canister was empty," Doctorow said.

"You wouldn't happen to have any idea who left us this message?" I asked.

"I wouldn't know anything about it," Doctorow protested, feigning alarm. "General, I am a peaceable man."

"Ellery, I'm not accusing anyone."

Doctorow seemed to regain his nerve. He said, "I don't think it was meant as a threat. Whoever left it, they probably meant it as a reminder."

"Probably so," I agreed.

"I happen to agree with whoever did this. It's high time you left," Doctorow said. "You and your men have outstayed your welcome."

"Does that go for all of us?" I asked. "Colonel Hollingsworth is under the impression that you only object to me."

"A simple misunderstanding," said Doctorow. "Don't take this personally, General Harris, but I don't really like having a military presence in my city. Armies are a tool of intimidation, and I don't believe governments should be in the business of intimidation."

"But you don't mind my Corps of Engineers," I said.

"What do you mean?"

"If you are evicting me and my men, I will need to take my engineers with me," I said. "How are you going to rebuild Norristown without them?"

"I would prefer for you to leave them, they make a valuable contribution," Doctorow said.

"They're military clones, just like the rest of us," I pointed out. "They came off the same assembly line and grew up in the same orphanages. The only difference between Scott Mars and Philo Hollingsworth is their training. When I give the order to leave, Mars and his men go with the rest of us."

"Are you threatening me, General?"

I answered with a wry smile, gestured with my head toward the empty gas canister, and said, "Not me, I'm just answering your message."

"I have every intention of leaving Terraneau as quickly as possible," I told Doctorow as I started the jeep. "I want to get off this specking rock, the sooner the better."

"Yes, you said that two months ago, General, but you're still here," Doctorow said. The farther we drove from the empty canister, the more he seemed to relax.

"Then you will be glad to know why I called for this little meeting," I said, and I told him that we were just about ready to send a ship through the broadcast zone. He listened carefully and said nothing. He probably did not care whether the plan worked or failed so long as it got me away from his precious society.

We stopped at the McGraw building, the building that served as a headquarters for the Corps of Engineers. Hollingsworth and several of his lieutenants attended the briefing as well.

Looking around the room, I saw that none of us had gotten much sleep. Thanks to the early-morning call to the armory, Hollingsworth and I had not returned to base until nearly 05:00. Mars had been on alert guarding the base. Doctorow looked tired as well. His eyes were badly bloodshot.

When Doctorow saw that he was surrounded by military men, he found a quiet corner where he could lean against the wall and watch the presentation unnoticed. I ditched him and drifted over to Hollingsworth. When I was close enough to whisper without being overheard, I said, "I brought your pal."

"We're not pals," he said.

I only grunted.

Lieutenant Mars booted up his holographic display, and we gathered around him for a closer look. Mars was a smart officer; he waited for me to get things started. When I asked him how things were progressing, he sighed and explained why everything was going wrong.

"Do you have any concept about the sheer mass of a battleship?" he began.

"I know they're big," said Hollingsworth. The other Marines laughed.

"We're talking about one hundred and thirty thousand tons of metal spread across three hundred thousand cubic feet."

"Why are you giving us a lesson on mass, Lieutenant?" asked Hollingsworth, who was clearly tired and edgy from the last night's activities.

Mars pointed to the display, and said, "Because the only way we are going to launch General Harris into that broadcast zone is by sealing him inside a battleship."

"Why are you choosing a big ship?" asked Hollingsworth. "Wouldn't it be easier to send him off in a frigate?"

"He'd never break through the ships blocking the zone; the smaller ships don't have enough mass," said Mars.

He pointed to the wall of derelict ships. Since our last meeting, the problem had gone from difficult to intractable. Hoping to blow the ships into tiny fragments, we'd talked about sending engineers to rig wrecks with charges. As far as I knew, he hadn't actually sent anyone.

"Break through?" I asked. "I thought we were going to clear a path."

"It doesn't look like that's going to work, sir," Mars answered, all of his former enthusiasm now absent from his voice. "We've tried conventional charges. We experimented with a small tactical weapon as well."

I should have seen this coming. The Morgan Atkins Believers had detonated an atomic bomb inside a Unified Authority fighter carrier. Parts of the ship fell away, but the frame of the ship survived.

"You nuked 'em?" Hollingsworth asked.

"Yes, sir, we nuked one. The device blew the outer hull off the ship, but the decks and the structure remained in place," Mars said.

"But a battleship could ram through?" I asked. I knew the answer. He would not have said he needed to seal me in a battleship if he did not believe it could break through. Still, I wanted reassurance.

Mars did not get a chance to answer. Hearing the ease with which the discussion had switched to tactical weapons, Doctorow spoke up. "Where, precisely, did you get a nuclear weapon?"

"Maybe we dug it up while we were out collecting gas masks," I said.

Doctorow glared at me, his fury coloring his face as red as rare roast beef, and sputtered for words. Finally, he said, "You son of a bitch. You raided the armory when you were pulling out those bodies."

I smiled, and said, "There's no call for profanity, Reverend."

"You lied. 'Bodies,' you said. 'I'm just collecting bodies so I can examine the armor.'" Doctorow threw his hands in the air.

"I wasn't lying," I said. "We only took bodies."

"Then you went back afterward. You still went back on your word."

"Last night was the first time I set foot past the fence since the day we dug up the armor. It was the first time any of us have been back, and we weren't the ones who tore down the fence," I said.

Doctorow did not take the bait. He ignored my jab about the fence, and asked, "Then where did you get a nuclear bomb?"

"Oh, that," I said, grinning as brightly as I could. "I didn't need to raid the armory to get that; we have plenty of nukes right here in Fort Sebastian."

Hollingsworth and Mars, both of whom knew I had been restocking the base with weapons, laughed softly as I spoke. "Remember when I offered to salvage food and rations from those derelict ships? I figured since we were up there, we might as well restock our armory while we were at it. You wanted rations, I wanted rockets. We both made out."

"You son of a—"

"You already said that," I reminded Doctorow.

"What do you plan to do with those weapons, General?" Doctorow asked. "Are you planning on recapturing Terraneau?"

I laughed. "We both want the same thing. You want me off your planet, and I can't wait to leave."

"But that didn't stop you from building your arsenal. Why stockpile weapons if you aren't planning a war?"

I shrugged my shoulders, and said, "I'm a Marine. Marines like things that are loud. It's all part of speaking softly and carrying a big stick."

Doctorow took a step forward and drove his right fist into his open left palm. "This is unacceptable. This is an act of—"

"We didn't leave an empty gas canister outside your door last night," I said. "If we ever do leave you a message, you can bet that the canister won't be empty."

Doctorow glared at me, but I didn't care. He had delivered his message last night, and I brought him to this meeting so that I could deliver mine. He now knew that I was leaving, and that if it came to a fight, I held all of the aces in my hand.

Now that everything was in the open, it was time to turn our attention back to the mission. "So you're suggesting that we light up the wrecks and bash through in a battleship?"

"Considering the situation, sir, that's the best we've come up with."

"What are the odds of success?" I asked.

Lieutenant Mars let a second pass before he answered. He was a young clone, maybe not even in his thirties. Fatigue and frustration showed on his face. "General, there are so many variables; I can't even begin to guess. It's a matter of velocity. With the right speed and God's good grace, this should work."

"It sounds like you've got everything you need," said Doctorow, suddenly sounding cheerful again. Perhaps hearing the suicidal nature of my mission had cheered him up. He bent over the display, looking the scene over closely. "Which ship is going to carry Harris?"

The display showed the entire battlefield, which was spread out over thousands of cubic miles of open space. With the camera panned so far out, the fighter carriers were indistinguishable from the fighters they carried. Everything was represented by tiny motes of light.

Mars said, "You won't really be able to see the ship from this angle." He adjusted the display so that it zoomed in on the

wreckage of a Scutum-Crux Fleet battleship. "I had originally
thought we would use a smaller ship, maybe even a minesweeper. A minesweeper would only have about one-tenth the
overall mass of this battleship.

"Setting a battleship in motion is going to be challenge."
He laughed nervously.

"What do you have in mind?" I asked. I was the one putting his ass on the line, not Mars, not Hollingsworth, not Doctorow; and I did not like the plan so far. The ideas sounded
too damn theoretical, and the wall of dead ships blocking my
way sounded too concrete.

"General, sir, we're going to attach a fleet of transports to
the hull of the ship and use them like booster rockets," Mars
said.

"What about the men in the transports?" asked Hollingsworth. "What about the pilots?"

"No live pilots; everything will be remote control," said
Mars. "This mission involves guiding a battleship into a
nuclear explosion. No one in his right mind would fly into a
nuclear blast."

"But that's what I'm doing?" I asked.

Nobody answered.

# CHAPTER
# NINE

The plan was to attach thirty remotely controlled transports to the hull of a derelict battleship to use as external
rockets. No one had ever used transports to move a derelict
battleship or anything of like size. Everything was theoretical, but Mars assured me that it would work.

When you place your life in other men's hands, you want to
know that they take their work seriously. The Corps of Engineers called their plan "Operation Chastity Belt" and referred

to the battleship as "Harris's Tool." They probably took the mission seriously, but they were also enlisted men; juvenile humor was part of their makeup.

They had *clever* names for every element of the operation. "Harris's Tool," the battleship, would travel nearly three hundred miles gathering speed in a linear acceleration before *poking* "Chastity Belt," the wall of destroyed Unified Authority ships that blocked the way to "Virginity," the hot zone. When the Tool was precisely forty-seven miles from Chastity Belt, the engineers would fire a series of nuclear devices that would both damage and superheat the U.A. ships, but the blast would not destroy them. They labeled this part of the operation "Foreplay." Just as the negative 450-degree temperature of space would set in, turning the metal brittle, the Tool would ram into the ships. If everything went right, the Tool would hit with sufficient velocity to break through the barrier.

Lieutenant Mars might have been counting on "God's good grace," but he carefully calculated acceleration and timing as well. Without the proper velocity, I would not have the power to smash through the ships.

My battleship/barge/battering ram would be wedge-shaped and wider from wing to wing than from bow to stern. This meant that I would have a better chance of survival traveling sideways, leading with the starboard wing while I hid in the landing bay on the port side of the ship.

I explained all of this to Sergeant Nobles, and he said, "It sounds like you're trying to kill yourself, sir." Nobles was a trained transport pilot. Officially, I did not have a personal pilot; but when I took rides in transports, he generally flew the bird.

We sat in the empty mess area of a vacant wing of Fort Sebastian. I wanted privacy as I explained the mission.

It was raining outside; gusts of wind blew a steady stream of water against the windows. The mess had a wall of windows overlooking Sebastian Commons—a park in the center of the base. The lawns outside those windows were as flat and even as a gymnasium floor. Even though we did not have enough men to fill the base, I had my men mow the grass. When forts become run-down, the men surely follow.

"Then it may be a double suicide," I said.

"Oh shit," he said. "You're asking me to come with you."

"I'll need a pilot," I said.

He'd been my pilot for nearly a year, making him one of my oldest friends on Terraneau; but until this conversation, I'd only known him as "my pilot." We'd flown missions in which we both nearly died, and I didn't even know his name. Was it because he was a clone? Had I become antisynthetic?

"Please say this is a joke, General," Nobles said.

"Once I get through to the other side, I'm going to need someone to fly the transport off the battleship."

"You mean the *Tool*?" Nobles asked.

"Yeah, okay, the *Tool*," I conceded.

"General, do you know where we'll be when we get to the other side?"

"I have no idea," I admitted.

"And you want me to come along for the ride?" he asked. "Are you ordering me to come?"

"I was hoping you would volunteer."

"Have you asked for other volunteers?"

I shook my head and told the truth, "There's no point placing additional lives in harm's way."

"No, sir. Why would you want to put anyone else in danger?"

I would not order Nobles to go. I could. He was a clone. In theory, his programming would make him comply. In theory, our battleship would break through the barrier, and we would sail into the broadcast zone safe and sound. In theory, military clones were incapable of fighting against the Unified Authority. I'd never placed much faith in theoretical solutions, but that wasn't stopping me from placing my life on the line.

"You've been my pilot since they transferred me to the Scutum-Crux Fleet. I'd hate to go without you," I said. It sounded weak, but Nobles liked the distinction of being my pilot. From what I could tell, he did not mind high-risk missions, either.

He gave me a sly, one-sided smile, and asked, "Since you put it that way, when do we leave?"

"Oh, our schedule," I said, feeling a bit ashamed. I had not told him about the mission until the last minute because, assuming he agreed to fly me, I did not want to give him enough time to change his mind. "We leave within the hour."

"Aye, sir, an hour," he said. "I'll go pack my things."

*He's a good man,* I thought. I'd seen so many good men die during the ten years I'd spent as a Marine.

I didn't give my pilot time to have second thoughts, but I also secretly hoped for a delay. One man's delay is another man's reprieve. I had not yet told Ava that I was ready to leave. She knew about the mission, but she had no idea about my schedule.

I went to visit her at work. She worked in one of the three skyscrapers left standing in a cluster in the Norristown financial district. One of the buildings served as a dormitory for orphaned boys, another for girls. Now that Mars and the Corps of Engineers had restored the power, the locals used the third building as a hospital, among other things. Ava taught literature and drama classes in the girls' dormitory.

I drove up to the building in my jeep, rain thrumming on the removable roof, making a noise like a thousand fingers tapping on a desk. The triangle of streets between the three buildings stood empty. One of the streets had been dug up and railed off from traffic. The Corps of Engineers had been laying cable there; but with my mission about to begin, the project had stalled as they were needed elsewhere.

I parked my jeep along the curb right beside the girls' dormitory. When I opened my door, a cold wind blew rain onto the dashboard. I jumped out, and the wind slammed the door shut behind me. My shoulders hunched against the cold and my right hand holding down my lid, I ran to the entrance. As I approached the covered walkway that led to the door of the building, an armed guard stepped out of nowhere and planted himself in my path.

He was a civilian, a kid in his twenties with a little beef on him.

"Where do you think you're going?" he asked.

A year ago, I would have planted the kid on his ass, but that was before the shoot-out with the U.A. Marines. I had not had a combat reflex since the Marines shot me with five neurotoxin-coated fléchettes. Instead of feeling the warmth of testosterone and adrenaline in my blood, I felt a slight tinge of nerves. That tiny glimpse of fear bothered me far more than the kid himself. I could not afford to hesitate when challenged, not even for a millisecond, so I responded with more prejudice than needed. Instead of explaining why I had come, I said, "Out of my way."

The boy started to raise his rifle; but my reflexes, quick as ever, were faster. I grabbed the gun, directing the muzzle away from me, and pulling as if trying to wrench it out of the kid's hands. When he yanked back, I gave the rifle a shove in his direction, driving the butt into his chest. The boy dropped to the ground, fighting for breath, while I held on to the rifle.

"Now if you will excuse me," I said. I dropped the gun a few feet from where the boy lay gasping and continued toward the door. Two more armed guards stood just inside the glass door, their rifles drawn.

Those two needed a lesson in depth perception that I would happily give them. They had miscalculated the distance between themselves and the door. I threw the door open, hitting the guard to the right on the nose. Some stupid instinct caused him to fire his weapon as he spun to the ground, and the bullets shattered the glass in the door, sending shards and blades across the lobby. The noise and destruction startled the second guard for a split second—long enough for me to grab his rifle and sweep his legs out from under him. The sound of the gunfire still ringing in my ear, I pulled the clip from the rifle, emptied the chamber, and dropped the gun to the floor. Then I turned to the first guard, and asked, "Excuse me, I'm here to see Ava Gardner. Could you tell her that I'm here?"

The kid scampered backward a couple of paces on his hands and ass, then climbed to his feet and disappeared into the building. I would not set foot beyond the lobby of the girls' dormitory; some taboos cannot be ignored. Doctorow might overlook my assaulting his three armed guards, but he would not look kindly upon my entering his home for orphaned girls.

As it turned out, my decision to semibehave proved wise. The next person to enter the lobby was not Ava, as I had hoped, but the Right Reverend Colonel Ellery Doctorow. He stormed out of the elevator, came halfway across the lobby, saw the shattered door, and froze where he stood.

"What happened here?" he barked in a voice that was nearly as loud as gunfire.

Only then did I notice the blood on the ground. There was a small puddle to my left, where the second guard sat wiping his face. Blood ran down from his cheeks and squeezed between his fingers. The flying glass must have slashed him.

"Your men pointed their weapons at me, I felt I had to take them away," I said. "The blood and the door, they did that on their own."

Outside the door, that first guard managed to sit up but remained on the concrete rubbing his chest, his rifle still resting on the ground beside him.

A dozen people crowded behind Doctorow gaping at the destruction that had been the door of the lobby. They chattered in tiny, half-whispering voices. No one came any closer than Doctorow, who remained thirty feet from me.

I had come unarmed, and I remained unarmed, having given the rifles back to the guards. Standing there in my Charlie service uniform, I tried to look as harmless as possible. If the locals ignored the bits of glass and blood on the ground, the injured men, and the rifles, they might have found me charming.

Attempting to compose himself, Doctorow asked, "What are you doing here?"

The words had barely left his mouth when an elevator opened, and Ava stepped into view. She saw the destruction around me and gave me a somewhat motherly smile—the smile mothers must sometimes give their children as they prepare to scold them. She worked her way through the crowd and stood beside me.

"What are you doing here, General? You know this building is off-limits to you and your men," Doctorow repeated. He was right, of course; I did know. Until this moment, I had always honored that rule. Even now, I stood just outside the building. I had barely entered its threshold. Once the guards were down, I could have waltzed in at leisure; instead, I remained at the door.

"I came to tell Ava good-bye," I told Doctorow.

"So you attacked my men and shot up my building?" Doctorow asked.

I did not know how to respond. The way he spun the story, I was the aggressor.

"Honey, next time, why don't you paint your message on a tank of poison gas and leave it outside the building?" Ava said in her tart voice. Her sarcasm was biting, but it was not aimed at me.

Ava saw things that completely skirted my range of vision. In the bigger scheme of things, Doctorow had fired the first shots.

He lifted a hand to his face and ran his fingers along his beard. "You're leaving?" he asked, sounding more in control.

"I came to say good-bye," I repeated.

"You stepped way out of line, Harris; but under the circumstances, I suppose we'll overlook it," Doctorow said. What else was he going to do? If he threw me in jail, I couldn't leave his planet.

Doctorow turned and went back to the elevators, his entourage following after him like a pack of well-trained dogs.

The three guards remained, though they now kept well away from me. Congregating in a distant corner of the lobby, they looked in my direction and whispered among themselves.

"Thank you so much for not making a scene," Ava said. Now the scorn focused on me, and I wished I hadn't come.

"Sorry," I said. It might not have made any difference to Ava, but I felt embarrassed. As we walked through the shattered doorway, glass crunching under our shoes, I wondered if Doctorow might have been right about me. Maybe I couldn't be trusted.

The rain continued to fall in windblown streaks. My Army green jeep blended in with the darkened streets and gray sky.

"When are you leaving?" Ava asked, as we reached the edge of the awning.

"Now," I said. "I'm driving to the airfield from here."

"That seems rather sudden. How long have you known you were leaving?"

"A week."

"You don't give a girl much notice."

"I thought maybe we could have lunch before I left." I used lunch as bait, but I had something else in mind.

"Harris, it's three in the afternoon."

"I haven't eaten," I said.

"I have," she said. I looked in her eyes and knew that she

understood what I wanted. Having run out of things to say, I fumbled for a moment, then decided to go for broke. "I could drive you home."

"What about my car?" she asked.

"We could drive in separate cars," I said.

"I have classes."

I could not tell if the wall between us was because she had already moved on from me or if she wanted to protect herself. The last two men in her life had cast her aside; maybe she built mental walls to insulate herself from pain. They were natural-borns, and they had dropped her because she was a clone. She was a clone, and I was a clone; we were together because society had very little use for us. Then again, she was beautiful, and beautiful women seldom hurt for company.

Hoping she had not simply moved on from me, I said, "I will come back."

I expected to hear more brass from her. I expected Ava to say some line that started with, "Honey." Instead, she drew close to me. I felt her warm breath as she pressed her lips to my mouth, then I tasted her. She held the kiss for most of a minute, then said, "Harris, you better come back."

With that, she spun on her heels and walked back into the dormitory, where she knew I could not follow.

## CHAPTER
# TEN

I pulled over in an empty area and changed into my combat armor, then drove to the airfield. The wind and rain picked up as I drove. A constant stream of droplets cascaded down my windshield.

I noticed the weather, but my mind was on Ava. If I came back, would we pick up where we left off? How long would she wait? Why hadn't she agreed to let me take her home? I knew the answer to that last question: She didn't want to have sex at that moment. But did that mean we were done? I had to clear my mind for the mission, but I didn't want to.

As I pulled along the edge of the airfield, I saw Sergeant Nobles waiting in his jeep. Like me, he'd come wearing combat armor. He stepped out of his ride as I approached. Nobles stood at attention and saluted, drops the size of toenails splattering against his armor. "Sir, we've fallen a little behind schedule, but we shouldn't be very late," he said.

"They won't start the mission without us," I said.

He laughed.

If things had gone the way I planned, we would have taken off an hour later, but I would have faced the unknown feeling a bit more satisfied. In the end, though, sex with Ava would have changed nothing.

As we walked around the transport, I watched to see if Nobles would comment on the boot-sized tube attached under the nose of the bird—a tube with a nuclear-tipped torpedo I'd had specially fitted. If he saw it, he didn't mention it. He might not have noticed the tube hidden the way it was. Me, I couldn't take my eyes off it. Amazing that such a tiny package could do so much damage.

We entered the transport, walking up the rear ramp into the darkness of the kettle, and my heart dropped. I had learned to live with saluting superiors and taking orders from banal-brained officers whose only qualification was that they were natural-born; but the gloomy feeling of entering a transport always gave me a chill. On this day, though, the chill turned icy.

Without saying a word, I crossed the kettle and climbed the ladder to the cockpit. Storm-filtered sunlight shone through the windshield.

A thick wall of mercury-colored storm clouds hid the sun but not its light. Driven by blustering winds, the rain fell at sharp angles and splash-landed in puddles along the side of the landing strip.

The airfield was little more than a landing strip with a couple of newly built hangars surrounded by a wall of chain link and razor wire. We had built guard towers in the corners of the fence to keep the locals out, but that was for show. No one manned the towers.

The landing strip was too short for anything but transports, a species of air-/spacecraft that took off vertically. You couldn't land so much as a fighter on this strip, but it had enough room for dozens of transports.

"What's that?" Nobles asked, pointing to the bright red switch one of Mars's engineers had installed over his throttle.

"Oh, that," I said, feeling a little bit guilty. "That fires the torpedo."

"We need a torpedo?" he asked, sounding nervous and more than a little skeptical. He probably wondered if there was more danger to this mission than I had let on about. There wasn't.

"It never hurts to be prepared," I said.

Nobles sat in the pilot seat but made no move toward the instrumentation around him. He folded his arms across his chest, and asked, "Prepared for what exactly?"

"Well, you know, there's no way of knowing where the broadcast will send us."

Nobles started to say something, but I put up my hand and stopped him.

"Hear me out," I said. "Admiral Warshaw flew his ships through this broadcast zone; it's going to be safe," I said. Having spent six years assigned to the Scutum-Crux Fleet, Nobles knew Warshaw. He might or might not have known Warshaw personally, but they'd both served on the *Kamehameha*, the flagship of the fleet.

"Did Warshaw strike you as having a death wish?" I asked. "If he used this zone to broadcast himself out, I'm betting it will send us someplace safe."

Nobles thought about this for a moment, then asked, "So where do you think we'll come out?"

"Where will we come out?" I repeated. "I have no specking idea, but I can make an educated guess. When the top brass decided to eliminate the cloning program, they shipped off whatever clones were left to twelve of the outer fleets. I don't know about you; but if I were Warshaw, and I had the Earth Fleet chasing after me, I'd send myself someplace where I could find reinforcements."

"And the torpedo?" Nobles asked.

"It's nuclear-tipped," I said. He knew what that meant.

When I arrived in the Scutum-Crux Arm, the Avatari had Terraneau sealed off from rescue by a layer of tachyons. By firing a nuke above the spot where the layer originated, we were able to poke a small hole through the layer. That was how we landed men on the planet.

Of course, with Terraneau, we knew the exact spot to hit with our torpedo. On this run, we might not even know what planet we were circling, let alone the right spot to hit.

"But it's just a precaution, right? We're not bringing it because we're going to fight aliens."

"Just a precaution," I agreed.

"And we won't need it?" he asked.

"No. Probably not."

He thought about this, nodded, and pivoted his seat so that he faced the flight controls. "You're a brave man, sir," he said as he fired up the engines. "It takes a lot of nerve to decide to fly a nuke through a broadcast zone."

"They used to do that all the time," I said, feeling relieved that we were finally going wheels up.

"Those ships were sealed. You've got us riding in a specking wreck," Nobles said. He looked back to see if I was suitably panicked, then fired the thrusters and lifted off the ground. "Good thing you're comfortable around nuclear weapons."

He knew I wasn't.

When I thought the situation through, I realized that anything that set off the nuke would probably toast us as well. Logic only went so far, however, when it came to my phobia of things I could not control. Trying to ignore my nerves, I sat in the copilot's seat and strapped myself in.

We crossed back over Norristown, passing over barren streets and thriving neighborhoods. Going up to gather food and weapons, I had flown over this territory dozens of times, but this time was different. This time I did not know when I would return. It was not just a question of survival. Even if everything worked out just right, I might never return.

Off in the distance, I saw the three towers of the financial district—the boys' dorm, the girls' dorm, and the hospital. Only a few minutes had passed since Ava sent me away. She'd still be in that building. Was she thinking of me?

"So if Warshaw broadcasted into wherever we're going, what's to say he stayed there?" Nobles asked. "I mean, maybe he wasn't any safer there than he was over here. Maybe he got there, patched up another broadcast station, and took his fleet to the next stop." As he asked this, Nobles took us out of the atmosphere. The sky turned dark and was no longer a sky but field of stars.

*And maybe the Earth Fleet caught up to him on the other side,* I thought. It was entirely possible that we were broadcasting from one graveyard to another.

"If it isn't the prodigal son come for a visit," Lieutenant Mars radioed in to us as we slowed to a drift and floated toward the wreckage. "I was beginning to think you changed your mind."

Nobles, who had become very serious, ignored Mars's greeting, and said, "This is Marine 1, do you have a target for us?"

"You mean Harris's Tool?" asked one of the engineers.

"Roger that," said Nobles.

"Harris's Tool," the engineer persisted. "Harris's Tool. That is the code name for the battleship. The only way Operation Chastity Belt can succeed is for us all to be on the same page. You need to call it 'Harris's Tool,' or we won't know what you are talking about."

"Come again?" asked Nobles.

"The names were Spuler's idea, not mine," Mars said, sounding somewhat apologetic. Seaman First Class Aaron Spuler was the resident joker of the Corps of Engineers.

"Fine, where is Harris's Tool?" Nobles asked.

"Where do you think?" asked Spuler.

Several people laughed. I did not, neither did Nobles.

"COE 1, where precisely is the battleship?" Nobles asked, his voice flat. "COE" was short for Corps of Engineers.

"Honestly, Spuler, you're acting like a ten-year-old," said Mars. Then he said, "Marine 1, I'll send over the coordinates."

The laughter stopped.

We picked our way through the graveyard. Terraneau, a giant blue, green, and tawny globe, spun in one corner of our vision. Far in a distance, a roiling orange-and-yellow sun

glowed. Seen from inside our transport, the dead ships floating around us looked as large as continents, their portholes
dark, the exposed areas of their decks even darker. Humanity
never conquered space, it just learned to travel in bubbles. All
around us, the dead ships hung as reminders of what happens
when that bubble breaks.

It took us twenty minutes to fly through the graveyard,
dodging around the ruins of capital ships, sometimes breaking through a fog of litter. We saw no bodies, though tens of
thousands of them floated around us. We pushed through bits
of armor plating, folds of molten glass, wings from fighters,
and more than one curtain of frozen water, all suspended in
space. My pilot might have been used to these sights; he always flew in the cockpit where he could see his surroundings.
I generally traveled in the kettle, blissfully ignorant of everything around the ship.

Off in the distance, a derelict battleship sat in a clearing like
an island in the night. Three rows of flashing lights ran along
the underside of the ship, winking on and off in a sequence of
red and yellow squares. At the far end of the ship, four flashing
blue lights marked the entrance to the landing bay.

The hull of the battleship was somewhere between beige
and gray in color, an enormous moth-shaped wedge with tears
in its skin where torpedoes had struck it.

"I don't like the looks of this scow," Nobles said.

I did not say anything. Somewhere in the back of my
mind, I wanted to treat this whole adventure as if it were a
bad dream. I would do what had to be done, but fear lurked in
my mind. I tried to ignore it, but I knew it was there.

All along the side of the ship, tiny dark spots stood out
against the gray of the hull. They looked no more significant
than slugs crawling on a garden wall. These were transports,
clamped to the hull on the ship in regular intervals, thirty of
them in all. We flew below one, and I stared up at it. No light
shone from within the cockpit. The transport looked every bit
as dead as the host to which it was now attached.

"They look like ants compared to the battleship," Nobles
said. I expected him to question whether they would be able
to move the big ship, but he didn't. A trained pilot, he understood the physics of space travel better than I did.

We approached the landing bay, a straight-edged passageway shrouded in darkness. In the dead of space, with the landing-pad lights extinguished, the inside of the bay was absolute black. The silhouette of a raven flying across a moonless sky would not have been as dark as the world inside that ship.

"COE1, this is Marine 1," Nobles began, and hesitated before completing his thought. "We have entered the battleship."

Spuler started to make another stupid joke, but Mars cut him off. "Understood," he said. I could hear Spuler grumbling in the background.

"Are the locks open?" Nobles asked. Landing bays incorporated enormous doors for atmospheric control.

"Everything is a go," Mars said. "We will seal the locks behind you."

"Yeah, we wouldn't want anything to shoot out prematurely," Spuler added.

"Stow it, Seaman," Mars snapped.

More laughter. Even Mars laughed this time. Then he said, "One more word out of you, Spuler, and you'll be cleaning the Norristown sewage system for the rest of your career."

Silence.

I knew Spuler. He had a mouth on him, but he was worth the trouble. Mars had one thousand men in his Corps of Engineers; Spuler might well have been the best of them. He'd probably done more to get this show rolling than all of the other engineers combined.

Moving no faster than ten miles per hour, we drifted into that dark hatchway, our runner lights illuminating small swatches along the runway and walls. This part of the ship was in immaculate condition—the walls, pipes, panels, doors, ceiling fixtures, and other furnishings all in perfect trim.

The runway was designed to accommodate transports, but it was wide enough for larger ships. Part of the design included an artificial-gravity field in which ships entering this passage were supposed to land. The field had not been restored. Instead of riding the sled system through the locks, Nobles had to fly the transport through that needle's eye.

"Marine 1, the outer hatch is sealed," Mars informed us.

Spuler said nothing. He probably had some smart remark

about restoring a foreskin or something along that line, but Mars had warned him off.

We slowly drifted past the first of the atmospheric shields, a massive iron door that weighed multiple tons. Behind it, in a discrete recess, a tiny red light winked on and off. I was glad to see it. It meant that while the rest of the ship was dormant, the engineers had restored power to the atmospheric locks.

Nobles pointed to a glowing lever on his flight stick. "Looks like we'll be able to open the doors from in here," he said, sounding relieved. I knew how he felt. Everything had gone according to plan so far.

We floated in past all three of the locks and settled onto the landing-bay deck. In the glare of our runner lights, I saw that Mars and his engineers had cleared as much debris as they could from the area.

I looked around the empty landing bay outside the window, a world so dark and silent it might have been at the bottom of a sea. Abandoned. Lifeless. How many people had died in this chamber? A crew of three thousand men had died defending this ship. That much I knew. Some had been flushed out to space. Undoubtedly, others were still aboard, floating statues that had once been sailors and Marines.

The Corps of Engineers had equipped the skids of our transport with special magnetic clamps to hold us in place during our upcoming collision. The magnets came on and locked us into place once we landed.

"COE 1, we are in place, repeat, we are in place," Nobles radioed, as our bird touched the deck.

I hated the sound of those words. They meant we were sealed into this orbiting tomb. They meant I could not turn back. Anxiety built in my gut. I wanted to tell Nobles that this was all a mistake. We needed to go back. Without my combat reflex to calm me, I had to deal with unadulterated fear.

"Copy that, Marine 1," Mars said.

And then, on a direct line that Nobles would not hear, Lieutenant Mars said, "General Harris, a lot of your men will be glad to see you go."

"So I hear," I said. Now it was Mars's turn to tell me what he thought of me. Why not give me an earful? He wasn't likely to see me again. I always thought the "born-again clone" liked me, but maybe he simply had a better poker face than Hollingsworth or Doctorow.

"Serving with you has been an honor, sir. I hope your mission goes as planned, and you return soon," he said, leaving me stunned. He signed off before I could respond.

Once again I found myself alone with my thoughts, trying to adjust to the alien feeling of unbridled fear. Flying always bothered me, even when I had a reliable combat reflex. It made me feel helpless. In the fight-or-flight of the battlefield, I had a measure of control. On a ship, I had no control of my fate. Whatever became of the ship would also become of me.

"Nobles, what's your first name?" I asked, mostly to clear the suffocating silence from my helmet.

"Chris, sir," he said.

"Short for Christopher?"

"Short for Christian. My parents must have been religious types." Like every other clone, he was raised to believe he was a natural-born. In fact, he was programmed to die if he discovered his synthetic heritage. As a Liberator, I was spared that last bit of programming.

"Must have been," I agreed. "Too bad you never knew them. Do you know how they died?"

"They died in a house fire," Nobles said.

*Funny,* I thought, *mine, too.* Lieutenant Mars broke up our conversation. "Prepare for launch initiation. Repeat, prepare for launch initiation."

"Shit, here we go," I whispered, not even thinking who would hear me.

"General Harris, we set up a video array if you want to follow the operation's progress."

I thought that he meant some kind of an interLink display. The last thing I wanted at that moment was images of transports dragging the carcass of a battleship showing inside my helmet.

Willing myself to sound calm, I said, "I'd rather keep the interLink open."

"They're not on the interLink, sir, they're on the screens behind your seat."

"What?" When I looked at the back wall of the cockpit, I saw five rows of four-inch video screens inlaid in the wall.

Most of the screens showed a small section of the battleship's hull and a bird's-eye view of cluttered space. The engineers must have placed cameras in the transports along the hull.

"That's was kind of you," I said.

"It was Spuler's idea," Mars said.

"Think of it as an in-flight porno," said Spuler. "You get to watch the Tool's penetration."

"Spuler," Mars said.

I tried to ignore them. Looking at the little displays, I realized just how much I wanted to scrub the mission. I felt the jittering in my hands and the throbbing in my temples. Now that the transport had landed, and the runner lights were out, I sat in darkness, seeing only by the light of the night-for-day lenses in my visor. I was scared already, and soon I would be terrified.

Trying to sound confident, I told Mars, "Pull the trigger." Then I did something I knew I would regret; I told Nobles, "I'm shutting down our Link until we get through," without giving him a reason why. I wasn't shutting down the entire interLink, we might need to contact Mars; I was just shutting down the Link between me and Nobles because I could feel the panic spreading through my thoughts like a cancer, and I did not want him to hear me.

"Yes, sir," said Nobles. He seemed preoccupied as he toyed with the switches and gear around his seat.

I removed the harness and climbed out of the chair. The artificial gravity drawing my boots to the deck, I walked to the panel of screens. When I took a closer look at some of the monitors, I saw the rear sides of transports in the corners of the screens. The engines were already running. We had started the flight without my noticing. Sometimes, that happens in space.

# CHAPTER
# ELEVEN

I couldn't stop myself from looking at the monitors. It didn't matter that I wanted to stick my head in the proverbial sand; the screens bore down on me like five rows of unblinking eyes. Even when I looked away, I felt their weight upon me.

Across the cockpit, Nobles busied himself checking systems and flight controls. He flipped switches, read gauges, then turned his attention to the video array I wanted so much to ignore. He settled comfortably, and there he sat, his gaze transfixed, the reflections of the little screens showing in rows of bright squares in his visor.

In the isolation of my helmet, I began to panic. "I'm not ready for this," I said to myself. I said it out loud. There was something comforting in hearing my own voice rolling around in my helmet; and what did it matter, I had shut off the interLink. No one would hear me.

"Did you say something, General?" For a moment I thought I might be hearing voices, then I remembered that I had not severed my Link with Lieutenant Mars.

"No," I said. "I'm just mumbling to myself." I thought for a moment, then I said, "I can't do this. This is crazy, we need to call this off."

The top screens of the array showed the view from the lead transport drones. The cameras looked out into space, but not open space. A tangle of wrecked warships filled the view, looking as impregnable as a castle wall.

I became aware of the way I was breathing, panting like a winded dog.

Light flared across thirty of the thirty-five screens, turning them white as an afternoon sun. The nuclear explosion. We'd just shot off enough bombs to destroy a small planet. The heat generated by the cataclysm would only last a moment. During that moment, metal would melt—and bodies—then the chill of space would return. What was the power of a few nuclear bombs against the immenseness of space?

The flash of the bombs vanished as quickly as it appeared, but it left ghosts on the video screens. Thirty of the thirty-five screens were outside the ship, placed in transports; the other five showed scenes inside the hull of the battleship . . . the *Tool*. These screens showed dark corridors and braced walls. Mars and his men had done a lot of work preparing the ship.

"I'm not ready for this," I told Mars. On the other side of the cockpit, Nobles sat comfortably, unbothered by what we were about to do. Apparently, flying through nuclear explosions left him unfazed.

"It's too late to call off the mission, General," Mars said in a voice meant to soothe me.

"Shut down the transports," I said. "You have control of the transports, shut them down."

"We can't do that, sir. There's already too much forward momentum."

"Shut them off," I said, feeling frantic. I had no control over the situation, and that terrified me.

"The Tool will still hit Chastity Belt whether we cut the engines or not," Mars said.

Now he was using the names Spuler had used, and that aggravated me. My anger cut through my panicked thoughts, and I said, "Lieutenant, shut off the specking engines."

Mars laughed. "Does Ava Gardner know that you're a coward?"

I heard the words, but it took a moment for them to sink in. I sat in the copilot's chair in stunned silence, as he added, "Harris, you're the best kept secret in the whole Marine Corps. Everyone thinks you're such a badass, and it turns out you're just another bed wetter."

"You son of a bitch," I said, looking away from the monitors. "You specking son of a bitch. If I get out of here . . ."

"Now I'm scared," Mars said. "General Bed Wetter is threatening me."

I could not think of anything else but how much I wanted to kill that son of a bitch. "Born-again clone" my ass. I would have hopped out of the battleship and dog-paddled to Terraneau if I thought I could do it. It was as I sat there fuming, trying to invent some form of revenge, that we struck the barrier. We did not slice through the broken ships, we smashed through like a hammer hitting glass, and the force nearly threw me from my chair.

I turned toward the monitors in time to see three of them go dead. The working screens showed a fractal kaleidoscope of shapes—shards of ships tumbling as they floated out of view. The five cameras located inside the battleship showed crumbled walls that looked like they might have been made out of paper.

Two of the screens in the first row showed the bow of one of the U.A. ships floating into open space. Strands of blue electricity formed around it, flexing and dancing; and then, in a flash, the section of ship was gone.

"You're through the barrier, sir," Mars said, suddenly sounding respectful once more. "For what it's worth, I would have resigned my commission before I would have done what you are doing."

"What?" I asked, my thoughts still entropic.

"You are traveling at a sustained speed of 273 miles per hour," Mars said. "I hoped you would come through at 290, but 270 is within the margin of error."

I still did not understand. I looked over at Nobles, who still sat staring into the monitors, looking so damned relaxed. He had his seat swiveled around, his right hand stretched across the arm of his chair and his left hand curled on his lap.

It took me another moment to realize that Mars had said those things to distract me. I took a deep breath, and said, "Thank you, Lieutenant."

"No problem, sir," said Mars. I could hear the smile in his voice. "Go with God."

My blood pressure returning to normal, I turned to look at screens and saw the beginning of the anomaly forming. The electricity of the anomaly was not as bright as the nuclear flare, but it was sustained. It looked like a bubble of light in the darkness of space. Jagged tentacles of electricity reached out from it.

"Here comes the dangerous part of the ride," I said.

"You'll be fine, sir," Mars said.

In less than a second, the lightning from the anomaly stretched and overtook the battleship. The screens on the first row of the array showed a brief flash of white and went dead. The screens on the second row showed lightning dancing on the hull of the battleship. They showed transports peeling away from the hull like dried leaves falling from a tree.

Electricity continued dancing along the hull. More screens went bright, then dark. Somehow, the electricity worked its way inside the battleship; I could see it on three of the internal screens. Unstable light danced inside the hallways, an obscene wattage, multiple millions of joules, more than enough power to stop my heart and sear my skin and melt my eyes.

The electricity ran through the ship like a flood, splashing glare everywhere. It happened so quickly, literally in a flash. One moment I saw monitors winking out of existence, the next moment all was silent. I sat in the cockpit aware that if a catastrophe were going to happen, it would already have occurred.

"Mars, can you hear me?" I asked.

No one responded.

*We've either made it through, or Mars has died,* I thought. Then I came up with another possibility—my communications gear might have fried.

I tried to raise Mars on several frequencies and had no luck. Then I tried Nobles. When he did not respond, it occurred to me that he might have had a heart attack. The poor son of a bitch might have died right there, sitting in his pilot's seat just a few feet away from me.

If he was having heart problems, there was nothing I could do. I could not open his armor; we had purged the oxygen from the cabin. Not knowing what else to do, I tapped my fingers on the glass visor of his helmet.

"What are you doing?" Nobles asked, his voice groggy.

"You fell asleep?" I asked, feeling both relieved and embarrassed.

"Sorry, sir," Nobles said. "When are we going to make the broadcast?"

"You slept through the entire thing?" I asked, now realizing why he looked so relaxed. Wondering if the sleep had helped him avoid a panic attack or if the sleep had been the attack, I patted Nobles on his armored shoulder, and said, "Let's take our bird out of here and find out where we are."

"Yes, sir," Nobles said, sounding as if I had woken him from a trance. He flipped a switch, and the lights came back online in the cockpit. The gauges in the instrument panel shone their low green-and-white glow. The runner lights along the base of the transport started, shining bright light all around the landing bay. Hitting our thrusters ever so slightly, he lifted us off the ground to rotate the transport so that our nose faced the runway.

He tapped a button and looked out the windshield. When he did not get the response he wanted, he tapped the button several more times. "COE 1, this is Marine 1. The atmospheric gates are not responding. Repeat, COE 1, I am unable to open the gates." He sounded so damn official when he hit the mike.

"Lieutenant Mars warned me that this might happen while we were prepping for launch," Nobles said.

"Come again," I said.

"The atmospheric locks are not responding, sir. Mars said that could happen. He said something about taking our fate in our own hands by flying a wreck," Nobles said. "I didn't think we'd survive the broadcast, that's why I took that sleeping pill."

# CHAPTER
# TWELVE

The doors of the atmospheric locks might have been knocked out of alignment when we crashed through the other ships, or the controls for opening the door may have been fried when we passed through the broadcast zone. We were trapped either way.

Nobles parked the transport and opened the rear hatch for me. The artificial gravity that rooted me to the deck of the transport did not extend beyond its ramp. I leaped into the void and floated across the open landing-bay floor as smoothly as a cloud rolls across the sky. Below me, I saw the rubberized insulation that the Corps of Engineers used to coat the floor, walls, and ceiling. The stuff had probably saved our lives; a lot of electricity had pulsed through this ship.

"Speck," I said.

"What is it?" asked Nobles.

I drifted right up to the wall and pounded a fist into the insulation. It was rigid. Hoping to peel the rubber away, I tried stabbing my fingers into the rubber. It did not give way.

"They sealed the doors to the ship," I said. I had hoped to search the ship for explosives or maybe a laser welder, something I could use to cut through the atmospheric locks.

"It's insulation," Nobles informed me. "That's what kept the electricity out of the landing bay."

"It's also sealing us in," I pointed out, my temper starting to get the better of me. I silently toyed with the idea of pulling my combat knife from my rucksack, but I knew I couldn't even nick industrial-grade insulation using a simple knife. "You wouldn't happen to have anything we can use to cut our way out?"

"You mean like a laser welder?" asked Nobles.

"Yeah," I said.

"No, sir. Did you bring any weapons we can use?"

"I have an M27 and a torpedo."

"Didn't you say the torpedo was a nuke?" asked Nobles.

"Affirmative."

"Maybe we should save that for a last resort, sir."

"There has got to be some way out of here," I said. Pushing off the rubberized wall, I launched myself past the transport and glided to the far end of the bay. With its electronics offline, the massive atmospheric lock was just another wall. It was designed to be bulletproof, fireproof, and radiation resistant. I might have been tempted to fire my M27 at it, but firing a gun in a vacuum with neither gravity nor air friction to slow the bullets down was never a good idea.

"Speck," I muttered as I kicked off the lock, sending myself past the transport. Gliding in the null gravity, I had no more capacity to steer myself than a bullet or a billiard ball. I sailed past the nose of the transport, then along the side and pushed a different wall, reangling myself so that I entered the transport through its ass, where the artificial gravity brought me to my feet.

Dragging my feet along the ramp to stop myself, I turned to take one last look across the landing bay. Surely there had to be a welding torch or a drill. Hell, even a particle beam might do the trick. A particle beam . . . A tiny pistol—its disruptive beam might tear through the insulation.

The standard-issue particle-beam pistol was small . . . so small you could throw one in your rucksack and forget it was there. I hit the button, closing the rear doors, then grabbed my rucksack and headed up to the cockpit.

"What are you doing?" Nobles asked, as I burst into the cabin.

"I have an idea," I said as I pulled out my clothes. I pulled out my Charlie service pants and blouse, not really flinging them away, but not watching where they landed. I had underwear, shoes, socks, toiletries, my M27, and three clips of ammunition.

And then, at the bottom of my rucksack where I hoped I might find a particle-beam pistol, I found nothing.

"What are you looking for?" Nobles asked.

"A particle-beam weapon," I said.

"Did you bring one?"

"Apparently not," I said. "I don't suppose you did?" I already knew the answer, but he confirmed it. Nobles was a pilot, not a fighter.

"So what do we do now?" Nobles asked.

I dropped into the copilot's seat, and said, "Isn't it obvious?"

"We die?" he asked.

"We wait," I said. "We're in a battleship that just sailed into occupied space. If the Scutum-Crux Fleet is anywhere near here, Warshaw will send ships out to investigate."

"Oh, hey, maybe I should send out a distress signal," Nobles suggested.

"Good idea," I said, no longer certain either of us imbeciles deserved to live much longer.

# CHAPTER
# THIRTEEN

The fighters came first. Unseen by us, they circled the battleship, listening to our distress signal for several minutes before asking us to identify ourselves. Trapped within the landing bay, unable to scan the area outside the battleship, we had no idea whether we were dealing with a couple of fighters or an entire fleet.

I identified myself as General Wayson Harris of the Enlisted Man's Marines.

"It doesn't look like you have much of a ship there, General," said one of the fighter pilots.

It occurred to me that the Unified Authority might well have tracked the SC Fleet to this stretch of the galaxy and defeated it. I might have been speaking to a Unified Authority fighter pilot, in which case my name, rank, and serial number would be more than enough information for a court-martial and firing squad.

The pilot had a clonelike voice, however. He sounded

pretty much like any man under my command. They were all built with the exact same vocal cords, after all.

"This battleship is deader than dinosaur shit," I said. "My pilot and I are sitting in a transport inside the battleship. The transport works. The battleship was just an empty husk we used to surf through the broadcast zone."

The fighter pilot repeated my story back to me to make sure he had heard correctly. "You say you rode a dead battleship through the broadcast zone?"

"That just about sums it up," I said.

He didn't believe me. I didn't blame him. "Tell you what, General, you just fly out, and we will escort you down to the planet."

"Um, I can't," I said. "The landing-bay hatch is broken."

"This just keeps getting more interesting," the pilot said. He thought for a moment, then asked in a suspicious voice, "Is this a readiness drill?"

"Pilot, what is your name?" I asked.

"Stanford, sir. Petty Officer First Class Jefferson Stanford."

"I assure you, Petty Officer First Class Stanford, this is not a drill. This is not a specking joke," I said, and I ordered him to call his commander and report his findings.

Another hour of silence followed. Nobles suggested we pipe air and heat into the cockpit so we could remove our helmets. Taking off the old lid felt good after what we had been through. A few minutes later, he suggested we air out the main kettle. Once that was done, he went to the head and relieved himself.

"Did I miss anything?" he asked when he returned.

I shook my head.

"What if they don't come back?"

"They will," I said.

Another hour passed, and they came back en masse.

"Harris, is that really you in there?"

"Who am I speaking with?" I asked.

"Are you a message in a bottle or a guinea pig?" The voice could have belonged to just about any clone, but the attitude sounded familiar.

"Who is this?" I repeated.

"This is Hank Bishop, Captain of the E.M.F. *Kamehameha*," he said, "E.M.F." being short for "Enlisted Man's Fleet." Just a few months ago, it was still the Scutum-Crux Fleet; but now that the break with the Unified Authority was formal, it was the Enlisted Man's Fleet, and the *Kamehameha* was its flagship.

"No shit," I said.

Bishop laughed. It was a friendly laugh. "Stay put, Harris, I have some engineers on the way. We'll get you out of there."

Another hour passed, and the atmospheric gates slid open. A squadron of fighters met our transport as we emerged from the battleship and escorted us to the *Kamehameha*.

# PART II

# IN DEFENSE OF EMPIRES

# CHAPTER
# FOURTEEN

Earthdate: October 28, A.D. 2517
Location: Providence Kri
Galactic Position: Cygnus Arm

When I first transferred to the Scutum-Crux Arm, my orders were to assume command of the fleet. Those orders changed when Gary Warshaw, the fleet's highest-ranking noncom, made an end run. He paid an unauthorized visit to the Pentagon to whine about a Marine taking command of the fleet.

He might have been acting like a weasel, but he was right. Admiral Brocius, the highest-ranking officer in the Unified Authority Navy, rewrote my orders. Warshaw took command of the fleet, and I became Commandant of the Marines. Then the Earth Fleet attacked, and our bickering came to an end.

The *Kamehameha*, flagship of the Enlisted Man's Fleet— formerly the Scutum-Crux Fleet, traveled out to meet us alone. That in and of itself suggested that something was wrong. Fighter carriers, particularly flagships, do not travel without support. But there she sat, in an isolated pocket of space, with no other ships in sight, the *Kamehameha*, flagship of the Enlisted Man's Fleet.

Five months had passed since the Unified Authority attacked Terraneau. I'd seen plenty of capital ships since the attack, but they were derelicts floating in space, as dark and lifeless as the vacuum around them.

The *Kamehameha*, for all her battles, was anything but dead. The entire ship was a patchwork of dark walls and bright spots, with light shining from viewports and observation decks. A squadron of fighters circled her bow.

My loyalty to the *Kamehameha* ran deep. She was the first ship on which I served, and I served on her twice, once as a newly appointed corporal still trying to earn his chops and more recently as a field-promoted general. But there was something even deeper between us.

We were the same, that ship and I. The *Kamehameha* was an Expansion-class fighter carrier. She was the only Expansion-class ship still in commission, a one-of-a-kind remnant of the abandoned past. Since her manufacture, the Unified Authority had introduced the bigger, more powerful Perseus-class ships. And now the U.A. Navy had yet another generation of newer, smaller, self-broadcasting ships, with better technology in their shields.

And me . . . well, I was the last of the Liberators, a class of clone that had been replaced before the Unified Authority abandoned its cloning program altogether.

"Transport, this is *Kamehameha* Flight Control. Come in."

"Flight Control, this is Transport," said Nobles.

"Do not raise your shields on your approach," the voice warned us. The man spoke in a perfunctory, monotone voice, as if he were reading from a script.

Nobles responded, "Copy that, Flight Control," then turned to me, and said, "That's pretty damn obvious. I wonder if they also have a recorded message in their officers' heads reminding them to wipe their asses after taking a shit."

Then he remembered something and scrambled for the radio. "Flight Control, please be advised that we are carrying a nuclear torpedo."

"Transport, please repeat," the voice said.

"Be advised that this transport has been outfitted with a nuclear-tipped torpedo."

"Transport, stop your engines and power down. Wait for further instructions."

Nobles stopped the transport and cut the power. Everything but the emergency lights went dark. The space outside our transport glowed brighter than the inside of our cabin.

"They're giving us a security scan," Nobles said. "They don't trust us. Can't say I blame them."

I had seen the litany of security tests—X-ray, spectrum analysis, gamma search, radiation readings. By the time they finished, they would know more about the contents of this bird than we did. All of this security told me that the fleet was still at war. They weren't just scanning for the torpedo—Nobles had already told them about that. They were looking for bombs, chemical weapons, maybe even robots and spies.

After no more than five minutes, they radioed back, and said, "Transport pilot, we have detected that your ship is armed. Can you confirm?"

"Affirmative. I already told you about it, we have a nuclear-tipped torpedo," Nobles said.

"What is the purpose of that torpedo?"

I placed a hand on Nobles's shoulder to stop him from answering and leaned in to the microphone. "It makes a hell of a conversation piece," I said.

"I will ask you again, what is the purpose of your weapon?"

I started to answer, but the controller asked me to wait. A moment later he returned and gave us clearance to land. Our escort led us to an open docking bay and left. Nobles piloted the transport into the bay and landed on the sled that would pull us through the three atmospheric locks.

I liked Nobles; he was not the kind of man who gets nervous when conversations die away. Too many pilots felt the need to chat while they waited for the locks, but not him. As the manufactured atmospheres equalized around us, and the gigantic metal hatches cut us off from space, he busied himself shutting down his flight controls, pausing only to say, "Bet they're surprised to see us."

I agreed, but I wondered how happy Warshaw would be about my reappearance.

I got my answer when the last of the atmospheric locks opened. A platoon of armed Marines stood at the ready inside the bay. So did a bomb squad.

"Please wait to exit your transport," said the voice on the radio.

Outside the transport, eight techs wearing the yellow soft-shelled armor of systems specialists, waved security sensors along our hull. Nobles seemed to find humor in all these precautions. He watched the men wheel an archway around the side of our ship, and said, "Security post. Man, these guys aren't missing a trick."

Whatever humor he found in all the precautions was lost on me. These boys were doing more than simply running a tight ship. Scrambling an armed escort, running five minutes' worth of tests, and now the posts; the only armies that ran that kind of security were the ones that had already been infiltrated. I wondered if the Scutum-Crux Fleet had escaped destruction only to become a fleet under siege.

"You may now exit your ship," said the voice on the radio. "If you are wearing armor, remove it before exiting your ship."

"Good thing I brought a change of clothes," Nobles said as he pulled out his rucksack and fished out some clothes. I did the same, and we dressed in the cockpit.

It occurred to me that they should already know if we had anything concealed in our armor. When they scanned our ship, they surely must have been able to scan inside our armor as well.

Once we were dressed in our Charlie service uniforms, Nobles tapped the radio, and said, "Flight Control, we're coming out." He hit the button that opened the rear of the transport.

We headed down the ladder and across the kettle. Our hands were empty and out where the Marines at the bottom of the ramp could see them. Between us and those Marines, a ten-foot-tall arch made of beige-colored plastic stood. The posts.

The column on the left side was "the sprayer." It shot a blast of air filled with a fine mist of oil and water vapor. The sprayer dislodged loose flecks of skin, dandruff, and hair, which the column on the right, "the receiver," drew in and analyzed. The findings were fed through a computer system. In the second it would take me to step through the posts, the techs on the other end of the security gate would know my make of clone, my age, any major illnesses I had suffered, and my blood type. For all I knew, they could even tell the last time I had sex.

The MPs at the bottom of the ramp signaled for one of us to pass through the posts. Nobles went first, not hesitating for even a moment. I followed a step behind. The perceivably moist breath of the sprayer blasted me on one side, and the receiver drew in the raw information. The entire process took less time than it took me to walk between the posts, and the results came up almost instantaneously.

Behind us, teams of docking-bay techs rushed to inspect our transport. I turned in time to see them scurrying up the ramp. As I watched the techs, a sailor in a captain's uniform came up beside me. He had the confident smile of an old friend who knows he will be recognized. He was, of course, a clone on a ship filled with clones. Though he did not know it, he had the exact same face as everyone around him. Fortunately, he did not wear the same uniform. I did know the man, but I would not have been able to distinguish him from any other clone had I not recognized the captain's insignia on his uniform. I saluted, and said, "Permission to come aboard?"

"Permission granted," he said, returning my salute.

"Are we near a front?" I asked.

Bishop shook his head. "Not out here in Cygnus. The only fighting in the Cygnus Arm is infighting."

"So what's with all the security?" I asked. "I half expected your MPs to check my body cavities."

"We are at war, you know," Bishop said, a nonanswer designed to brush off the question.

"This isn't wartime security," I said. "Wartime security is a fighter escort and armed guards at the door."

He took a deep breath, held it for just a moment, then exhaled. "It's not the war that's got us worried. The war is going well, everything else is falling apart."

# CHAPTER
# FIFTEEN

Four Marines followed from a few feet back as Bishop led me out of the landing bay. The rest of the platoon hung back with Nobles as he secured the transport.

The *Kamehameha* was a warship with a complement of fighters and Marines, but it was also the mobile administrative headquarters of the Enlisted Man's Fleet. Fleet headquarters was spread across an upper deck of the ship. At least, it used to be there. We did not take the lift to the fleet deck. Instead, Bishop led me to the bridge.

"We're not going to Fleet Command?" I asked.

"Not now, no," Bishop said.

"Is Warshaw up there?" I asked.

Bishop stopped walking and turned to face me. I saw deep-seated suspicion in the way he examined my face. "Why are you in such a rush to see Warshaw?" he asked.

Oh, there were so many good responses, both politic answers and flaming. Warshaw was the only officer in my pay grade in the fleet; I wanted to congratulate him for saving the fleet, but I also wanted to poke him in the nose for leaving me stranded on Terraneau. Instead, I said, "I get the feeling I'm still being screened."

"Something like that," Bishop admitted.

I didn't know him all that well; we'd only been on the same ship for a few months before the Earth Fleet attacked. We occupied different worlds—he was Navy, I was a Marine. We'd gotten along, but the standard prejudices applied. Sailors thought of Marines as cargo.

"I'm not a spy," I said. "You don't really think the Unified Authority captured me, trapped me in a battleship, and sent me through that broadcast zone."

"General, I don't know what to think. You're not even supposed to be alive."

"I walked through the posts. What did your computers tell you?"

"You've got the DNA of a Liberator Clone. We've verified that."

That was my genetic fingerprint. That was as specific as the computers could get with clones. They could tell one natural-born from the next by their DNA; but since clones were cut from the same helix, genetic fingerprinting only went so far. The security station could identify our make and our age and catalog any major or recent illnesses.

"That should narrow the field," I said. "How many Liberators do you know?"

Bishop did not answer my question.

We went up to the bridge deck, but we did not enter the bridge. With his MPs still tailing us, Bishop led me into an off-bridge conference room. Wanting to believe Warshaw would join us, I took a seat at the table. The room was empty, except for a table, chairs, and a media/communications display.

We sat in silence for a moment, then I asked, "What am I missing here?"

"What do you mean?" Bishop asked, playing the role of the obtuse ship's captain.

"You say the war is going well," I said.

"I believe I said it was going better than we could have hoped for."

"Okay, but you're hiding like a mouse in a hole. What's with the siege mentality?" I asked.

I waited several seconds for him to answer. To this point, I had not yet become angry, but my tension level was rising.

"What happened on Terraneau?" he asked.

"Is that an official question?" I asked.

"No," he said.

"Who else is listening in on our conversation?"

"No one," he said, shaking his head.

"I don't believe you," I said.

Before the big attack, the Corps of Engineers set up a prison called Outer Bliss on Terraneau. They rigged a mike and a camera in the prison's interrogation room that were so small, trained experts would need equipment to locate them. When I interrogated prisoners in Outer Bliss, Warshaw listened in on the conversations from the *Kamehameha*. I suspected he would listen in on this conversation as well.

"What happened on Terraneau?" Bishop repeated.

"Do you mean before or after you guys ditched the party?" I asked.

"What happened on the planet?" he asked. "How did you get out alive?"

"The Unified Authority landed three thousand Marines; I had five thousand men. The cocky bastards didn't even bother landing more men after you left. That's how sure they were that they would win."

"You faced their Marines, and you survived?" Bishop asked, ignoring the obvious evidence that we were having a conversation, not a séance.

"Something like that," I said.

"Was there anything unusual about their troops?" Bishop asked. Now he was probing.

"Do you mean the shielded armor?"

"Maybe," he said. "Tell me about it." The son of a bitch was testing me.

"They had shielded armor," I said. "What do you want to know? Their armor was just like ours except that it projected a shield. Even the palms of their hands were shielded; they couldn't carry guns. They fired fléchettes from tubes that ran along their arms inside their armor. Sound familiar?" I placed my right hand on the table, palm up, and showed him pea-sized scars in my wrist and forearm. The fléchettes had passed through my arm and armor with the ease of a sewing needle poking through a cotton sheet.

"You were shot?" he asked.

"Five times," I said.

"You're lucky to be alive."

"I wouldn't have the pleasure of sitting through this interrogation if I had died," I said. "And Warshaw wouldn't be listening in on us," I added, hoping to get Warshaw's goat and flush him out of hiding.

"Just answer the specking questions, okay, hotshot?" said

the voice that came out of the ceiling. Admiral Gary Warshaw had the same voice box as every other clone, but he had his own way of talking.

Bishop winced. I smiled.

"They're using poison on their fléchettes now," Warshaw said. "They hit you, you die."

"That's how it went on Terraneau, too. They killed everyone they hit," I said.

"Everyone but you," Bishop pointed out.

"Genetics. I'm a Liberator. I had the mother of all combat reflexes. The doctor said there was so much adrenaline and testosterone in my blood that I should have died of a heart attack."

"But you survived."

"More or less. That may be my last combat reflex. The poison injured the gland." In truth, the gland had mostly healed, but I decided to keep that to myself. With Bishop holding his cards close to the vest and Warshaw playing hide-and-seek behind a camera, I would hold on to my secrets as well.

"That's how you survived the fight, but how did you win it?" Warshaw asked.

I explained how we lured General Mooreland and the U.A. Marines into the underground garage, then demolished the structure while we escaped through the subterranean train station in the back.

"And you just left them there?" Warshaw asked. "You just left them there to starve?"

"Yes."

"You specking bastard." Warshaw meant this as a compliment. "Bastard" is one of those all-purpose words in the military. "Your doctor was wrong about you, Harris; you don't have adrenaline running through your veins, you've got ice."

"Brilliant move," Bishop said in a voice just slightly above a whisper.

"Damn specking right it's brilliant," Warshaw said. "And I bet our boy Harris came up with the idea all on his own. Am I right, Harris?"

It was my idea, but I did not say so. I did not respond. I felt like Warshaw and Bishop were herding me somewhere I did not want to go.

Bishop asked, "What happened after you buried the Marines?"

"What do you mean?" I asked.

"Why didn't the fleet send more Marines?" Bishop asked.

"I don't know," I admitted.

"So they just left?" Bishop asked.

"Some of them left, some of them stayed," I said. "You sank twenty-three of their ships."

"Twenty-three," Warshaw said. He sounded pleased. "I wondered what kind of damage we left behind."

"They lost twelve ships trying to chase you into your broadcast zone," I said.

"They didn't even need to send more men down to the planet," Bishop said. "Why didn't they just bombard you from space?"

He still did not trust me.

"Maybe they didn't think we were worth the trouble," I said. "We were landlocked; they probably didn't consider us a threat."

"Then they didn't know you as well as I do," Warshaw said. "Anyone who knew you would be scared. He's clean. You can bring him down."

# CHAPTER
# SIXTEEN

Bishop told me the fleet decks were empty, then offered to let me inspect them for myself if I did not believe him. I believed him.

He remained, however, unwilling to explain the situation. When I asked what happened to Fleet Command, he put up a hand, and said, "Take it up with Warshaw."

"You can't tell me anything?" I asked.

"Not my pay grade, sir. I just steer the ship."

We had that discussion over an early dinner in the last vestige of Fleet Command, a mess reserved for captains and up. Bishop ate chicken, I ate beef, and we both had potatoes and salad. There was a linen sheet across the table, and the utensils appeared to be made out of silver instead of some chrome-coated alloy.

"Can you tell me where we are?" I asked.

Bishop laughed, and asked, "You don't know your galactic position?"

"How the speck would I know that?"

He thought about that, and said, "It takes real balls to fly into a broadcast zone without knowing where you'll come out." He shook his head, and added, "I've got to hand it to you.

"You're in the Cygnus Arm, Enlisted Man's territory." He pointed to the viewport, and added, "The planet down there is Providence Kri."

"Is that where Warshaw is hiding?" I asked.

Bishop shook his head. "Nope; he's not even in this arm."

"Are you going to tell me where he is?"

"He's in the Tube."

"What is the Tube?" I asked.

"It's our high command. The Unifieds have their Pentagon, and we have our Tube," Bishop said, clearly enjoying my frustration. "Times have changed, General. Admiral Warshaw has thirteen fleets under him. We don't just have an Enlisted Man's Fleet anymore, we have an Enlisted Man's Navy."

"You're shitting me," I said.

"I told you, the war is going well."

"So where is the Tube?" I asked.

Bishop's smile spread so wide, it looked painful as he said, "That's on a need-to-know basis. You're not navigating, so you don't need to know."

You could broadcast from one end of the galaxy to the other and never know it inside a big bird like a fighter carrier. At some point, the *Kamehameha* entered a broadcast zone. We might have entered several for all I knew. I went to my temporary billet to wash up and rest. A few minutes later, I got a message informing me that we had reached Naval Command and directing me to report to the landing bay.

Bishop met me at the bay and escorted me into my transport. We traded salutes.

"Well, General, you're Warshaw's problem now," he said.

"Anything I should watch out for?" I asked.

"You'll be fine, sir. He's happy to see you," Bishop said.

I looked around the transport, and asked, "Am I flying with the same pilot I came in with?"

"You have a personal pilot?" Bishop asked, sounding surprised.

"More or less," I said.

"You're stuck with a loaner pilot for this trip. Your identity checked out, but we haven't started on the guy you flew in with."

I nodded and crossed the kettle on my way to the cockpit. The door of the transport slowly closed behind me, clapping shut as I reached the top of the ladder and stepped onto the narrow catwalk.

We launched into space, and I immediately saw that we were not headed for Providence Kri. The term "Kri" was given to planets with "engineered" atmospheres. Back in the days of the great expansion, the Senate selected planets based on several factors, location being the most important. If a planet with a breathable atmosphere was roughly the same distance from its nearest star as Earth was from the sun, it became a candidate for colonization.

Some planets were "retreads," meaning they had all the ingredients to support life but needed the right infusions of hydrogen and oxygen along with some plant life to sustain the mixture. Seen from space, Providence Kri was a green-and-blue marble with layers of clouds and ice caps. It looked a lot like Earth. "God makes 'em good, and terraforming makes 'em better" was the old motto of the now-defunct Unified Authority Planetary Engineering Corps.

The planet we were heading for was arid, the color of sand, with few clouds and bone-dry poles. In the distance, a hot sun blazed. I could see its flare peeking out beyond the equatorial horizon.

"What a shit hole," I said.

My pilot smiled but did not respond.

"What planet is that?" I asked, thinking perhaps he had been told to ignore my questions.

"Gobi, sir."

"Gobi?" I asked, then I laughed so hard he must have thought I'd lost my mind. I began my career on Gobi. Wanting to make sure this was the same planet, I asked, "If that's Gobi, then we must be in the Perseus Arm, right?"

"Yes, sir."

Nearly ten years ago, in 2508, I had meandered into Gobi Station as a new Marine fresh out of boot camp. Now, almost a decade and three wars later, to Gobi I returned, a general.

Hundreds of ships crowded the space around the planet. A trio of fighter carriers floated in the distance. Beyond them, a broadcast station blended into the darkness around it. Had it not been for the ring of lights along its mile-wide discs, I would never have spotted the station.

Closer to the planet, Navy ships hovered in silhouette against the atmosphere. Squadrons of fighters flew in and out of view. A school of battleships passed around the wide equatorial curve of the planet at a lazy pace. The first time I had landed on Gobi, it struck me as a backwater planet and a dead end for my fledgling military career. It had the galaxy's smallest Marine installation and the Navy, Army, and Air Force were nowhere to be seen.

We dropped into the atmosphere.

"Last time I came here, the fort looked like a house of cards after an earthquake," I said. The old base was a sandstone fortress made more for show than warfare. When the Mogats attacked, the bulky walls caved in around us.

"You've been here before, sir?" the pilot asked.

"Yeah, but it's been a while. I was stationed here."

"No offense, sir, but you must have really pissed someone off. I wouldn't station a dog on this planet."

I felt the same way.

The new Gobi Station rose out of the desert like a modern-day minaret, a single, nearly indefensible column as sleek and straight as an old-world rocket preparing to launch into space.

The original station, the fort I'd once called home, was built along the side of a cliff. Not this building. The desert spread out in every direction around it.

The structure stood thirty stories tall. As we approached,

I spotted a ring of bunkers around the base of the structure. Tawny and mostly submerged in the sand, those bunkers could have housed five thousand men. Particle-beam-cannon and missile arrays ran along the sides of the cylindrical fort like rows of spines. "How long has this building been around?" I asked. It sure as hell had not existed ten years ago, or we wouldn't have been living in a prehistoric rat hole.

The pilot shrugged, and said, "It was here when we got here."

I always hated the way transports handled in atmospheric conditions. They were built for space, relying on boosters and skids instead of wings and wheels. They had wings, but they were small and useless for gliding. Cut the power in a bird like that, and it would fall like a rock. My pilot knew his trade, but he wasn't good at it. As we approached the landing pad, he missed a mark, and we dropped sixty feet below the platform; then he righted the bird, and we had to fly around the building and come in again.

"Sorry about that, sir," he said as he fumbled with the controls.

We touched down on the second pass, and the ground crew converged on our transport. The landing pad was open-air. Why not? Rain was never a problem on this planet.

A security station with armed guards hiding behind a wall of bulletproof glass waited just inside the doorway. The glass formed a funnel that led to a set of security posts. As I walked through the posts, a team of security techs confirmed my identity while men with M27s kept close watch on me.

The techs only needed a moment to clear me, and the guards waved me on.

Even after all of the other precautions, two of the guards paired off with me. They herded me into a lift, and down we went. Judging by the lights, the numbers, and the length of the drop, it seemed clear we had gone deep underground. When the elevator doors opened, we had arrived at another security station with another set of posts.

There was no way to enter this building without passing through posts that scanned your DNA, and yet they scanned me again when I left the elevator. These people weren't just digging in for a war; they were terrified.

# CHAPTER
# SEVENTEEN

If you did not know that Gary Warshaw was a clone, you might have mistaken him for a natural-born. He didn't have general-issue standard brown hair. In fact, he didn't have any hair at all. The man shaved his entire head from his crown to his chin, including the eyebrows. He shaved in the morning. By the end of the day, dark grainlike stubble covered his chin, neck, and head. The eyebrows, though, he might have removed with lasers. They never grew back.

From a distance, Warshaw looked shorter than other clones. He wasn't, of course. He stood the standard five-foot-ten just like every other government-issue clone; but he looked smaller because he was wide. A fanatical bodybuilder, Warshaw began and ended every day in the gym, then supplemented his achievements with ample doses of chemistry.

He had the basic facial features of a clone—the correct shade of brown in his eyes, the right shape of nose and mouth; but his skull seemed to have stretched to keep up with the tree-trunk diameter of his neck. His face had taken on a flattened appearance. A skein of veins bobbed in and out of view along the sides of his neck.

Warshaw had an office the size of a basketball court, which he divided into distinct areas that did not blend into one another. We met in the conference area, which included a desk and a ring of chairs. No more than forty feet from us, and not partitioned off by walls or screens, was a gym with weights, exercise equipment, and a personal sauna. Scanning the space, I saw a drafting room, a chartroom, and a lounge.

Warshaw looked at me, his eyes sparkling, and he said, "I doubt you'll believe me, but I'll say it anyway. If I thought there had been the slightest chance that you survived the attack, I would have gone looking for you."

He sat behind his desk, looking both lost and out of place. He had a weight room, and food, and men to command; but he was an engineer, and one thing he did not have in his fortress was an engine room. He belonged on a ship.

"It wouldn't have been worth the trouble," I said. "No point sending your fleet clear across the galaxy to pick up a few thousand Marines." As a commander, Warshaw tended to err on the side of caution. He wouldn't have risked a trip to Terraneau.

"It depends on the Marines. For guys like you and Thomer—"

"Thomer is dead," I said.

"The Unifieds got him?"

"He survived the attack and died a few days later," I said. Kelly Thomer had been my second-in-command.

"Sorry to hear that," Warshaw said. He sounded gloomy. "He was a good man, Thomer."

We both gave Thomer a spontaneous and perfunctory moment of silence; and after that, neither of us seemed to have anything to say. For my part, I had so many questions that I did not know where to begin. I wanted to ask about the war with Earth and about the size of our fleet. Just as I was about to ask my first question, Warshaw spoke up.

"Look, Harris, I don't feel like playing 'twenty questions' with you, so I'll lay it all out. The Unifieds are running scared. We hooked up with twelve of the abandoned fleets. That gives us thirteen fleets and twenty-three planets. Throw in Terraneau, and I guess I have twenty-four planets. You think that speck Doctorow wants to play ball with us?" Warshaw asked.

I shook my head.

"Then he's an asshole, and we don't need him," Warshaw said. "And he's alone. Earth isn't looking for new colonies, especially colonies on the far side of the galaxy. The Unifieds may be down to two planets, but they're not looking to grow their operation.

"They still have New Copenhagen, but we took something else they wanted to keep. We got the Golan Dry Docks, for all the good that does us. The Unifieds destroyed the computers and evacuated most of the personnel before we got there."

"You went after the Golan Dry Docks," I said. I was impressed.

"They have better ships than we do. I figure one of theirs is as good as three of ours in a fair fight, so we don't fight fair. Anytime we see one of their ships, we send ten of ours. It's good policy. It cuts our losses."

Warshaw stared down at his right hand as he spoke. He clenched the hand into a tight fist and squeezed, causing the veins to rise in his massive forearm. He traced the patterns with his eyes, then relaxed his hand.

"Have they launched any counterattacks?" I asked.

Warshaw laughed. "Harris, their ships are better than ours, but they're still only as good as the crew sailing them. Their officers are scared. We catch a glimpse of them outside our planets, and they run away like little girls."

It all sounded so good, so victorious. And then I remembered all of the security stations Warshaw had dotting his base.

"If the war is going so well, what's with all of the security? You've got posts at every door."

"You noticed that?" Warshaw asked.

"And why place your headquarters on Gobi; it's the shittiest planet in the galaxy." Until I said those words, I never realized how deeply I resented beginning my career on this planet.

"I didn't come here for sightseeing," Warshaw said in a cold, matter-of-fact voice. He waited a moment, then decided that he trusted me, and said, "It's not the war that's the problem. It's the cancer that came with it. We've been infiltrated.

"The Unifieds can't beat us in a fight, so they're just going to hang back and wait for us to die."

There were guards and posts right outside Warshaw's office. There were guards and posts right outside the elevator on Warshaw's floor. There were guards and posts outside the elevator five floors down, and more guards and posts outside the door of the infirmary. I began to wonder if I would find guards and posts at the opening of the toilet stalls in the officers' head.

Walking like a man who means business, Warshaw led me through the front of the infirmary into its darker reaches.

"At least this building is secure," I said, as we stepped into an antiseptic world of plastic sheets, stainless-steel tables, and air that smelled of formaldehyde. Tools both primitive and modern arrayed on chrome-plated trays, coffin-sized tables, laser saws, and bladed scalpels—this part of the infirmary reminded me of a medieval dungeon.

"You would think a place like Gobi Station would be safe," Warshaw said, starting a new conversation. He waved to a doctor—a short, skinny natural-born in a lab coat. Warshaw asked, "Can you get Admiral Thorne?" and the doctor left the room.

"Thorne? He's on Gobi?" I asked.

Thorne—Rear Admiral Lawrence Thorne—was a natural-born who had allied himself with the clone cause. He had been the commander of the Scutum-Crux Fleet when Warshaw and I took over. The rest of the natural-borns transferred out, but he stayed on with us.

"Yeah, as of last week," Warshaw said.

The double doors spread open, and the doctor rolled a gurney into view. Until I saw that gurney, the significance of our surroundings had not occurred to me. We had walked through the infirmary and entered the morgue. We had entered the meat locker.

The man whom I had mistaken for a physician must have been a coroner. He pulled back the sheet, and there was Lawrence Thorne, flat on his back, his hands by his sides, an old man with skin so bleached and wrinkled he might have spent the last twenty years sitting in a bath. His legs were as skinny as a bird's, but a roll of flab orbited his gut. Seeing Thorne laid out in this butcher shop, I felt a pang of regret.

"What happened to him?" I asked, still staring down at the body. He looked small and frail.

"His neck was broken," said the coroner.

"How did he break it?" I asked.

"Somebody broke it for him," Warshaw said. He looked to the coroner for confirmation.

"There's bruising along the jaw," the coroner said. Showing the coroner's familiarity with the dead, he turned Thorne's head to one side. Along the bottom of his wrinkled cheek, faint bruises showed in bluish ovals. The death tech placed his hand over the bruises, his fingers reaching toward the spot where the jaw met the ear. It wasn't a perfect fit, but the spread of his fingers matched the angles of the bruises.

I'd killed a man or two using that very technique.

"Can you tell anything about the killer from the bruises? Size? Weight? Anything?" I asked.

Warshaw answered. "Yeah, they tell us something." He walked to the door and asked one of the guards to join us. Clearly nervous around Admiral Warshaw, the petty officer approached the table.

Warshaw pointed at Thorne's corpse, specifically at the dead admiral's jaw, then said, "Put your fingers over the bruises."

The man hesitated.

"Don't worry, he won't bite. This old boy won't bite anyone ever again."

The petty officer slowly lowered his hand over Thorne's cheek. He spread his fingers so that they covered the bruises. It was a perfect fit. He kept his trembling hand on the dead man's face and turned to look at Warshaw.

"That will do," Warshaw said.

The hand shot up.

"Go wash up and get back to your post," Warshaw said.

Still looking shaken, the petty officer said, "Aye, aye, sir," and left in a hurry.

Warshaw grimaced, and said, "It's like Cinderella; only this time, everybody's foot fits the slipper."

"He was killed by a clone?" I asked.

"Yeah. Doesn't narrow down the list much, does it?" Warshaw said. "The only ones on this base we can be sure did not do it are you and me. I'm natural-born and you're a Liberator; our fingers don't fit."

The coroner said, "I'm not synthetic."

Warshaw said, "Yeah, and the good doctor here, he's natural-born, too."

Warshaw's fingers would fit, of course, but I saw no reason to point that out.

"It's not just Thorne. They killed Lilburn Franks," Warshaw said. "They got him the same way—broke his neck. One of his lieutenants found him on the floor in his quarters.

"Specking nasty way to go, a broken neck."

Actually, in the litany of ways to go, a broken neck ranked just below death by sexual exhaustion in my book. Thorne might never have known he was in danger. He might have simply walked around a corner, felt a quick tug, then never felt anything again.

All of the swagger had washed out of Warshaw. He spoke quietly. "They killed three of my top five officers, Harris. Two of them were killed right here, right in this base.

"They hit us even harder a few pay grades down. The Unifieds hit so many officers in the Central Norma Fleet that we had to shut down one of our fighter carriers. We didn't have enough officers for the chain of command.

"How do you fight back against something like this? It's like they hit us with a specking ghost. You know what the worst part is? I don't know what to do about it. It's like we conquered the whole specking galaxy, and now we're dying of cancer."

I did not know what to say.

We left the morgue. Warshaw invited me to have dinner with him, and I told him I needed to rest. My mind was reeling. I had started the day on Terraneau, spent hours sealed in a derelict battleship in the Cygnus Arm, and now I was talking mass murders on Gobi.

Warshaw laughed when I declined his invitation. "Rest? Harris, I'm about to paint a specking target on your back, and you want a nap? I haven't even begun your briefing."

# CHAPTER
# EIGHTEEN

Warshaw gave me a couple of hours to rest before dinner.

I had a tiny billet, not much more than a rack and a head, with a writing desk that folded out of the wall. I went to the head, shaved and showered, and used the Blue-Light to laser clean my teeth. And then I crawled onto my rack, not to rest, but to think.

The "Enlisted Man's Empire"—that was what we called ourselves now that they had twenty-three planets and thirteen fleets. None of that conquest would have been possible had Warshaw not created his own miniature version of the Broadcast Network. The Unified Authority had built broadcast stations near each of its planets, now Warshaw was using them to link our planets together. He'd built his own pangalactic superhighway using the ruins of another empire.

He could even reach Earth. In fact, reaching Earth would be easy. Any of our broadcast stations could be rigged to send ships there. Getting back would be another story. The Mogats had destroyed the Mars broadcast station, the station that used to broadcast ships out of the Sol System. Without the Mars Station, any ships we broadcasted into Earth space would be stuck there.

The U.A. Navy did not have the same constraints thanks to its fleet of self-broadcasting ships. It was a small fleet, too small to confront us; but the U.A.'s ships could travel anywhere at any time.

My thoughts drifted to the late Admiral Lawrence Thorne. Why would they kill Thorne? Was it revenge for changing loyalties? Maybe Warshaw was right, and the Unifieds were after senior officers. Thorne was a thirty-year man, the most experienced man in our fleet and the only one ever to attend Annapolis; but he had little combat experience. I liked him.

He was a capable administrator, but from a strategic point of view, his death was not much of a loss.

They had also killed Lilburn Franks. That was another story. Franks was a clone with an inordinate amount of command experience. He'd seen war firsthand, riding on the bridge of some of the Unifieds' most decorated warships. He knew tactics, and he didn't back away from a fight. Warshaw always struck me as a bit of a coward. Franks came across like a man spoiling for a battle. They balanced each other out.

Two dead admirals, the number two and number three men in the fleet. No wonder Warshaw dug a hole for himself on Gobi. Hiding in a backwater desert must have sounded good once his lieutenants started dying; but if the Unifieds did have clones working for them, posting guards and analyzing DNA samples would not do a lick of good.

I tried to consider all of the angles as I turned off the lights in my quarters. I would sleep for an hour, then meet Warshaw for dinner. We had a lot to discuss.

"Hope you don't mind eating in my office. I eat all my meals here."

Warshaw had a dining room tucked away in one corner of his office/living complex. The table was large enough to seat a dozen officers. Sitting alone at that table, he looked big and strong and terrified. He had two armed guards posted inside the door to his complex and four more just outside.

A steward waited by the door as well. He watched me sit, gave me a moment to get comfortable, then came to ask what we wanted to drink.

"Just water," I said.

"Give me a beer," Warshaw said.

The steward brought us our drinks and left without another word.

"I served on this planet," I said. "We were stationed in an old sandstone fortress with a swamp for a courtyard. We drank filtered sludge from the swamp."

"I know the place. It's out near Morrowtown, right?" Warshaw asked. "I went out to see the ruins."

I nodded, and asked, "Is that far from here?"

"Other side of the planet," Warshaw said. He looked so

unhappy. He sat slumped in his chair, his arms folded across his lap and his shoulders hunched. "When I first got here, they told me there were these ruins from the original Gobi Station. It's like a historic site, you know, something for tourists . . . as if any tourists ever came to this place.

"They treat the place like a museum exhibit. They have guides and tours, and they take you into the living quarters and shit. There's a plaque that says something about the attack on Gobi being the first shots fired in the Mogat War."

I had never thought about it that way; but as I considered it, perhaps those were the opening shots of the war.

"I was there during the attack," I said. "The fort had a regional armory. That's what the Mogats were after. Crowley led them on that one." "Crowley" was General Amos Crowley, a U.A. Army officer who defected to the Morgan Atkins Believers.

Warshaw whistled, and said, "Crowley? No wonder the fort got so banged up."

"I was lucky to get out of there alive," I said.

"Yeah, well, speaking of being lucky, you got lucky on Terraneau. Every time my Marines run into the Unifieds, we get our nuts flattened."

As I started to say something about that, the steward came back to take our orders. Since I had no idea what was on the menu, I decided to order whatever Warshaw did. He ordered salmon.

When the steward left, I asked, "They have salmon here?" We were on a planet with no lakes or oceans.

"It's flown in," Warshaw said. "So you got any ideas for stopping U.A. Marines that don't involve demolishing an underground garage?"

"I do: Wait till their batteries run out, then stick it to 'em," I said, and I explained about the short-life batteries. He laughed. "Good call, Harris. You'll beat the whole damned Unified Authority Marine Corps as long as they don't bring spares."

I laughed politely, then said, "We dug some of them out."

"You dug them out? That doesn't sound like you. An act of compassion? That's something new. I didn't know you had it in you."

"After they were dead," I said. "I wanted a better look at their armor. That was how we found out about the batteries."

Warshaw nodded.

Our fish arrived, sautéed and dusted with almonds. The smell of salmon and onions filled the air. It was the best meal I had eaten in over a year. My plate was large and buried under enough fish and wild rice to last me a week. The meal came with white wine.

Warshaw took a sip of wine, loaded salmon and wild rice onto his fork, then paused to ask, "Did you test the batteries yourself?"

"Do you remember Scott Mars?"

Warshaw toasted Mars with his wine. "Yeah, I know Mars. Good engineer. I heard he went born-again Christian."

"They call him the 'born-again clone,'" I said.

"And Mars found out about the batteries?"

"The shielding works off a forty-five-minute battery," I said. "The battery drains even quicker when anything touches the shields."

"Mobility versus power," Warshaw observed. He had more than twenty years in the Navy, all of them spent in engineering. As an enlisted man and a clone, he would never have qualified for engineering school, but he had plenty of practical education. "They can't make the battery too big or the Marines can't move."

Warshaw put down his fork and stretched his arms, moving his bald head from side to side. He had the physique of a buffalo, overstuffed at the chest and shoulders, tiny at the waist. Staring at me, a slight smile on his face, he said, "The Enlisted Man's Marine Corps needs a Commandant. Of course, now that we know you're alive, you get the job. From here on out, Harris, you and I are equals."

"You didn't believe that back at Terraneau," I said.

"Things have changed," Warshaw said. "We need a man like you."

"Someone to wear a bull's-eye on his back," I said.

"I wouldn't put it in so many words," Warshaw said.

"How would you put it?"

"How would I put it? I'd put it this way. We've got a security problem, General. I want you to find our rats, lead them into some underground rat hole, and bury them for good."

# CHAPTER NINETEEN

Earthdate: October 29, A.D. 2517
Location: St. Augustine
Galactic Position: Orion Arm

Warshaw had one lead, one thin lead to help me track down the security breach. That lead came in the form of three dead bodies on a planet called St. Augustine.

Back in my billet, I pulled on a pair of mediaLink shades and read about the planet. It didn't take long to realize that if I wanted to track down a breach in security, St. Augustine—the rest-and-recreation capital of the Enlisted Man's Empire—was a promising place to start. If there was a place where our sailors would let down their guard, it was St. Augustine, a planet with beaches, hotels, and very few men.

Several years ago, when the Avatari attacked St. Augustine, the Unified Authority had left the locals to fend for themselves. The people of St. Augustine fought to the figurative last man. Once they ran out of men, the women and children went into hiding, and the aliens simply went away. That was how the Avatari ran things. Once they captured a planet, they left you alone as long as you didn't disturb their toxic mining operations.

When the Enlisted Man's Empire liberated the planet, the women of St. Augustine welcomed our sailors and Marines. Having lived without men for more than two years, they welcomed us rather intimately.

One of the first factories to open on St. Augustine manufactured condoms. Now, the clones in the Enlisted Man's Empire were as sterile as a surgeon's gloves—"built to copulate, not populate" as the saying goes; but they were also programmed to think they were natural-born, so some enterprising resident came up with the idea of selling condoms to a population of "dead-end Joes" who thought they were potent.

If the news stories were true, that factory did a lot of business. On a planet with a population of six million adult females, more than one hundred million condoms had been sold.

I left for St. Augustine the following day.

As the Commandant of the Marines, I traveled with an entourage. Warshaw assigned me a staff that included a one-star admiral, three captains, and enough lieutenants to man a small fleet—all of them tainted. These were men who had played the power game and come up short for one reason or another; now they wanted to redeem themselves. I brought them along as camouflage, but I did not trust them. I did not like traveling with remora fish in my wake; but fleet officers were expected to have an entourage, and a lone-wolf general would elicit suspicion.

Admiral J. Winston Cabot, supposedly my liaison to Warshaw and Naval Command, was officious, petty, politically motivated, and, I suspected, something of a coward. I decided that much about him during the fifteen minutes it took us to travel from Gobi and land on St. Augustine.

A simpering politician by nature, Cabot all but attached himself to my person. Once Warshaw introduced us, the little ferret swooped right in on me, warning the other officers of the entourage away with a threatening glance. He chattered mindlessly in the beginning, but giving credit where credit is due, the little bastard read me accurately after a couple of minutes and settled down, allowing me to think.

Had he known what I was thinking, Cabot might have given me more space. What came to my mind was how incredibly interchangeable he was, like a gear in an old-fashioned clock. There he sat, a fifty-two-year-old general-issue clone with brown eyes and slightly grayed brown hair, and nothing to distinguish himself beyond his uniform.

And therein was the problem.

If the Unified Authority had developed some kind of new cloning program, there would be no way to stop them from infiltrating our military. If their clones truly had the same DNA as ours, they would be identical. We could place posts by every hatch on every ship and run hourly DNA scans of every sailor, and the bastards would slip through our net.

We flew from Gobi to St. Augustine on the *Kamehameha*. Bishop walked me to the landing bay, where I expected to see a shuttle waiting. As the Commandant of the Marines, I should have traveled down to the planet in a shuttle, but nothing was available. Instead, I would fly down in the familiar steel-and-shadows world of a transport.

"That's the best you could get me?" I asked Bishop. "I'm the specking Commandant of the Enlisted Man's Marines."

"That's the best I have."

My entourage hung around me like flies. I told them to board the transport, and all of them did except for Cabot. He lingered, having decided that the order was meant for everyone but him.

"Do you need something, Admiral?" I asked.

"No, sir," he said.

"Then board the transport," I said.

He reluctantly left.

"How do you put up with this shit?" I asked.

"You'll learn to love it," Bishop said.

"Bullshit," I said.

We traded salutes, and I boarded the transport. I started the trip in the kettle with my entourage. After five minutes, I found myself so irritated by their company that I excused myself and climbed up to the cockpit. And there, through the windshield, I saw St. Augustine.

After reliving the uniform dryness of Gobi, I had a greater appreciation for the greens and blues of St. Augustine. The planet had oceans, rivers, and lakes. It had pastures, mountains, and ice-capped poles. From space, Gobi looked like a ball carved out of unfinished wood. By comparison, St. Augustine looked like a well-polished opal.

Cabot came up to the cockpit to check in on me. "General, will we have time to inspect the officers' R & R facilities while we are on St. Augustine?" he asked. "I haven't tried them myself, but I hear good things."

"We're not here to inspect the facilities," I said.

"Yes, sir. I'm just saying that I understand they're supposed to be nice, you know, if we get the chance." When he saw that he wasn't getting anywhere, Cabot asked, "Why are we here?"

"We're here to look at corpses," I said.

The transport shook and rattled as it punched into the atmosphere.

"Corpses?" Cabot asked.

"Three of them," I said. "Maybe more if we're lucky."

"Who died, sir?" He did not know that the Unified Authority had infiltrated our security. Warshaw would not have trusted a weasel like Cabot with that kind of sensitive information. I felt bad for the bastard. Not knowing that I was little more than a moving target, he still believed that being assigned to me would help his career.

"Clones," I said. "There are three dead clones on St. Augustine, but none of the ships have reported any of missing men."

"I'm not sure what you are getting at, sir," Cabot said.

"Three men died on R & R, right? So they couldn't have reported for duty when their leave ran out. Only they found these guys last week, and none of our ships have reported anyone missing."

"Someone must have reported in their place," Cabot said. "Spies?"

"Worse," I said. "Assassins."

# CHAPTER
# TWENTY

By prewar standards, St. Augustine qualified as an emerging world. The planet had a fledgling banking system, a global government, and a world market. The Avatari had knocked out the planet's mediaLink during their invasion; but other than a lack of communications services, the planet of St. Augustine had all the amenities.

St. Augustine had three continents and twenty-five cities, each of which had a police department manned by MPs. It did not take long to determine that the various law-enforcement groups did not share information among themselves.

"Bodies found in other cities?" asked the commander of the Petersborough police—a lowly ensign on loan from one of our ships. The Petersborough Police Department consisted of seven officers and thirty-five enlisted men, an unsatisfactorily small count, especially considering that Petersborough was the capital city of St. Augustine.

"Yes," I said, and I repeated my question, "Have you heard anything about dead clones turning up in other cities?"

"I . . . I haven't, sir. Nothing," he said.

We stood in the morgue, three occupied body bags lying on tables before us. I had come with my entourage, and the ensign had come with his as well. It made for a crowded room.

"Perhaps you could get one of your men on the horn to find out," I suggested.

"Yes, sir." He turned to one of his men and communicated his orders without speaking. The man saluted and left, making the room one body less crowded.

"Do you have information on any of these men?" I asked the ensign. "Names? Units? Which ships they came from?"

"No, sir."

Pushing my way through the crowd, I approached the first

bag and opened it far enough to reveal the head and face within. The mess that stared out at me did not look like a clone. Its skin was the purple of a fresh plum. The face was moon-shaped, a fat blue tongue poking out between black lips. The hair was the correct color—regulation cut and the right shade of brown.

Seeing the body, a few of the men in my entourage groaned. Sailors . . . They were not as used to dealing with death as Marines.

"What happened to him?" I asked.

"He drowned," said the ensign.

"Are you sure he's a clone?" asked Admiral Cabot. He looked pale, his eyes locked on the corpse's flat doll's eyes. "He doesn't look like a clone."

The ensign looked back into the crowd. Obviously not seeing the person he wanted, he called, "Andy, can you come in here? Tell the general what you told me."

Unlike everyone else in the room, Andy was a natural-born, probably a local doctor pressed into performing forensic medicine. He was a short man with fiery orange hair and heavily freckled skin. He looked at the body, then at the ensign, then settled his gaze on me. "He was three days dead when he washed up."

"Are you sure he was a clone?" Cabot repeated.

Andy nodded up and down like a horse, and said, "Oh, he's a clone, there's no doubt about that. I ran a tissue sample. I checked his teeth, too. You can always tell by the teeth." He reached down and squeezed the corners of the dead man's mouth, making the lips open in a puckered smile.

"Jeez," Cabot hissed. "Show some respect."

"Respect." The word hung in the air as the examiner unzipped the body bag farther, revealing open incisions in the cadaver's throat, chest, and gut. I wondered if it was possible to respect a body and run an autopsy at the same time.

"We drained a quart of water from his lungs," the examiner said.

"So he died of natural causes?" asked Cabot.

In my mind, "natural causes" meant a heart attack or kidney failure. Death by drowning seemed no more natural than eating poison or having an underground garage cave in around you.

"We didn't find anything to suggest he was murdered if that's what you mean."

"How about this one?" I asked, taking a step toward the next table. I opened the bag enough to reveal the badly deformed face. Great pains had been taken to clean this corpse, but the skin around the cheeks looked like melted plastic. Bone showed through his skin along the top of his forehead. Despite all of the wreckage to the rest of his face, the man's undamaged eyes stared up at the ceiling.

What was left of the dead man's hair had been singed and turned to wire. If he'd had any facial hair, the fire had burned it away. The merely blackened strip of skin along the point of his chin reminded me of a beard.

Hoping to demonstrate his command of the situation, the ensign said, "This one died in a fire."

"Yes, I see that," I said. "One man drowns and the next one burns. St. Augustine is a dangerous planet."

"Actually, he died of asphyxiation," the examiner said. "It's fairly common. Most people choke on the smoke long before the fire gets them."

"Did you find anything to suggest—" I started.

"Foul play? Murder? It's hard to tell," said the examiner. He probed the skin along the cadaver's throat with his fingers. "No broken bones; but on a body like this, burning can hide contusions and abrasions." He pulled one of the man's hands free of the body bag, holding it up by the wrist for me to get a closer look. "There's not much we can get from this. His hands could have been cuffed or tied together before he died, and we wouldn't know, not when the body is this badly burned."

"That's very convenient," I observed.

"We didn't find any cuffs or rope at the scene," the ensign said.

"Have you investigated the cause of the fire?" I asked.

"We haven't looked into it, sir."

"Maybe you'd better get someone on that," croaked Cabot, his face pale and clammy.

"Yes, sir." The ensign hesitated, then said what Cabot should have known. "Um, sir, I don't have anyone with that kind of MOS."

Investigating arson was not a typical "military occupation specialty," and none of the local MPs had any experience in that field. These guys knew how to break up street fights and how to haul drunken sailors to the brig. The Navy trained them to handle "drunk and disorderly" conduct, not forensics and crime-scene investigations.

"Tell me about this one?" I asked, moving to the last of the corpses.

"He didn't die of natural causes. Someone snapped his neck," the examiner said as he opened the bag.

The dead man had a startled expression, his glassy eyes open so wide they looked like they might roll out of their sockets. His skin was the color of curdled milk, and a familiar set of bruises ran along the base of his jaw. He'd died like Admiral Thorne—somebody had twisted his head around until the spinal column broke.

"Ensign, why weren't we notified about this?" one of the lieutenants from my entourage demanded. He sounded outraged.

"We were notified," I said. "That's why we're here."

"Yes, sir," the lieutenant whispered. He sounded contrite. Perhaps he had read my mind . . . more likely my expression. I was tired of seeing the officers in my entourage grandstanding.

"Lieutenant, come here," I said, making no attempt to hide my annoyance.

He came over, his steps short and tentative. He reminded me of a pet dog being called over to a scolding.

Normally, I simply ignored fools, but in this case I made a point of reading the lieutenant's name tag. When we got back to the ship, I would assign him to some other duty.

I pointed to the dead man's jaw, and said, "Lieutenant Granger, place your fingers over these bruises." He was a sailor, not a coroner; the order must have seemed ghoulish to him. To show that I was not making sport, I demonstrated. The spread of my fingers did not fit the bruises.

"I don't see what you're—"

"Just humor me," I said.

He placed his hand across the point of the jaw, his thumb on one side and the fingers on the other. The fit, of course, was perfect. He stared down at the way his fingers covered the bruises in shock.

"Sir, you can't possibly think . . ."

"Not at all," I said. The lieutenant did not know why his hand fit the bruises so perfectly, but everyone else understood my point—the killer was a clone.

The body tally was at thirty-nine and counting.

St. Augustine had twenty-five cities and one hundred thirty resort areas. We had military police patrolling most of the big resorts, but the smaller ones provided their own security. Apparently it never occurred to the locals to call for help when bodies trickled in.

"We just heard back from Goshen Beach Station," one of my lieutenants reported. "They've got four stiffs."

The room was warm and crowded. It smelled of chemicals and perspiration. The men in the body bags smelled of soap and formaldehyde, but that might have been my imagination. I did not mind the morgue or the bodies, but the entourage and the politicking made me claustrophobic.

"I'm going for a walk," I said.

"Where are you going?" Admiral Cabot asked, sounding like a little child afraid his parents are abandoning him.

"Out for fresh air," I said. He started after me, so I added, "Alone."

"There may be a murderer out there," he said.

"At least one," I said.

"Maybe I should—"

I put up a hand, and asked, "You don't really think I need you along for protection?"

He gave a nervous laugh, and said, "That's a good one, sir."

*Officious prick,* I thought as I escaped out the door. It was early in the evening. The sky had not gone dark, but the streetlights had come on.

From the reports, I expected to see nothing but women, children, and clones on the planet. That was not the case. Groups of teenage boys roamed the streets. Old men worked the shops. And there were fighting-age men as well, locals who had survived the invasion. Maybe half the men I passed were clones, maybe only a third.

Petersborough was no resort town. It had probably been an industrial center before the Avatari invaded. Though I saw an occasional empty lot heaped high with debris, most of the buildings had survived the war in one piece. The aliens hadn't set out to destroy this city, but they sure as shit did nothing to improve it.

I walked along streets decorated by an odd combination of iron doors and glittering storefronts. One block gave way to the next. As I neared an open-air casino, I saw scores of sailors with women on their arms. In the alley behind the casino, I passed couples groping and kissing and thought of Ava.

Another block, and I had entered an abandoned industrial district with dilapidated warehouses made of cinder block and steel. Even though they were only a few streets back, the storefronts and casinos seemed like a memory from another town.

Wandering off by myself was asking for trouble, and I knew it. I stopped, searched the street. Seeing that I was completely alone, I returned to the bright lights and amorous crowds of the hospitality district.

A parade of couples marched by me—clones with natural-born dates, their loud laughter carrying on the breeze. I saw unattached women on the prowl outside several bars. The Marine term for these women was "scrub." I sometimes wondered what names they had for us.

It was nearing 20:00, and I had not eaten since lunch, so I found a promising-looking restaurant/bar and headed in. Ironically enough, the place was called Scrubb's, spelled with two Bs. The name could have been an accident, but I doubted it.

Two hours after the dinner hour, the place was still half-full, with a few couples leaving as I came in. The clones who remained eyed me nervously as I came through the door.

The tall, well-curved hostess approached me and introduced herself as Debbie. I stood six-three, and she came up to my eyes. She studied my blouse for a moment, smiled, and said, "You must be an important man."

"How do you mean?" I asked.

"You have a lot of ribbons," she said, pointing to my chest.

She had olive skin and silky brown hair that hung straight down past her shoulders, then formed curls at the end. She had blue eyes that were narrow and small. Her eyes had an angry set, but her smile was friendly. She wore a dark blue dress with a cut that showed the tops of her breasts.

"You see action, and they give you ribbons," I said.

"You must have seen a lot of action."

I could have taken that comment several ways. I chose to take it as innocent, and said, "More than I like to admit."

"Is that how you got those stars?" she asked, pointing to my collar. "I've seen men with bars and leaves pinned on their collars, but I've never seen stars."

"Lieutenants wear bars, majors wear clusters."

I expected her to say something stupid such as asking if that made me a sergeant. Instead, she said, "Let me find you a table, General."

When I asked, "How do you know I'm a general?" she just laughed and led me across the floor.

The eatery was not all candles and violins, but it wasn't burgers and fries, either. The lighting was low, and the waitresses wore dresses instead of uniforms. Some customers spoke in hushed tones, and others told stories and laughed in voices that boomed like kettledrums.

Debbie sat me at a table near the back of the restaurant, about ten feet from a hearth with foot-tall flames dancing on a stack of logs. Cool air poured out of the ceiling, causing the temperature to remain comfortable. It reminded me of a hot shower on a cold night, leaving me relaxed.

I half hoped she would give me a card, a phone number, or a slip of paper stating what time she got off work. At the moment, Ava seemed far, far away. Debbie touched me on the shoulder, and said, "Your waitress will be right with you."

I wondered what would happen if I pursued her? Ava was more beautiful than this girl, but not as young . . . smooth-skinned youth had its own kind of beauty. Not that gravity had caught up with Ava; it probably wouldn't for another few years. I watched the girl walk away and knew that I might well fantasize about her for the next night or two.

Compared to the hostess, my waitress seemed positively plain. She was short and slender, with shoulder-length blond hair. Before taking my order, she asked, "Are you really a general?"

"I am," I said.

"Can I ask you a question?"

"You mean besides what I want to eat?" She didn't laugh. "Sure. What is it?"

"Are we safe now? Are the aliens gone for good?"

I studied the girl closely. The restaurant was dim, so I could not see every detail. She might have been twenty or maybe twenty-five years old.

I saw no scars on her skin, but I heard them in her voice and decided to lie. "Gone for good," I said, unwilling to say anything further. I so wanted to believe my own words that it almost made them true. Modern alchemy—turning lies into gold.

She said nothing, and I wondered if she believed me. Maybe she realized the same thing I did, that sometimes it is better not to know what lurks around the corner.

"What's your name?" I asked.

"Lyra."

"Lyra, those aliens weren't soldiers, they were business-men," I said. "They didn't come looking for a war, and when we gave them one, they went to bother someone else."

Lyra saw things as they were. I spoke to her the way I would speak to a scared child, but she knew war and death as intimately as I did, and she took no comfort from my reassur-ance. She let me say my piece, thanked me, then recited the specials of the day. I ordered baked fish and wild rice, hoping it would be as good as the meal I'd eaten with Warshaw.

Looking around the restaurant, I saw only couples. A meal in this place would cost more than most sailors or Marines wanted to pay; but men on leave will sometimes pony up the credits if they think it will change the outcome of their date.

Scrubb's had a bar near the front, the kind of place that would attract conscripts and officers alike. The bar sat on a slightly raised floor that overlooked the rest of the restaurant. Debbie, the hostess, must have worked the bar as well as the restaurant floor. I saw her walk in, heads turning to follow her, and disappear into the darkness of the bar.

That was when I spotted the phantom. He sat alone at a

small table, quietly looking around the floor. He might have been either a Marine or a sailor, a clone to be sure; but dressed in a bright tropical shirt and slacks . . . the typical serviceman on leave.

Like any other single man drinking alone in a room filled with couples, he looked out of place as he scanned the floor around him. Something did not seem right about him. I could not put my finger on it, but he just came across wrong. *Like a tree in a desert or maybe a wolf among sheep,* I thought to myself.

The man was not trolling for girls, that much was clear. Time passed as he slowly nursed his beer. A waitress ran her rounds in his part of the bar. When she saw his untouched glass, she approached the table and said something to him. He answered, and she rolled her eyes and walked away.

The man leaned back and rested his arm on the rail that separated the bar from the rest of the restaurant. He casually surveyed the bar, then the eatery. The move looked so relaxed, so subtle. Too relaxed, it felt calculated to put people at ease.

*Why would he come here alone?* I asked myself; but even as I thought this, I realized that I had come here alone, and just like the phantom, I was looking around the floor and studying the wildlife. Did I make him suspicious? But this guy wasn't drinking. His beer was a prop.

As he scanned the restaurant, his gaze eventually drifted to my table. I saw him looking in my direction, and he saw me staring back. I expected him to turn away, but he didn't. His eyes stayed on me as he took in my insignia or possibly counted the stars on my collar. He met my gaze with a look that showed neither fear nor nervousness, then calmly pulled out his wallet and dropped a few bills on the table. Without looking back, he abandoned his money and his half-finished beer.

I started to go after him. I stood, then questioned myself. What did I have? Why would I stop him? He didn't finish his beer, big specking deal. What did that prove? I only hesitated for a moment, then I went after him; but that moment was enough. By the time I reached the street, the phantom was gone.

I went back into the restaurant wondering if I had made

a mistake. As I tried to reason out my suspicions, my fish arrived.

I sat, and I ate, and I rewound the scene and watched it over and over again in my head—a clone comes into the bar. He sits alone. So what?

I took a bite of fish and chased it with a forkload of wild rice. The rice had pepper and butter. The food tasted good, but it was wasted on me. I would have been just as happy eating bad food camouflaged with ketchup. I took another bite of fish and realized one difference me and the phantom—I was eating my fish; he had only been hiding behind his beer.

## CHAPTER
# TWENTY-ONE

After my meal, I returned to the police station and found Cabot.

He saw me, growled, "General," then caught himself and paused.

"Spit it out, Cabot," I said. For a moment, the little ass-licker had shown a bit of backbone.

"Where the hell have you been?" he asked. He looked relieved to have said his piece, then he winced as he braced himself for me to respond.

Finding humor in his discomfort, I smiled, and asked, "Did you just say 'hell'?"

Cabot turned red and stared at the floor.

"Did you just ask me where the *hell* I went?" I continued, sincerely enjoying his discomfort.

"Sorry, sir," he said.

"I went out for a quick dinner."

Cabot looked up from his feet, and said, "You left three hours ago, sir. We have MPs combing the city for you."

"Good Lord. You're like an obsessive mother and a nagging wife all rolled into one." I said this in a chiding tone, not really caring how derisive it sounded. "You called the police because you didn't know how to find me?"

"General, you were gone three hours. We were just looking at bodies, sir. I have every MP in the city searching for you. The station is on high alert."

I looked around, and said, "High alert? Cabot, we need to do some serious field training on police procedures down here. I was able to walk in here without anyone even noticing me."

Cabot pursed his lips as he fought to control his anger. He might have been a hanger-on, but he was also a one-star admiral, the kind of man who normally talks down the chain, not up. When he next opened his mouth, he spoke in an even tone as if the conversation had started anew.

"We've received body counts from every precinct on the planet except for one, a town called Sunmark," he said.

"What's the count at?" I asked.

"We're up to 503 bodies found in the last three weeks."

"That's a lot bodies," I said. "Five hundred stiffs, and it never occurred to anyone that there might be an epidemic?"

"General, that's 503 bodies planetwide on a planet that doesn't have centralized communications," Cabot said. He had a point; no one on St. Augustine knew what anyone else was doing.

"Any idea when we'll hear from the last station?" I asked.

"We haven't been able to reach them. The town is not very far from here; I sent some men to knock on their door."

Cabot heard back from his men an hour later. The Sunmark police station was empty. As far as anyone could tell, all our MPs were M.I.A. and probably worse.

The ghost precinct was less than one hundred miles away. By the time I arrived with my entourage to investigate, it was 00:13, a cursed time if such a thing could exist.

Bright light shone through the windows of the precinct building as we pulled up. A few men searched the alley around the building. The inside of the precinct building looked as busy as an anthill, with MPs bustling in every direction.

I did not recognize any of the men beyond their uniforms

and the fact that they were clones, but some of them had undoubtedly come as my support staff. At that moment, another piece of the puzzle fell into place for me.

*What if somebody killed a member of my staff?* I thought to myself. *I don't know them well enough to tell them apart. If someone quietly murdered one of my men and showed up in his place, I wouldn't notice it.*

As I waited by the car, Cabot went to the door of the building and spoke to the officer in charge of the investigation. He came back a moment later, and said, "Someone attacked the building."

"Have they found any bodies?" I asked.

Cabot shook his head. "No, sir."

Sunmark was only a hundred miles from Petersborough, but the air was slightly cooler here and far more humid. This was a coastal town. I enjoyed the combination of warm night and ocean-chilled breeze. Taking a deep breath and letting the moist air hold in my lungs, I walked toward the building, Cabot hopping close on my heels.

The men outside the precinct building snapped to attention as I walked past them. I saluted and told them to carry on.

Standing outside the building, I saw rows of flood lamps through one of the windows. I heard a generator purring in the distance.

"What happened to the lights?" I asked a nearby officer.

"Someone shut off the power, sir," he said.

The station was two stories tall and rather narrow. It was shaped like a book. My men must have set up an emergency generator behind the building. Arteries from the generator covered the floor, a confusion of power cords that led in every direction. The Marine sergeant who met me at the door was not part of my entourage, and I was glad to see him. When it came to dirty work, I preferred having Marines around me.

"Found anything?" I asked.

"They fought a small war in here, sir."

"Any survivors?"

"So far, we can't tell, sir. The people who were manning the station are M.I.A.," he said.

"No bodies?" I asked. I stepped around him.

Just inside the door, the first splash of dried blood started about five feet up on the wall and stretched to the floor in dribbles. A foot-wide, rust-colored pool had formed below it.

*They'd caught their first victim off guard,* I thought. He'd been standing tall when he was shot in the head. I was no detective, but I'd participated in a stealth operation or two. I knew how men reacted when they spotted you, and how they died when you took them by surprise.

"Was this the only victim?" I asked.

"The whole goddamned building looks like this, sir," the sergeant said. "We're taking blood samples and scraping shit off the walls."

"Good idea," I said. It wasn't, though. All of the blood would be the same general-issue clone blood. If we knew anything about these assassins, it was that they were clones just like us. The good guys and bad guys would have the exact same makeup in this fight, right down to their DNA.

The next victim had been caught unawares as well. He must have been at a desk. The chair he'd been sitting in lay on its back on the floor. There was no blood on the chair, but blood and brains covered the wall and the filing cabinet behind the desk.

"Do you have any idea about what happened to the bodies?" I asked.

"No, sir." That was the proper answer, no excuses, no promises, no explanations, and no speculation. "Marines never speculate. They always speck you right on time"—wisdom I picked up from my drill instructor in boot camp.

The sergeant interrupted my thoughts. "Sir, whoever attacked the station destroyed the computers."

"Destroyed them?" I repeated.

Across the floor, computer cases and cabinets lay spread across the floor like trash. No big loss, though. A platoon of MPs had been temporarily assigned to man a precinct on a stretch of sandy beach. They probably had not kept careful records.

"Do we know how long the power has been out?" I asked.

"No, sir. Not yet."

"Do we know what happened to it? Do we know if the neighbors still have power?" I asked. I looked out the window and saw light in some of the windows across the street.

The sergeant peered out the window as well, and said, "This appears to be the only building without power."

I nodded and moved on. "Shit," I whispered to myself.

Whatever happened in this building was not a war or a battle; it was an assassination. Someone had come in with suppressed weapons and caught the entire staff off guard. Judging by the gore and bullet patterns, they might have gone through the entire building without any of ours returning fire.

Magic restored.

In the old days, communication signals were routed across the galaxy using the Broadcast Network. Somehow, Gary Warshaw and his enlisted engineers had restored pangalactic communications using their limited broadcast network. It was nothing short of a miracle.

Warshaw called me that evening.

"Where are you?" I asked.

"I'm on Gobi," he said, sounding a little surprised. "Something wrong with that?"

"I didn't know you had pangalactic communications," I said. It should have occurred to me back when I was on the *Kamehameha*. Warshaw wasn't even in the same arm as the *Kamehameha*, but he had been able to watch Bishop interrogating me. I should have figured it out back then.

"Yeah, well, we got a network up, so why not?" he asked. "You making any progress on your investigation?"

"We've found a lot of bodies," I said. "Over five hundred of them so far."

"All clones?"

"Yeah," I said, "all clones. There were a few in every city."

"Murdered?" Warshaw asked.

"Drownings, car accidents, fires . . . a couple of outright murders. St. Augustine is a revolving door with eighty thousand men running through at any time." *Five hundred men . . .* I wondered if it was a revolving door or a meat grinder.

"I bet we haven't even found half the breakage yet," I said. "All we have are the bodies that floated to the surface."

"That's what I like about you, Harris, always the optimist," Warshaw said.

"I contacted the ships that went to St. Augustine on leave and had them check their service logs. In the last two months, less than thirty men were reported absent without leave. Every last one of them showed up sooner or later. According to the logs, none of those five hundred stiffs came from your ships."

"But you think the logs are wrong," said Warshaw.

"They have to be," I said. "And that's five hundred bodies so far. Who knows how many bodies we'll find by the time we finish here."

"You think I have five hundred saboteurs on my ships?" Warshaw asked.

"Sooner or later, it's going to get ugly." I thought about the clone at the restaurant. We had no hope of ferreting them out, not with camouflage like that.

"Are you keeping yourself safe?" I asked.

"Maybe I'll move my operation back to the *Kamehameha*," he said. "How are they going to hit me on a big ship like that?"

"Where was Franks when they got him?" I asked.

"On the *Obama*."

That was another fighter carrier.

"Yeah, well, Franks didn't know what he was hiding from," Warshaw said. "I have a better idea, thanks to you."

"Glad to be of service," I said. "So what are you watching for?"

"Anything that moves." Warshaw let the comment ride for a moment, then asked, "How about you? What are you doing to keep safe?"

"If you wanted me to play it safe, you shouldn't have painted a specking target on my back."

He must have expected a different answer. Sounding defensive, he said, "At least you've got the toe-touchers brigade watching your back, and I hear you called in an intelligence unit."

"Toe-touchers brigade?" I asked.

"Yeah, Cabot didn't tell you why he lost his command? Remember Fahey?" Perry Fahey was a ship's-captain-turned-spy for the Unified Authority.

"Cabot was a spy?" I asked.

"Shit, Harris, I just told you, he was a toe-toucher. He lost his command for conduct unbecoming an officer. I thought having him along might help you relieve any stress."

"Get specked," I said. In the years that many of our fleets were stranded in deep space with no hope of rescue, some of our sailors and officers had traded unfulfillable heterosexuality for a convenient alternative.

Warshaw laughed. "At least I didn't paint the bull's-eye on your ass."

He still did not get it. Every Marine and sailor in the entire empire was a potential assassin. Thinking he had deflected the danger onto me, he did not notice the noose tightening around his own neck as well.

When I did not respond, Warshaw said, "You'll survive this one, Harris. You always survive." Perhaps he meant the comment as an olive branch, but it was meaningless.

I changed the subject. "I'm in a town called Sunmark. Ever heard of it?"

"Can't say I have," Warshaw said.

"It's a small coast town surrounded by a lot of jungle."

"Yeah, so?"

"I have two hundred men searching the jungle for bodies. Let's say one of my guys gets nixed while taking a leak in the woods, next thing you know, one of the men watching my back is an assassin. Then how safe will I be?"

"You sound paranoid."

I laughed. "Paranoid? The last time I saw you, you were hiding in a high-security base in the middle of a desert with guards and DNA-reading posts by every entrance and elevator."

"What's your point?" Warshaw asked, though he damn well knew exactly what I meant.

"How many guards are you going to have around you on the *Kamehameha*?"

"Four, same as always."

"How many guards are you going to have posted on your deck?" I pushed.

"Having a platoon is standard operating procedure."

Posting an entire platoon to guard the deck of a ship was hardly standard operating procedure. "Are you going to tour the ship?" I asked.

"Maybe."

"Are you going to take the whole platoon with you?"

"Okay, I apologize for calling you paranoid. What are you going to do next?"

I thought about this. "First we find out how badly we've been infiltrated, then we stop the leaks, then we catch a spy and figure out what makes him different from a run-of-the-mill clone."

"And that fixes everything?" Warshaw asked.

"Then we need to round up the enemy clones. That's going to be the hard part."

The ax came down that afternoon. We might have been able to stop the leaks, we might have been able to catch a killer clone and examine him under a microscope, but it did not look like we would ever untangle how badly we'd been infiltrated.

At 15:00, Admiral Cabot informed me that the intelligence unit had found a mass grave in the jungle. Bored stiff from two days spent sitting in an office, I took the news more enthusiastically than he expected. In fact, I insisted we drive into the jungle and oversee the excavation.

By that time, a large security detail of locals and clones had arrived in Sunmark. Armed civilians patrolled the streets. MPs and militiamen manned the police station. The town was beginning to look like a prison.

I had hoped to escape all of the security precautions by going out to the grave site, but it didn't work that way. Cabot arranged for a convoy escort. As we left town, I watched the trucks and guards, and muttered, "You'd think we were headed to a battle, not a burial."

"Did you say something, sir?" Cabot asked. His mind had been elsewhere.

My driver heard me, though. He was a Marine. I caught his sardonic smile in the mirror.

I wondered how many men we might find in that grave. No one had given me the details. The grave could have been huge or small.

We drove away from the coast and into the jungle, trading bright sun for dappled light and shadows. Following a guidance signal from the site, we turned down a dirt path that led through trampled plants and into heavy undergrowth. The road led us through a maze of broad-leafed plants that looked like bloodred banana trees, vines, bamboo, and tall trees with wide trunks.

"It's going to get bumpy from here, sir," my driver said. Hearing this, Cabot sighed and slumped back in his seat.

Fortunately, we had a heavy troop mobile ahead of us. The big truck bashed all obstacles out of its way. It slowed and took turns wide, practically paving the path for us. We bounced along for another fifteen miles before we reached a clearing in which men in fatigues prowled a low ridge.

The first man to reach my car wore an air filter over his nose and mouth. He pulled it off, and said, "General, you will probably want to stay in your car unless you have an oxygen mask."

When I asked, "That bad?" the man simply nodded.

"Poisonous or just smelly?" I asked.

"Reeking," he said.

"I hate this shit," I said as I climbed from the car. I would not like what I saw, but I'd seen death and decay before. Over the last ten years, I'd lost my emotional virginity.

The steamy air hit my chest like a hammer, and blood rushed to my head as I adjusted to the heat. There was not so much as a breeze in this blasted hellhole. The leaves on the plants sat so still they might have been painted on, and the flies were everywhere. They filled the air, their buzzing so strong it sounded electronic.

The men near the grave wore jumpsuits that were wet and soiled. They wore full face masks with clear hoods over their ears, hair, and necks.

The air smelled bad, sweet and putrid at the same time. I recognized the scent of rotting bodies in the liquid air. I also smelled the acrid scent of vomit. Whatever they had seen had left seasoned men sick.

The pit was twenty feet long, no more than six feet wide, and shallow. A small silver canister lay on the ground beside it. The word NOXIUM ran down the length of both sides.

Suddenly, looking into that pit was the last thing I wanted to do. Thinking of a long-ago battle on a distant planet in which scores of men had been killed with Noxium, I wanted to return to the air-conditioned comfort of the police station. I wanted to put on a pair of mediaLink glasses and read a good book, maybe something philosophical or religious . . . something that explained the meaning of life.

There were no bodies inside the grave, not even so much as a human finger. What I saw was a writhing carpet of pearly white maggots feeding in the flesh-colored soup that might once have been forty or fifty men. Soggy uniforms lay in the mix along with boots, belts, and weapons.

# CHAPTER
# TWENTY-TWO

"Quarantine the solar system? You mean blockade it, right?"

"You already have a blockade, and it didn't work," I said. "It didn't keep the bad guys out; but that's not the problem now. Now we want to keep the bad guys in."

"We haven't caught anyone running our blockade," said Captain Tom Wesker, commander of the fleet Warshaw had assigned to guard St. Augustine.

Something about Wesker; he was a defensive speck.

"That makes sense," I said.

"What's that?" He sounded nervous.

"It makes sense that you haven't seen them running your blockade. If you had seen them, you might have caught them, and we wouldn't have five hundred dead clones on our hands."

"That's not fair! We've only been here two months. Maybe they got here before we did," Wesker whined like a little kid.

"Good point," I said, trying to be diplomatic. On the other hand, Warshaw had only liberated St. Augustine three months ago. "Unless the enemy landed during the alien occupation, they pretty much had to have arrived on your watch."

I decided to make things easy on him. "Look at it this way. You should have an easier time keeping ships on the planet than you did chasing them away; it gives you a smaller area to patrol."

He wanted to tell me that was bullshit, but he knew better. He was a captain, I was a three-star; if he pissed me off, I'd have him scrubbing toilets for life. He took a deep breath, drank back his anger, and asked, "What are you trying to keep on the planet?"

"The same people we wanted to keep off the planet for the last two months," I said.

"Who exactly is that?" he asked, his frustration so close to the surface his eyes twitched.

"If I knew who the speck they were, don't you think I'd arrest them?" I asked. "I can tell you this much, they look like us, they talk like us, and they kill senior officers. If I were you, I'd do everything in my power to keep them on the ground, you know, as if the planet were under quarantine."

"Yes, sir. Understood, sir."

"Also, put every available man on security at all times," I said.

"On the planet?"

"On your ships. I'm betting you've already been infiltrated."

I had traveled from Gobi to St. Augustine on a battleship with a crew of 1,800 enlisted men and 150 officers. I returned on a frigate, a small ship with a crew of 170 men. I felt like I was rowing home on a dinghy.

The man I had seen in the restaurant looked like he might have been in his midtwenties, making him slightly on the young side for the Enlisted Man's Navy. We hadn't seen a new cadet since the Mogats destroyed the clone farms six years ago. Our youngest clones were twenty-four, and most of our men were in their thirties.

One of the benefits of flying in a frigate was that the ship was so small I could assemble my own crew. I had undoubtedly assembled the oldest crew in the short history of the Enlisted Man's Navy. By the time I finished, the youngest man on the ship was in his early forties. It was possible that some infiltrator might have stowed away aboard the ship, but he would stand out once he left his hidey-hole.

Why had I hesitated before going after that bastard at Scrubb's? Even if I'd had to kill him, we might have found something to go on. The autopsy might have provided clues about how we could identify the infiltrators. And maybe I would not have had to kill him. With any luck, I might have captured him alive with nothing worse than a broken leg or spine.

On the frigate, my quarters were both my billet and my stateroom. It didn't matter much. My time on the ship was short. We spent fifteen minutes traveling untold trillions of miles and then another two hours circling Gobi as I considered my options and decided where I should go and what I should do.

Someone knocked on my door, and I knew who it was. When I opened the door, Admiral J. Winston Cabot saluted and asked for permission to enter. I did not like the guy. I would dump him when I got the chance. I had already abandoned half my entourage on St. Augustine.

I asked him in.

"Did you send for me, sir?" Cabot asked. It must have galled him, calling me "sir." He was nearly twice my age, and he had reached the rank of admiral. Once you obtain a certain rank, you expect to leave the sirs and salutes behind.

"Have a seat," I said.

"Yes, sir," he said.

"Let's forget the senior officer stuff for now," I said.

Cabot nodded and quietly sat down. He had aged well. He had plenty of white in his hair, but he had neither put on pounds nor turned frail after fifty. He looked fit, like a man who runs five or six miles every day.

"I think I may have seen one of their assassins," I said.

Cabot perked up. "On St. Augustine?"

"Yes, in Petersborough, after I left the morgue. Remember when I went off on my own?"

"I remember," he said.

"I walked around for an hour, then I ended up at a restaurant. There was a man in the restaurant . . . a clone."

"What makes you think he was the killer?" Cabot asked.

"He was alone in the bar. Everyone else came with friends or dates, but he was there alone, looking around the room like a man on a hunt."

"Maybe he came looking for a date," Cabot suggested.

"Yeah, maybe," I agreed. "But he wasn't there for the girls." Considering Cabot's reputation as a "toe-toucher," I wondered if that was a sensitive topic. He seemed unfazed, so I went on. "He sat by himself in a corner. He didn't eat. He didn't talk to anybody. He ordered a beer, but he didn't drink it. When he spotted me watching him, he paid his tab and left."

"What makes you think he was an assassin?" Cabot asked.

"He left when he spotted me."

"Maybe you scared him."

"Maybe, but let's go on the assumption that he is a Unified Authority assassin."

"Was there anything besides the beer that made you think he was an assassin?" Cabot asked. It was a fair question.

I sighed. I had nothing to go on, just my instincts. "I don't know."

Cabot shook his head. "It sounds pretty thin, sir. I mean, what are the odds? The entire Navy uses St. Augustine for R & R. How many bars do you think there are in Petersborough? I bet there are hundreds, maybe even thousands; and here you stepped into the one bar in the entire city where a Unified Authority assassin sits waiting. Do you really think we got that lucky, sir?"

I knew why he added the "sir." It was like telling someone they look like shit, then finishing up with, "No offense."

*So he's not all bad,* I thought. *At least he speaks his mind.*

"You thirsty?" I asked. "I brought a bottle of Scotch for the ride."

Cabot shook his head, and said, "I'll pass." Maybe he didn't like me any more than I liked him. Until this moment, it hadn't occurred to me that my lack of respect for him might be mutual.

"Of all the gin joints in all the towns in all the world," I said. It was one of those ancient sayings you heard from time to time, though nobody actually knew where it came from anymore. "Maybe it wasn't a coincidence. What if there's a guy like that in every bar in every city on St. Augustine?"

"I think we would know about something so massive,"

Cabot said. "Sooner or later, somebody is going to notice something like that."

"Maybe somebody did notice," I said. "Maybe one of the MPs guarding Sunmark got curious, so they killed him; and then they killed off everyone else in the precinct just in case he told someone.

"Maybe that's what happened. They killed him, then they killed the others, then they dragged their bodies into the jungle and dissolved them with Noxium."

"It's a possibility," Cabot said slowly as he considered the theory. "That would explain who did it and why."

"But you don't think that's what happened?" I asked.

"I don't have any better explanations, but I'm at a disadvantage here, this is the first time you've told me about your mysterious barfly."

He thought for a moment, then shook his head. "It doesn't wash, sir. They couldn't land that many replacements on the planet without people noticing."

"There are eighty thousand clones on St. Augustine taking leave at any moment. Who's going to notice a few hundred infiltrators?" I asked.

"They'd notice if a bunch of clones disappeared . . ." Cabot began, but he stopped himself.

"We found 550 victims give or take a few. Did anybody notice anything before we started counting bodies?"

We had thirteen fleets filled with clones who had not been ashore for at least two years. For the men on leave, St. Augustine was a bottomless supply of booze, women, and freedom. From the moment they landed to the moment they returned to duty, they left their brains behind.

I had a slightly different view of the planet. I saw St. Augustine as a malignant tumor that had metastasized and was now spreading cancerous poison throughout the Enlisted Man's Empire.

Cabot and I spoke for another few minutes before I dismissed him. He'd done his job.

An hour later, I had typed up my report and my recommendations, weak as they were. The only answer I could come up with was to be on the lookout for clones in their midtwenties who seemed alienated from the rest of the crew. Maybe we would catch a spy, and maybe he would break under interrogation. Then we would have more.

In the short term, I was placing my investigation on hold. I knew someplace where I could assemble an elite brigade of Marines that I knew had not been infiltrated. The only question in my mind was, "Would they follow me?"

## CHAPTER
# TWENTY-THREE

Earthdate: November 3, A.D. 2517
Location: Terraneau
Galactic Position: Scutum-Crux Arm

I sailed out of the Scutum-Crux Arm on a wrecked battleship and returned on a yacht . . . more or less. I rode a frigate to Gobi, then requisitioned the *Salah ad-Din*, a Perseus-class fighter carrier.

In demographic terms, the *ad-Din* had the oldest crew of any carrier in the Enlisted Man's Navy, its youngest sailor being thirty-two years old. Beyond that, having not yet been granted leave, the crew of the *Salah ad-Din* could not have picked up pests from St. Augustine. If any ship was secure, it was the *Salah ad-Din*, and she had plenty of space for transporting Marines since the eleven-thousand-man Marine compound on her bottom deck now sat vacant.

There were twenty-two hundred Marines stationed on Terraneau. The *ad-Din* had room to spare.

I toured the Marine complex as the *ad-Din* broadcasted out through a station that was specially programmed for a single broadcast to Terraneau. Walking through the barracks,

I imagined them filled with men. I went to the firing range, the ghosts of ancient gunfire echoing in my head.

"General Harris?" The voice of Captain Pete Villanueva spoke to me from a squawk box on the wall. I wondered if his voice had sounded from every speaker in the Marine complex or if some onboard system had tracked my movements.

I went to the box. "Harris here."

"We are in Scutum-Crux space, sir."

"What is the situation?"

"All clear, sir."

Several months had passed since the U.A. Navy attacked Terraneau. If the Unifieds were coming back, I figured they would have done it months ago.

"Have you made contact?" I asked.

"We reached Fort Sebastian, the Marines are expecting you, sir."

"Very well. All I need now is a transport and a pilot," I said.

"Your staff pilot is ready and waiting for you, sir."

"My staff pilot?" I asked. He might have meant Nobles, but to the best of my knowledge, Nobles was still on the *Kamehameha. Maybe I picked up a tick on St. Augustine,* I thought, and the thought made me smile.

"Captain, please send a security detail to the landing bay," I said. "Have them seal off the bay and wait for me in the hall."

"Yes, sir."

"Under no circumstances are they to enter the bay before I arrive," I said.

"Aye, aye, sir."

I didn't need to worry about them arriving before me as the Marine complex was on the same deck as the landing bay. Running through the hall, I arrived in about three minutes. My security detail—six men armed with M27s—arrived a few seconds later. Villanueva ran a tight ship; I was impressed.

"There's a transport waiting for takeoff," I told the men. "The man piloting that transport may be a Unified Authority assassin."

If these men had been SEALs instead of MPs, I would have sent them in first. I'd seen SEALs at work; they could slip into a hangar, sneak onto a transport, and knock out the pilot more smoothly than most men could zip their pants.

MPs had a different calling. They arrested drunken sailors and escorted troublemakers to the brig. "I'm going in first. I want you to come in fifteen seconds after me. If there's an enemy in there, I want to take him alive," I said.

They answered with nods and sirs.

"Fifteen seconds, then you come in with your fingers off your triggers. I don't want you shooting me in the back," I said.

Months had passed since the last time I'd seen combat. During that time, I had not so much as fired a gun at a range; so as I entered the landing bay, it came as no surprise that I felt a nervous rush of adrenaline. I had not slipped into a combat reflex, but it wasn't far off.

I stepped through the hatch, took three steps forward, and heard the familiar greeting.

"General Harris." Sergeant Nobles waved and greeted me like an old friend. Then he remembered himself, stiffened, and gave me a proper salute.

"Nobles?" He fit the profile of the U.A. assassins—a clone in his twenties. He was neither heavy nor thin, neither muscular nor frail. Put him in any platoon, and he would blend in.

I had burst through the hatch and run toward the transport, then I slowed to the speed of a drill sergeant inspecting his platoon. A few seconds passed and the hatch opened again and six M27-carrying MPs charged in behind me and ground to a stop. I did not even need to look back to know they had confused expressions on their faces.

They had come in locked and loaded, expecting a fight. Instead, they got a dawdling general and an unarmed man standing at attention.

I ignored them and returned Nobles's salute.

"Are we bringing an escort, sir?" he asked. The guy was so positive, so innocent. Six armed MPs had just stormed the transport, and it never occurred to him that he was under suspicion.

I said no and dismissed the MPs.

Thus began one of the more dismal missions of my career.

\* \* \*

I did not expect Philo Hollingsworth to greet me with open arms, but I thought he would be interested in what I had to say. As things currently stood, he commanded a tiny base on a backwater world that was cut off from the rest of the universe.

No cars waited as we touched down on the airfield outside of Norristown. I wasn't hoping for a ticker-tape parade, but I expected something. Nobles secured the transport, and we stood there wondering if perhaps we'd landed in the wrong place.

Two jeeps arrived fifteen minutes later. Colonel Hollingsworth did not come himself. Instead, he sent a couple of enlisted men to drive me. Glad for the chance to gather his gear, Nobles rode back to base in one of the jeeps. The driver of the second jeep took me to Norristown.

"Where exactly are we going?" I asked, as we drove past the road to Fort Sebastian.

"To the capitol building, sir," the man said.

I did not know that Terraneau had a capitol building.

We drove almost all the way across Norristown. I had seen the city in ruins, now I saw it in reclamation, like a forest three years after a major fire. Collapsing structures had been torn down. Lots had been cleared. The locals had begun work on a scattering of small buildings, nothing too aggressive, just two- and three-story affairs. In another year, they might begin work on new skyscrapers.

Hollingsworth must have ignored my orders and alerted Doctorow that I was coming if we were headed to the capitol. I didn't like it, but it could have been worse. Hollingsworth could have sent a firing squad out to shoot me when I stepped off the transport.

# CHAPTER
# TWENTY-FOUR

We drove into the prewar government sector.

For a moment, I thought we might end up outside the collapsed garage, with Doctorow telling me he had excavated the weapons; but the new fence we had built around the lot remained closed, and the ground looked undisturbed.

We stopped in front of a building with a polished onyx façade and working fountains. Its windows, once crusted with dust, now sparkled in the sun. A stream burbled down the tiered waterway that ran along the front of the building. The buildings in this part of town had not been destroyed, but they hadn't been in use when I'd left. Someone had done a lot of work in a very little time on this structure. Taking in the amazing restoration around me, I hopped out of the jeep and entered Terraneau's new "government center."

The lobby of the building was a giant cavern paved in black marble and sparsely populated by men in expensive suits. The room could have held five hundred people. I saw no more than two hundred.

Hollingsworth met me at the door, his expression belying something deeper than anger. He saluted. I saluted.

"Did you really go through that broadcast zone?" he asked in a whisper, his eyes switching between me and the lobby. "It wasn't just a trick?"

"What do you think?" I asked.

"Did you find anyone on the other side?"

We were just inside the door. Across the floor, maybe one hundred feet away, Doctorow spotted us and started in our direction. Others noticed us as well, and the din dropped noticeably.

"I found Warshaw," I said.

"He made it?"

"He's got a growing empire with twenty-three planets," I said in a soft voice. "Looks like the Unifieds want their planets back."

Sarah Doctorow floated in her husband's wake. She smiled in my direction, her lipstick the bright red color of oxygenated blood. Her face was as round as a full moon, and her body was tapered up like a pyramid. She moved through the gathering with the grace of a queen.

"I don't believe it. You were right about everything," he said in a voice that betrayed aggravation instead of admiration.

And then Doctorow was upon us. I had never seen him dressed like this before. He wore a freshly pressed dark suit. He'd trimmed his beard so that it no longer covered his neck. He had also cut his hair. It still hung past his ears, but gone were the dried-out tresses that had once brushed his shoulders.

"Welcome back," Doctorow said as he approached us.

"General Harris, thank God you're safe. It's just a miracle," Sarah said, sounding too enthusiastic to be sincere.

"It's good to see you," I told Sarah, my pleasure in seeing her every bit as genuine as her gratitude for my safe return.

Doctorow came up beside me. We traded handshakes and glances with about as much affection as boxers touching gloves before a fight.

The last time I had checked, Doctorow had been running Norristown out of his house, with his wife snooping over his shoulder. As for this building, I did not notice any cleaning crews in the government complex the last time I came by. Now it had a gleaming chandelier cascading from its ceiling, water fixtures decorating its lobby, acres of shining black marble, and air-conditioning.

"When did you move here?" I asked.

"This is our new capitol building," Doctorow said, the friendly smile never leaving his face.

"For Norristown?" I asked.

"For all of Terraneau," Hollingsworth said.

"Now you're the governor of the planet," I said. "Congratulations on your promotion."

"We all have our ambitions, General," Doctorow said in a booming voice. "You want to conquer Earth. My plans are not nearly so grand. I'll settle for rebuilding Terraneau."

The small crowd that had gathered around us chuckled . . . everybody but me.

We adjourned to the assembly room. It reminded me of the capitol building on Earth, only in miniature. The men Doctorow had assembled to help him run his utopian planet were the inquisitors; I was the criminal.

We entered a three-story auditorium in which a lectern and a couple of seats waited on a stage at the bottom of the well. Doctorow led the way down the stairs, bounding each step with energy I would not have expected from a man in his sixties, his excitement unmistakable.

He led me to the stage and asked me to take a seat. Behind us, extending out like a small wall, stood the type of raised bench that judges use in courtrooms. The stand rose a full eight feet above the stage, and Doctorow sat behind it, leaving me alone on display.

The audience quietly assembled along the tiers of the auditorium. Were they Doctorow's appointees or elected officials? How had so many changes happened so quickly? I'd only been gone a week. Doctorow must have started the ball rolling before I left. Maybe that was why he'd wanted me off his planet so badly.

Hollingsworth sat the meeting out, leaving me to the lions . . . the bastard.

Once everyone was seated, Doctorow started the meeting by congratulating me on my safe return. He assured me that the "assembled body" had been briefed about the circumstances of my departure and that the meeting was nothing more than a briefing. "We're simply curious about what you found," he said, sounding so specking diplomatic. He must have seen himself as cordial, but his demeanor made me think of a rancher giving a steer a friendly pat before leading it to the slaughterhouse.

Instead of letting me speak, Doctorow invited the gallery to ask questions. Not a moment passed before five or six people stood in place, signaling that they wanted the floor. Doctorow called each of them by name.

"General, you left to find your fleet. Did you find it?" asked the first man.

"Yes," I said.

"Was it destroyed?" the man continued.

"No. I returned on the *Salah ad-Din*, one of the ships from the fleet."

Back when the Unified Authority ran the galaxy, every planet had security stations monitoring nearby space. If a ship broadcasted in within a couple of million miles of that planet, the equipment detected the anomaly and tracked the ship. Judging by the nervous twitters filling the room, I got the feeling that the *ad-Din* had slipped into Terraneau space unnoticed. Doctorow would have that problem fixed. He'd make it a priority.

"The *Salah ad-Din*, General, isn't that a fighter carrier?" the man continued.

I nodded.

"Is there any particular reason you chose to return in a fighter carrier, General?" he asked, the first strains of hostility beginning to sound in his voice.

"Are you asking if there was a reason other than its being a ship capable of traveling through space?" I asked.

"I am trying to ascertain why you chose to travel in one of the largest and most aggressive ships in your fleet when you returned to Terraneau. Are you trying to send us a message, General Harris?"

Arguments broke out throughout the gallery.

Doctorow spoke up from behind me. "Please. We are getting ahead of ourselves. Give the general a chance to explain what he found on his mission.

"I apologize for this outburst," Doctorow said, holding his right hand over his heart to show his sincerity. "Please, tell us about the status of your fleet."

The well of the auditorium was three stories deep, with rows forming rings around the stage. Only the area directly behind me was blocked off.

I felt no fear facing down these politicians . . . these nouveau-bureaucrats. That these men and women had promoted themselves to a planetary council meant nothing to me. What did I care about glorified postmen pretending to be governors and heads of states? When I came to Terraneau, these people lived in fear like rabbits cowering in a warren, and now they'd made themselves kings. What a joke.

I no longer gave a damn about getting along with the Right Reverend Colonel Ellery Doctorow, governor of Norristown and apparently emperor of Terraneau, or with the pompous men and women who made up his choir, so I told it to them straight. "The Enlisted Man's Empire controls twenty-three planets and thirteen fleets. The empire has not attacked Earth, but no one is ruling out the possibility."

The initial silence that filled the auditorium pushed in on my eardrums like the pressure from a deep-sea dive. Pandemonium replaced silence. Half the representatives stood to ask questions. When Doctorow did not call on them, they started shouting.

"Are you saying the Clone Navy is preparing to attack Earth?" Doctorow asked.

The room went quiet.

Unsure how I could have stated it any more clearly, I said, "No, I did not say that. I simply stated that attacking Earth is an option."

A woman ran down the stairs shouting, "But you can't do that! That would be an act of aggression. The clones would be declaring war on their—"

"Let me make this clear to you," I said, raising my voice so it would be heard above the din. "We did not break off from the Unified Authority, they abandoned us. We owe them nothing. *They* abandoned their clone military. *They* abandoned their outworld territories. *They* discarded their fleets."

My comments were greeted with a scared silence.

"You say you have twenty-three planets in your empire? Did you conquer them, or did they join willingly?" Doctorow asked, shattering the hush.

He didn't understand. He was so lost in his vision of a perfect society that he could not comprehend anyone's rejecting his views. He resented any outside authority, and he instinctively believed that everyone else felt the same way.

"No one held a gun to anyone's head," I said, not entirely sure that was the case. I hadn't asked.

The meeting lapsed into some form of order—even chaos runs out of energy. The wildfire conversations burned out, and I explained the situation as I understood it, leaving out one small detail—that our forces were infested with U.A. assassins.

"Is it still your goal to conquer Earth?" Doctorow asked, his voice solemn and flat.

I turned and looked up at him. From his lofty seat, Doctorow stared down on me, the light forming shadows across his face. The shadows added grim punctuation to his solemn expression.

"I am not the one who would make that decision," I admitted.

"I'm sure you're an important man in your empire," Doctorow persisted, then he dredged up ghosts from a distant conversation, and asked, "Do you want revenge?"

Revenge? I'd spent the last week concerned with survival.

"Conquering Earth makes no sense. Why declare war on the Unified Authority? Why fight a war at all?" Doctorow asked. "The Unified Authority is not your enemy."

"I would not call them my friends," I mumbled in a voice that no one else would hear.

"You came in a fighter carrier. Do you plan to force us to join your empire?" Doctorow asked.

"No," I said. I felt an odd sense of defeat. I had not come expecting a warm welcome, but this mix of fear and hostility caught me off guard. "You're welcome to join, I suppose," I said. And there it was, I had reverted back to acting like a guest on Doctorow's planet.

"We'll consider your offer, General Harris, but I don't expect the people of Terraneau will want to join you."

"No, I suppose not," I said. I hadn't really offered them membership. In truth, Terraneau was far more trouble than it was worth.

The auditorium had become so quiet that I could hear people breathing. "My vote will be against any form of treaty," Doctorow told the auditorium. "I will resign before I sign a treaty with the clones or with the Unified Authority, and I will do everything in my power to ensure that Terraneau remains a neutral planet."

"Not even for protection?" I asked, more out of curiosity than concern.

"General, men like you bring wars upon yourselves," Doctorow said, sounding so damn sympathetic as he condemned me with his words. "We don't need protection. Take away the armies and the battleships, and we won't need to protect ourselves.

"Nations, empires, armies . . . we don't want any of that on Terraneau. We'll vote on your offer, General Harris, but I can tell you the outcome already."

"You probably can," I agreed. I didn't care. With a government like this, Terraneau would make an unreliable ally at best.

"My vote is for you to take your Marines and go away," Doctorow continued.

Applause broke out in the auditorium. A woman rose to her feet, nodded, and clapped her hands. More representatives stood and joined her. Pretty soon, every person on every tier had risen to their feet and begun to applaud Doctorow's statement. The sound echoed through the well, drowning everything else out.

I did not hate these people, but I did not care what became of them.

## CHAPTER
# TWENTY-FIVE

What should I have called it? An interrogation? An inquisition? Doctorow might have described it as a hearing, but that sounded too benevolent by my book. I was glad when it ended.

As we drove away from the government center, Hollingsworth asked a question that came so out of the blue that it took me aback. He asked, "What if it came to a choice between her and us?"

"You sound like a jealous girlfriend," I said. "The relationships do not overlap. She's my girl, you're my Marines. It's completely different."

Night had fallen over Norristown. Streetlights blazed, as did lights in windows and headlamps on cars. Just a few short months ago, nothing but fires and flashlights had lit the city after dark, now it sparkled.

"Not all that different," Hollingsworth said. Now that I had returned, he had not once bothered using the word, "sir." "You screw her. You screw us. It's a different kind of screwing, but you're still screwing us."

If I'd been driving, I would have pulled over and hit the bastard. We could have had it out with our fists. It sounds primitive, but it's better than letting things fester. A couple of black eyes, a bloody nose, and maybe some bruised ribs, and we would get on with our lives. Unfortunately, he was driving.

I worked with what I had. I pulled the corner of my collar and held it out for Hollingsworth to see. "Listen here, you self-pitying waste of speck. See these stars? You may not like it, but these stars make me a more important person than you. You got that? You've got a bird and I've got stars and that means you will either show me respect or I will throw your ass in the brig."

He did not speak for several seconds. Finally, he said, "Sorry, sir."

"Get this through your skull, Hollingsworth, I did not start the war with the Unified Authority. If you haven't figured that out, it's time that you did. They sent us out here to use us for target practice. You got that?"

"Yes, sir." He stared straight ahead as if driving through hazardous traffic instead of empty streets, his hands wrapped tight around the steering wheel.

"I wasn't the one who started the war. So if you are going to blame me for something, blame me for saving the specking fleet."

This woke him from his stupor like a slap across his jaw. He looked at me, and said, "Begging your pardon, General, but the way this Marine sees it, Admiral Warshaw saved the fleet when he started up the broadcast zone."

"Who came up with the idea of salvaging broadcast equipment in the first place, asshole? Who came up with the idea of hijacking those self-broadcasting battleships?" I asked.

Hollingsworth went back to staring straight ahead. He did not answer my questions.

"By the way, I hope you don't plan on staying on Terraneau," I said. "Your pal Doctorow told me to pack up my Marines and leave."

More silence.

This was not how I wanted the conversation to go. When we left the meeting, I had half expected we could have a friendly conversation. I thought we might stop somewhere to talk over a couple of beers. As I saw Hollingsworth seething with anger, I realized that friendly conversation would never happen. He and I would never be friends.

"Turn up here," I said, pointing to a road that headed to the northern edge of town.

"I thought you wanted to head to base," Hollingsworth said.

"I changed my mind," I said. I told myself I was being logical, that Hollingsworth could order the men to pack; but logic had nothing to do with my decision. I felt alone, and I wanted reassurance.

I knew the way to Ava's house like I knew the scars on the back of my hands, and I told Hollingsworth every turn well in advance.

"Do you want me to send a jeep for you, sir?" he asked, as I climbed out.

"No, Colonel, I think I'll find my own way back to the base," I said.

He saluted and drove away.

I knocked on the door, but no one answered. I had to laugh. I had just traveled across three galactic arms only to find myself stuck in a suburb without a phone or a jeep. Maybe Ava was working late, maybe she was having dinner at a friend's house, maybe she was spending the night in the girls' dorm. She might arrive any minute or be gone all night.

The house was completely dark. I tried the door, but it was locked. For no real reason, I knocked again. No one answered. I walked to the edge of her front porch, sat, and waited. Time passed. Night turned to early morning.

By the time she finally arrived, the first streaks of sunlight showed in the sky. The car pulled into the driveway, stopped, and Ava climbed out of the passenger's side. She started toward the front door, then she saw me and froze. A look of anger replaced her surprised expression.

*Why did I come back?* I asked myself when I spotted the silhouette of a man in the driver's seat. I wished I hadn't returned.

Ava and I stood staring at each other for a few seconds.

"You're back," she said.

"I told you I would come for you," I said. I wished the driver had been a clone. I would have accused the bastard of being an infiltrator and performed his autopsy on the spot, but he was a natural-born.

She saw where I was staring, and said, "I'm sorry," her voice as cold and hard as marble.

"I was only gone for a week," I said, not feeling so much angry as sad. Anger might come later, but for now I felt a deep sense of loss. A strange numbness spread across my brain, and with it came feelings of helplessness.

"Harris, we need to talk," she said, not trying to disguise the scene as anything other than how it looked.

"No, we don't," I said. I stepped off the porch and walked past the car, not even bothering to look inside.

"Where are you going?" she asked.

I did not answer her. I had no idea where I would go.

"I'm sorry," she said, as I reached the end of her driveway.

"Yeah," I said. I might have said, "Me, too," but it would have been a lie. I was no longer sorry. Sadness had already turned to anger.

I reached the end of the block before I realized that I had no way of calling for a ride. I could have gone back and called the base from Ava's house, but my pride would not allow it.

Ellery Doctorow lived a few miles away. I could have found my way to his house easily enough, but that pompous bastard was the last person I would go to for assistance. I would not give him the satisfaction.

Deciding that a good walk would give me time to think things through, I turned the corner and started down the hill. I wanted to be alone with my anger, so I walked.

Your perspective changes when you walk streets you've only driven in the past. Rises stretch into hills, and slopes become steeper. Seconds turn into minutes. It took me twenty minutes to reach the bottom of Norristown Heights, and Fort Sebastian was still twenty minutes away by car.

The air had a cool morning chill. Dew glistened on the grass. Cars passed me on the road every few seconds, speeding down streets that were nearly empty. I ran across a four-lane road, the nearest cars so far away that I could not hear their engines.

A few moments later, a Marine sped by in a jeep going at least eighty miles per hour. He spotted me, and his head turned to track me as he drove past.

I expected him simply to drive away, but he didn't. The jeep did not screech to a halt, but the tires did squeal just a bit as the driver pulled a U-turn. He cut across several empty lanes, then drifted in my direction, pulling to the side of the road about ten feet ahead of me.

"General Harris?" He said my name as if it were a question.

"Yes," I said.

"Colonel Hollingsworth sent me to pick you up, sir," he said.

"Did he? Well, that's excellent," I said, remembering full well that the last thing I told Hollingsworth was that I would get myself back to base.

"Yes, sir," the sergeant said.

It was possible. Ava might have called Hollingsworth and told him what happened. They did not know each other well, but they had run into each other a time or two, and she might have wanted to make sure I got back to Fort Sebastian safely. He might have decided to send a car even if she did not call. It wasn't likely, but it could happen.

Instead of climbing into the rear of the jeep, as I might normally have done, I stepped into the passenger's seat.

"Where are we going?" I asked as we pulled away.

"The colonel is waiting for you at Fort Sebastian, sir," said the sergeant.

"Excellent," I said. I spoke the words around a yawn. I'd just spent the entire evening standing outside Ava's house. We headed south and east, the right general direction for Fort Sebastian, skirting downtown Norristown but still driving through other urban districts. My driver did not speak. I sensed an odd intensity in his focus.

I asked him a few questions, and his answers seemed right enough, but something about him, some indefinable quality, left an unpleasant impression. He was the kind of guy who can't tell a joke because nothing he said could ever be funny. Here he sat, saying all the right things, and I had already decided that I did not like him.

"What is your name, Sergeant?" I asked.

"Lewis, sir," he said. He sounded respectful enough, but he looked away from me as he answered and gave off a sense of disregard.

"Is that your first name or your last?" I asked.

"It's my last name, sir. My first name is Kit . . . Kit Lewis," he said.

"Well, Kit Lewis, you just missed the road to Fort Sebastian," I said. We had actually passed the turn two miles back, but I decided to wait until we had passed any likely detours before mentioning it.

"A work crew is laying a cable on the main road, sir," he explained. "The regular roads are closed."

"Is that so?" I asked.

"Yes, sir. We need to take a service route."

"I see," I said. "It must be quite a project; this detour of yours is taking us pretty far out of the way."

"Yes, sir."

Lewis shrugged his shoulders, then faked a laugh, and said, "Oh, we're not going to Fort Sebastian, sir. Colonel Hollingsworth wants to meet you at the airfield."

The road we were on would take us past the field, that much was true. "So he's at the airfield? I could have sworn you said we were meeting at Fort Sebastian," I said.

The sergeant responded with another nervous laugh. "Did I? I always do that, sir. I was thinking about Fort Sebastian when I meant to say we were meeting the colonel at the airfield, and I switched it around." His voice was friendly, and he said all the right words.

It was a trap, of course. I had suspected it from the moment I saw the jeep. Stuck behind the wheel, though, he could not pull a gun on me. I had control of the situation.

We were driving at eighty miles per hour. A few miles ahead of us, the edge of the airfield was visible behind a row of small buildings. I pretended not to notice it. We passed two roads that wound around to the airfield. Lewis did not slow down as we reached the third. I doubted he would slow down at the fourth.

"How long have you been here, kid?" I asked.

"Six years, sir," he said.

If this kid operated like the ones on St. Augustine, we'd find the real Kit Lewis's body in a day or two. I wondered if he had been strangled, drowned, burned, or dissolved.

"I'm not asking how long Kit Lewis has been here," I said. "I'm asking how long you have been here."

"Three days," he said, the friendly sheen missing from his voice. If he had a gun, he made no move to draw it. He did not need to worry about me. Traveling in a jeep at eighty miles per hour, I would not attack the driver.

The stalemate would last until we came to a stop. He might pull a gun at that point, but I doubted it. The kid showed no signs of fear. He clearly thought he could kill me anytime he wanted. I felt the same way about him. Only one of us could be right.

# CHAPTER
# TWENTY-SIX

"How did you get here?" I asked. "You're a long way from Earth."

Lewis laughed, and not in the friendly way that he laughed when he still wanted to convince me we were going to Fort Sebastian. Now he sounded disdainful and possibly unhinged. "Are you going to interrogate me right up to the end?"

"It's better than dying curious," I said.

"Sorry to disappoint you, General, but I didn't come here to answer questions."

"I suppose not," I said. "But out of curiosity, how did you get here?"

He laughed. "I don't know the name of the ship."

We were rapidly approaching the east end of town. The

buildings became smaller, and the lots became larger. Civilization gave way to countryside. We passed a stand of trees. Off in the distance, I saw hills and forests. *The end of the road,* I thought.

"Are you working for the Unified Authority?" I asked, pretending to be a little afraid. I wasn't afraid at that point, not in the least. My combat reflex had not kicked in, but I didn't care. I did not think I would need it. The fight would not last long. I'd fought this make of clone a thousand times. He was just a clone, just an ordinary standard-issue clone.

"Sure," he said.

He slowed to thirty miles per hour as we approached the trees.

"So you're not Avatari," I said.

"What the speck is *Avatari*?"

"Alien," I said.

"I'm property of the Unified Authority Marines, just like you."

"You're a different make," I pointed out.

He slowed the jeep to fifteen miles per hour as he turned onto a small dirt road. When we bounced over a bump, I grabbed Lewis behind the neck and slammed his face into the steering wheel, then I slammed the bottom edge of my fist into the base of his skull.

During the moment that he blacked out, I slipped the gear into park, hoping the jeep would come to a stop; but its gears ground together, its engine whined, and the wheels locked as we skidded into a ditch. Bracing myself for the slow collision, I watched Lewis's already bloody face slam into the wheel a second time, tearing gashes across his forehead and eyebrows.

We landed nose down in a three-foot ditch. I climbed out of the jeep, pulling Lewis out as well, carrying him away from the ditch and slinging his limp ass down on the hard forest floor. I checked his pockets. He'd come unarmed. No gun. No knife.

He moaned as he started to wake, so I kicked him in the ribs, probably shattering two or three of them. The man did not call out in pain. He made a grunting noise, but he did not writhe or cough up blood. He was awake enough to know that I'd kicked him, but he did not curl up to protect himself.

"Get up, asshole," I said, and I kicked him again, in the same spot, doing damage to organs that were no longer protected by bones.

"You kick me again, Harris, and I'll break your specking legs," he said calmly.

"I don't think so," I said, and I kicked him again. I kicked him hard, and I felt the side of his body give way like the side of an overripe melon.

Lewis sat up coughing. When the coughing stopped, he looked to his right and spat blood.

"How many of you are there?" I asked.

"I don't know," he said, sounding as if he did not take my question seriously.

My next kick was not to the ribs. It was a roundhouse, and it struck him across the cheek. Had I connected two inches higher, I would have shattered his eye socket, but I did not intend to inflict that kind of damage. Not yet.

The kick to the face knocked Lewis flat. He lay there, rubbing his cheek, and said, "I'm going to break your arms and legs and your ribs before I kill you." The words rang hollow, but his voice radiated anger instead of fear.

"I don't think you understand what's going on here. See, now, I am the one standing, and you are the one on the ground who just got his face kicked. Correct me if I'm wrong; but the way I see it, you are in the shithouse, pal."

"It looks that way," he said as he sat up.

I kicked him again. This time I kicked him in the ribs first, and then doubled up on the kick and fetched him a simple soccer kick across the face.

Lying on his back, staring up at me as he felt his injured ribs, he said, "Stop kicking me."

"I don't think so," I said.

"You won't get anything out of me if I'm dead."

I wasn't sure that was true; his autopsy might provide all kinds of answers. "Tell me what I need to know, and maybe we can both walk out of here," I lied.

"Why the speck would I let you walk?" he asked. He rolled backward, toward the jeep and slid into the trench headfirst. I felt sorry for the bastard, until I saw how quickly he sprang to his feet.

The expression on his face looked more animal than human. His eyes focused on me to the exclusion of anything else, his lips formed a sneer.

My combat reflex kicked in quickly. A reviving soup of adrenaline and testosterone flowed through my veins, clearing my mind and sharpening my reflexes. There was no *fight or flight* once the reflex began, there was only fight. Lewis lunged at me quickly, striking first high, then low, then crashing into me with all of his weight. I fell backward, with him attaching himself around my waist, still slamming his fists into my ribs and gut. I hit the ground hard, knocking the air out of my lungs. As I struggled for breath, he pounded his left hand into my chest and his right hand into my face.

Ignoring the flashing lights that filled my eyes, I fought back. I grabbed his blouse and pulled him toward me as I hit him in the face again and again. I worked a knee loose and drove it into his ribs. That slowed him, and I threw him off me; but I was dizzy, and it took me a moment to climb to my feet.

He recovered more quickly than I did. As I tried to clear my head, he jumped to his feet and came at me again. I kicked at his knees and struck his broken ribs with the heel of my right hand. The blow should have put him down, he had to be badly injured; but he grabbed me and threw me backward to the ground, then stomped a heavy boot into my gut, knocking the fight and the air out of my lungs.

Lewis dropped a knee into my chest and wrapped his fingers around my throat. "I'm going to enjoy this, Harris," he said in a voice that sounded triumphant and insane.

A single shot rang out, echoing through the forest, and Lewis flew off me, smashing into a tree a few feet away. A quarter of his head was missing, from the right eye to the top. Still gasping for oxygen, I sat up and stared at the bloody mess of his head.

The air slowly returned to my lungs. It felt like fire inside my chest.

Sitting on that rocky ground, fighting for breath, the pains in my back and arm and shoulder starting to register, I knew who had saved me even before I saw him. A few moments passed before he stepped into my view.

Seven feet tall, thick as an oak tree and just as stout, his shaved head as bare as a billiard ball and his skin as dark as mahogany, Ray Freeman came and stood over me, his sniper rifle hanging loose in his right hand. Here was a powerful man who could snap a man's bones or crush his skull with his bare hands, but he preferred the work of the sniper.

"Nice shot," I said, my throat not quite able to add voice to my words.

My vision was still a bit blurred. The light was to Freeman's back, so I could not see his face. I didn't need to see it to know that I would find no sympathy in his gaze.

He was not a man given to compassion. We were friends, of a sort; but the last time I had seen him, he fired that very rifle at me. He'd shot me with a "simi," simunition, a gel cartridge loaded with fake blood used to simulate an assassination. He'd come all the way across the galaxy to deliver a message for the Unified Authority. They wanted me to know that I was not beyond reach. The U.A. attacked Terraneau the following day.

Despite the burning in my chest and throat, I inhaled enough air to speak. "You could have popped him before he started choking me."

"I wanted to see how you would do."

Freeman spoke slowly, and his voice was so low it sometimes didn't sound human. His voice was the sound of cannon fire or a lion's roar.

"How did I do?" I asked.

Freeman did not answer. He wasn't the kind of man who wastes his breath stating the obvious. He was a man of few words.

# CHAPTER
# TWENTY-SEVEN

The jeep wasn't going anywhere, not without a winch and a tow truck to pull it out of the ditch. Even if we did pull it out, I wasn't in any shape to drive it. My right eye was nearly swollen shut, and I could barely stand, let alone drive.

Freeman offered to take me back to the base in his car. He'd only parked a few dozen yards from the jeep, but I covered the distance like an old man suffering acute appendicitis. I'd walked one hundred times the distance earlier that morning when the only things that hurt were my feelings. Now my head was spinning, and the ground seemed to roll under my feet like the deck of a ship in a storm.

"So what brought you to this neck of the woods?" I asked.

Freeman did not respond. He did not take well to humor. I knew this, but it only made me wisecrack around him all the more. His sphinxlike persona presented a challenge.

Speaking in a language he was more likely to answer, I asked, "How did you find me?"

"I followed the clone."

"Was there any reason why you followed that particular clone?" I asked.

We reached the car. Anyone else might have opened the door for his poor, crippled friend, but Freeman climbed in, started the engine, and waited for me to catch up.

I opened the door, jerked my head back toward the trees, and said, "I want to bring him along."

"Get in," Freeman said. I got in without knowing whether he would refuse to pick up the stiff or if he planned to back his car into the forest and get it. He backed the car up the dirt road and stopped a few feet from the abandoned jeep.

"Put him in the trunk," Freeman said.

Having barely been able to walk to the car, I wanted to protest, but I knew better. I was the one who wanted the corpse, not Freeman, so it stood to reason that I should be the one carrying the corpse with a head like a smashed-in gourd.

I climbed out of the car, limped over to the dead faux sergeant, and lifted him from where he had landed beside the tree. Rigor mortis had not yet set in. As I lifted him, his shattered head bounced backward, then rebounded forward and rested on my shoulder. His arms hung limp.

I slung Lewis over my shoulder like a dockworker carrying a sack of potatoes, then tossed him into the trunk. Noticing blood and brain tissue and skull fragments on my shirt, I cursed under my breath as I slammed the trunk and hobbled back into the car.

"How did you know where to find me?" I asked as I closed the door.

"I told you, I followed the clone," Freeman said.

"There are a whole lot of clones living in Fort Sebastian. How did you know which one to follow?"

"I followed him here from Earth," Freeman said.

"He said he arrived three days ago," I said.

Freeman did not respond. I took his silence as confirmation.

I tried to imagine Freeman hiding near Fort Sebastian, hoping to observe the base without being seen for three days. It didn't sound possible. Freeman stood seven feet tall and weighed well over three hundred pounds. He was a black man living in a galaxy that had spent centuries diluting its races. The man stood out.

"When I heard that the Navy was sending an assassin to Terraneau, I figured he was coming after you," Freeman said.

"The Navy thinks I'm dead. They all think I am dead."

Freeman shrugged. "There's no one else on Terraneau worth shooting."

I had my own opinions about who should be shot on Terraneau, but I kept them to myself, and asked, "So why send someone now? They could have sent someone to finish me five months ago."

Freeman said, "They saw the anomaly."

"They saw the anomaly," I repeated. "From the broadcast

zone . . . from when I broadcasted out," I muttered to myself. It didn't make sense. How the hell would they spot an anomaly from Earth? Even if they had a telescope pointed right at us, the light from that anomaly would not reach Earth for one hundred thousand years.

Feeling uncharacteristically chatty, Freeman filled in the gap without my asking. "The Navy has spy ships cruising your territory. They have satellites monitoring your broadcast stations."

Spy ships and satellites . . . I had gone through that broadcast zone a week ago, and the clone in the trunk landed on Terraneau a few days later. Until we sent a ship through that zone, it really didn't matter if I was alive because I was cut off.

"What are we dealing with?" I asked. "Should I send some fighters out to look for the satellite?"

Freeman shook his head. "Don't bother. The satellites are too small to locate."

"And the spy ships?"

"You don't see them unless they want you to."

I did not bother thanking Freeman for saving me. In his ruthlessly self-sufficient heart, Ray Freeman didn't care about my gratitude. He didn't need gratitude or approval, and he did not concern himself with things he did not need.

Freeman and I had once been partners. We might have been friends, too, but you could never tell with him. As far as I could tell, Freeman did not have friends. Raised by Baptist colonists before becoming a mercenary, he was an outcast among his own people, and he just plain didn't care what the universe thought of him.

We drove in silence. As I said before, Ray Freeman was a man of few words. If I'd tried to strike up a conversation, he'd probably have ignored me.

When we pulled up to the security gate at Fort Sebastian, I heard the guard radio in. "Holy shit, he's got himself a specking giant," before coming to my side of the car, saluting, and letting us in.

Freeman pretended not to notice, but I knew he'd heard the guard as well. He could do that. Freeman could outwait you. He had many strengths, patience was among his best.

We drove to the administration building, where Hollingsworth and a small group of junior officers waited to meet us. It was still early in the morning. A lot had happened, but it was only 09:00, and dew still glistened on the grass.

Hollingsworth walked up to the car, took one look at my face, and laughed. "Let me guess, the big guy caught you stealing his car," he said, pointing at Freeman.

When I did not say anything, Hollingsworth laughed even harder, and said, "No? Don't tell me. Your girlfriend hit you with a shovel?" His entourage joined in on the joke.

Hollingsworth was still busy laughing as I climbed out of the car and opened the trunk. I smiled, and said, "You think I look bad? Have a look at the other guy." As I said this, I reached in, grabbed the faux Sergeant Lewis by his collar and belt, and flipped him onto the ground.

By that time, some rigidity had entered the body, and the arms remained bent at the elbows. The blood on his forehead, what remained of it, at least, had crusted over.

"What the hell?" Hollingsworth asked, shocked and serious.

"I'll tell you about it sometime," I said. "In the meantime, would you mind putting him on ice? I want a coroner to have a look at him."

"Is he one of ours?" asked one of Hollingsworth's cronies.

"He said his name was Lewis, Sergeant Kit Lewis. Ever heard of him?" I asked.

Hollingsworth shook his head. So did his friends.

"That's funny. He swore you sent him to pick me up at Ava's."

"I didn't send anyone after you."

"No? How'd he know where to find me?"

"A lot of people knew where you went. I mean, it wasn't classified information. I—I mentioned it to . . ." He stopped. "Why did you kill him?"

"I didn't kill him," I said. "Freeman did." I tapped on the roof of the car, and Ray Freeman came out. The top of the car came up to my chest. It came up to his stomach. He stood there, hulking, huge, intimidating, silent.

"The late sergeant said you wanted to meet with me, then he drove me out to the woods west of town. That was when things got physical."

"Shit," Hollingsworth hissed.

"Wrap him up and throw him in a cooler," I ordered. "There's something special about this clone. We're going to need an autopsy to find out what it is."

"Yes, sir," Hollingsworth said, suddenly sounding like a proper Marine.

"Something else. If this son of a bitch called himself Sergeant Lewis, that means there's probably a dead Sergeant Lewis lying around here somewhere. Send out a team. I want to know what happened to him."

# CHAPTER
# TWENTY-EIGHT

Ellery Doctorow summoned me to his office, the political equivalent of a master whistling for his dog. Worse yet, I responded. Even knowing what he was going to tell me, I came running. Some duty-bound voice inside me reminded me that this was his planet. I would be gone soon, and he would still be here, the emperor of this little rock. He whistled, I came, and the chain of command was preserved, goddamn it.

So I climbed in a jeep with a twentysomething-year-old corporal I did not know. I took two precautions before climbing in the jeep with the kid. I asked his platoon leader if the corporal had been acting strange lately. When the sergeant asked what I meant, I simply said, "Never mind." If the guy had to ask, there was no point in explaining.

I also brought a sidearm. That last infiltrator clone had nearly killed me even after I'd dealt him enough damage to leave him spitting blood. I was in no mood to go for a second round. But the corporal did not give off the same aura of outrage and danger that the faux Sergeant Lewis had. This kid just came off nervous.

We drove to the capitol building, and the corporal waited

for me in the jeep as I went in to see Doctorow. Armed guards watched me from inside the door as I approached. I saw them and remembered a little more than a week earlier when guards had tried to stop me from going to see Ava . . . Going to see Ava, had it really been such a short time ago?

I asked myself if I still loved Ava, and I had no answer. Whatever I once felt for her, it was the closest I had ever come to love. And now? I told myself that I would get over her the same way I had with so many other girls. She was just more scrub, I told myself, but I didn't believe it.

The guards stayed out of my way as I entered the building. They did their best imitation of the sentinel statues in a giant cathedral, eyes straight ahead, standing silent and stiff. Maybe they knew me by reputation. Perhaps one or two of them had been at the girls' dorm.

I did not need to introduce myself to the man at the reception desk. He greeted me by name and called Doctorow's office to let them know that I had arrived. A few moments later, an aide came to escort me in.

Ellery Doctorow, former Right Reverend, former Army chaplain, and former colonel, had gone grand. He had an office the size of a small parade ground. His floor had a foot of black marble running like a border around two-inch-thick carpet. Bookshelves and paintings lined the walls. In the center of this opulence, Doctorow had an oak-and-mahogany desk that looked large enough to use as a landing pad.

As I entered the office, Doctorow met me at the door and shook my hand. Not even a second passed before he noticed the breakage on my face. How could he miss it? My right eye was a purple goose egg. I had multiple bruises on my jaw, a badly swollen cheek, and cuts on my lips. I saw disapproval in the way his eyes narrowed. He pursed his lips, but he said nothing.

"General Harris, I am glad you came," he said as he shook my hand.

"I had the impression attendance was mandatory," I said.

"Oh please," he said as he led me toward a set of chairs. "You have twenty-two hundred fighting Marines and enough weapons to destroy this planet three times over. You don't take orders from me, and we both know it."

He sat down behind his fortress of a desk. I sat in the wood-and-leather seat in front of the desk.

"The planetary council rejected your proposal, General. We won't be joining your empire," he said. "We would like you and your Marines to leave Terraneau as soon as possible." He did not say this in an angry fashion or in a demeaning way. If anything, he sounded serene.

"Are we making way for the Unified Authority?" I asked, though I already knew what he would say.

"No. When and if they contact us, we will give them the same answer we gave you. Terraneau is a neutral planet."

"I see," I said.

"A few council members felt we should join the Unified Authority," he confessed. He sounded so specking magnanimous, it was a bit surreal. Here he was telling me, "Thanks for rescuing us from the aliens, now close the door on your way out," but he managed to convey this in the comforting voice of a father telling his son about the facts of life.

"They wanted to join the Unified Authority?" I asked, hardly believing my ears. The Unified Authority had abandoned these people. We saved them, and they still preferred the U.A. to us.

"After we discussed the issues, there was a nearly unanimous vote to remain neutral. In the meantime, we all agreed that we wanted you and your Marines to leave our planet.

"I've always been up-front with you, Harris. You and your Marines and your warships represent nothing but a threat to us. I mean, look at you. You've been here one night, and what happened?"

"I was attacked," I said.

"By my people?" Doctorow asked. He sounded concerned.

"No," I admitted.

He said nothing. He did not need to say anything; I had already made his point.

"So you're done with us?" I asked. "That's it."

"What are you looking for, General? Do you want me to thank you for rescuing us?"

"We also restored your power and fixed your roads," I said. "The Corps of Engineers is military, too."

That shut him up for a half of a second. "I wanted to speak with you about that. As we discussed before, we would like you to leave your engineers here, on Terraneau. We could use their help for another year or two."

It was hard not to smile, but I managed it. "You certainly have a set of balls on you," I said.

"General, there is no cause for profanity," Doctorow said, and this time he showed no signs of embarrassment for saying it.

"You don't want me around, but you want me to leave my engineers."

"Engineers aren't trained killers. They pose no threat to our goals. Engineers don't carry guns.

"Harris, you and your men and the whole military way . . . You bring trouble on yourselves. Look at you. You're like a lightning rod. You attract violence."

"That's a bit simplistic," I said. "We didn't bring the aliens."

"Yes you did. They came back when you arrived."

"They never left. They were always here, always destroying the planet, you just didn't know it."

"Have you had a look at yourself in the mirror this morning? Your face is covered with bruises," he said. "I'm sure it wasn't your fault. You were attacked. I understand that, but what happened to the men who attacked you?"

"One man," I said.

"Where is he now?" Doctorow asked. "Is he dead? Did you kill him?"

"Dead, but I didn't kill him," I said. I hated this. The bastard had put me on the defensive.

"You didn't kill him, but he's still dead," Doctorow said. "That is why we don't want you or your kind on our planet."

"How will you protect yourselves?" I asked.

"Protect ourselves from what? With you and your Marines off the planet, we won't need to defend ourselves. Without you, we'll be safe."

"What happens when the Unified Authority arrives?" I asked.

"With you gone, they won't have any reason to come here. We're not at war with them."

"Do you think they will respect your sovereignty?" Actually, I was pretty sure they would. They'd given up colonizing years ago.

"Yes, I believe they will. Look, we don't want you here. I really don't see that there is anything else for us to discuss."

"What happens if the aliens come back?" I asked.

It was my ace in the hole, but I had played it too often, and I knew it. This time Doctorow was ready for it. "That's a possibility, I suppose," he said. "Personally, I am less concerned about that possibility than I am about getting you and your men off my planet."

"You didn't feel that way when we chased them away," I said.

"If you recall, we did feel that way. We asked you to go away. I'm glad you ignored our request, but we didn't want you here in the first place. And now, General Harris, it is time for you to leave."

I stared at him angrily, he returned my gaze, looking calm and smug, neither of us willing to look away.

"We'll leave," I said, "but we are taking our engineers with us."

"Have you asked them what they want?" Doctorow asked.

"I have. I took the liberty of speaking with Lieutenant Mars last night."

"You ran an end run to my engineers?" I asked, barely able to contain my anger. Why the speck had I come back to Terraneau? My girlfriend left me, an assassin nearly beat me to death, now this bastard was kicking me off the planet. "Have you spoken with anyone else? Perhaps you want my pilot."

"I spoke with Ava this morning," Doctorow volunteered.

"You spoke with Ava." I muttered.

"She wants to stay," he said.

"I saw her last night," I said. "I got the same feeling."

Doctorow's composure never wavered throughout the interview. My temper flared. I became sullen. I wanted to kill the bastard. My emotions betrayed me and made Doctorow look all the more prescient.

"Hollingsworth would probably stay if you asked him," I said.

"I don't plan on extending that invitation," Doctorow said.

"So I guess we are done," I said as I started to stand.

"Not yet," Doctorow said. "What are your plans, General? The Council would prefer for you to leave within the week."

My thoughts had become a double helix. One strand contained logic and the other emotion. I never wanted Terraneau to sign a treaty with the Enlisted Man's Empire; but now that they had rejected me, damn it, I felt judged and devalued by the people whose worthless lives I had saved.

"It won't take long for us to pack," I said, admitting my defeat.

"And your engineers?" he asked.

"I'll speak to Mars. They can decide for themselves." The Enlisted Man's Empire would have plenty of engineers. If Mars wanted to stay, we'd get by without him. He'd earned that.

"Good man," Doctorow said.

Had he just called me a "good man"? Had this specking antiestablishment son of a bitch just called me a "good man"? I quietly contemplated ripping his throat out of his neck.

He stood up to signal that the interview had ended, then he did something that almost set me off. As we walked to his door, he patted me on the shoulder and repeated his comment that I was "a good man." *Shoot me, stab me, kick me off your specking planet, but for God's sake don't make a show of being magnanimous in victory.*

"So, I suppose that concludes our business together, General," he said as he led me toward the door.

I turned to say something to Doctorow and found that I could not look the bastard in the eye. I wasn't ashamed, just angry beyond reason.

And so I left. I walked out of that marble-lined office and found my own way out of the building. I stormed out to my car and told my driver to take me downtown.

He wanted us off his planet by the end of the week. I wanted us off by the end of the day.

Ava looked so pretty in her cream-colored blouse and sky blue skirt. The blouse was loose, but it showed off her figure. She wore her hair down, and her makeup was perfect. She applied her makeup discreetly so that it blended with her face. I wouldn't have known she was wearing makeup had I not seen her without it. She looked at me and smiled.

"I'm leaving," I said.

"L told me," she said. "L" was the name Doctorow's closest associates used to address him. Apparently Ava had joined that elite circle of friends. Maybe she had joined it long ago, and I had never noticed.

"So I guess that's it. I'm done here," I said, feeling rather foolish for having come to see her again.

Tears formed in the corners of her eyes. Were they real? I reminded myself that she was an actress.

"You can come with me?" I said.

"And live on a battleship?" she asked. "Honey, I've done that before. I think I'm done with big guns and seamen."

She'd slipped into her brassy persona. For a moment I felt hope. Then she dashed it. She looked at me with deep-seated sympathy and touched me on the cheek. "I can't come with you, Wayson," she said. "There's nothing for me out there."

"I'd be there," I said, sounding so specking pathetic I thought I might never forgive myself.

One of the tears broke free from its nest and slid down her cheek. "You? You were never there for me. After the Unified Authority attacked, when you were in the hospital, and you were so weak, I thought you needed me. I thought maybe we had a chance.

"But once you got better, you started looking for a way off the planet."

"I told you, I wouldn't leave you here."

"You never needed me. You had your big plans and your Marines, and that was everything you needed." She smiled for a moment, brushed a tear from the corner of her eye, and said, "You never even pretended to need me."

"So when did he happen?" I asked, not bothering to explain that I meant the other man.

"I fell in love with him while you were planning how to escape Terraneau," she confessed.

"In love?" I whispered.

"I'm sorry."

I swallowed and asked the question I had to ask. "Did you ever love me?"

"Back in the beginning, you asked me how you compared to other guys. Do you remember that?" She took my hand in hers, and said, "You are the only one who ever broke my heart."

I smiled when I heard this though it meant nothing to me.

# PART III

# DEALING WITH CANCERS

# TWENTY-NINE

This was my day for good-byes. Within the last two hours I'd already said good-bye to Ava and Ellery Doctorow. In a few more hours, I'd bid a happy farewell to Terraneau, which had lately replaced Gobi as my least favorite planet in the galaxy. Now Freeman was leaving.

I looked at Freeman's Piper Bandit, a private commuter craft that the Unified Authority had outfitted with a tiny broadcast engine, and remembered the days when I had a Johnston R-56 Starliner of my own. The Johnston was a nicer ride—a twenty-seat luxury corporate number flown by rich executives with private pilots.

Civilians were not allowed to own self-broadcasting planes; hence, broadcast engines were never offered as standard equipment. The Unified Authority Navy had placed the broadcast rig under the hood of my Starliner. The jet had been built for a four-star admiral, and I sort of inherited it when he died.

My Starliner was considered a luxury ride. Freeman's plane was known in some quarters as an "interplanetary mosquito."

It was supposed to be a two-seater, apparently designed to fit two anorexic midgets. Ray Freeman was not fat, but his seven-foot frame was thick and filled with muscle. To wedge himself into that tiny cockpit, he would need to curl his legs in odd angles under the instrumentation. The seats were narrow, and his massive shoulders would probably rub against both walls of the cockpit. Worst of all, he'd have to fly with his head bowed to fit it under the low ceiling. As we stood beside the Bandit, I gave it a dubious glance. That cockpit would be a tight fit for me, and Freeman had nine inches and a hundred pounds on me.

Not only was the Bandit too small for Freeman; it was also too small to house a broadcast generator. Someone had outfitted the plane with a tiny broadcast engine that had a single destination setting—Earth—instead of a broadcast computer. In lieu of a broadcast generator, it had a one-use battery. You got one broadcast out of this bird, and the preprogrammed computer made sure it ended up near Earth.

"Where'd you get this?" I asked.

"I took it from a clone," he said.

"This is what infiltrator clones fly?" I asked. "No shit? Did this one belong to the guy who tried to kill me?"

Freeman shook his head.

"You mean there's another one in Norristown?"

Freeman did not answer. If Freeman had the plane, the guy who was supposed to fly it was dead.

There had to be at least one more of these planes hidden somewhere around Norristown. I wondered how many I would find when I searched St. Augustine. Now we had something to look for—clones traveling in Piper Bandits.

"How does it fly?" I asked.

"Slow," Freeman said. "A half million miles per hour."

That was slow. Most naval ships had a top speed of thirty million miles per hour. You needed that kind of speed when you traveled billions of miles.

I changed the subject and asked Freeman the question that had been bothering me since he'd first shown up. "What are you doing here?"

"Besides saving your ass?"

"Are you here for money or revenge?" I asked. He was a mercenary first and foremost. Those were the only reasons he did anything besides eat, shit, and sleep. "You didn't come all this way just to save me."

"We were partners," he said.

"You didn't come here for old time's sake," I said. "How did you know about the clone in the first place?"

Then, recognizing the flaw in the story, I said, "You wouldn't have known about him unless you were already in the war. What's your stake?"

Freeman said nothing, and I would not push it. When the

time came, he would tell me his reasons. He was ruthless and violent, but he also lived by a personal code of conduct. I trusted him.

"You can't fly that into the broadcast zone," I said. "You know that, right?"

Again, he did not answer. It was a stupid question.

"It's a one-way zone," I said, another inane comment. "It goes straight to Providence Kri."

I wanted to make sure he knew how to find me. "Any chance that I will see you there?" I asked.

Freeman opened the door of his plane and folded himself into the cockpit. He slid his right leg all the way across the cabin and into the well for the passenger's feet, then exhaled all the air from his lungs before wedging his chest behind the yoke. He pressed his chin to his collarbone as he crammed his shoulders and head into the tiny space under the ceiling.

Once he was in, he snaked a hand out to close the door, then paused. "How do I find you?" he asked.

I told him about Scrubb's, the restaurant on St. Augustine, and promised to check the restaurant the following Thursday night.

"Doesn't sound very private," Freeman said.

"So we meet and go for a walk," I said.

He nodded and closed the door of his plane. The Bandit was small and he was a giant. He filled the cockpit as snug as a bullet in the chamber of a gun.

There were many lessons they never taught us in the Marine Corps, foremost among them was instruction on how to be magnanimous in defeat. Trash a Marine, and you have an enemy for life.

At the moment, I did not feel especially charitable toward Ellery Doctorow; but what I had in mind for this visit might just save lives, Ava's life in particular. He'd kicked me off his rock and made an end run on my engineers; his last-minute concern about my well-being struck me as gloating. I considered him a pompous, arrogant, self-important windbag, and that was why I hated what I had to do next.

Before returning to Fort Sebastian, I would visit Doctorow

one last time. If he was no longer in his office, I would go to his home. I would find him, and, despite my desire to break his neck, I would do him a favor.

I told my driver to take me to the new capitol building.

Freeman had found his Bandit on a civilian airfield on the south side of town. The south and west sides of Norristown had taken the brunt of the war against the aliens. The Corps of Engineers, formerly my Corps of Engineers, began restoring the west side as soon as we liberated the planet. The south side, however, remained in tatters. If I were trying to hide a plane near Norristown, I would hide it in the wreckage of a southern suburb.

I stared out at broken buildings and empty space as we headed north, then I saw a massive work project—the Norris Lake Tunnels. The southern edge of Norristown fronted on a large lake that sparkled like a giant mirror across the landscape. The sun shone across its endless blue surface and shimmered. At one corner of the lake, a pair of tunnels grew out of the water like a set of sleeping leviathans, their four-lane mouths stitched shut by a latticeworks of scaffolding and heavy equipment.

*So they're working on the tunnels,* I thought to myself. That was why Doctorow wanted my Corps of Engineers. It would have taken the locals a decade to finish the project; Mars and his engineers would polish it off in a few weeks. The tunnels ran three miles along the bottom of the lake. Once they finished, Norristown would be reconnected to Ephraim, its long-abandoned sister city.

Driving from the south side of town to the governmental seat took fifteen minutes. We started in a place of ruins and ended in a canyon of marble and glass. I had my driver wait in the car while I went to speak with Doctorow. As I reached the door of the capitol, two guards blocked my way.

I told them whom I had come to see, and one of them escorted me to the receptionist. The receptionist, in turn, contacted Doctorow's office and told me that an aide would come out and speak with me.

I was not impressed, but at least the charades were over. Doctorow had my assurance I was leaving. He had everything he wanted from me, the bastard, so I was no longer worth his time.

A few moments later, out came this snooty kid in a nice suit and silk tie. His wrist went limp as he shook my hand, then he suggested that we sit and talk in the lobby. As far as he was concerned, he was as close to Doctorow as I was going to get.

When the kid asked, "What can I do for you?" I wanted to tell him to douse his hair with gasoline and light up a cigar; but I behaved. I looked him in the eye, and said, "You can tell Colonel Doctorow—"

"President Doctorow."

"Excuse me?" I asked.

"His title is president."

"Oh, I see. Well, that's different. I had no idea," I said, trying to sound contrite. "You can tell *Colonel* Doctorow that I am here and wish to see him."

"The president is a busy man," the kid said.

"Yes, so am I," I said.

"Perhaps if you have a message—"

"I just told you my message. I am here, and I wish to see him."

"Perhaps you would like to tell me what this is about," the kid said, his patience wearing thin.

"If I wanted to tell you why I was here, I would have already done so," I said.

The kid controlled his temper better than I would have. He sat unmoved by my sarcasm. "If you would prefer to write—"

"If I wanted to send the *president* a letter, I would have written one."

The kid just sat there. He started to say something, but only said, "Hmmmm."

I stood up.

The kid thought I was leaving, and said, "What should I tell President Doctorow?" He started to get up and reached out to shake hands.

"I'll tell him myself," I said, and started for the door to the offices.

The kid threw himself in front of me as the guards from the entrance came trotting across the lobby. The receptionist started speaking frantically into a panel on his desk. I had not come to make a scene, but I was about to make one just the same; then the door to Doctorow's office flew open, and out came "the president."

"Are you quite finished, General Harris?" Doctorow asked in a loud but calm voice.

"Do you see anybody bleeding?" I asked.

"That is precisely why we want you off our planet." Doctorow pronounced this judgment with finality.

"You know what, I can't wait to leave," I said.

Doctorow took a deep breath, and asked, "What do you need, Harris?"

"I came here to do you a favor, but you probably don't want anything from someone like me."

"No, I probably do not," he agreed.

I took a deep breath, and said, "I came to give you an escape hatch . . . in case the aliens ever return."

Now I had Doctorow's attention. He surveyed the scene one last time, then said, "Perhaps we should speak in my office." He turned to leave without speaking, and I followed, like an obedient dog.

Doctorow returned to his seat behind his desk. "How are your preparations going?"

"I hope to be out of here tonight," I said.

"Well, that is good news."

"Look . . ." I paused to take a deep breath because if I didn't, I might have killed the bastard. I didn't even know what to call Doctorow anymore. I did not want to call him president, the title was bullshit. I would not call him by his first name, we were not friends.

In the end, I decided not to call him anything, and simply said, "Listen, there's a small plane hidden somewhere in Norristown, a Piper Bandit. If I had to guess, I would say it's somewhere just south of town."

"Why should I care about a small plane?" Doctorow asked.

"Because it can reach Earth," I said.

"How is that possible?" Doctorow asked, sounding more than a little concerned.

"It's self-broadcasting," I explained. Even as I said this, I realized that I had overlooked an important question. Freeman said the battery was only good for one broadcast. That meant the Unified Authority had ferried the plane and its pilot to Terraneau space and dropped it off. But how had he, Freeman, traveled to Terraneau?

"A self-broadcasting plane," Doctorow repeated.

"It's very small, just a two-seater, and the broadcast engine is only good for one use. If the aliens come back, you can use it to send for help," I said. I hated handing the plane over to Doctorow. I specking hated it. I was doing it for Ava. If the aliens did come back, I hoped like hell these assholes would send their distress signal in time for us to help them. I had my doubts.

"I appreciate your telling me about this," Doctorow said. "Now if you could direct us to the plane before its owner returns."

"I wouldn't worry about that," I said.

"No?" Doctorow asked.

"The original pilot will be leaving with me and my men," I said. It was true. What I neglected to mention was that he'd be traveling in a body bag.

# CHAPTER
# THIRTY

There was not a single trained surgeon in the entire Enlisted Man's Navy. We had medical technicians who could set broken bones, remove a bullet, or treat a burst appendix; but medical school was the domain of natural-born officers. The closest clones got to that kind of education was training as a nurse.

I didn't need a surgeon to run the autopsy, but I wanted someone who knew his way around a corpse. I needed someone with the right eyes and skill set to examine the body of the late faux Sergeant Kit Lewis, someone who could tell me what the security posts had been missing.

"I don't know the first thing about forensics," said the chief medical officer of the *Salah ad-Din*. We were in sick bay. The body, still wrapped in a self-chilling body bag, lay on the table before us.

"Understood," I said as I unzipped the bag. There he was, Sergeant Lewis, his remaining eye staring straight ahead, the jagged remains of his skull poking out from areas where his face had shriveled.

The doctor looked at the corpse and swallowed, then quickly recovered. "Want my official opinion about what killed him?"

"I know what killed him. I was there," I said. "What I want to know is what makes him different than everyone else."

"Half his skull is missing, that's different," said the doctor.

"Besides that," I said.

"Besides that he's exactly like everyone else, he's a clone," the doctor said.

I gave up and started to leave. When I reached the hatch, I looked back, and said, "This boy was different. I want to know why."

I left the sick bay and walked to the bridge.

The *Salah ad-Din* was a Perseus-class fighter carrier—a moth-shaped monstrosity that measured fifty-one hundred feet from wingtip to wingtip and forty-five hundred feet from bow to stern. The walk to the bridge took nearly ten minutes.

Captain Villanueva sat waiting for me when I arrived. He was a clone, of course. Villanueva was in his late forties. The crow's-feet along his eyes stretched down to his cheeks when he smiled. His tiny sideburns had gone white, and he had a spackling of white hairs.

The man was twenty years older than me, but he showed proper respect for my rank. I liked him. Unlike so many officers, Villanueva had no political ambitions. He had his fighter carrier and his crew, and he was satisfied.

"I hear you brought luggage aboard my ship," he said. When he saw that I had not caught his meaning, he said, "A dead man. I just got a call from sick bay. They said you dropped off a dead guy."

Maybe I was having trouble focusing. Try as I might to

ignore her, Ava still haunted my thoughts. I was angry and jealous; but more than anything else, I just wanted to know that someone would protect her.

"What do you want with a dead clone?" Villanueva asked.

"He's got secrets," I said.

"What kind of secrets?" Villanueva asked.

"If I knew, I wouldn't bother lugging him around," I said. It seemed like a polite way of telling the captain to mind his own business, but Villanueva did not take it that way. He bobbed his head like a fighter ducking a punch, and said, "Yes, sir."

Villanueva's lack of ambition made him easy to work with, but it also left him a trifle unmotivated. With remora fish like Admiral Cabot, ambition meant initiative. Cabot might have been preening for glory, but he got things done. Cabot did not wait for orders, he looked for ways to draw attention to himself. Villanueva, on the other hand, would happily stand around letting the proverbial moss grow under his feet.

As we spoke, I saw officers glancing in our direction. There was no privacy on the bridge of the *ad-Din*, the deck was designed with no interior walls so that its officers could synchronize a thousand separate operations during attacks. The decks of the big ships were filled with desks and computer stations. Even the helm had more to do with keyboards and touch screens than steering yokes. The *ad-Din* was nearly a mile wide. You didn't control a big bird like that using a stick and pedals.

"Is there somewhere else we can speak?" I asked.

Villanueva nodded and led me to a closet-sized conference room off the bridge floor. I sat across the narrow table from him, and asked, "What is the status of our evacuation?" I hated the term "evacuation"; it made it sound as if Doctorow had chased us away. In my mind, we were abandoning Terraneau, not evacuating it. The semantics mattered to me, but not to anyone else.

"Your Marines are on board, sir," Villanueva said.

"All of them?" I asked, feeling a bit stunned.

"All twenty-two hundred men are accounted for, sir. Are you sure you want to leave all of that equipment behind?"

The equipment was the rather extensive arsenal of weapons I had procured from the graveyard of ships. It must have seemed strange to Villanueva that I would leave guns, grenades, rocket launchers, tanks, and even a half dozen transports in the hands of the local militia. Maybe it was a bad idea, but I wanted Doctorow to have the weapons. If the Avatari came back, he'd need them . . . she'd need them. Ava. Everything was about protecting Ava.

"The Marine compound on this ship is fully stocked," I said.

"Aren't we arming a potential enemy?" he asked.

"You see Terraneau as a potential enemy?" I asked. "It's an undeveloped planet with leaders who want to create a utopia. Hell, the locals probably don't even want our guns.

"I've got more important things on my mind." I did. I had a complement of two thousand two hundred Marines that needed screening. We would leave for St. Augustine immediately, but I would keep my men under quarantine until I had searched them for infiltrators. With that many men, it could take a full day to check them all out. I gave Villanueva the order to take us to St. Augustine and excused myself.

I was still feeling the effects from a couple of long days, and I should have gone to my quarters for an hour's rest. Instead, I went down to the Marine complex for a quick inspection.

The men were unpacking, and most of the barracks were dark. A team had begun setting up the shooting range. The cooks and their assistants clanged pots and fired up the stoves in the mess. Hollingsworth met me as I watched a few of his men mopping their barracks. I asked him how the move was progressing, and he told me he had it under control. Our conversation lasted a few antiseptic seconds, and I left for my billet.

Villanueva sent an ensign to my quarters with the news that we had reached St. Augustine. When the ensign asked if I had any orders for him to relay back to the bridge, I shook my head and closed the door on the kid. I was genuinely tired, but I did not want to go to sleep. I had too much to do.

I decided to rest for a few hours, then I would check my troops for intruders, then I would return to St. Augustine. I was stalling. I did not want to return to St. Augustine. It wasn't the planet that bothered me; it was the group of ambitious officers who awaited me there.

I hated having an entourage, but I had little choice in the matter. My preference was to travel quietly and alone, and to drop in on bases unannounced. I preferred traveling under the radar; but if I wanted to flush out the infiltrators, I needed them to see me coming and make the first move. Having a troop of worthless comfort-class officers in my wake made me easy to spot. So I would go back to wearing a bull's-eye and waiting for someone to shoot.

There was something else I wanted to avoid as well—contacting Admiral Warshaw. He wanted regular progress reports; but unless a coroner found something useful about the late Sergeant Lewis, I would have nothing to report.

I turned off the lights and lay down for a nap, wondering what secrets the autopsy would reveal. A ship's medic might not find anything, but that coroner on St. Augustine was another story. He'd know what to search for and how to find it. *Yes,* I told myself, *I would bring in a trained coroner, then there would be results.*

My thoughts ran their course. *Had I been Lewis's first victim? No, of course not. We never found the body, but he must have killed a real Kit Lewis.*

*What would have happened if Freeman had not followed us?* I asked myself. The answer was obvious. I would have died. The answer was as obvious as the bruises on my face, arms, and neck.

I drifted into a light sleep.

If the man had waited a few more seconds, he might have caught me fast asleep instead of just dozing off. He had his gun ready when he slipped through the door, but I had already heard the soft hiss of the pneumatic piston and rolled off the bed.

He must have thought he'd found an empty room. He stepped in and closed the door behind him, pausing when he saw my unmade rack. Peering from a gap between my desk and my bed, I saw the man's legs and the silenced pistol he held in front of him.

My billet was small, a bed, desk, closet, and head all built around each other as tightly as the pieces of a jigsaw puzzle. The lights of my communications console blinked on and off on the far wall; someone was trying to reach me. I hoped they would come to check on me when I did not answer.

His gun at the ready, the man took a step toward my bed. Maybe he knew I was in here, maybe he thought I left it unmade like a guest in a hotel; but he took no chances. He walked to the edge of my rack, and said, "You might as well come out."

I heard uncertainty in his voice. He didn't know I was in the room.

"I know you're here, Harris. I saw you come in."

I did not believe him. I sat quiet and waited. Hidden by the desk, I managed to crawl along the far side of the bed toward the bathroom. I was as silent as a cat on the prowl, and I felt the beginning of a combat reflex running through my veins.

The man laughed, and said, "I can see you." The stupid son of a bitch had his back to me when he said that. He was aiming his gun into my closet when I lunged at him from the door of the head.

The bastard had lightning reflexes. He spun and clipped me across the jaw with his pistol. Lights popped behind my eyes, and my head spun for a moment, but I grabbed his gun hand with both of my hands as my momentum slammed both of us into my tiny work desk. He smashed a fist into my head as I knocked the pistol out of his hand.

The man brought his knee into my chest as I slid to the floor and grabbed the pistol. He stomped at my hand, then kicked me across the jaw; but I held on to the gun. The fight was as good as over. He kicked me in the chest, sending me to the floor, then he bolted from the room. I took a moment to recover, then I leaped to my feet and ran through the door. By the time I reached the hall, the speedy bastard was gone.

I reported the attack and placed the ship on alert even though I knew it was a waste of energy. Captain Villanueva placed security posts throughout the *ad-Din*, he set up security cameras and posted MPs to guard vital areas.

He reacted thoroughly and by the book; but if stopping the infiltration had been that easy, Warshaw would have nipped our infiltration problem long ago.

That night I received a message from Warshaw summoning his admirals to Gobi for a summit. As the "highest-ranking" officer in the E.M. Marines, I was required to attend.

St. Augustine would have to wait. Screening my men would have to wait as well. They would be trapped on the *ad-Din* with an infiltrator in their midst. I had Villanueva send a transport to retrieve Cabot, then we set off for Gobi.

## CHAPTER
# THIRTY-ONE

Earthdate: November 6, A.D. 2517
Location: Gobi
Galactic Position: Perseus Arm

I brought the dead sergeant with me to the summit.

Before wheeling him out of sick bay, I opened his cryogenic body bag to make sure it held a stiff instead of a stowaway. Frozen mist rose out as I spread the seam. The dead and partially dissected Kit Lewis stared back at me with his one remaining eye, little folds of skin peeled back from his cheek, ear, and neck.

Seeing the frozen body, I realized that no one in their right mind would hide in a cryogenic bag. The temperature inside the bag remained a constant zero degrees, and there was no air.

"You know you wouldn't be in there if you had just dropped me at Fort Sebastian," I said as I closed the bag. I slung it from the table to the cart and wheeled it toward the landing bay.

In the meantime, a team of twenty MPs swept the landing bay and the transports for signs of tampering or unwanted visitors. After I heard the bay was clean, I posted the MPs by the door. The only people allowed in the landing area were me, Admiral Cabot, and my pilot—Sergeant Nobles.

I found Nobles and Cabot when I arrived at the landing

bay. They met me as I came up the transport ramp. Nobles, clearly uncomfortable around Cabot, shrugged off his generally casual attitude and stood at attention as he said, "Sir, this Marine does not mean any disrespect, but that body bag looks full."

"A coroner is going to have a look at him while we're on Gobi," I said.

"From what this Marine has heard, sir, there are plenty of dead men at Gobi Station. Do you have any idea what killed them?"

I nodded toward the gurney, and said, "He did."

"Sir?" asked Cabot.

"Before I bagged him, our passenger was a Unified Authority infiltrator clone," I said. Both Cabot and Nobles stared at the bag as if its contents might try to climb out; but Cabot understood, he'd been in on the investigation on St. Augustine. Nobles, like most of the men in the fleet, had no idea that Unified Authority had cooked up a new line of clones.

"How soon can we go wheels up?" I asked Nobles, stealing him from his thoughts.

"Whenever you are ready, sir," he said.

"I'm ready," I said.

I sent Cabot to go sit with Nobles in the cockpit while I remained in the kettle with the cadaver. The cabin was silent, filled with shadows and cold. I looked over the still form of Kit Lewis in his blue-gray body bag and remembered his fury as he attacked me. He'd had murder in his eyes and charged at me with not so much as a moment's hesitation.

These bastards could kill, no doubt about it. If we did not discover their secrets, they would spread and destroy us.

I left the *Salah ad-Din* in lockdown. The ship was quarantined, and a search had begun for the man who attacked me in my quarters.

Every ship in the fleet was under lockdown. Until we figured out some way to protect ourselves, the best we could hope to do was stop the disease from spreading. For now, we would settle with a tourniquet approach, but soon enough we would upgrade to amputation.

# CHAPTER
# THIRTY-TWO

The summit began the next day.

For lack of a safer place, Warshaw decided to hold his summit in Gobi Station. Why not? He had a small army guarding the place. He had posts taking meaningless DNA samples at every door. Gobi Station was the safest spot in an entirely unsecured empire.

Warshaw assigned human guards and robot sentries to patrol the grounds outside Gobi Station. Armored vehicles ran the perimeter. A battery of rocket launchers waited inside the gates. Gobi Station was prepared for war, not infestation.

Inside the station, fleet officers mingled, followed by entourages of high-ranking hangers-on. As far as I could tell, I was the only Marine in attendance. I wore a tan uniform in a sea of white.

Warshaw kicked the meetings off with a banquet. I sent Cabot in my place and used the time to hold a summit of my own in the morgue.

Warshaw had brought two coroners in from Morrowtown, the capital of Gobi. When I entered the morgue, I found them hard at work, standing over gleaming steel trays holding carefully washed body parts. In the background, Sergeant Kit Lewis's cadaver lay partially skinned and disassembled. It reminded me of the holographic "visible man" display my teacher used in physiology class.

The coroners had peeled the skin from Lewis's right cheek and pulled the pipes from his throat. The skin and ribs had been removed from the left side of his chest, revealing layers of soft pink meat. Any blood had been washed away. The cavity that once held his heart now sat empty like a secret compartment in a waxwork dummy.

Whatever portion of the faux sergeant's brain remained

in his head had been scooped out, washed, weighed, and examined. Seeing the eviscerated body with its cubbyholes and cavities left me queasy, but seeing the organs on trays and in bowls did not bother me much. They had been carefully cleaned so that they were no more offensive than the meat in a butcher case.

When I stepped into their lab, the two coroners turned to greet me. I walked over to the table, took a look at Lewis, then turned to them, and asked, "Have you found anything?"

The taller of the two men, a man in his forties with bushy red hair and round glasses, asked, "Were you the one who brought him in?" In his gloved right hand he held a waxy-looking organ.

I nodded.

The second man, a pudgy kid who stood no more than five feet and five inches, spoke through his mask. He said, "It was the gunshot that killed him."

I'd heard that joke too many times already. "Yes. I was there," I said in an officious voice. "What else can you tell me?"

"Were you the one who shot him?" the taller, older man asked. When he placed the organ in a tray, I realized he'd been holding the dead clone's heart.

"I didn't pull the trigger," I said.

"Was this an execution?" he persisted.

"No," I said. *It was supposed to be my execution,* I thought.

"You were putting him out of his misery, right?" the younger coroner asked. He sounded slightly cocky, the promising young apprentice who believes he knows more than his master.

The older man turned to his student and corrected him, saying, "You're jumping to conclusions, Sam. All he said was that it wasn't an execution."

"What are you talking about?" I asked.

The older coroner pointed to a spot on the cadaver where the ribs had been cut away, and said, "This fellow was badly beaten. When I first saw him, I thought he had been hit by a car, but then I got a closer look at the damage. Was he tortured?"

The younger man picked bone fragments out of a dish.

Some of the pieces were an inch long. Some were shorter. "These are pieces of his ribs. We pulled them out of his lungs. His liver was so badly traumatized it was leaking like a sponge."

"Injured that badly," I said, thinking about how quickly he moved when he attacked me.

"Not just injured, he was dying," the younger man said.

The older coroner glared at me, and asked, "Aren't there laws against torturing prisoners? Do you know who did this? It's, it's inhuman." He looked down at Lewis and shook his head.

"No one tortured him," I said.

"What happened?" the old man asked.

Staring down at the cadaver, I said, "He got in a fight. All things considered, I'd say he won it." When I looked up, I saw that both coroners were staring at me and I became very self-conscious. The bruises Lewis had given me had not even begun to heal before I was attacked on the *ad-Din* and given a new set of gashes.

"I assume you were involved," the older coroner said. His posture stiffened, and he looked nervous.

"Yes," I said.

He must have believed that I'd tortured and murdered the dead clone. Carefully choosing his words, he said, "This man was in no condition to defend himself at the time of his death. Many of his bones were broken, and his internal organs were hemorrhaging. He had a collapsed lung. He could not defend himself, not with a collapsed lung. I doubt he even had the strength to stand.

"General, you didn't need to shoot him. If you'd given him another minute or two, he would have bled to death."

"If he'd had another minute or two, he would have taken me with him," I said.

"That simply isn't possible," said the older coroner.

I saw no reason to argue the point, so I asked, "What else have you found? Have you taken a DNA sample?"

"DNA? You're joking, right?" asked the young coroner.

I shook my head.

"You brought us here to check his DNA? He's a clone. He's a Unified Authority military clone. He has the exact same

DNA stuff as any other soldier. It's the most common DNA in the galaxy."

"There's got to be something more," I said. "Is there some way his DNA could have been altered?"

The older, wiser coroner let his apprentice field the questions. The younger guy said, "Alter it to do what? I mean, look at this guy. He's a normal, garden-variety clone. The only thing different about him is that he got pounded into mush, and half of his frigging head is missing."

Lying on that table, his skin peeled away, Kit Lewis did not look like other clones. He might have looked like other cadavers, but nothing about him looked specifically clonelike.

The senior coroner said, "Sam, read back what we have so far."

The younger man tapped a computer screen and read in a flat voice, "Subject, Male; Unified Authority military clone; approximate age 28; weight at time of autopsy, 168 pounds . . ." He looked up from the screen, and said, "With his brains and organs intact, he'd probably go 180."

He turned back to the monitor and continued reading. "Hair: brown; eye: brown . . ." That might have been coroner humor—the cadaver came in with only one eye.

"Yes, I see that," I said. "If that was all I was looking for, I would not have asked for your help."

"What are you looking for?"

"You see those broken bones," I said, pointing to the tray holding the broken ribs. "I did that to him. I kicked him, and he got up, so I kicked him again. I felt his ribs go, but he still got up. It didn't matter what I did to him, he just kept coming at me.

"The last time I hit him, it was like he didn't even have any ribs. It was like hitting a water bag. Do you know what he did when I hit him that time?"

"Collapsed to the ground and coughed up blood," the younger coroner guessed.

He had coughed up blood, I remembered that much. "He lunged at me, threw me down, and started strangling me," I said.

"I don't blame him," said Sam, the younger coroner.

Wanting nothing more than to hit the kid, I shook my head,

and said, "You say he was dying. You say he was bleeding internally. Fine. I believe you. That makes him even more dangerous, because he still almost killed me."

"He's dead now," Sam said.

"He's a specking clone! They can make more of him!" I heard my words echo across the morgue and realized I was yelling at them.

I dialed my voice down, and said, "This man damn near beat me to death when he was supposedly bleeding to death, I want to know how the hell he did that. Pull his genes apart under a microscope, run chemical tests on what's left of his brains. I don't care what you do, but get me answers."

Sam, the younger of the coroners, reached down, turned the skull so that it stared back at him, and said, "Maybe he had a surge of adrenaline."

For a moment, I wanted to scream in frustration. Instead, I said, "Look, there's got to be something different going on here. I need you to find out what it is."

We began the summit with reports from the thirteen fleets.

Unified Authority Navy cruisers had been spotted throughout our territory. They may have been testing our security measures, they may have been spying on us. Cruisers were small and fast, better suited for hit-and-run tactics than confrontations. Phantom U.A. ships had been spotted in all six arms and near most of our twenty-three planets. We never got more than a brief glimpse of them, and they were always cruisers. The most sightings occurred around St. Augustine and Olympus Kri, the only two planets we held in the Orion Arm. Apparently, there had been dozens of incidents around St. Augustine.

Admiral Glenn Nelson, Commander of the Orion Inner Fleet, shared his opinions freely. "The Unifieds want Orion back because we're too close to Earth. They're going to try to run us out of the Orion Arm, the gutless pricks.

"We should take the fight to them . . . end the war once and for all."

I had my own theory about what the Unified Authority wanted and how we should respond, but I was in no rush to share my opinions in a room filled with admirals. They were Navy. I was a Marine.

"Have any of you gotten close enough to fire at one of their cruisers?" Warshaw asked.

"I got within a million miles," Nelson answered. "We were down to about six hundred fifty thousand when the ship broadcasted out."

"Was she one of the new ships or an older model?" Warshaw asked.

"New. We got a signature reading from its shields," Nelson said. Other admirals grunted approvingly.

"Did you have enough guns to win if she stood her ground?" Warshaw asked.

Nelson frowned and nodded. "Three carriers and a battleship . . . it wouldn't have been much of a fight."

The commander of the Sagittarius Central Fleet came even closer to nailing a U.A. ship. "She broadcasted in five million miles off Donwyn Kri. We had four ships in the area. We were almost on top of her."

"But she got away," Nelson said in a bored voice.

There was one exception. One of the Unified Authority ships put up a brief fight in the Norma Arm. Norma was the innermost arm, the vortex of the six spiral arms—or in sailor terms, the "asshole of the galaxy."

"If they want Norma, we should give it to them," one of the admirals offered. This comment earned him laughs and nods.

Sitting in a room filled with clones wearing admiral's uniforms left me feeling slightly disoriented. They all looked alike, more or less. Some were as old as fifty and one was barely thirty, but they had the same face. Warshaw, the fanatical bodybuilder, stood out. He outweighed the next heaviest clone in the room by a good twenty pounds. Also, the others had hair. Warshaw shaved anything resembling hair from his head . . . though, judging by his nearly comic overabundance of muscle, the absence of hair might have had more to do with steroid use.

"So you think they're up to something? What are they up to?" Warshaw asked, looking for volunteers. "We know they're watching us. Obviously, they're infiltrating us with assassins. Are they running scared? Are they planning an attack?"

No one answered.

"They're going to attack us," said Admiral Nelson. "Sooner or later, they are going to attack us. They have to. They don't have any choice."

"They don't want to fight us," said Admiral Swift, the officer in charge of guarding the space around Olympus Kri. "Those are cruisers they're sending. Cruisers are the most expendable ships in the U.A. Navy. I bet they even have clone crews flying them, the bastards.

"If they wanted to fight, they'd send carriers and battleships. They're running scared."

"So why are they spying on us?" Warshaw asked Swift.

"Because they're scared, sir. They want to make sure we're not coming after them."

"Bullshit! They are planning their attack," said Nelson.

Swift turned on Nelson, and said, "You don't know your shit from your ass. We're talking about Alden Brocius. I've seen rabbits with bigger balls than Brocius. The bastard is going to play it safe as long as he can. He'll send scouts to make sure we're not planning anything, then he'll wait until he has the biggest fleet and the most guns before he commits. That son of a bitch will take us into the next century before he attacks. Guys like Brocius don't make their move till they're sure they'll win."

At that point, the meeting moved on its own inertia. Warshaw tried to take control, but no one was interested.

I watched the quagmire with some satisfaction. I found the officers pretentious. Not a one of them had attended Annapolis or received any other form of officer training. They grew up in the same orphanages as the clones they commanded, and yet they had already adopted the air of superiority I despised in natural-born officers.

Sitting beside me, Admiral Cabot ignored the confusion. He looked pleased just to be in attendance. The summit was officially for fleet commanders, admirals with two stars and up. Cabot, a lower-half rear, had only one star. He would not get to speak unless I invited him to say something on my behalf, but he did not seem to care.

I sat through the meeting, biding my time, speculating about the cadaver in the morgue. When speakers droned on too long, I let my thoughts wander to Ava. I listened for items of interest as the admirals pontificated; but they were talking Navy, I spoke Marine.

When the meeting adjourned for lunch, I found a quiet table where I hoped to sit alone. I did not have the table to myself for long. Cabot came to join me. Like any successful entourage officer, he knew how to read his benefactor. He instinctively knew that I did not feel like talking, so he sat and ate, silent and serene.

A few moments later, Warshaw slid into the seat beside Cabot.

"Mind if I join you?" he asked.

Cabot leaped to his feet. He snapped to attention so quickly that his thigh struck the edge of the table and it slid an inch. Fortunately, I had sipped enough of my water that it did not slosh out of the glass. Cabot's water splashed on to his plate, though. "Good thing we weren't eating soup," I said. They both looked at me curiously, not understanding my joke.

Warshaw, a man who'd risen to master chief petty officer before the Unified Authority gave us field promotions and cut us loose, returned Cabot's salute as he dropped into his seat, and said, "At ease, Cabot. Let's just enjoy our meal."

"Yes, sir," Cabot said, sounding embarrassed. He sat down and proceeded to stare into his plate.

"Harris, do you plan on joining the discussion, or are you here to enjoy the show?" Warshaw asked.

A waiter came and placed dishes before Warshaw, took his drink request, and left.

Warshaw looked at the plate, and said in disgust, "Is this a chicken or a dove?"

"It's a local game bird," I said. "I guess they don't grow too big in the desert."

Warshaw changed the subject. "Harris, I get the feeling you've been avoiding me."

"Avoiding you?" I asked. "Why would I do that?"

"You tell me," he said.

"Nothing comes to mind," I said.

"Made any progress on your investigation?"

"Some," I said.

"Okay, I want you to present tomorrow. Tell us what you got so far."

"I won't have much to talk about," I said.

"Maybe you can tell us what happened to your face. That should be a fascinating story," Warshaw suggested. Cabot had probably wanted to ask about it as well but had lacked the guts and the rank.

"As a matter of fact, that's not a bad idea," I said.

"And you brought a stiff with you," Warshaw said.

"Yeah, he's down in the morgue."

"One of ours?"

"Theirs," I said. "Our first confirmed infiltrator."

"And he's a clone?"

"He was. Now he's a cadaver."

"Sounds to me like you've got a lot to talk about. Look, Harris, right now you're the highest-ranking target in the Enlisted Man's Empire. I bet you have some harrowing tales."

After that, we mostly ate in silence. Warshaw asked me a few friendly questions. Except for a question about touching his toes during his morning stretches, Warshaw pretty much ignored Cabot. I did notice that Warshaw emphasized the word "rear" when he referred to Cabot's rank.

Just as I finished my lunch, one of Cabot's lieutenants came to deliver a note. Cabot read it and passed it on to me. It was from Villanueva, informing me that his MPs had located a suspicious clone on the *ad-Din*. The note ended with an offer to "detain" the man.

I thought about the last infiltrator and wondered what would have happened if MPs had tried to arrest him. I had the feeling it would have ended up with wounded MPs and another bullet-ridden corpse.

I wrote, "Keep him bottled up. I am on my way," and sent the note back.

"I may be late to the next meeting," I told Warshaw. "Something important has come up."

"Something you can discuss in your briefing?" he asked.

"If everything goes right, we'll be doing show-and-tell instead of a lecture."

# CHAPTER
# THIRTY-THREE

Where do you look for a cold-blooded killer? The MPs guarding the *Salah ad-Din* found theirs in a cargo hold, inventorying food supplies.

We huddled together in a small room a few doors from the cargo hold watching him on a security screen. The man looked like a general-issue clone, just another enlisted sailor counting crates on an inventory tablet.

"He's been in that exact same spot for sixteen hours now, ever since you left for Gobi," Villanueva explained.

"What's he doing, counting every specking noodle?" asked Nobles. No one had briefed Nobles on the situation.

Villanueva ignored him. Nobles was a Marine. As far as Pete Villanueva was concerned, that made him my problem.

"Camouflage," I told Nobles. "He's a stowaway, and he's trying to blend in."

"So he's hiding?" Nobles asked.

Hoping he would just keep quiet and figure things out by listening in on the conversation, I ignored him.

"Is he a spy or something?" Nobles asked. He was too comfortable around me. Maybe that happened with pilots and drivers; they spent so much time with superior officers that they thought of them as friends.

"Spy, assassin, saboteur, the bastard's a one-man wrecking crew," I said.

Noble dropped out of the conversation after that.

"Have you sent anyone in after him?" I asked Villanueva. I'd warned him not to send anyone in, but orders sometimes slip through the cracks.

"No, sir."

"Do you know if he's armed?"

"We can't be sure, sir, not without sending a team in to apprehend him," said one of the MPs.

"But you haven't seen anything?"

"No, sir," said the MP.

The clone on the screen did not look dangerous. If anything, he looked neurotic. He had that tablet, but he wasn't writing anything. He kept yelling something, maybe even screaming like a man out of control. Every so often he stopped talking and smacked himself on the head with the tablet.

"Is there any way to pick up what he's saying?" I asked.

The MP controlling the monitoring station fielded the question. "No, sir. The camera does not have audio. It's for checking inventory."

"Too bad," I said.

"He's been doing that the entire time," Villanueva said, sounding somewhat disgusted.

"Doing what?" I asked.

"Beating himself up. Watch his lips. When you see him pucker and grimace like that, he's saying the word, 'SPECK.' He says 'speck' just about every other word."

As Villanueva said this, the man rapped himself across his forehead with his tablet three times in rapid succession. He puckered, then grimaced, puckered, then grimaced, puckered, then grimaced. Watching his lips move, I imagined him shouting the word.

"Dangerous or not, he sure as hell is crazy," Villanueva said.

"He's both," I said.

If everything the coroners had said about Sergeant Lewis proved true, he'd kept fighting long after he should have curled up and died. Guys like that don't throw in the towel. You can pull a gun on them, and they just keep fighting.

"I'm going in after him," I said.

"You don't need to go in there yourself," Villanueva said. "I have plenty of men . . ."

"Alone," I added. Was I afraid? Was I facing my fears? Was I climbing back on the proverbial horse? God, I hoped not.

"Sir . . ."

"I have a better shot at nabbing this guy without your boys getting in my way."

"That's bullshit," one of Villanueva's MPs whispered to the man beside him. Then in a louder voice, he said, "Sir, may I suggest that we send in ten men and piggy-pile him, sir."

It was not a question of climbing back on the horse; I wanted a rematch. I hadn't taken Lewis seriously, and he'd damn near killed me. If this lunatic was the same clone who'd attacked me in my quarters, I'd managed to scare him away the first time we met; but I was the one on the ground when he ran away.

Commanding officers do not generally participate in arrests, and I should have sat this one out. At most, I should have notified Hollingsworth and had him send Marines to assist in the arrest. I was running this operation too far from the rule book, but I didn't care.

"You really plan to go in alone?" Villanueva asked, the mirth in his voice too apparent.

"I do," I said.

"General, we'll be able to watch you on the surveillance cameras," said one of the MPs. "I'll have men waiting right outside the door if something happens."

"That's good, but I don't want you jumping the gun on this one."

"No, sir."

"This is almost sure to come to a fight," I said. "Don't come running at the first sign of trouble."

"At what point should I send in help?" Villanueva asked.

"Good question," I said, not sure how to answer the question. "If I give the distress signal, come in running."

"What's the signal?" The MPs sounded worried. They didn't want a general dying on their watch.

"If you see me flat on my ass and begging for mercy, come in after me."

The MPs laughed. Villanueva did not. "Begging your pardon, sir, but I hope that's not the same signal you used last time?"

The MPs stifled their laughter, but the point was well taken, I still had plenty of bruises on my face.

"I've got the situation under control, Captain," I said, fixing Villanueva with my coldest glare, "and you have your orders. Give me five minutes, then send your men after me."

Villanueva followed me as I left the security room. "You do know that this is crazy, right?" he asked, as I headed toward the cargo hold.

"I know," I said. He was correct, but a combat reflex had already begun to flood my veins with hormonal courage, and I felt the old excitement. "Don't sweat it. Just get my safety net ready. I seriously doubt he will kill me in the time it takes your MPs to break things up."

The cargo hold had twelve-foot ceilings lined with bright lights. It was a maze with crates and shelves instead of walls. I entered, heard someone shouting, and followed the sound. The infiltrator's tone of voice reminded me of a man scolding a dog. As I got closer, I heard the *thwack* of him smacking himself with his tablet.

"Stupid. Gawd, you are so specking stupid. And now you're stuck here! And what, you think he's ever specking coming back?" A pause, then he shrieked the word, "SPECK!" Agony and probably insanity rang in his voice.

When I turned around a corner, the clone, the sailor, the infiltrator heard my footsteps and turned. There was nothing spectacular about him, just a standard-issue clone, standing five-foot-ten, with brown hair cut to regulation length and wearing a sailor's uniform. His brown eyes fell on me, and I saw recognition. He went silent, dropped the hand with the tablet to his side, and saluted.

I returned the salute, and asked, "Who are you speaking to, sailor?"

He gave me an embarrassed grin, and said, "I was talking to myself, sir. It's an old habit." In his eyes, recognition turned into hope. I was his target, and I had returned.

I pretended to think about what he had said, then responded, "You might want to work on that; people won't understand. They might think you are dangerous."

"Dangerous, sir?" he asked.

"I don't think you're dangerous. I don't think you're dangerous at all."

"No, sir?" he asked.

"No, not in the slightest," I said. "You couldn't even finish me off when you had a gun, and now you're not even armed."

Still standing at attention, he smiled. "Maybe you got lucky."

"Maybe I did. On the other hand, maybe you got lucky, too," I said.

His smile faded as he said, "Maybe." Then he said, "You know who I am and you still came. Doesn't that seem a little foolish?" Amazingly, he remained at attention, chest out, shoulders back. I'd seen how fast he could make his move, though. I wasn't fooled.

"I know what I'm doing," I said.

"How do you know I'm not armed?" he asked.

"Because my MPs have been watching you for hours. If you had a gun, you would have shot yourself instead of trying to beat your head in with an inventory tablet." I pointed to a camera hanging from the track along the ceiling. It was not the small and discreet kind of camera preferred by security personnel. The camera hanging from its bracket was as big as a boxing glove and had robotic claws for pulling cases.

"You were watching me on an inventory drone?" he asked.

I shrugged. "You were entertaining." As we spoke, he seemed to collapse in on himself. He was like the kid who comes into the game full of bravado, then misses a shot and falls apart.

"Are they still watching us?"

"Sure," I said. "But I can signal them to look away if you think you want another shot at me." I was kicking a handicapped man, taking candy from a kid. He was broken. He was still trying to stand at attention, but now his shoulders slumped, and his expression fell.

"Are you going to arrest me, sir?" he asked.

"Unless you give me a reason to have you shot," I said.

"No, sir," he said. "I won't do that."

The clone made no move as I signaled Villanueva to send in his MPs.

*Like Samson without his hair,* I thought. He stood at dazed attention as a pair of MPs entered the cargo hold and put him in cuffs. I watched the scene with bemusement, my combat reflex fading into a pleasant memory.

# CHAPTER
# THIRTY-FOUR

"I heard you brought in a live one," Sam, the apprentice coroner, said. He sounded impressed.

"More or less," I said.

Seaman First Class Philip Sua was bound, drugged, dressed in a straitjacket, and placed in an incapacitation cage. He had remained awake for the trip down to Gobi, but that didn't make him lucid. A river of drool cascaded from his lips, and his eyes stared straight ahead, unblinking and corpselike.

"I don't get it," I said. "The first clone is beaten until his insides turn to pudding, but he keeps fighting. The second clone surrenders without a fight. A coward and a maniac cut from the same DNA, that doesn't add up. Maybe something went wrong with their neural programming."

It was now 03:00, Gobi time, and the station was silent except for the swarms of guards patrolling the corridors. Down in the subterranean levels, the halls remained bright as ever.

"The first one must have known he was going to die," Sam guessed. "You know, maybe he knew he was as good as dead, so he kept fighting as one last act of defiance."

"Okay, that explains why the first one fought to the death, but why did the second one give up so easily."

"Was he bleeding?"

"No."

"Injured in any way?"

"No."

Sam thought for a moment, then said, "Maybe he didn't feel like committing suicide."

We were alone in the morgue, well, mostly alone. Sergeant Kit Lewis was in the room. He was all over the room. His mostly skinned carcass lay on a table. What was left of his face, now rolled inside out and pulled below his chin, hung like the collar of a turtleneck sweater.

Sam blinked to clear his tired eyes, and asked, "Who do you have examining the live one?"

"They're flying some kind of crime shrink in from Morrowtown," I said.

"Dr. Morman?"

"You know him?" I asked.

"I've worked with Morman before," he said, speaking quickly, as if giving the doctor short shrift.

*Why couldn't Terraneau have been like Gobi?* I asked myself. The locals respected us here. And it wasn't just Gobi. We were greeted as heroes on all of the worlds we had liberated except for Terraneau.

"Have you found out anything more about Lewis?" I asked. *Anything more than cause of death?*

"Good timing. If you'd asked that question an hour ago, I wouldn't have had anything to show you," the kid said. "Then I had another look at the DNA. How much do you know about DNA?"

"I thought DNA was a dead end," I said.

Sam shook his head, and said, "It is and it isn't. The DNA itself isn't much help."

"I don't follow," I said.

"There's gene expression and gene regulation. With gene expression, you can create two radically different creatures using identical strands of DNA. You said this man was unusually strong. It's basic epigentics—same DNA, different cell divisions."

"And in English?" I asked.

"Instead of looking at his DNA, I had a look at his chromosomes."

"Chromosomes? The stuff that make you a boy or a girl?"

"I take it biology is not your strong suit," Sam said as a joke, but it sounded so patronizing that I wanted to hit him.

He pointed to a slide on the wall. "Lewis, here, has the exact same DNA as any other military clone, it's just arranged differently."

"If Lewis had the same DNA as every other clone, why isn't he like them?" I asked. "Same DNA, same everything, right?"

"That's what I am trying to explain," Sam said, his irritation starting to show. I think he was used to being the student. Now I was the one with a million questions, and he lacked the patience to answer them.

"DNA is the basic building block. Genes are made of DNA; but you can change genes by changing the layout of the DNA."

Seeing I was still confused, he picked up a syringe and a glass dish. "What do these have in common?" he asked.

"They're lab equipment," I guessed.

"They're made of glass. Glass is made of sand. If I have molten glass, I can make a bowl or a syringe, right. Once I melt the sand, I can use the glass to make a bowl or a syringe."

"Okay, I get that," I said.

Apparently I didn't get it, though, because he sighed, and said, "It's not like bowls are made from bowl sand and syringes are made from syringe sand. Glass fruit sand doesn't come from glass fruit deserts. It's all the same sand from the same desert."

"Yeah, okay, one desert, one kind of sand," I said, slowing as I finished the sentence because the meaning of what he had said finally dawned on me.

"Okay, so they don't make bowls out of 'bowl sand' and syringes out of 'syringe sand.' It's just sand. What you do with the sand once you melt it is up to you," Sam said, making sure I understood.

I thought about what he was saying and saw a problem with it. "But it's not the same with DNA," I said. "They selected the specific genes when they made us. They spent—"

He put up a hand to stop me. "You said this clone was created as a spy. They designed him to break into your forts, right? Can you think of better camouflage than making him out of your DNA?

"Do you know what chromosomes are made of? You pair a strand of DNA with a protein. Do your security posts test for chromosomes?"

"I don't know," I said.

"His DNA is identical to any other clone's, but his chromosomes are different. Once I started with his chromosomes, the difference became obvious," said Sam.

"Chromosomes?" I asked, shaking my head. It didn't make sense to me. "I can see how you might make different chromosomes, but what does that get you. That's the stuff that determines your sex, right? Women have two X chromosomes and men have an X and a Y."

"Women have two Xs, most men have an X and a Y, but Lewis had an X and two Ys. He has the same DNA but a different set of chromosomes."

"Two Y chromosomes? And the Y is what separates men from women. Does that make him more . . ." I almost said "manly." "Would that make him strong?" Even as I asked the question, a more pressing concern came to mind—*Could we configure the posts to read chromosomes instead of DNA?*

"It could make him much stronger than other clones. The potential exists. Lewis was like any other clone on the surface, but his muscles could have been stronger, his heart was stronger . . ."

"What about his brain?" I asked. "What would that do to his brain?"

"Oh, yes, his brain. You know, the autopsy would have been a lot more productive if you hadn't shot the subject in the head."

"I didn't shoot him," I said.

"Okay, well, whoever shot him really specked up the works," Sam said, holding both hands up in frustration. "The bullet blew more than half of his brain out of his skull, and the part that was left was in bad shape."

He walked over to Lewis and placed his fingers around the bone-and-muscle remains of his chin. "It wasn't a complete washout."

He turned the head so the empty brain cavity faced toward me. "It's not conclusive; but considering the amount of trauma done to this man, we're lucky we found anything."

"Found what?" I asked.

"I took a tissue scraping from the area just inside here." The kid stuck his hand into the gaping brainpan and pointed to the part of the forehead that had not been destroyed by the bullet. During my time as a Marine, I had shot, stabbed, strangled, and exploded enemies, but I never played with their remains. I did not peel away their skins or pull out their organs. Watching Sam the cocky student coroner twist and turn the body made me queasy.

"We got this from his brain," he said, using tweezers to hold up a gauss-thin strip of meat. "Its NAAs are so low, they're almost not there."

I asked the obvious question, "What is NAA?"

"N-acetylaspartic acid."

"That doesn't tell me anything," I said.

The kid was many things, but he was not a snob. When he continued, he did not speak in a condescending way. "It's a compound you find in a normally functioning brain. Things go wrong when it's not there. The lower the NAA level, the bigger the problems, and this guy's levels were really low."

This information was interesting but not practical. I asked a practical question, "Is there any way we can configure our security equipment to track this?"

He smiled, nodded, and said, "Dead men don't walk, blind men don't see . . ."

It was a limerick or maybe a line from an old song. The second half went, "I gave her my heart, and she crucified me."

"General," he said, "I checked your chromosomes when you came through the door. A coroner can't be too careful."

Before leaving the morgue, I asked the kid to write up his findings and send them to Station Security along with recommendations about how the posts could be upgraded to scan chromosomes instead of DNA.

I returned to my quarters and stripped and showered and ran a laser across my teeth, then went to bed, all the while asking the same questions I had been asking before seeing the coroner—Why would one clone fight to the death and another surrender?

Part of the answer was obvious, self-determination. Clones start out alike, but that does not mean they stay that way. I grew up among clones. I knew brave ones and not-so-brave clones, but I never met a clone who was an outright coward. I went to boot camp with men who would not flinch in the face of death and clones who might hesitate before a charge but none who would run from the field.

But the clones I knew had been raised from infancy. These

new clones had to have "crawled out of the tube" in their twenties. The Unified Authority did not have time to raise their clones, they needed them out and killing.

As I slid onto my rack, I thought about bowls and syringes and manufactured chromosomes. Sleep did not come so easily that night because along with the bowl and the syringe came images of the cadaver. I'd seen worse. I'd seen rotted, maggot-infested bodies of men. I once stepped on the body of a man killed by Noxium gas. My boot crushed through his chest. It was like stepping on overripe fruit.

It wasn't the cadaver that bothered me; it was the casual way the damn apprentice coroner handled it that got under my skin. Lewis was a maniac and assassin, but he was still as human as me.

As I played the scene over in my mind, thoughts gave way to fitful sleep, and I dreamed of men fighting a war in which they killed each other with glass bullets. The men who died were buried in glass coffins in a cemetery with glass headstones. Watching them lower the coffins, I wondered if the men who lived and the men who died were made from the same kind of sand.

I could not tell if it came the minute I fell asleep or six hours later. I woke up disoriented, groped for the communications console beside my bed, and croaked the word, "What?"

The voice on the other end belonged to a woman. "General Harris, this is Jennifer Morman."

"Morman?" I asked. I did not recognize the name or the voice.

"I'm the forensic psychologist you brought in from Morrowtown."

I recognized each of the words as she spoke them, but it took a moment before I pieced them together into a coherent stream. Sitting up, I said, "Right . . . right. Have you had a look at the clone I brought in?"

"I've never seen anything quite like him," she said.

I glanced at the clock in the console. The time was 05:28. It no longer mattered whether it was 01:00 or 10:00; it was time for me to get moving. "Have you made any progress?" I asked as I climbed out of bed and slipped into my uniform. I still had sixty minutes before I had planned to wake up.

"Oh, I've made progress all right," she said. "I've made a lot of progress."

I told Morman I would be right over and headed out of my billet. Gobi Station did not have a "forensic psychology" lab, so I'd stuck her in an unused office in the station's lowest basement. Five armed guards stood outside the lab . . . just in case.

The guards knew me by sight. They stood at attention and let me through. Morman, on the other hand, had never seen me. She heard the door open, turned to say hello, and froze. A strange smile formed across her lips as she said, "Oh my Lord, you're a Liberator."

Feeling a bit awkward, I said, "Dr. Morman, I'm General Harris."

"You are a Liberator, aren't you?"

"Yes, I am a Liberator clone. Is that going to be a problem?" Even the most open-minded people were afraid of Liberators. We were the pit bulls of the synthetic crowd.

"God, no," she said. "It's exciting to meet you. I thought the Liberators were extinct."

"As far as I know, I'm the last," I said, no longer caring whether or not she felt comfortable around me. She made me uncomfortable. I got the feeling she was dissecting me with her eyes.

"General, for a forensic psychologist like me, you are a gold mine. I'd love to sit down with you and maybe pick your brain."

Images of Sam the coroner manhandling Sergeant Lewis still played in my head. I did not want this woman giving me the psychological equivalent of an autopsy. "We'll see," I said, making a mental note not to spend any unnecessary time down here.

As if she had read my thoughts, Dr. Morman nodded and became somewhat guarded. "Maybe we should stick to Sua," she said.

"What can you tell me about him?" I asked.

"Oh well, he's an interesting study," she said in an all-business tone. "I don't believe his name is Sua."

"It's not. We found the real Philip Sua shortly after we arrested this man. Your patient had stuffed him into a meat locker."

"Was he all right?" Morman asked.

I pulled a Freeman and answered the question by ignoring it.

"Have you looked at Myron's report?" she asked.

Maybe I was still tired. It took me a moment to figure out that *Myron* must have been the older coroner. *Myron and Sam,* I told myself. "I've spoken with his assistant," I said.

"Okay, well, did he tell you about the low brain activity?" she asked. "I would have come to the same conclusion without Myron's help. I mean, you don't need to spend more than a minute with Sua to see what's wrong with him, but the autopsy confirmed my findings. Philip Sua's problems wouldn't be any more obvious if he had three heads."

*Or if he was a Liberator clone,* I thought as I asked, "And what exactly is his problem?"

"What are his problems? Sua's problems are legion, General. This man has more devils in him than anyone could ever hope to exorcise."

"I don't understand. Are you saying he's insane?" I thought about the bastard standing for hours in that cargo hold, hitting himself with his tablet and berating himself. *A lunatic?* It made sense. *Maybe a sociopath, too.* His kind killed easily enough. Maybe the Unified Authority had developed a strain of mass-murderer clones. "Is he psychotic?"

"Psychotic," she said, the word lingering on her lips. She was an older woman, maybe in her forties, the first traces of gray showing in her hair. She wore glasses. She was trim and energetic, and she approached her work with this queer enthusiasm. I might have described her as a playful authority. Maybe she found irony in the notion of a Liberator clone accusing anyone else of being psychotic.

"Clinically speaking, he is not psychotic. He hasn't lost contact with reality," she said. "Sua's problems are more along the lines of neurosis than psychosis. I mean, he does have an induced physical condition, but his behavior is clearly neurotic."

She must have thought I knew more about forensic psychology than I did. I knew a few psychological terms, but Marines used those terms as pseudoobscenities not diagnosis. When an officer goes out of control, we may report him as a "loose cannon," but in private conversation we'd refer to him as a "psychotic bastard."

"What do you mean by neurotic?" I asked.

In answer, she winked, and said, "Let's go have a word with Mr. Sua, shall we?" She led me through the door at the back of the office into the area that had become her makeshift lab. The only furniture in her lab was a desk, a few stools, and three long-necked floor lamps bunched close together like a trio of storks.

In the center of the room, Philip Sua lay on the contraption that law-enforcement professionals referred to as an "incapacitation cage." The cage did not rely on anything as primitive as bars or straps or clamps. If Sua managed to sit up, he could have walked right out of the laboratory. The problem was, his muscles weren't listening to his brain.

He lay on a table with two diodes a pin's breadth away from the nape of his neck. Metal filaments inserted into the base of his skull channeled the steady stream of electricity running between those diodes through his spine, rendering his body helpless from the neck down. He could not turn his head or uncurl his fingers.

Sua lay conscious on the table, watching us as we entered the room. His eyes switched back and forth between us; but he did not speak. If I expected a psychotic madman with a confident grin and dangerous eyes, that was not what I found. Sua looked nervous.

"Can he speak?" I asked.

"Oh yes, see, hear, speak . . . everything but move. He's been very cooperative," Morman said.

I stepped closer to the cage. I did not hear the crackle of electricity or feel a tingle on my skin. The current running through Sua's body was a mere trickle. "Hello, Sua," I said.

Dr. Morman introduced me as well. "Philip, this is General Harris."

"We've met," he said, his brown eyes on my face but never quite meeting my gaze.

I was glad to see two MPs standing in the far corner of the lab with guns on their belts. Despite her ghoulish fascination with Liberators, I liked Dr. Morman. She struck me as smart and competent, but also as a delicate woman playing with forces far more dangerous than she understood.

That thought reminded me of the question that had been

nagging me since we arrested Sua. Still watching the captive clone, I said, "Doctor, I've run into two of these clones so far. There is the tissue donor down at the morgue, then there is Sua.

"The one in the morgue wouldn't give up. He was coughing up blood, and we still had to shoot him.

"Then there is Sua. He gave up without a fight."

Morman had her answer ready. What she said made me forget all about sand, syringes, and bowls. Her answers were far more enlightening. Once she explained herself, everything fell into place.

I asked her if she would be willing to present this information to the admirals during the afternoon session, and she said that would be fine. With the pieces of the puzzle she had given me, I finally understood the infiltrators. What the coroners found was good. What she uncovered was gold.

"They built his brain with a slight abnormality," Dr. Morman told me. She sat on her rolling stool, I stood. We were still in the lab, close enough for Sua to overhear our conversation.

"You said that Myron and Sam told you about the slowed activity level in the dead clone's frontal lobe."

I nodded.

"It's a symptom of BPD, Borderline Personality Disorder. It's not uncommon . . . well, not among clones, it's not. Mr. Sua is something of an extreme case."

I got as far as, "I don't understand. What is Borderline Personality—" but she interrupted me.

"Borderline Personality Disorder. It's a neurophysiological condition that interferes with the patient's ability to regulate emotion. It affects the way they interpret social questions. If someone told you or me that we had lint on our clothing or a smudge on our face, we'd go clean up and not give it a second thought. It's a normal interaction, something you fix and forget.

"Someone like Mr. Sua would take it as a personal affront."

"So he's crazy," I said.

"Not crazy."

"And you think the Unified Authority purposely made him this way?" I asked.

"The tissue from the clone in the morgue suggests he had the same disorder." Dr. Morman took a long look at Sua, then turned back to me, and said, "Judging by the NAA samples, he was an extreme case as well."

"Why in the world would the Unified Authority want an army of pathologically insecure clones?" I asked.

Dr. Morman took a deep breath, then spoke in a whisper. "People with BPD have a nearly debilitating fear of abandonment. If his superiors threatened him, maybe told him to kill you or they would give him a dishonorable discharge, Sua would see you as the cause of all his fears. He'd rather die than have his superiors abandon him."

"Okay, that explains Lewis's behavior," I said. When Dr. Morman gave me a funny look, I said, "The one in the morgue.

"But Sua didn't put up a fight at all. I came unarmed, and he surrendered."

"I asked him about that. He said you caught him off guard when you came in unarmed and alone," said Dr. Morman. "BPD creates a fascinating dichotomy. Patients have a false sense of confidence. In extreme cases, like Sua's, the patient thinks of himself as undefeatable. He had unreasonable over-confidence; but once you challenged that confidence, he was crushed. He said you disarmed him the first time he attacked you."

"The only time he attacked me," I said.

"Right. The second time you found him, you came in alone and unarmed, and that made him believe that you had no fear of him. When you treated him like a helpless child, he decided he did not stand a chance against you and gave up."

"So he's useless," I said.

"So he's dangerous," Dr. Morman corrected me. "This man hates you. He has personalized his fight with you. If he were to get free, he would dedicate his life to destroying you, and he would find a way to do it.

"And something else, he feels that way about the entire Enlisted Man's Empire. He believes you and the other clones left him behind on Earth to die."

"That's ridiculous," I said.

"General, it's not ridiculous to him. That is how he interprets information. He's not just an enemy soldier, not just some kind of spy; because of his built-in insecurities, this man takes every offense as if it were personal. He is strong, he is intelligent, and he is willing to dedicate his life to your destruction.

"If you're not worried by an enemy like that . . ." She shook her head. "You are a Liberator. Everyone knows what you are capable of doing; but I would hate to have someone like him hunting me, General Harris."

# CHAPTER
# THIRTY-FIVE

During breakfast, I gave Admiral Cabot an assignment. We sat alone at a small table in a corner of the mess. I was tired from my early-morning meeting with the forensic psychologist. He looked well rested.

"I need you to do something," I said as I downed my third cup of coffee. "I need you to get me some information about cruisers."

Cabot put down his coffee and pulled out his notepad. "What are you looking for?" he asked.

"I need to know about landing bays on cruisers."

"Okay, what about the landing bay?" he asked. He sounded confident, like he already had the answers.

"The measurements. I need to know the number of bays and the square footage."

"One bay, it holds four transports. I'd put it at three thousand square feet, not including the tunnel."

He leaned forward, put up a hand as if blocking outsiders from overhearing what he had to say next, and added, "I spent three years on a cruiser."

"Not our cruisers," I said. "Theirs. I need to know about the new ones, the cruisers the Unifieds have been using to spy on us."

"Oh." Cabot sounded disappointed. He knew I wanted the information right away, and that meant missing part of the summit. I was getting in the way of his ass-kissing and politicking; and from his expression, I could tell that he resented it.

"You can start by going to Navy Intel; you might get lucky," I said.

"What if they don't have the information?" he asked.

"Then fly out to the *ad-Din* and have Villanueva take you to Terraneau. There's all kinds of wreckage floating around out there; you're bound to find a cruiser."

"You want me to measure a wreck? How am I supposed to do that?"

"I don't care if you use your dick, just get me the specking dimensions. You got that?"

It was crude talk, but I needed to get through to him. As we spoke, Cabot sat there watching the other admirals enter the briefing room. I could read his thoughts. He wanted to pawn the assignment off on an underling. He wanted to be in the summit rubbing shoulders with the two-stars.

"By the way, don't use your dick," I said. "You're going to need something longer." *And something that doesn't change size every time a superior officer walks past,* I thought.

"Aye, aye, sir," he said, barely trying to disguise the snarl in his voice.

I had my reasons for wanting Cabot to handle this himself. Like him or hate him, J. Winston Cabot got things done. When I gave him orders, he executed them as if his next promotion depended on it. The information he brought me would check out; and since he would not be able to enter the summit until he got those dimensions, he'd be fast.

"You better get going, Admiral," I said. "I'm presenting this afternoon. I need that information before I start my presentation."

"Yes, sir," he said. He took one last fawning look at the door to the summit, then put down his coffee and headed off.

The morning's meetings went quickly. We discussed fleet readiness. Warshaw had run a series of drills to test how quickly he could shift forces to meet an invasion. When he simulated an attack on the Golan Dry Docks in his first exercise, only six fleets responded. While the first ships arrived in thirteen minutes, the bulk took between forty minutes and an hour. The final three ships to arrive on the scene did not broadcast in for three hours.

Heads rolled. High-ranking officers were offered early retirements. Rumor had it that one man shot himself rather than face Warshaw's wrath.

The next fire drill went better. It took less than ten minutes for the first few carriers to arrive. The entire armada broadcasted in within fifty minutes. Some of those ships went through four broadcast transfers, traveling as many as eighty-three thousand light-years to arrive on the scene.

This time Warshaw acknowledged that his captains had carried out their orders. He then took his frustrations out on the officers who designed the ERP—the "Emergency Response Protocol," stating that the response times could be cut in half again if the routes were better organized.

All of this came as old news to everyone else in the room; but I had never heard any of it. Until a few weeks ago, I had been safely tucked away on Terraneau worrying about the locals breaking into an underground parking lot. Now I had galactic security on my mind, and spy ships, and infiltrator clones.

When Warshaw's staff simulated a surprise attack on Olympus Kri, twenty-six fighter carriers and sixty-three battleships arrived on the scene within seventeen minutes. Another fifty ships arrived by the half-hour mark.

As he spoke, I came to realize that Gary Warshaw had morphed into the Napoleon specking Bonaparte of his time. *Maybe all clone brains weren't created equal,* I thought. But then again, maybe they were. Maybe the U.A. had accidentally packed two brains into Warshaw's wide, bald pate.

Standing at the lectern, looking mildly deformed with his hairless head and endless stream of muscles, Warshaw smiled and announced the results of his most recent exercise. Twenty-eight ships had responded to a simulated attack on Gobi within six minutes. Within twenty minutes, fifty-two ships had arrived on the scene.

"You know what that tells me," Warshaw said. "That tells me that the Enlisted Man's Navy has the will to survive."

Applause rose from the audience. Were they applauding themselves for their fast response or Warshaw for working miracles? I didn't know, and neither did he. I doubt the admirals knew, but they clapped until Warshaw raised his hands, signaling for them to stop. Warshaw's presentation included charts and holographic displays. It lasted four hours. By the time he finished, it was time for lunch.

I was next on the agenda, right after lunch. With a sinking feeling, I searched the dining hall for Cabot. He was nowhere to be seen.

Not feeling especially hungry, I went to my billet. I called Station Security to see if Cabot had returned. They checked their records and reported that he'd left Gobi Station shortly before the morning session began. He had not yet returned.

I left orders for them to rush Cabot to the summit the moment he passed through security. Even if it meant interrupting a closed session, they were to send him in.

Before rejoining Warshaw and his fleet commanders, I contacted the morgue. Sam had gone home for the day; but Myron, the senior coroner, was there. He gave me some very good news.

I returned to the summit slightly before 13:00, just in time for the meeting to begin. Warshaw stopped at my desk, and said, "I didn't see you at lunch. I hope you don't get all weird when you make presentations."

"Just nailing down a few loose ends," I said.

"So are you ready to present?" he asked.

I nodded, and he headed to the lectern. Introducing me only as "Harris," he told the group that I would report about a "special intelligence operation" under my command. He then turned the next session of the meeting over to me.

Not feeling especially nervous, I walked up to the stand. I knew a few of the men, but not many. With the exception of Warshaw, not a one of them had done anything to earn my respect. Their idea of combat involved sitting on the bridge of a carrier while Marines and fighter pilots did the heavy lifting.

I began with a bombshell.

"The Unified Authority is tracking our movements," I said. I turned to Warshaw, and added, "When you ran that last ERP, you revealed your fleet movements, emergency protocols, and readiness to the Pentagon."

I doubted there was so much as a single officer in the room who believed me. I was a Marine speaking to Navy men. They trusted me to shoot guns and throw grenades, but they didn't respect my intelligence-gathering ability any more than I respected their hand-to-hand combat experience.

Repeating the scraps of information I'd learned from Ray Freeman, I continued. "The Unified Authority has set up spy satellites to monitor our broadcast activity. Every time our ships broadcast in or out of an area, those satellites read the anomaly."

The room went quiet. Men who had originally doubted now began wondering just how much I knew. Spy satellites reading distant anomalies, the technology was basic and nearly impossible to track. Reading anomalies was child's play, and the data could be synchronized to track the entire empire's movements.

"Why haven't we spotted any of their satellites?" one admiral asked. He sounded cynical. I didn't blame him.

"Have you looked for satellites?" I asked. "We're talking satellites the size of golf balls floating in millions of miles of open space. What are the odds of finding them?"

That shut him up. There was no point sending ships out to look for the satellites. It would be like combing a ten-mile stretch of beach for one specific grain of sand.

"How are they deploying them?" another admiral asked.

Warshaw stood, and the room went quiet. He asked, "Is that what the cruisers were doing, dropping spy satellites?"

"If we chart the cruisers' courses, maybe we can find their satellites," another admiral suggested. The idea had not occurred to me. It touched off a discussion.

As the admirals discussed ways to search for satellites, the door opened, and in walked Admiral Cabot. He stared at me, waited until we had eye contact, gave me a nod, then went to the desk where I'd been seated. I breathed a sigh of relief. The pretentious little bastard would not have come without completing his mission.

An admiral sitting a few tables from Warshaw yelled, "If they really have those satellites, then they've analyzed our

Emergency Response Protocol." His voice rose above the din.

"We need to destroy the satellites," somebody yelled. I did not see who.

"Don't be in too big a hurry to destroy them," I said, quieting down the room. I repeated this, and added, "It's always a good idea to give your enemies a little misinformation before killing their spies."

A general hush fell over the room as the admirals considered this.

"Misdirection, I like it," Warshaw said. "Norma ships responding to Orion . . . Perseus ships covering Sagittarius. Do it right, and we could really speck with their intel."

With the meeting dissolving into many conversations, I asked Warshaw if he would mind giving me a fifteen-minute break. I used the time to catch up with Cabot.

"We had to go all the way to Terraneau," he complained.

"What did you find?"

"Their cruisers are built for spying, not combat. They have cloaking equipment, and they're fast. They have a top speed of thirty-eight million miles per hour."

Our ships topped out at thirty million.

"So you found one at Terraneau?" I asked.

"Three of 'em. I boarded one myself. It had three landing bays, all kinds of spy gear, and no weapons . . . just bays and bunks. And the landing bays were big, almost ten thousand square feet of parking space."

I heard him, but it didn't sound possible. "Ten thousand feet per bay?"

He nodded.

I considered the ramifications, and said, "Oh, shit."

# THIRTY-SIX

I started the meeting with another explosion.

"I caught the assassin who killed Admiral Franks," I began. It was sort of true. Whoever killed Lilburn Franks, his DNA would be identical to Philip Sua's DNA. His chromosomes would match as well.

Firing a gun into the ceiling would not have captured their attention as quickly. From the moment an aide had found Thorne's and Franks's bodies, these men had been living in fear. With the Unifieds killing top officers, every man in the room was a target.

I waited for the admirals to respond, but no one spoke. No one challenged me.

"The Unified Authority breached our security by creating a strain of clones based on the same DNA as our clones. That made their clones impossible to detect."

Silence. I went on. "Over the last few days, we have managed to isolate two of their clones. We arrested one and killed the other."

I spent the next five minutes talking about Sergeant Kit Lewis, feeling every man's eyes on the bruises that still covered my face. I told them how I had, for all intents and purposes, beaten Lewis to death, and how he nearly killed me in return. Then I told them about Seaman First Class Philip Sua, who allowed MPs to arrest him without a fight.

"These new clones have the same DNA as general-issue clones, but they don't have the same chromosomes. I've issued orders for Gobi Security to update its security posts. If any of the new clones have infiltrated Gobi Station, we should have them shortly.

"Any questions?"

Only one admiral, one I did not recognize, raised his hand,

and asked, "How can you have the same DNA but different chromosomes?" It took guts to ask the question that everyone else was afraid to ask.

I pretended to mull over my answer, then I stole the bit about glass and sand and bowls and syringes. Trying to come across like a man-in-the-know, I damn near quoted Sam the coroner verbatim.

"I'm impressed," said Warshaw. "I never realized you knew so much about science."

Feeling more confident now that I had spoken with Cabot, I continued on to the topic I had meant to discuss before the break. "Those cruisers you've been spotting, they've been carrying more than satellites. They have been ferrying infiltrator clones into our space. The infiltrators are flying into our territory on cruisers, then penetrating our blockades in planes with stealth shields.

"While we've been looking for battleships or cargo carriers, they've been using private planes. They're flying Piper Bandits."

Warshaw put up his hand. "Bandits? You mean the little two-man jobs? That thing's got a range of what, one or two hundred thousand miles."

"Not if they are outfitted with broadcast engines," I said.

"Out of the question," one of the admirals said. "There is no way anyone is going to wedge a broadcast engine into a little two-seater."

The natives were getting restless. A dozen private conversations ignited across the room.

"I've seen a modified Bandit," I said. "The broadcast engine is not much bigger than a shoebox. Instead of a broadcast generator, it has a single-use battery. You use it once, then you have to recharge it."

"That's it? That's your big theory of how they are getting here?" Warshaw asked. "You think they are flying them in on cruisers? How many Bandits do you think they can fit on a cruiser, Harris? I started out on a cruiser. You'd be lucky to fit five planes on one."

Entourage officers, men like J. Winston Cabot, live in a black-and-white world in which they judge everything by the way it impacts their careers. They view anyone or anything that slows their career as the enemy, and they remember every indiscretion.

By sending Cabot to measure a cruiser, I had made myself his enemy. I could probably have repaired the damage by citing him as the source of some of my information. Instead, I called him up to the dais.

He came up slowly. I had caught him off guard, and that made him nervous.

"Admiral, tell us what you were doing this morning and what you found."

He looked across the gallery and focused on Warshaw as he said, "I took the *Salah ad-Din* to Scutum-Crux space looking for a U.A. cruiser."

"Did you have any luck?" I asked Cabot, trying to prompt him. God he was stiff.

"We found several in the wreckage around Terraneau. Per your orders, sir, I boarded one and measured her landing bays."

"What did you find?" I asked.

"The new Unified Authority cruisers have three landing bays. Each landing bay has ten thousand square feet of floor space, sir. If you packed them carefully, you could fit eighteen Piper Bandits in each bay. That means they can transport and launch fifty-four Bandits per ship per mission."

Stunned silence.

Cabot seemed to inflate before my eyes.

I turned toward Warshaw, and said, "Your fleets have spotted cruisers near every planet in the empire. Is that correct?" Not waiting for an answer I already knew, I added, "The cruisers have been particularly active around St. Augustine. Is that correct?" And then I told them about the massacre on St. Augustine.

I had hoped to finish my presentation by having Jen Morman report her findings, but she never appeared.

# CHAPTER
# THIRTY-SEVEN

I rounded up a squad of MPs and rode the elevator down to the basement. As the elevator descended, I warned them that we would find armed killers, and that was all the briefing I gave.

We reached the bottom floor of the station.

The doors slid apart, and the light from the elevator formed a stripe across the leg of the dead guard lying on the hallway floor. I saw the body and hit the emergency button, setting off an alarm and causing the elevator doors to close. So much for the element of surprise.

The two men beside me had seen the body as well.

"Why did he close the door?" asked an MP in the back of the lift.

"We're sitting ducks," I said. "It's dark out there and bright in here."

"I thought I saw a dead man," one of MPs said.

Another one whispered, "I wonder if there is any connection between this and that plane we saw in the desert?"

"What plane?" I asked.

"We found a plane in the desert, sir," the MP said. "We found it while we were patrolling for bandits."

Which explained why they had not notified me, the silly pricks saw the word "bandit" in their orders and thought I meant robbers.

"When was that?" I asked in as measured a voice as I could muster.

"Last night, sir." He sounded nervous.

"You," I said, singling out an MP with an earpiece in his ear. "You just became my radioman. Contact Station Security. Tell them to place the entire station on emergency lockdown. I want the exits sealed, the elevators stopped, and the emergency stairwells closed off while they run a floor-by-floor search of the entire facility."

"What about the landing bays?" the MP asked.

"That goes double for the landing bays."

"Yes, sir." He turned and faced the wall, his shoulders hunched, and whispered in emphatic tones.

The panel beside the emergency cutoff held a flashlight, an oxygen mask, and a fire extinguisher. I took the flashlight.

"Who wants to hold this?" I asked.

Two men volunteered.

"You'll be a target," I warned them. "Those bastards out there are going to aim at the light."

One of the men lowered his hand. I handed the flashlight to the other.

We were trapped in a cramped elevator. Seven men pressed together like fish in a barrel.

"There are enemy assassins out there," I said. "I'm guessing that there are two of them. They'll look like general-issue clones. At least one of them might be dressed like an MP.

"One of them will have just come off a cage, and the sides of his head will be shaved. If you see him, shoot him and keep shooting him until you are sure he is dead. If he's got a friend with him, shoot them both."

That was all the advice I had to give them. It wasn't much.

We pulled our guns—the thirty-shot pistols preferred by military police, with limited muzzle velocity that made them safer for indoor use. Fire a powerful weapon like an M27 in a building, and the bullets could bore through two or three walls.

I used my first bullet shooting out the light in the elevator. The lift went dark, and the elevator buttons lit up. I found the button that opened the door and pressed it.

The infiltrators had shut off the lights, but they had not been able to shut off the emergency power. Rows of tiny colored lights winked on and off on a far wall.

The first shot hit the man with the flashlight. A single shot, the muzzle flash appeared and disappeared like a drop of lightning, the sound from the suppressed weapon no louder than a muffled cough.

I leaped from the elevator like a swimmer diving from a starting block. I landed on the dead MP with the flashlight and rolled across the floor, ending up in a crouching position, my gun out. The other MPs clambered off the elevator, at least one of them stumbling over the guards. An infiltrator fired two more shots, and two more of my men died. I heard them groan as they fell, then I heard silence instead of labored breathing, and I knew that they were dead.

I returned fire, aiming at the flares of the muzzle. Neither shot hit anything except the wall, but I must have come close. The man panicked. He ran past a communications panel and I saw his silhouette against the lights on that panel. I squeezed off two shots and hit the bastard, pausing to listen to the sound he made when he crashed into the wall and collapsed. I didn't think I'd killed him, but he wasn't happy. I heard him rolling around on the hard, cold floor.

"Sound off," I called to my MPs.

Only three men answered.

We closed in around each other in a protective circle, our backs pointing in, our guns pointing out. We remained in a crouch as we slithered toward the spot where I had hit the infiltrator, feeling our way through the darkness.

Another shot. Hidden by the darkness, the bastard fired a single shot, then we were three. I returned fire, wasting three bullets. The guy next to me returned fire, too. Neither of us hit anything.

The clone I'd shot continued to spasm as we neared him. He kicked at me, but he was weak. I'd aimed low, hoping to hit him in the gut. If I'd shot right, he should have lost a lot of blood. I heard him wheezing, fighting for air. I might have hit him in the lungs or the stomach.

He kicked at me again as I knelt beside him. I grabbed his ankle with one hand and fired two shots along his leg. He went limp. Trying to emulate a coroner's disregard for the dead, I worked my way along the body and found the dead man's head. I wasn't checking to make sure of my kill. I wanted his goggles.

No more than twenty feet away from us, but hidden by darkness, the second infiltrator clone made too much noise as he entered the hall, and I fired at him. My two surviving MPs fired as well. We didn't hit the bastard, but we chased him away long enough for me to grab the goggles from the dead clone's head.

Warm liquid smeared along my forehead as I pulled the goggles over my eyes. As a Marine in combat mode, I was trained to ignore the feel of the other man's blood; but as a Liberator, I took a certain pleasure in it. It added to the combat reflex already spreading through me.

Now wearing night-vision goggles, I could see in the dark. I had not hit the man in the chest as I had thought. My shot had hit him where his shoulders met his neck, leaving a messy wound. Anyone else would have quietly bled to death, but this infiltrator tried to kick me as his life bled out of him.

The goggles had bulky, thick lenses, but they cut through the darkness. I could see the hall around me as clearly as if the noon sun shone through it. I glanced at the body beside me and knew that it was Sua, the sides of his head shaved clean. Filaments as fine as an old man's whiskers stuck out of the bald patch—the wires that had conducted the electricity into his brain to disable him while he was on the cage.

Keeping my gun out and ready, I grabbed my last MPs by their shoulders and stood them up. As they fell in behind me, the infiltrator peered out from behind a corner, and I caught a glimpse of him. He wore Marine combat armor. Even if he went to the morgue, the armor would have gotten him through the updated security posts. With that armor, he would have been able to pass through posts without them reading his DNA.

I fired a shot and missed. He answered with a grenade.

"Shit!" I yelled as I turned and shoved my men around a corner. Three seconds passed before the grenade exploded. By the time it finally went off, we had dashed around one corner, then the next, working our way back toward the elevator.

I pushed one of my MPs into the elevator, then forced the second one down to the floor. He must have felt the blood and known what I was doing because he smeared the gore on his chest and face.

I left him there, lying still as a corpse with his gun hidden under his ass.

For me, with my combat reflex in full swing, I might have taken a perverse pleasure lying there, blinded by darkness, knowing an assassin lingered nearby. The MP did not have the benefit of a gland flooding his blood with synthetic courage. Instead, he had nerve.

Marine combat armor had many uses, but it was not designed for stealth. The infiltrator's armored boots clattered on the floor. His body plates clacked softly when they brushed against the walls. Me, I was dressed in a Charlie service uniform. My shoes had hard soles, but they weren't extruded from a compound of plastic and steel.

Time was on my side. The infiltrator could hide if he wanted, but sooner or later an army of MPs would show up. It might take one minute, it might take ten; but once they finished securing the upper corridors, the MPs would arrive. The lights would come on and he would be trapped. He had to know that.

I reached a corner, knelt low to the floor, flashed around the wall for a fleeting look. The two men guarding the psychology lab lay dead on the floor. One was inside the open entrance to the lab. The door slid partway closed, struck his body, then slid back into its recess. A moment later, it repeated the process.

I moved toward that door slowly, my gun ready, my eyes searching for the slightest hint of motion. The way the door chewed on the dead man distracted me. Staying low and searching the hall around me, I darted into the lab and kicked the dead guard out to the corridor.

A moment after I entered the lab, I heard a shot followed seconds later by more shots in rapid succession. Not waiting for the shooting to stop, I hurried back to the elevator. I did not run. I moved ahead slowly, methodically, always expecting a trap.

When I reached the elevator, I saw my MPs sitting on the floor, talking. One held a gun in his hand, the other held the flashlight. They heard me coming, spotted me with their light, then shined it on the heap of combat armor lying dead on the floor.

I went to the dead clone and kicked him hard enough to send his helmet spinning across the floor. I kicked him again. These were dangerous clones, the kind of enemy who plays possum, then shoots you in the back as you walk away. Not this one, though. He was dead.

* * *

The cavalry finally arrived, and only ten minutes too late. At least they figured out how to restore the lights.

With the lights in the hall shining brightly above me, I returned to the psychology lab. Two MPs lay dead in the anterior office, their guns lying lame beside them. They'd tried to cover the door, but they were blind in the dark. At least they'd stayed at their post to the end.

I hesitated a moment and entered the lab. There was the cage, now little more than an empty table. Beside it, toppled to the floor, was the stool Dr. Morman had used as she interviewed her captive patient.

She wasn't by the stool. Her body lay in a bloodstained heap in a corner of the lab. Sua—it must have been Sua—had beaten her to death. Uncontrolled outrage had been built into his psyche. From the angle of her neck and the twists in her body, I got the feeling that simply killing Jennifer Morman had not been enough to quench Sua's fury.

# PART IV

# BETTER THAN WAR

# CHAPTER
# THIRTY-EIGHT

The dynamics of the summit changed on the final day.

Gobi Station Security sent gunships on hourly sweeps of the desert. When they found fifteen Piper Bandits hidden in caves and under tarps, they issued an order to fire on any unidentified vehicles or people seen within a ten-mile radius of the base.

The first speaker of the day was Lieutenant Pearce, the naval engineer who modified Gobi Station security posts so that they would read chromosomes instead of DNA.

"It was easy," he began. "We've had no problems reconfiguring the posts to catch double wise."

Warshaw put up a hand, and asked, "What is a 'double wise'?"

"Double wise, you know, clones with two Y chromosomes. The infiltrators. Now that we know what they are, the guys down in Security call them 'Double Ys.' Fixing the posts to read chromosomes instead of DNA was a snap."

"So the posts can detect them?" Warshaw asked.

"Yes, sir, no problem. We had some up and running yesterday. We would have caught the one who killed that woman, except he was wearing armor. Not much we can do about that."

"I understand that," said Warshaw, his frustration rising to the surface. "I want to know how quickly you can convert the entire fleet over. What equipment do you need to send out so you can fix the posts on our ships?"

"They won't need new equipment, Admiral. They've got everything they need built right in."

Pearce was a clone, of course, and a man in his twenties. He fit the exact demographic for which we would soon be screening. If he'd shaved the sides his head and implanted a couple of wires behind his ear, he could have passed himself off as the late Philip Sua.

"Turns out you can use the posts for MRIs as well," Pearce added.

"You can fix meals with them?" asked an admiral.

"That's MREs, asshole," snapped Warshaw. He massaged his brow and shook his head, looking so miserable I felt sorry for him.

Another admiral, possibly the only honest man in the room, put up a hand and asked, "What is an MRI?"

I knew what an MRI was because I'd read the late Dr. Morman's report. None of the admirals would have bothered with something so mundane as a psychological inventory taken by a forensic psychologist. They commanded fleets, what did they care about psychological profiles and medical reports . . . now that we knew how to catch the infiltrators?

Lieutenant Pearce used more tech-speak than he should have for communicating with admirals. They pretended to listen, but now that they knew the problem could be solved, they didn't really care about the details.

"Magnetic imaging? A resonance scan," Pearce explained. "The clones you're looking for . . . their brains are slightly deformed. It was in the lab report."

According to the late Dr. Jennifer Morman, MRI scanning could be used to detect reduced activity in the limbic areas of the brain. In her final report, she recommended running MRI scans as a secondary method of identifying clones like Sua.

Pearce clearly enjoyed presenting to the admirals. I got the feeling he saw them as dumb, dependent, and ignorant, and he liked talking down to them. He smiled, and said, "There's a side benefit to running MRIs, we'll be able to spot brain tumors as well."

Thinking he was joking, several admirals laughed.

"It really will spot tumors," Pearce said, sounding a bit defensive.

"If you can configure the posts to cut hair, maybe we can use them for barber duty," one of the admirals suggested.

Everybody laughed. The mood in the room had turned jovial, almost euphoric. A few of the admirals stood and applauded Pearce.

Warshaw did not join in the festivity. He sat in his seat, quietly watching. I suspected that he and I shared a common concern. Identifying armed and dangerous enemies would be the easy part, arresting them would be another story.

After Pearce finished his presentation, Warshaw went to the lectern, and said, "You did good work, Harris. You did good." It was a magnanimous statement, but his handing out kudos reemphasized for everyone who was in charge. Warshaw and I might have been peers coming into the summit; but now that he no longer needed me as a decoy target, he would return to the role of supreme commander.

"We still have a problem," I said.

"What's that?" Warshaw asked.

"Combat armor. It's like Pearce says: The clone we caught in the psychology lab got around the posts by wearing combat armor."

"Do you think he knew you were reconfiguring the posts?" Warshaw asked.

That was one of those million-dollar questions. If he knew . . . He would have had to have breached Station Security to have known what we were doing. As I thought about it, I realized he must have breached our security; he knew we had Sua. "He might have," I said. "There's a chance we got him before he reported anything. We should have picked up the signal if he transmitted from here."

Warshaw thought this over, and asked, "So it is your opinion, Harris, that the other infiltrator clones do not know that we can modify our security posts." When I nodded, he said, "Okay, then we're still in business. Order your Marines to turn in their armor."

"Won't that tip our hand if we issue a fleetwide order recalling all combat armor?" asked one of the admirals. It was a fair question. I thought it might.

"What if we said we were going to update their armor with shields? We could say we know how the Unifieds added shielding to their armor," another admiral suggested.

"No one would believe it," Warshaw said.

"We could say we were going to update our interLink hardware so the Unifieds can't pick up our signals," I suggested.

The best lies were the ones that incorporated the truth. Since the Unified Authority designed and manufactured our armor, there was no doubt that they eavesdropped on our conversations.

"I like it," Warshaw said. "Tell them that the latest intel shows that the Unifieds have been listening in on us. We'll say that we have a new circuit that will keep the Unifieds out."

*Co-opting my ideas and pretending like they're his, he really is in charge,* I thought. Maybe it was part of my programming, or maybe it was just conditioned into me as a Marine, but I needed to know who was in charge. Once I knew who was boss, I instinctively stepped in line behind him. I was not made for command, and neither was Warshaw; but he had adapted to it much better than I had.

"We're going to have to root the infiltrators out like weeds," I said, and I told them about Philip Sua and how he hid in a cargo hold pretending to take inventory for sixteen hours.

"One quick cut," Warshaw said. "We do it all at once, one swipe, all the way across the empire. We send out teams to update the posts on every ship and base, then we scan everyone all at the same time. That way, they can't warn their friends."

"What about the planets?" an admiral asked. "What about the men on leave?"

"Maybe we don't get them all," Warshaw agreed, "but we'll get most of them, and the residuals will run for cover. They'll know we are onto them, and they will run."

He was right, of course. Then he said something cold and calculating and true. "All that leaves are their planes. You see someone flying a Piper Bandit, don't even ask them for identification, just blow them out of the sky."

The last time I saw him, Ray Freeman was flying one of those planes.

# CHAPTER
# THIRTY-NINE

Earthdate: November 11, A.D. 2517
Location: St. Augustine
Galactic Position: Orion Arm

We searched the airports, the fields, even the open deserts, and we came up with 6,323 Bandits on St. Augustine. A few of the planes belonged to legitimate civilian pilots, but most were U.A. modified with a tiny broadcast engine, a single-use broadcast battery, and an energy-efficient stealth shield. Considering the odd places in which we located a few of these planes, I suspected we had not yet found all of them.

One Bandit turned up in the parking garage of an abandoned sewage treatment plant. Another was hidden in a cave filled with bats, its wings and windshield buried in guano. The most creative hiding place was a pawnshop for high-ticket items. The local police located that particular plane during an investigation; the man who ran the shop had been murdered.

Some of the planes had been on the planet for weeks. There was no telling what had become of the clones who had piloted them or how much damage they had done.

By the time I arrived on St. Augustine, the Easter egg hunt had ended. I hadn't come looking for planes.

I went to Scrubb's, the restaurant where I had spotted an infiltrator clone my first night on St. Augustine. Having no other means for contacting Freeman, I had suggested this restaurant as a place where we could meet. I told him I would come here every Thursday night.

I spotted Freeman the moment I entered.

He sat at a two-man table, looking as out of place as an

adult at a child's tea party. His knees arched above the top of the table, and his feet poked out the other side. Had he tried to wedge himself into a booth, he would not have fit.

Freeman spotted me but made no move to invite me over. He sat quietly, pretending to look the other way while watching me in his peripheral vision.

Piano music wafted on the air in the bar, weaving its rhythm through soft conversations. The floor was busier than the last time I had come, heavily packed with sailors and Marines in civilian clothing.

"There are a lot of clones in here. Are you sure they're all friendly?" I asked as I sat down.

"One of them wasn't," Freeman said.

"Where'd you leave the corpse?" I asked.

"In a bin out back," Freeman said.

"Was he much of a problem?"

Freeman's gaze floated past me and across the floor. He gave his head the slightest shake. "No. Not much of a problem."

I wondered how he identified the clone; no one had told him about Double Y chromosomes. He probably went by his gut instincts. If I had to choose between chromosome scans and Freeman's gut instinct, I'd go with the latter. I had that much confidence in him.

I wanted to tell Freeman about chromosome scans and how we would soon take care of the infiltrators, but I kept quiet. I only trusted him so far. He was a mercenary. In the end, he was loyal only to himself.

"They're going to invade Olympus Kri," Freeman said. Had anyone else said this, I would not have taken it seriously; but Freeman did not suffer small talk or gossip.

"You're behind on the news," I said. "They're already on the planet. We found a couple of hundred Bandits hidden—"

"I'm not talking about clones," Freeman said.

"When?" I asked, surprised that the Unified Authority would launch a full-scale invasion on an E.M.E. target.

"Five days."

"Are you sure about that?" I asked.

He didn't answer, not so much as a shrug. He just looked at me and gave me the standard penetrating glare, his coal black eyes boring into my head. "They want the Orion Arm back. Sooner or later, they'll come here, too."

"That doesn't sound like Brocius," I said. "We have more ships, more men, and more resources. That puts the odds in our favor, and he never moves unless he has the upper hand."

I'd had plenty of experience with Admiral Alden Brocius. He was a competent officer, but he was also the kind of officer who refuses to play unless he gets house odds.

"Brocius is out. Brocius, NewCastle, Smith, they're all gone. The Linear Committee cleaned house two months ago." The Linear Committee was the executive arm of the Unified Authority government.

Now that was news to bring a smile to my face. I could only come up with one reason for the committee finally giving those bastards the boot—our little rebellion. They were the ones who lit the fuse. They were the ones who came up with the idea of stranding us in nonbroadcasting ships and using us for target practice.

"Have I met any of the new brass?" I asked.

"Hill is still around. He replaced General Smith at the top."

"Nickel Hill?" I asked. General George Nicholas Hill had run the Air Force effort on New Copenhagen during the alien attack. Not the bravest officer in the military, but a bright guy and a man who spoke his mind. He always struck me as fair.

"All the new leaders served on New Copenhagen," Freeman said. "That's the new litmus test. Officers who ducked New Copenhagen get field assignments."

"The Linear Committee only trusts veterans of New Copenhagen . . . I don't suppose that means they want to kiss and make up with the clones who actually won the war?" I asked, feeling bitter indeed. The Linear Committee had sat back and watched as Congress placed the thirty thousand clone veterans of New Copenhagen in concentration camps.

Most of the officers who fought on New Copenhagen kept well away from the front line. Us clones . . . we were the front line. They gave the orders, we paid the price. The normal ratio of enlisted men to officers was six to one, but the ratio on New Copenhagen was fifteen to one. The survival rate among clones sent to New Copenhagen was one in seventeen. Out of every seventeen clones sent to fight, sixteen ended up dead. The officer corps had it better. Out of every one hundred officers on New Copenhagen, eighteen were killed, and eighty-two returned home to a hero's welcome.

A waitress stopped at our table, and I ordered a beer. She looked at Freeman's drink and said nothing to him. Like that infiltrator I'd spotted, Freeman used his drink for camouflage, not that a seven-foot man can hide behind a single glass of beer. Every person in the bar was aware of Freeman. He was tall, he was dark, and even when he smiled, he was menacing.

"Hill isn't stupid," I said. "He's got to know we have ten times more ships than he does. Even if he takes Olympus Kri, we'll just take it right back again."

"You have a hundred times more ships," Freeman said. "Their self-broadcasting fleet took a real hit on Terraneau."

"I knew they lost ships," I said.

"A lot of ships. They had to decommission half the ships that returned home," Freeman said.

We'd lost a lot of ships, too; but we could better afford to lose them. "If that's true, it only makes an attack on Olympus Kri more ridiculous. That doesn't sound like Hill."

When Freeman did not answer, I asked, "What aren't you telling me? There is something you aren't telling me."

He shook his head.

"Why should I trust you?"

He didn't answer. Instead, he changed the subject. "Have you figured out why the Pentagon sent out those clones?"

"The Double Ys," I said, hoping the name would irritate Freeman. He had no patience for clever nicknames.

"Is that what you call them?" he asked, obviously unperturbed.

"I don't know if you heard about their chromosomes, they have an X and two Ys. Apparently that makes them more dangerous. Sending out saboteurs isn't going to sink our fleet."

Freeman sat still and placid, but his eyes burned holes in my head as he said, "You still don't get it. Hill doesn't want to sink your fleet; he wants to take it back whole.

"You're looking for war while he's slipping you rat poison.

He figures if he kills off enough of your officers, your enlisted clones will just hand the ships over. He doesn't care about clones. It's the ships he's after."

"Then he's out of luck," I said. "We've pretty much cracked our infestation problems."

"They're tracking your movements, too," Freeman said.

"Right, the satellites. You were the one who clued us in about them, remember?" I felt frustrated. This was Ray Freeman, nothing ever slipped his mind, yet here he was, telling me things he had already told me. The pieces did not fit.

"So if it comes to a fight, are you taking sides?" I asked.

"We're talking," Freeman said.

"Are you looking for work?" I asked. "If you have an angle on Olympus Kri, name your price."

Freeman did not answer right away.

I downed my beer and signaled to the waitress for another one. She brought it over.

I watched him closely. Freeman wasn't in this for the money; he'd made over a billion dollars on New Copenhagen. "What are you looking for?"

"We're all after the same thing."

"Yeah, and what's that?" I asked, not even bothering to hide my irritation. He wasn't being straight with me, and I was tired of it.

"Survival," he said. As he said the word, his fingers tightened around his unfinished beer.

# FORTY

I called Warshaw to give him the news.

"The Unified Authority is planning to attack Olympus Kri," I said. A simple announcement that I hoped would start the gears of war turning.

"Tell me something I don't know," Warshaw said. "If they ever get around to picking a fight, that's where they're going to start it. Everyone knows that."

"In five days," I said.

"Five days?"

"The attack is coming in five days?"

"No shit? Who's your source?" He wasn't taking me seriously, but I had his attention.

"Ray Freeman, the same guy who warned us about the satellites," I said. Warshaw had never met Freeman, but he'd certainly heard tales about the man.

"Wasn't he the bastard who shot you on Terraneau?"

"And told us the U.A. was about to attack," I pointed out.

"But he was working for them," Warshaw countered. "He was delivering a message for Admiral Brocius. What if he's still working for them?"

"He says he isn't."

"You believe him?"

"I don't know," I admitted.

"He sounds like a real saint, Harris."

"He was right about the satellites," I said.

"Maybe he was right. We still haven't found one. It makes sense that they're spying on us, but that doesn't make it true.

"U.A. spy satellites and God . . . you can't prove either exists, but your questions are answered the moment you accept they're out there."

Warshaw had no interest in taking a leap of faith based on

Freeman's word, and I didn't blame him. The Unified Authority had apparently stopped sending cruisers into our territory, and there was no way we would find those satellites without U.A. cruisers leading us to them.

"I've never met this friend of yours. Do you think he knows what he's talking about?"

"He always knows what he's talking about. That's not the problem. It's not a question of confidence, it's a question of trust. Freeman's out for himself. Even when he picks a side, he's still out for himself. He keeps his cards hidden and plays his angles tight. So far, he hasn't even told me why he's helping us."

"So why trust him?"

"History," I said. "Until now, he and I always ended up on the same side. He makes a damn good ally."

"Harris, that doesn't even sound like you. You're a brute. You're a specking Liberator clone. If he's not telling you what you want, catch the bastard and beat it out of him?"

I laughed. I could not stop myself. "Beat information out of Ray Freeman?" Killing him might not be too much of a problem, not with satellite surveillance and high-altitude air strikes; but trying to interrogate the son of a bitch would be like trying to tackle a bull elephant.

"If you think he's a spy . . ."

"Not a spy," I said. The man stood seven feet tall. He was an "African-American," living in a time when races had been abolished. He was a purebred living among synthetics and mutts. Stealth was not among his long suits. Brutal strength, patience, and cunning intelligence were. He was a mercenary and an assassin, not a spy.

I felt tired. It had been a long day. I wished I could do something about the buzzing in my head, and sleep seemed like the best solution.

Planets had time zones, but outer space did not. The Space Travel Clock (officially Coordinated Universal Time) coincided with a zone that used to be known as Greenwich Mean Time on Earth. To avoid confusion, the Unified Authority had set up an arbitrarily selected twenty-four-hour clock for an endless void with an infinite number of suns but neither sundown nor sunup. St. Augustine, which had a faster rotation than Earth, had twenty-two-hour days. Warshaw and I spoke at the same time every night by his clock, but each of our meetings kept getting later and later by mine.

"It sounds like a trap," Warshaw said.

"Maybe, but we'd still better get more ships out there," I said. "I don't see that we have any other choice."

"What about the Double Ys?" he asked.

"We take care of them first. We can close that chapter today if we need to. All the pieces are in place." Before leaving for St. Augustine, I had put Hollingsworth in charge of the project. Reconfigured posts were set up on every ship and in every fort. We could recall the armor in the morning and spring our trap in the afternoon.

"Hollingsworth says everything is ready. All he has to do is pull the trigger." Warshaw knew Hollingsworth, they'd served on the same ship.

"Then pull the trigger," he said. "The sooner we close that door, the better."

"That still leaves Olympus Kri," I said. This conversation was not going as I had hoped.

"I'm not sending more ships," Warshaw said.

"What if the Unifieds have figured out a way to knock out our broadcast stations?" I asked.

"Not very likely," Warshaw said, but he didn't sound confident. Without a broadcast network lacing it together, the Enlisted Man's Empire would come apart.

"Probably not," I agreed. "I'm just thinking out loud."

But my comment had the desired effect. Still nervous, Warshaw said, "I could send a few more ships . . . just in case."

"I'm going to take the *ad-Din* out there," I said. "I want to get as many Marines on the ground there as possible."

# FORTY-ONE

We were coming down to zero hour for the infiltrators. Hollingsworth began the day by sending out a fleetwide order recalling all combat armor. Until we sent out new orders, any man caught in armor would be detained, questioned, and ultimately have his chromosomes scanned.

With the cogs quickly falling in place, Freeman and I met at Fort Greeley, the local Marine base, for breakfast. Wanting to stay alert, I ate light that morning, a boiled egg, a cup of coffee, and toast. Freeman ate relatively light as well, four eggs, a whole damn pig's worth of bacon, two cups of juice, no coffee, no toast.

"How did you get to St. Augustine?" I asked.

"I flew here," he said.

"Another one-way ticket?" He could not have flown in on a stolen Bandit; the broadcast computers on those ships were set for Earth.

He shook his head. "I caught a ride in your broadcast network."

Ships with onboard broadcast equipment blew up when they entered our network. If Freeman was telling the truth, he would have had to have come from one of our planets. I had a good idea which one it was.

"How is the weather in Odessa?" I asked. Odessa was the capital city of Olympus Kri.

Freeman favored me with a half smile, and said, "It depends how you feel about rain."

"It beats the hell out of living in a desert," I countered. I thought about the summer I'd spent in that concentration camp in the Texas badlands.

"I thought you liked the sun," Freeman said.

I liked St. Augustine, with its coastal cities and languid

days. I liked waking up to tropical mornings and going to sleep on balmy nights. I had no trouble forgetting time and seasons in places like this. Before the Avatari invasion, I'd spent a year living like a civilian in the Hawaiian Islands on Earth.

"Does Olympus Kri have the same seasons as Earth?" I asked.

"More or less," Freeman said. "It rains hard in Odessa during the winter."

I looked at the calendar on the wall and saw that the Earth-date was November 12.

In the time we were talking, Freeman methodically cleared his tray, occasionally gulping down an egg in a single bite.

"I'm not sure I can get any more ships to Olympus Kri," I said. "Warshaw wants proof."

Freeman nodded, and said, "Tell him to get used to having twenty-two planets in his empire."

"We have a fleet circling the planet. We'll outnumber them. Even if they send everything they have, we'll still outnumber them."

"You have sixty-eight ships in the area," Freeman said.

"You know the size of our fleet?"

Freeman said nothing.

Sixty-eight ships, that was just a small fraction of what we'd had at Terraneau when the Unifieds came knocking. The Unified Authority attacked Terraneau with eighty-five ships and sent the four-hundred-ship Scutum-Crux Fleet running for cover.

"And you do not think that's enough to protect the planet?" I asked.

Freeman did not speculate. When he knew the answers, he gave them; but he was not one for guessing.

"Have they figured out a way to attack our broadcast stations?" I asked.

Freeman downed a large glass of juice. "I haven't heard anything either way," he said. His low voice gave the words a rumbling timbre. His father had been a minister. Had he followed in his father's shoes, Ray Freeman would have been one of those preachers who seemed to call down the heavens when they speak.

"Once the attack begins, we can call in a thousand ships if we need them," I said.

Freeman said nothing.

I wondered what card he was hiding.

"I'm taking the *ad-Din* to Olympus Kri. If you want a ride back, I can take you," I offered.

"I have a ship," he said.

"What are you hiding, Ray?" I asked.

He did not answer.

At 11:00 STC (Space Travel Clock), Captain Villanueva held a shipwide briefing; attendance was mandatory. I personally prescreened two hundred Marines to run the security posts and patrol the corridors during the briefing. Villanueva screened a team of officers to man the bridge and Engineering.

On the *Salah ad-Din*, Marines and sailors did not commingle, not even for an all-hands briefing. The leathernecks attended a broadcast on the bottom deck, in the Marine complex. Sailors attended their briefing in a huge auditorium on the third deck.

I watched the scene outside the third-deck auditorium from an overlook as men lined up in crooked queues and waited to file through the doors. The talk was loud and came in indecipherable waves. I could not focus on a single conversation, there were too many going on at once, and I could not untangle the chatter of four thousand simultaneous discussions.

The MPs stood out with their helmets, armbands, and batons. At this stage, they would make no arrests. They had one standing order: "Everyone has to enter the auditorium through the security posts, no exceptions. Anyone discovered to have the Double Y chromosome will be quietly pulled aside."

We had recalibrated posts on the inside of the auditorium doors. Prescreened MPs manned the computers. An army of MPs monitored the lines. If anyone tried to slip away, he was escorted back to his place.

Immediately below me, a sailor broke ranks, and four MPs descended upon him. They formed a circle, blocking his way. I tried to listen to what was said but could not hear a word of it.

Looking almost straight down on the scene, I could not see

faces or expressions. Two of the MPs brandished their sticks, one of them slapping the end of it into his palm in a way that suggested he would gladly hit the sailor. The conversation went on for several seconds. When the sailor did not turn back, one of the MPs reached out and grabbed his shoulder. The man jerked free, then turned and returned to his place in line, unescorted.

Maybe he had argued that he needed to go to the head. Maybe the MPs had convinced him that he would not find his equipment in working order if he did.

As the sailor approached the door to the auditorium, he made a few furtive glances over his shoulder; but the MPs were right behind him. They remained in place, watching him as he stepped through the door.

A fight broke out in another line. A man grabbed the sailor in front of him and threw him to the floor. Three MPs ran to break up the fight, pushing gawking sailors out of their way and stepping between the downed man and his assailant.

They moved like cattle, these sailors did. They took slogging steps. They formed fuzzy lines that snaked down the hall. They moved slowly, more interested in talking and searching the crowd for friends than getting where they were going.

The sailor who had started the fight took a menacing step toward one of my MPs as he arrived on the scene. The MP drew his baton, but that seemed to mean nothing. The sailor took another step. When one MP tried to club him, the man caught his wrist and stopped the blow.

The other two MPs stepped in to help. One of them hit the man in the ribs, causing him to wince and cover the wound. Pressing his elbow over his battered ribs, the errant sailor returned to his spot in line. He might have been tough, but I did not think he was a Double Y.

Watching the drama closely, I almost missed the man at the end of the hall as he stole into the shadows with the grace of a phantom.

I shouted for help, but no one could hear me over all of the noise. Using the security Link built into my collar, I called for backup, then I charged after our rabbit. I dashed along the corridor, running in the same direction as the phantom, but one floor up. I could not see him; if he turned right or left, I would not know, and I would lose him.

Sprinting, swinging wide around a corner, I dashed down a set of stairs. I leaped the first flight, my arms pinwheeling as I flew through the air, and I crashed on the deck and into the wall, turned, and leaped the second flight.

"Where are you?" I yelled over the Link when I did not see MPs coming my way.

"They're on their way. These halls are packed."

"Get them here quickly," I shouted.

The short sprint did not wind me, but my legs took a jolt as I came down the stairs. Behind me, I heard the cloud of conversations coming from outside the auditorium. I was at a T-junction. The corridors were empty to the right and to the left. I turned right, then changed my mind, and sprinted left.

The halls of the *ad-Din* were a labyrinth, with offshoots and avenues and hatches. Without seeing which way my rabbit had run, I had no prayer of finding him. And then I heard three shots. I ran back in the direction from which I had just come and spotted the blood on the wall and the two dead Marines. One sat with his back against the wall like a man taking a rest; the hole in his chest was large enough for me to fit my fist into it. The other man lay on the floor with his arms stretched before them.

So much for my backup. I radioed in for more reinforcements.

I was only a few seconds behind the clone. Now I could hear him running. It was the only sound in the hall.

If I could hear him, then he could hear me. He must have known I called in for help. Now in full pursuit, I ran around a corner, spotted the gun, and stepped back behind the wall in time to make him miss. He fired one shot, then silence. Hoping he was not waiting to ambush me, I jumped forward, dropped to my knees, and returned fire.

He was already gone.

My combat reflex began. I ran faster now, and the world seemed to slow down around me. I could hear the clone running and knew I would catch him. I sprinted down one hall, took a right turn, and spotted him. He spun, fired, missed by more than a yard, and took off running. I did not return fire.

He'd fired at least five shots. I suspected he took the gun from one of the dead MPs, meaning he had a clip that carried thirty rounds, with at least five spent.

He took a right turn into a long, narrow passage where he didn't dare turn to shoot because there was nowhere to duck for cover. I was right behind him, my gun out. In the time it would take him to stop, spin, and aim, he knew I could cap him.

He was forty feet ahead of me, and I was gaining on him. My legs were longer. Another moment, and he was thirty-five feet ahead of me, then thirty, then twenty-five, my footsteps drowning out the sound of his. He was one of those full-body runners, every inch of him swinging with every step. His elbows cut through the air like pistons.

His steps slowed, his stride shortened, and he glided, then coasted, then stopped. He held his hands in the air, the muzzle of his pistol pointing to the ceiling, and he slowly turned to face me.

"Drop it," I said.

He hesitated for just a moment, undoubtedly calculating the odds in his head, and the pistol fell from his hand. Without my giving the order, he stepped on the gun and slid it toward me.

The hallway was no more than ten feet wide, but it extended for hundreds of feet behind and before us. We stood there staring at each other, both of us panting from the long sprint. We were not alone for long. Two MPs came dashing around the corner about one hundred feet ahead of us, their pistols drawn.

I wanted to kill this rabbit. I wanted him to scream and wave his arms in the air like a madman on fire, then rush me. If he did, I might have shot him, or I just might have thrown my gun away and beaten him to death. I thought about Dr. Morman lying dead, a quirky woman with a dark obsession who meant harm to no one.

"Are you going to shoot me?" the rabbit asked, his eyes not on me but on my gun.

*Few things would give me more pleasure,* I thought. I said, "No. You're missing a mandatory briefing. We're going to escort you back to the auditorium."

I didn't even cuff the bastard. Of course, I hoped he would

run or put up a fight. He didn't. And when he passed through the posts and the computer identified him as a Double Y, we cuffed him. He lowered his head and said nothing as we led him to the brig.

We captured seven infiltrator clones on the *ad-Din*. We caught seventeen thousand Double Y clones in our net as we swept every ship and base. Next, we had to decide what to do with them.

<br>

## CHAPTER
# FORTY-TWO

Warshaw held an emergency convocation on the *Kame-hameha* to discuss plans for disposing of the Double Y clones. This was a meeting for fleet commanders and fleet commanders only—attendance mandatory. Much to Winston Cabot's displeasure, attendees checked their entourages at the door.

Warshaw held the meeting in a conference room on the fleet deck. He was still in the Perseus Arm, still circling Gobi, but he no longer feared for his life. He still had MPs manning posts around the ship, but guards no longer stood inside and outside his office door.

He began the meeting by saying, "From what I hear, we have seventeen thousand prisoners of war. How the speck did the Unified Authority manufacture seventeen thousand new clones in under a year? I thought the Mogats destroyed all the old orphanages."

I had an idea of where they might have come from. Toward the end of the Mogat War, an enterprising admiral created his own private clone farm for making SEALs. It was secret and small, which was why the Mogats missed it. Small as it was, that clone factory might have been able to mass-produce seventeen thousand clones in a few short months if its assembly line was on overdrive.

I kept my mouth shut though.

"Ah well, at least we tagged 'em and bagged 'em," Warshaw said. And then he banged me with a stealth attack. He said, "Any of you ever worked with Philo Hollingsworth before? He ran the tagging operation . . . did a pretty good job."

None of the other officers seemed to know Hollingsworth. Hearing this, Warshaw said, "I served with him in Scrotum-Crotch for a few years. Smart guy."

*Message received,* I thought to myself. *Message received.*

The operation, of course, had been mine. I planned it, I directed it. By giving all of the credit to Hollingsworth, Warshaw played down my involvement and consequently my value to the empire, the bastard.

"So what do we do with our prisoners?" Warshaw asked.

Several admirals made nebulous suggestions, broaching the subject of executing the Double Y clones but never quite coming right out and saying it. One admiral said, "They're too dangerous to keep in prison."

Everyone agreed.

"So what do we do with them?" Warshaw repeated.

No one spoke. The answer loomed in the air like a ghost, like an intangible presence that anyone could see but no one wanted to acknowledge. I had the feeling that Warshaw had come to the same conclusion as all of his men but wanted someone else to say it first.

Admiral Nelson of the Orion Inner Fleet took the bait. "We should dump the bastards in deep space," Nelson said. It made sense that he would speak up. Of all the officers in this meeting, he was the one living closest to the front line.

"Kill them?" Warshaw asked, as if the idea had not occurred to him.

"We wouldn't be *killing* them; we would be *executing* them," Nelson said. "They're spies. They were caught wearing our uniforms."

That was not exactly right. Since designing new uniforms had never been a priority, we were still wearing the uniforms that the Unified Authority had provided us. No one felt like arguing the point. I sure as hell did not. Now that we had them behind bars, I felt a certain sympathy for the Double Ys. I didn't like the idea of exterminating the pathetic bastards, but I sure as shooting would not let them go free, either.

Admiral Adrian Tunney, commander of the Orion Central Fleet, bawled out, "Speck! Why are we even having this discussion? Those bastards aren't human; they're deformed clones. They're synthetics gone wrong."

I always considered Warshaw a deformed clone, but I kept that opinion to myself.

"Deformed clones," Warshaw repeated. To his credit, he treated the comment with contempt. "Why don't we eliminate all the synthetics?" he asked. "That way I won't have to hear so many stupid comments during my staff meetings."

Almost every officer in the room laughed, but they sounded nervous. Each man at the table incorrectly believed that the joke was about everyone but himself. Unlike the other officers, I had no delusions.

Warshaw roused me from my contemplations by asking, "Harris, you helped us catch them. What do you think the Unified Authority hoped to accomplish with those clones?"

Now there was a question for the ages. "I have no idea," I admitted. I kept thinking about what Freeman had told me, that the Unified Authority wanted to kill off our officers so it could take control of our ships. The idea sounded too simplistic to me.

"You have no idea," Warshaw repeated, his frustration showing. "That's it? Not even a theory?"

"You want a theory?" I asked. I wanted to tell him that "Marines don't speculate." I wanted to tell him that the Unifieds probably told the Double Ys to kill every officer whose brains were bigger than his balls, and that after Franks and Thorne, the killer clones ran out of targets. "Here's a theory," I said. "Maybe the Unified Authority wants its ships back."

"And they don't have the brass to come after us in a fight," Warshaw said. Clearly he liked that line of thought. It stroked his ego. He saw himself as the hero of Terraneau. If the Unified Authority was scared, that meant they were scared of him. Maybe he deserved the credit, too. He'd come up with the idea of using the broadcast stations to create a new network.

Warshaw nodded, and asked, "So they kill off the officers,

and anyone left is so scared they just hand over command of our ships? Is that what you're saying?"

"Something like that," I said. "It's just a possibility." Most clones lacked the initiative to take over once the officers went down.

We had found a solution to the Double Y problem before we fully understood its significance. Interrogating the Double Ys didn't help, the pathetic bastards did not even know as much as we did.

Freeman understood what was going on, though. I would ask him again.

"What are we going to do about Olympus Kri?" I asked.

Warshaw must not have told the other admirals about Freeman's warning. I heard confusion in their whispering.

There was a moment of silence in which Warshaw sat glaring at me, clenching his right fist, then letting it relax, making his forearm and biceps bulge. If he had not mentioned this bit of intelligence to anyone, it was because he did not take it seriously. He probably hoped it would just go away. Now I had thrown it back in his face in front of his admirals.

By way of explanation, Warshaw said, "Harris believes the Unifieds are going to attack Olympus Kri."

"That's a pretty safe bet," said Admiral Nelson. Of all of the admirals, he had the biggest stake in the matter. As the commander of the Orion Inner Fleet, protecting Olympus Kri was his responsibility.

"He says they're going to attack early next week," Warshaw said.

"How solid is your information?" asked Admiral Nelson.

"Pretty solid," I said, not offering any details. Had any of them asked me that question a week ago, I would have vouched for Freeman without question. Now, though, I had reservations.

"How many ships do we have patrolling the planet?" Warshaw asked.

"Sixty-eight," I said.

All heads turned to stare at me. That was not the kind of information admirals expected to hear from a Marine.

Nelson looked at his pocket computer and confirmed my number.

"How did you know that?" Warshaw asked.

"From the same source that told me the Unifieds were on their way," I said.

"Maybe your man isn't blowing steam after all," Warshaw said. "What do you think we should do?"

"We need to send more ships to the area and land more Marines on the ground," I said. I kept one recommendation to myself—that we needed to pray Freeman was really on our side.

## CHAPTER
# FORTY-THREE

Philo Hollingsworth met me as I arrived back on the *ad-Din* to tell me about his promotion. He waited for me in the landing bay and waylaid me as I came off my transport.

"Has Admiral Warshaw contacted you?" he asked. He gave me a proper salute. I did not yet know why he had come, but I could tell he was uncomfortable by the way he approached me. I half expected him to inform me that I had been relieved of command.

"I was just in a meeting with Warshaw," I said. The staff meeting had ended a couple of hours ago. While the other officers rushed back to their ships, I went down to the officers' mess and ate a leisurely meal.

Hollingsworth bobbed his head in agreement a bit too quickly, his eyes never quite meeting mine. Whatever news he had, he knew I would not like it, and he seemed almost apologetic. "Warshaw gave me a promotion," he said.

He'd been a full-bird colonel; the next step up was general and the promotion was well deserved. Hollingsworth and I did not get on all that well, but he was a good Marine.

"You got your star," I said, putting out my hand to shake his. "It's about specking time."

"Three stars, sir. He promoted me to major general."

I had no doubt Warshaw had made that promotion to send me another message, and he'd been none too subtle. The promotion put Hollingsworth and me in the same pay grade.

"Congratulations," I said, though I already had a premonition that his rise in the ranks signaled my fall.

I wished him luck. Hollingsworth suffered from the same character flaw that got in my way as an officer. He had the temperament of a combat Marine, not a fleet officer. Infighting and backroom deals did not appeal to him.

"When are you shipping out?" I asked.

"I'm not shipping out; my orders are to remain on the *ad-Din*," he said.

That sealed the deal, I was on my way out. Warshaw might leave me marooned on Olympus Kri, or he might send me back to Terraneau. One thing was certain, the *ad-Din* did not have enough room for two three-star generals. Hell, there wasn't enough room for two three-stars in the entire Enlisted Man's Marines.

For now, I still had the upper hand. I'd held the rank longer. Trying to sound unconcerned, I said, "The last update I received, we were heading for Olympus Kri. Is that still the case?"

"Yes, sir," Hollingsworth said. "I wanted to speak with you about that."

I nodded and started toward the exit. Hollingsworth fell into step.

"Admiral Warshaw says you think the Unifieds are going to attack."

"I do," I said.

"We have a half million troops stationed on Olympus Kri," Hollingsworth said.

"I did not know that," I said, wondering why Freeman had neglected to mention it.

"Yes, sir." Now that we were on equal footing, Hollingsworth seemed more anxious to get along.

"That's a lot of men," I said.

"I gave them orders to look for sonic cannons . . . in case the Unifieds attack."

I had to think about that for a moment. Finally, I flashed

back to Lieutenant Mars's findings on Terraneau. "In case they have shielded armor," I said. I vaguely remembered the conversation, as if it had happened years earlier instead of weeks.

"It was your idea," he said.

I smiled and answered, "Yes, and if it doesn't work, we can always try to get them to chase us into an underground garage."

There were always wild cards in battle. If a sniper targeted you from two miles away, for instance, you would never know what hit you until God gave you the details. Even factoring land mines, snipers, and atom bombs, I always felt that as a combat Marine I had more control of my fate than sailors had of theirs.

When the shooting started, I could attack or run for cover. If I stayed alert, I would probably survive. Sailors, on the other hand, lived and died with their ships. Speed and reflexes cannot save a man when his ship explodes around him. Maybe it was a phobia; but I felt helpless riding into a combat zone on the *Salah ad-Din*.

Most of my Marines shared that phobia. The twenty-two hundred Marines on the *ad-Din* had survived the land battles of Terraneau, then seen what happened to the men on the ships. Walking around the Marine complex, I felt the tension. Fuses burned quickly. Tempers ran short. Stumble into another man, and he might curse at you. Step on another man's toe, and a fistfight would likely follow.

Olympus Kri was not an especially large planet. With the *Salah ad-Din* and two more carriers transferring in, the space around it became even tighter. Admiral Nelson had his ships arrayed in perfect order. His sixty-eight ships patrolled well-defined routes. Battleships and carriers patrolled larger zones. Frigates and cruisers stirred in smaller circles. The blockade formed a nearly perfect net.

Nelson was that rare officer who comes off cocky, smart, and competent. I did not appreciate the logic of his tactics until Captain Villanueva explained the blockade.

"I don't see any holes. How about you?" I asked.

Villanueva looked at the displays, and said, "Here. This

one is probably the biggest." He pointed to a spot near the top of the planet, circumscribing the vulnerable area with his finger.

"Think you could squeeze a ship through there unnoticed?" I asked.

"Not a big ship," said Villanueva. "Maybe a frigate. I could slip a whole squadron of Piper Bandits through that hole unnoticed if they were cloaked."

"So he did a good job blockading the planet?" I asked.

"Textbook," Villanueva said.

"If the Unifieds attack, do you think we'll be able to fight them off?" I asked.

"Depends what they send."

I nodded, taking a certain satisfaction from the feeling of being prepared.

"How about your Marines?" Villanueva asked. "Can you hold out if you need to?"

"It depends what they send," I said.

Villanueva laughed.

The Olympus Kri broadcast station floated 230,000 miles above the planet. We kept the blockade well clear of the station. The last thing we needed was for our patrolling ships to stumble into a broadcast zone and end up in the Cygnus Arm.

"What if they go after the broadcast station?" I asked.

"He has two carriers and three battleships watching it," Villanueva said.

"Is that enough to keep it safe?" I asked.

He gave me a wicked smiled. I interrupted him before he could answer. "I know, it depends on what they—"

"Ain't that the truth?" Villanueva said. "The way Nelson has his blockade set up, he can shift fifteen ships to any spot at any time. It's a thing of beauty.

"See these ships over here? They can shift over to the broadcast station in under a minute." He pointed to a battleship, three dreadnaughts, and a couple of cruisers. "I never liked Nelson, but the bastard knows his tactics."

We had all the pieces in place, but I still worried. If Freeman knew how many ships we had patrolling the area, who else knew? What other secrets did Freeman know? I wanted to trust Freeman. I wanted to think of him as a friend; but Ray Freeman did not have friends.

"You look worried," Villanueva said.

"I am," I admitted.

"The blockade is solid," he said, no doubt trying to re-assure me.

Thinking there must be a flaw, I took another look at the plans. I saw nothing. We still had time to make changes. If Freeman had his facts right, the Unifieds would come in another day and a half.

The plan was for me to meet Freeman on Olympus Kri. I went to my billet, packed a small knife and a fléchette-firing pistol, and left for the landing bay. Sergeant Nobles met me at the door and told me he had requisitioned a new ship for me. He smiled like a boy with a new bicycle as he said this. He rubbed his hands together, and he had more spring in his step.

We entered the bay, and there it sat.

"A shuttle?" I asked. "Where the hell did you find a specking shuttle?"

Compared to the boxy transports around it, the shuttle looked sleek and modern. Transports had tiny wings that looked more like stubs. Shuttles had broad graceful wings.

"All of the admirals have them," Nobles said. "I put in a requisition while you were at the summit."

We entered the shuttle. It had a living-room-like main cabin, which included couches, chairs, and a wet bar. Aft, there would be a small office complete with sleeping accommodations.

"You bucking for a promotion, Sergeant?" I asked.

"No, sir," he said. The man was always so damn cheerful.

"Well, that's too bad," I said. "Anyone who can pull off a coup like this belongs in the officers' corps."

He did not know if I was joking and looked at me, hoping to find a sign one way or the other. "I'll put in your paperwork when this business is over, Lieutenant."

"Are you serious about that, sir?" he asked.

"Just don't start angling for captain, or we're going to have a problem," I said. "I hate wasting a perfectly good enlisted man by giving him bars."

So the always cheerful Christian Nobles made his way to the cockpit a happy new officer. I sat in the cabin, still troubled. As we taxied through the atmospheric locks, I looked around my luxurious new digs. This bird was made for officers with entourages, Cabot would have felt at home.

I did not even notice when we took off, we moved so smoothly. Our entry into the atmosphere went the same way. Military transports entered most atmospheres like a hammer battering a nail. They rumbled and they shook, their fuselages audibly rattling as they pounded their way in from space. Not this shuttle. It sliced into the pocket like a sharpened scalpel cutting through skin.

I pivoted my armchair so that I could look out a window. It was nighttime on this side of Olympus Kri, the clouds below us were so thick that they blocked out the city lights below as we flew through. For a moment, the world outside my windows was all mist and cotton, then sheets of water streaked the glass, and I saw Odessa below me, a million million tiny amber-colored lights forming patterns that arranged themselves into streets and neighborhoods and tall buildings and riverside docks.

Odessa, capital of Olympus Kri, had survived the Avatari invasion pretty much intact. During the darkest days of the war, with the aliens closing in on Earth, the Unified Authority all but ceded Olympus Kri to the aliens. Without an army to defend it, the planet fell quickly; and because no one put up much of a fight, the Avatari ignored the people. They dug their mine, filled it with gas, and moved on to New Copenhagen.

"We're coming in for a landing, sir," Nobles radioed from the cockpit.

Looking out of the rain-coated window, I saw the sprawling lights of the spaceport. Runways stretched more than a mile in five different directions, their blue lights forming a pentagonal constellation.

We touched down smoothly, then taxied toward the multifaceted glass castle that served as Odessa's air terminal. Once we stopped taxiing, the shuttle's pneumatic struts compacted until the fuselage was only a few inches from the ground.

A car waited for me on the runway. I trotted the few feet to the car and was surprised to see who waited inside.

"Admiral Cabot," I said. "Aren't you supposed to be on St. Augustine?"

"Not much left for me to do over there," he said.

The clouds were so thick that I could not see stars in the sky. The rain fluctuated somewhere between drizzle and mist, forming a film on my skin and uniform.

I patted beads of water off my shoulders and stepped into the car.

"How did you know where to find me?" I asked.

"Colonel Hollingsworth sent me your itinerary, sir," Cabot said.

"General Hollingsworth," I said.

"Warshaw made him a general?" Cabot said.

I nodded, not sure if I should tell him how many stars came with the promotion. I changed the subject. "I'm here looking for a civilian named Ray Freeman. Heard of him?"

"He's waiting for you at Camp Marshall." Camp Marshall was the largest military base in Odessa. It had been an Army base; but, the Enlisted Man's Empire did not have an Army, so it now housed Marines.

"Are you sure he's there?" I asked.

"He's a hard man to miss," Cabot said.

I watched the surroundings out the window as we drove through the city. We crossed a suspension bridge, and I saw a shoreline bustling with life. Rows of skyscrapers lined the freeway like the cliffs along a river canyon. "I have not seen a city like this for a while," I said.

"Yes, sir. It's like the war never came here," Cabot agreed.

*You can only dodge bullets for so long,* I thought. These people might have ducked the Avatari; but the Unifieds would make up for it. The next war would begin in a day and a half.

# FORTY-FOUR

"Evacuate the planet?" I asked. The suggestion was ridiculous. It didn't matter what the Unified Authority had up its sleeve, evacuation was out of the question. "I have five hundred thousand men here."

"I'm not just talking about your men, I mean the civilian population," Freeman said. He sat unflinching, his eyes narrowed in on mine.

"That isn't going to happen," I said. Then I thought about what he had just said. "The Unifieds aren't going after civilians."

We sat alone in the camp commander's office. The pictures on the walls were placed there for soldiers, not Marines. They showed scenes with tanks and gunships and fighting men wearing fatigues. The clock showed 22:13.

"You are talking about millions of people. I couldn't evacuate them if I wanted to. I don't have enough ships."

"You're going to need more," Freeman agreed.

"You wouldn't happen to have a few lying around that you could loan me?" I asked with so much sarcasm that even Freeman could not ignore it.

"I have twenty-five of them," he said. "They carry a quarter of a million passengers apiece."

That gave me pause. I would have accused him of joking, but Freeman never joked. He was more likely to build twenty-five gargantuan ships than tell a joke.

"Bullshit! Nothing but a planet can carry a quarter of a million people," I muttered, though I already knew that the ships must exist.

"They're barges," Freeman said.

"Where the speck did you find something like that?" I asked; but as soon as I asked, I realized the only possible answer. I shelved that information away, Freeman was on the verge of showing me his hidden cards. Taking a deep breath, I asked, "Ray, why do we need to evacuate?"

Always enigmatic, Freeman did not answer. He studied me for a moment, his expression impassive, then he reached into his pocket and pulled out a small device that looked like a notepad with a screen. Whatever it was, it looked tiny in Freeman's gigantic right hand.

He placed it flat on the table.

The two-way communicator was six inches long, less than three inches wide, and flat as a shingle. The edges of the communicator were shiny black plastic. The screen that filled the frame was already lit. A face I recognized stared up from it.

"Good morning, Harris," said the familiar gravelly voice.

"Good morning," I said, wondering if somewhere along the line, I had lost my mind.

"We hear you've been promoted to general. Congratulations."

"Thank you," I said, staring at the screen and trying to figure out its magic. Few people had earned my respect as thoroughly as Dr. William Sweetwater. He died more bravely than any man I knew.

## CHAPTER
# FORTY-FIVE

William Sweetwater died on New Copenhagen. He led the team of scientists that unraveled the aliens' technology. He was a brilliant, fearless dwarf who always referred to himself in the royal plural.

I started to ask Freeman if this was some sort of a prank, but he put up a hand to stop me. He had pointed the communicator toward me, so that the pin-sized camera mounted under the screen would not catch his movements, then he put up a finger across his lips.

On the screen, Sweetwater continued chatting amiably. He watched me with eyes that I had seen burned by toxic air. He spoke with lips I had seen blister so badly they burst. In this new incarnation, the little man was once again whole.

The diminutive scientist chattered on. "We hear you've been busy resurrecting planets, Harris."

I almost spoke up when I heard his use of the word "resurrected." He looked real enough, but any schoolkid could scan a photograph into a computer and convert it into a three-dimensional animation. Making the animation interactive, though, giving it the exact right voice and mannerisms, that would require familiarity with Sweetwater and extensive audio files. The character on the screen not only looked and sounded like Sweetwater, it acted like him.

"You mean the revolution?" I asked. Now Freeman waved his hand to stop me, then picked up the communicator and turned it toward himself.

"Doctor, give me a moment to speak with General Harris?" Freeman asked.

The avatar on the screen smiled, and said, "Certainly, Raymond."

Freeman switched the two-way off, then told me, "He doesn't know you are at war with the Unified Authority."

"Of course he doesn't, he's been dead for three years," I said. "The only thing going through his mind is worms."

"He thinks he's alive and that he has been assigned to the Clarke space station." The Arthur C. Clarke Space Station, or the "Wheel," as most people called it, was a scientific observation post on the extreme outer edge of the Orion Arm. The Wheel was huge, three miles in diameter. It took its name from a prehistoric science-fiction writer who had popularized ideas like spinning space stations and spaceflights to nearby planets.

"He doesn't think anything," I pointed out. "He's dead. He's more than dead, he's incinerated. We left him lying next to a fifty-megaton bomb."

"He may only be a V-job of Sweetwater, but he thinks he's real, and we need to keep it that way," Freeman said. "They replicated Sweetwater's brain."

"What about Breeze?" I asked. Arthur Breeze had been Sweetwater's partner in science and his polar opposite. Sweetwater was barely four feet tall, plump, with a scraggly beard and long reddish brown hair. He was mildly cocky, acted hip, walked with a swagger.

Breeze, on the other hand, stood six-foot-four and weighed a bony buck fifty at best. He was forehead-bald past the crown of his head with a garland of cotton-fluff hair that ran between his ears but no lower. He wore thick glasses that were always smudged with fingerprints and dusted with dandruff. He had teeth the size of gravestones that would have looked just about right in the mouth of a horse.

"Breeze is in there, too," Freeman said. "No point having one without the other."

"In there? On the Wheel?"

"They believe they are alive and that they are on the Wheel for their own protection," Freeman said.

"For their own protection," I repeated. "Protection from what? They're dead?"

"From the Avatari," Freeman said.

Hearing Freeman mention the Avatari, I felt a moment of elation. I'd been expecting Freeman to play whatever ace card he'd been hiding, but he didn't have a card at all. Instead, he had the missing piece of a very frightening puzzle.

The Double Y clones, the rush to get as many ships to Olympus Kri as possible, the way the Unified Authority never pressed the attack . . . they all fit together in a flash of clarity. The Double Y clones were never meant to destroy our Navy, they were meant to behead its leadership, to kill the officers and leave the ships and crews operational. Once our Navy fell apart, the Unifieds hoped to assimilate the ships and the crews. Clones were designed to follow orders, not to give them. Kill all the leaders, and the followers might well give up without a fight when ordered to surrender. Then what? Then send the ships here? Send the entire Navy to Olympus Kri to . . . *If the Unifieds weren't planning to attack, why did Freeman want me here?* I asked myself, and I knew the answer.

The Unified Authority wasn't going to invade Olympus Kri, but somebody else might, somebody the Unifieds feared . . . the Avatari.

"The barges you were talking about, they're U.A. ships, right?" I asked.

Freeman nodded.

"It's New Copenhagen all over again," I said, now starting to feel a chill as the reality of what this meant set in.

Freeman shook his head, fixed his eyes on mine, then said in rumbling whisper, "This isn't New Copenhagen. This is Armageddon."

Before resurrecting Sweetwater on the two-way, Freeman gave me one last warning. He said, "Sweetwater doesn't know that he's dead. Neither does Breeze. It's got to stay that way. There is no way of knowing how they will react if they find out they are dead."

*The psychology of the virtual soul,* I thought. Clones die when they learn they are synthetic. Do virtual people shut down when they find out they exist only on a computer?

"What about the mine on New Copenhagen?" I asked.

Sweetwater came with my platoon as we entered the underground cavern that the Avatari had created. The bottom of that mine was filled with corrosive gas, the fumes of which slowly dissolved the little man's skin and lungs. He insisted on accompanying us as we delivered the bomb, even though we did not have armor that would fit him. His heroism cost him his life in one long, slow, painful, installment.

"He doesn't know about it."

"And Breeze doesn't know he was torn apart by a giant spider?"

Freeman shook his head. "They think we evacuated them from New Copenhagen. They know you liberated some planets, but they think you did it for the Unified Authority."

"And I'm supposed to lie to them?" I asked.

"Lives are depending on it," Freeman said.

"Lives are depending on my lying to a computer?" I asked. If it had really been Sweetwater, instead of a computer program, I wouldn't have agreed to lie to him. Sweetwater deserved better.

"If you can't be trusted—" Freeman began.

"What do you care about saving lives? You've never cared about anybody."

He did not answer.

I might have walked away from this meeting; but Olympus Kri belonged to the Enlisted Man's Empire. If the Avatari annihilated this planet, they would be killing citizens of the Enlisted Man's Empire, not the Unified Authority.

"You haven't become some kind of homicidal humanitarian, have you?" I asked.

"Are you ready to talk to Sweetwater?" Freeman asked, ignoring my question.

"Not even remotely," I said. The cogs were clicking together in my head. I nodded toward the two-way communicator, and asked, "When did they boot up the ghost?"

"When we lost New Copenhagen."

"Lost New Copenhagen?" I asked. The pieces finally fell into place. "I bet that was right about the same time you showed up on Terraneau."

Freeman said nothing.

"They sent two clones to kill me . . ."

"Five clones," Freeman said. "I hit three of them before you came back from St. Augustine."

"They sent the clones, then they lost New Copenhagen, so they sent you to keep me alive."

Freeman sat silent and impassive. He was big and dark and powerful and oddly serene. Here was a man who avoided friendships, who might never have loved anyone, even as a child; but now he exuded a sense of ominous serenity.

"Why attack Olympus Kri?" I asked. It didn't make sense. Granted, Olympus Kri was the closest colony to New Copenhagen, but astrogeography did not matter to the Avatari. They had the technology to leapfrog entire galaxies when they chose to.

"New Copenhagen was the first planet we liberated from the aliens," Freeman said. "We liberated Olympus Kri next."

"No we didn't. The first planet we liberated was Terraneau," I said.

Freeman shook his head, and said, "The Inner Orion Fleet landed here while you were still in Bliss." He meant Fort Bliss, the concentration camp the Unified Authority built as a home away from home for the clones who fought in the battle of New Copenhagen.

"Oh," I said. Then I mumbled, "That's not good . . . not good at all." If the Avatari were taking planets by the order of their liberation, Terraneau was next in line. And here I learned something about myself. I thought I had washed my hands of Ava Gardner and Ellery Doctorow and the stupid, stupid people who lived on Terraneau; but now, knowing that they might all be killed, I had a change of heart. Fantasizing about them getting what I felt they deserved was one thing; knowing that they all might die was entirely different.

I thought about Ava and wondered if we could possibly evacuate Terraneau before the zero hour.

"You ready to talk to Sweetwater?" Freeman asked.

I nodded. He was a ghost, just one more ghost with which I would have to reckon, one more occupant in a life already overpopulated by the dead.

## CHAPTER FORTY-SIX

Peace does not always come with a signed treaty. Sometimes it is foisted upon sworn enemies when they realize they must either work together or perish.

"Do you trust them?" Warshaw asked, when I reported to him about my meeting with Freeman. He was still on the *Kamehameha*, still orbiting Gobi.

"Who? Freeman, the dead scientist, or the Unified Authority? I think Freeman is telling the truth," I said. I believed him from the start, I just didn't trust him. "Sweetwater is—"

"I don't care about Sweetwater, he's just a cartoon."

"I believe Freeman," I said.

"Yeah? You believed him when he said the U.A. was going to invade us. That turned out to be a lie."

"He never said it was the Unified Authority. I misread him."

"It sounds like he was counting on you misreading him," Warshaw said.

"Probably," I agreed.

"I don't see any reason why I should trust Freeman. He's your pal, not mine," Warshaw said.

"What if he can prove what he's saying?" I asked.

"How is he going to do that?"

"I'm flying out to New Copenhagen in an hour," I said.

"New Copenhagen? That's off our broadcast grid. How are you going to get there?"

"As a guest of the Unified Authority; they're sending out an explorer," I said. Explorers were unarmed research vessels. The first self-broadcasting ships were explorers. The U.A. used them for mapping the galaxy.

"Sounds like a cozy arrangement," Warshaw said, hinting at all kinds of sins. "They're just going to send a ship, and you're just going to specking climb aboard. It sounds like you're getting in bed with them."

"We're running out of time," I said.

"I did some checking, Harris. There are seventeen million people living on Olympus Kri. Evacuating the planet is not going to be easy," Warshaw said.

I had witnessed a planetary evaeuation once. I saw the chaos and the confusion. Warshaw was right. Those new barges would simplify matters, but some tasks take time. Persuading families to leave their homes, then leave their planet would not be easy. Ferrying seventeen million people out of the atmosphere would take more time.

"Did your friend happen to mention where the aliens are going after Olympus Kri?" Warshaw asked, sounding more than a little suspicious.

"Terraneau."

Warshaw laughed. "Terraneau? Oh, that's rich. Serves those assholes right for kicking us off their specking planet."

I did not appreciate the irony. Warshaw was thinking of Doctorow. I was thinking of Ava. "We need to clear them out," I said.

Looking like a god in a Greek statue display, Warshaw folded his arms across his barrel chest, fixed me with a cold stare, and said, "We can't evacuate every specking planet."

"We have to try," I said. "We're talking about millions of people."

"Not our people," Warshaw said. "Remember, Harris, they didn't want anything to do with us."

"We can't just sit back and watch it happen," I said.

"Where would we put the refugees? We can't keep moving them from planet to planet. We can't even specking fit that many passengers in our ships. Even if the Unifieds come out with a fleet of million-man barges, we can't fit 'em all.

"And that's assuming that Freeman and the Unifieds are telling us the truth. I'm not convinced."

"They sent me a video file taken by a satellite over New Copenhagen. Want to have a look?" I asked. I'd had the file queued and ready before I called Warshaw, now I simply touched a corner of the screen to upload the file.

I studied Warshaw's reaction as he reviewed the devastation. For the first twenty seconds, he scrutinized the images with the air of detachment one would expect from a high-ranking officer. After that, wrinkles appeared across his broad face, and his scowl went slack.

"Did you get to Valhalla?" I asked.

"Valhalla?"

"The city," I said.

"I'm there now. It doesn't look as bad as Norristown did after the aliens attacked."

*It was and it wasn't,* I thought. "Look at the buildings. Look at the windows. Everything is burned." Everything was charred, so that even the bricks looked like they were covered with soot.

"Did they set off a nuke?" Warshaw asked.

"The Avatari don't use bombs," I said. He was right, though, Valhalla had that burned-out look you see in the aftermath of a nuclear blast; but it didn't have the blasted look. Most of the buildings were standing; and the buildings that had collapsed looked like they had been crushed from the top. There was no rhyme or reason to the destruction.

"Maybe they did it to themselves," Warshaw said. He did not look up as he said this. His eyes remained fixed on the images of New Copenhagen, taking in every last prurient detail.

"What are you saying? Do you think this was some sort of accident? You can't possibly think they did this on purpose. You don't believe that any more than I do."

Warshaw grunted some indistinguishable response.

"Sweetwater says the destruction was global, not an inch of the planet was spared. The Unifieds couldn't do that even if they wanted to. They don't have anything powerful enough to do that. If they did, they would have used it on us instead of themselves."

"I don't trust them," Warshaw said.

"Yeah, me either."

The anomaly spread like a budding flower, and an explorer emerged. The explorer had neither the sharp edges of a warship nor the boxy profile of a transport. It had a long, cylindrical fuselage with wide, jutting wings that could provide glide in an atmosphere.

The explorer was not outfitted with weapons or armor, not even shields. It had barely cleared the corona of the broadcast anomaly when two squadrons of E.M.N. Tomcats circled in behind it. If the ship varied from its prescribed course, the fighters would blow it apart.

Seeing our fighters close in tight around the explorer stirred an odd emotion in me. Fighters were small ships. The sight of them attacking a capital ship always reminded me of bees going after a bear. This time, though, they had surrounded another small target. The explorer was nearly twice as long as the Tomcats and considerably wider; but it looked helpless ringed by our birds of prey.

Decelerating as it glided toward our armada, the explorer approached the *Salah ad-Din*. Coming to Olympus Kri in a lone ship, unescorted and unarmed had been an act of faith and desperation. A rodent among lions, the little U.A. ship threaded a path between battleships and fighter carriers. Any ship in our fleet could have destroyed that scientific explorer with a swipe of its shields or a single shot from its cannons.

The explorer and its escort slowed down to three-minute miles as *ad-Din* security ran tests for explosives, weapons, and chemicals. Once cleared, the explorer retracted its gangly wings, then hovered into a landing tunnel. I waited and watched as the explorer cleared through the locks.

"Are you sure you want to go alone?" Hollingsworth asked.

We stood at the edge of the track. A team of MPs dressed

in ground-crew uniforms crowded around the explorer with pistols in their pockets and tools in their hands while a genuine traffic ace guided the explorer into its parking slot.

The hatch opened, and our armed MPs/ground crew boarded the ship to "service" it. They weren't fooling anyone. They boarded like Marines, not engineers, rushing up the steps, stopping to scan for enemies as they entered the cabin, then bowling ahead.

A few moments later, a second crew entered the explorer and checked the engines and batteries. Before entering the bird, I made a show of telling Hollingsworth to keep our fleet on high alert, as if he had any sort of authority in the fleet. We traded salutes, then I entered the U.A. ship alone.

Three men met me as I stepped into the cabin. I recognized all of them—Tobias Andropov, the newest member of the Unified Authority Linear Committee; General George "Nickel" Hill, now the highest-ranking officer in the U.A. military; and Gordon Hughes, a native of Olympus Kri who had risen to the highest seats of power in the Unified Authority before defecting to the Confederate Arms Treaty during the Mogat War.

Like me, these men had made a show of good faith, arriving without guards or weapons. Of the three, I knew Hill best, having served with him on New Copenhagen. We'd attended briefings together. I'd met Hughes once before as well. He'd torn me apart on the floor of the House of Representatives.

I'd never met Andropov though I felt like I knew him better than the others. He was one of the architects of the program that placed clones in concentrations camps and ultimately abandoned us in space. Hill and Hughes had played forgettable parts in my life, Andropov had made a memorable contribution.

I had no time for sulking or harboring grudges on this outing, though. Andropov and I shook hands. We greeted each other with somber smiles and looked each other in the eye as we exchanged pleasantries.

"General Harris, I have heard so much about you. It's good of you to meet with us," Andropov said.

"Sounds like we have a lot to talk about," I said.

Next came Hughes, an old man with the face of an ancient.

The bags under his eyes were the color of dead skin. His hair was brown, with large shocks of white. It tapered off around his temples. A fine network of blue-black arteries formed a fishnet pattern on the right side of his nose. Years back, this man had cut a heroic figure, one of those rare politicians who had fought in the wars. Now he had red-rimmed eyes and bleached skin. His handshake was firm, but his palm was a sponge.

"It's been a while, Congressman," I said as I shook his hand.

"How is my planet?" he asked.

*So asks the once-powerful representative of Olympus Kri,* I thought. Still shaking his hand, I pledged, "We will do everything we can to protect it."

General Hill and I traded salutes grudgingly. We were members of antagonistic forces. He did not recognize my authority, and I despised his.

"So," he said, "back to New Copenhagen."

"Back to New Copenhagen," I agreed. Hill had been against the deportation of clones. I felt anger toward the man, but it was unjustified. The politics that made us enemies were not of his making.

The ground crew turned the explorer around, and we launched. Fighters followed us as we flew away from the *Salah ad-Din.* To me, they no longer looked like protection. They looked like my last line of support. It occurred to me that I was now a prisoner of the Unified Authority. If we broadcasted to Earth instead of New Copenhagen, I would be tried and executed.

We flew out into space for several minutes. Our fighter escort fell away, and soon the fleet vanished in the distance.

"I was always very interested to meet you, General," said Tobias Andropov. He was the youngest man in the cabin. Well, he was the youngest natural-born among us, younger than Hill and a great deal younger than Hughes. He was forty-four, making him fifteen years older than me. His black hair had the flat look of hair that is dyed, but his skin was smooth, and his blue eyes were clear of veins and bags.

"I read a lot of military history as a boy. I don't know if you knew this, but my father was a general in the Marines."

"I didn't know that," I said, though, in fact, I was very aware of his father. Brigadier General Mikhail Andropov never shied away from a fight, and he never lost, but he maintained that perfect record by drawing deeply from an endless pool of cloned conscripts.

"I've read a lot about Liberators, and I found something interesting. They never lost a battle, not even so much as a skirmish," he said.

"There was Little Man," I said. That was a famous land battle in which 2,300 Marines were sent to capture a planet. Only seven of them survived. "We had four Liberators in that battle." I was the only Liberator who made it out.

Sounding surprised, Andropov said, "We won that battle."

Historians would see it as a great victory, but the survivors didn't. We had seven survivors, and the Mogats had none. As our forces fought the Mogats on the planet, the Scutum-Crux Fleet ambushed and destroyed three Mogat battleships. From the historian's point of view, we had won a great victory, destroying three of their ships and all of their ground forces.

Tint shields formed over the windows. Hill and Hughes, deep in a conversation of their own, probably did not even notice the anomaly as we broadcasted across the Orion Arm.

"What about New Prague and Albatross Island?" I asked.

"Those weren't battles, General; they were police actions, and the Liberators came out on top."

"They went berserk and killed civilians," I said.

"You're not looking at it with a clinical eye," Andropov said. "They accomplished their objectives in both cases, then lost control of themselves afterward. It wasn't the battles that they lost; they destroyed the enemy."

"That's one way of looking at it," I said.

"And you are the last of the Liberators. I find it interesting that even after you defected to the Enlisted Man's Empire, you're still winning every battle," Andropov went on.

*Defected to the Enlisted Man's Empire?* I thought. First this son of a bitch had me locked in a concentration camp, then he had me marooned in space, where he planned to use me for target practice; and now he says I defected. I decided to shut him out. From here on out, I would only pretend to listen to him.

As I started to let my mind wander, Gordon Hughes joined our conversation. He said, "But we're not here to discuss military history; we're here to plan an evacuation."

"Right," Andropov agreed. "That is why we've come."

"Mr. Andropov is of the opinion that we might be able to fight our way out of this situation," Hughes said.

"I suggested the possibility," Andropov said. He turned to me, and explained, "I simply meant that there are other avenues to explore besides evacuation. We could make the entire Navy available for the fight thanks to your empire's new broadcast network. Should the aliens try to capture Olympus Kri, well, we now know how to blast through their ion-curtain defense."

General Hill spoke a word into the intercommunications system, then leaned into our conversation and spoke softly. "Mr. Andropov, our pilot informs me that we are about to enter the atmosphere."

The explorer did not inject itself into the atmosphere with the grace of my shuttle, but it broke through more smoothly than a transport would have. The sky outside our ship was dark with clouds as fine as lace.

"Before you experiment with military options, you'd better evacuate the planet," Hughes reminded Andropov. "We all agreed that the first thing we need to do is to evacuate Olympus Kri."

He looked so old, a caved-in, wilted wax model of the one-time political heavyweight known as Gordon Hughes.

Andropov drummed the fingers of his right hand along the top of his armrest, then asked, "Where do you suggest we take them, Gordon?"

"Take them to Earth," Hughes said. "God knows there's enough room for them there."

"What are we going to do with the population of Terraneau?" Andropov asked.

"As I understand it, there are only five million people left on Terraneau," Hughes said. "There's plenty of room for them on Earth."

"And Providence Kri? What about the people on Providence Kri?"

"Take them all to Earth."

It sounded like the bastards expected to evacuate our whole damned empire.

The lower we descended, the more grim the atmosphere became. I could see the planet below through a hazy sky that was black, but not pitch-black. It was a dirty, rusty black.

The thing that surprised me most was the snow. A fresh layer of fluffy gray snow covered the burned-out countryside, blanketing forests in which the burned-out hulls of pine trees pointed into the sky, as straight and naked as sewing needles.

There could be no question that this was New Copenhagen, I'd fought in these woods under very different conditions. I recognized the terrain. I recognized the roll of the forest floor, even spotted clearings in which our Marines and soldiers had ambushed the enemy.

Clearings? The entire specking forest was a goddamned clearing. I could not see so much as a hint of a leaf or a pine needle.

"What kind of weapon does something like this?" I asked.

"Sweetwater thinks the Avatari ignited the atmosphere," said General Hill.

"Ignited the atmosphere?" I asked. "What the hell does that mean?" I was angry. I was irritable. I was scared.

No one responded. They didn't know.

"Have you debriefed the survivors?" I asked.

Hughes answered in a hushed voice. "That is the point, General. There are no survivors."

When I looked back out the window, we were flying above Valhalla, the capital city of New Copenhagen. I had seen this city destroyed; but in the three years since I left, the residents had undoubtedly rebuilt it.

"It looks a lot better now than it did when the Avatari left the first time," Nickel Hill said.

"Igniting the atmosphere" had toppled some buildings and left others standing. I saw no logic in the buildings that remained and the ones that fell. We flew over tall buildings that stood and piles of rubble that might have once been great skyscrapers. On one side of the street a three-story building might stand untouched, while across the street, a building of seemingly similar size lay in ruins.

Our pilot took us lower and lower until the roofs of the tallest buildings passed only a few feet below our wings. I saw melted roadways below us and streetlamps with posts that had wilted like old sticks of celery. We flew over an intersection in which cars had sunk axle deep into the road below them.

The cars were all the same color now, the dull nickel gray of burned metal.

"We landed drones down there to gather data," Hill said. He always struck me as a man with a love of gadgets and an appreciation for science. "The radiation levels are normal. The carbon monoxide is off the charts, but that's predictable. Whatever did this, it killed off the plant life. It burned everything. We haven't found a patch of ground that has not been burned."

Flying low to the ground, we passed a tall skyscraper that reached well above us. The glass in some of its windows had melted and run down the side of the building like wax from a candle. The entire building was covered with soot.

"I can tell you what Sweetwater says happened here if you're interested," General Hill said. Of all the generals stationed on New Copenhagen, George Hill was the only one who took Sweetwater seriously. "Sweetwater doesn't think we fought the Avatari Army that first time out. He thinks they sent their exterminators, maybe only their janitorial squad. He says they sent their C-team to sweep us cockroaches out of the way. That's what we fought.

"He thinks they're sending their army this time. Last time they wanted us to leave. That was before we took our planets back. Now they're sending their army."

I turned from Hill and stared out the window. Below us was a park in which a blackened and mostly melted slide stood on a glittering mound that looked like it was made of glass. Scanning the grounds, I did not see so much as a single blade of grass.

We left the city, flying no more than fifty feet above a residential suburb. Some of the homes below us had exploded. For the most part, the neighborhood looked like it could be washed clean with a hose, just spray the soot away and move right in.

"I don't want to fight them again," Hill admitted. "I think we got lucky last time. I think we got lucky, and they didn't take us seriously, and they were fighting with one arm tied behind their backs, and they were still almost won."

"We don't have any other options," Andropov said. "Even if we move everyone to Earth, how long do you think it will be before they come kill us there?"

The pilot banked and turned so that he could take us back

for another pass across Valhalla. As he did, I saw a park with a large reflection pool. The pool was empty, but the ground reflected our lights in smeared streaks, as if it were made of crudely made glass.

"Did you ever hear the story of the gossamer moth?" Hughes asked. He stared out the window, his eyes drinking in the devastation. Did he see New Copenhagen or Olympus Kri below?

"I used to tell my children a bedtime story about a moth that lived near an air force base. It watched the fighters as they flew in and out of the base. It watched them dogfight and studied their maneuvers. One night a lizard crawled up into its tree, and the moth attacked the lizard, using the tactics it had learned by watching the fighters; but it forgot that it was just a moth, and the lizard ate it.

"I don't know what the Avatari are like; but I think to them, we're just another moth."

We passed over a section of street with fancy-looking storefronts and outdoor restaurants, the kind of place that gets crowded on weekends. I looked for bodies or signs of life and saw nothing. No clothes. No toys. No shoes or hats. *Anyone stuck down there must have been cremated,* I thought; but what I said was, "Just a million moths."

## CHAPTER
# FORTY-SEVEN

Apparently Freeman wasn't the only person with a direct line to important ghosts. He did not attend the negotiation with the Unified Authority, but a member of the U.A. Academy of Science with a direct link to Sweetwater and Breeze did. He was the liaison. He was the buffer. His job was to keep Sweetwater and Breeze informed while weeding out any information that might tip them off to their virtual reality.

We sat in the conference room on the *Kamehameha*. Andropov, Hughes, Hill, and the scientist sat on one side of the table. I sat across from them. I was alone. Warshaw sat at the head of the table, running the meeting. Andropov, representing the highest power in the Unified Authority, should have conducted; but Warshaw would not allow it. We were in Enlisted Man's space on an Enlisted Man's ship. He insisted on calling the shots.

Warshaw sat at the head of the table, making no effort to hide his disdain for everyone else in the room, including me. Methodically flexing his muscles in an effort to make himself more menacing, he sneered, "You give the orders in your corner of the galaxy, and I give the orders around here."

His eyes still locked on Andropov, he asked, "Harris, are you sure that was New Copenhagen they showed you?"

"Yes," I said, letting my annoyance show. We all knew Warshaw had big muscles, big specking deal. His physique wasn't intimidating anybody in the room.

"How do you know?" he asked me.

"I recognized it," I said.

"I thought it's all burned up," Warshaw said. "How did you recognize it?"

I saw no point answering; he would not accept anything I said. He wanted to make a point.

"Admiral, we have to get moving," Hughes said climbing partway out of his chair. "We need to begin the evacuation immediately. There may not be enough time as it is."

Appearing to weigh his options, Warshaw rubbed his jaw and sat in silence. His forearms bulged, then his biceps, then the muscles in his neck. The way he worked his muscles was impressive, but it was also pathetic.

Hughes dropped back in his chair and threw his hands up in frustration. "Look, we'll fly you to New Copenhagen, we'll fly a team of clone scientists to take soil samples, we'll do whatever it takes to make you believe us; but we need to start the evacuation. Every second could mean lives lost."

Warshaw turned to face him, smiled, and said, "I'm not convinced."

He was playing with us, with all of us. He wanted to show everyone who was in control.

Accustomed to working with self-important officers and

politicians, the academy scientist tried to get the meeting back on track. "Admiral, we can provide scientific findings. We've sent drones to run tests on several of your planets."

"My planets?" Warshaw asked. "What planets are my planets?"

"The planets you stole from the Unified Authority," Andropov said.

"Oh, stole them. So you were trespassing on some of the planets we stole. Which ones?" Warshaw asked.

"Olympus Kri, St. Augustine, Terraneau . . ." the academy man began.

"Yeah? And how did you run tests on those planets?" Warshaw asked.

"They sent in Double Ys," I said.

"What's that?" Hughes asked.

"Those were the clone assassins Andropov and his pals sent to kill me and my officers," Warshaw said.

Andropov flushed with anger. Hill looked nervous as well.

"I didn't know about that," said Hughes.

"You didn't know about the clone assassins? Don't worry about it; we've got the situation under control," said Warshaw.

"We found traces of a particle we're calling 'Tachyon D' on New Copenhagen. There are large concentrations of that same particle on a few of your planets," said the scientist.

"Oh, we're back to them being my planets," Warshaw said, clearly trying to be unreasonable.

"The highest concentration is on Olympus Kri. We also found it on Terraneau."

"So you think we should abandon our planets because you found this particle?" Warshaw asked.

"There's no point staying," I said. "Whatever hit New Copenhagen, it didn't leave much behind."

Warshaw softened, and asked, "How many people died on New Copenhagen?"

Had I not been sitting right across from him, I would not have heard Andropov quietly whisper, "All of them." I could not tell if the comment rose out of sarcasm or pain.

"Seven million," said Hughes.

No one said anything for a few moments after that.

Warshaw broke the silence. "What is the population on Olympus Kri?"

"Seventeen million," said Hughes, answering quickly, sounding desperate. "We have twenty-five barges capable of transporting 250,000 people at a time."

"Big boats," Warshaw said, sounding impressed. "Are they self-broadcasting?"

Hill answered, "No, sir, they are not."

"So how are you going to get them here?" Warshaw asked.

Hill answered again. "We need you to link the Mars broadcast station into your network."

"Mars station? I thought the Mogats busted it," Warshaw said, finally sitting up straight and taking the meeting seriously. Now it wasn't just a question of saving lives; our military security was at stake. Warshaw might not have cared about lives and evacuations, but he took security seriously.

"We've constructed a temporary station," Hill said. "It's primitive, but it will do the job for now."

Warshaw's eyes narrowed and hardened. His mouth worked itself into a sneer. "So we open the gates and let you roll your horse in. I'm not biting," he said. He turned to me, and added, "And you, Harris, I never figured you for a collaborator."

"Admiral . . ." Andropov began, at the same time as Hughes, Hill, and the scientist from the academy.

But I was the one who had been challenged. I spoke over them. "Get this through your head, you overinflated son of a bitch. We have a new enemy, someone too big and mean to beat. There's no question who is going to win this one. The only question is how many people we are going to lose."

"If they're telling the truth," Warshaw muttered.

"Oh, right, we can't trust the Unifieds. Tell you what. Let's run a test on Olympus Kri," I said. "We'll just wait and watch, and after seventeen million people burn, then we'll know it's time to evacuate Terraneau. Is that what you want?"

An angry silence filled the room. We all sat staring into the table.

"Okay, so let's say you're right. Even if we get everybody off Olympus Kri, where do you plan on putting them?" Warshaw asked. It was the closest thing to an olive branch that he was willing to offer. He sat rigid in his chair, no longer flexing his muscles.

"We have to save them," Hughes said, sounding tired and discouraged.

"If you're routing them through Mars and taking them to Earth, your barges better have broadcast engines," Warshaw said.

"I told you, we've got a temporary station by Mars," Andropov said.

"Check the orbits. The jump from Earth to Mars is over one hundred million miles at the moment. That's a three-hour trip, even for your ships." Warshaw held up a little handheld computer he must have been hiding under the table.

I did not know the positions of Earth and Mars in their orbits, but I had considered the problem. "There's a way around that," I said.

The solution should have been obvious. "We can store the evacuees in the Mars Spaceport," I said.

"The spaceport is closed. We haven't used it since the Mogat War," Andropov said. The stupid bastard still wanted to fight the Avatari. He wanted to send out the clones like his father did in the good old days. Of course, he would not lead the fight himself. His bravery extended only as far as declaring wars, not fighting them.

"The military used it as a processing station before the battle on New Copenhagen," I said.

"All of the equipment was operational when we shut it down," Hill said. He sounded enthusiastic. The Mars Spaceport had dormitory rooms for hundreds of thousands of workers and enough floor space to accommodate millions of visitors. "We should be able to get the power and oxygen running."

"But that still leaves us with your Trojan horse," Warshaw said. "I don't trust you." He looked directly at Andropov as he said this. "And I don't want your specking ships in my broadcast network."

"Admiral, what if you took Olympus Kri off your broadcast grid?" Hughes's voice was low and nervous and hollow.

"Are you saying I should give the planet away?" Warshaw asked.

"He's saying we should amputate it," I said. "The planet is as good as gone. Once we remove it from our network—"

"I won't know if the aliens came or the whole thing was a fraud," Warshaw said.

I looked across the table at Gordon Hughes. When we went to New Copenhagen, he saw one planet and thought of another. Now I was doing the same thing. "I'll stay and oversee the evacuation," I said, speaking of Olympus Kri and thinking of Terraneau . . . not even Terraneau, really, just one of its residents.

# CHAPTER
# FORTY-EIGHT

Earthdate: November 16, A.D. 2517
Location: Olympus Kri
Galactic Position: Orion Arm

The rescue had been going on for three days now, and I still had not gotten used to the look of the Unified Authority's new barges. They were little more than biospheres. They looked like floating warehouses as they grew out of their anomalies. They had a nub in the front for a cockpit and enormous rocket engines in the back, but they lacked even the semblance of wings or aerodynamics. They did not have landing bays or atmospheric locks. Transports would land along the hulls of the barges, on special pads with automatic clamps that would fasten onto the transports' skids. Passengers would enter the barges through umbilical walkways.

*Only an idiot would broadcast in something so feeble,* I thought to myself. I almost said something, then I remembered that I had traveled out of the Scutum-Crux Arm to the Cygnus Arm welded into a derelict battleship.

"Those barges have got to be the ugliest ships I have seen in my entire life," Hollingsworth said, as one of the barges floated toward the *ad-Din*. We were on the observation deck watching the Unified Authority ships arrive.

The barge passed beside a U.A. battleship, positively dwarfing it. "It looks like a packing crate for mailing battle-ships," Hollingsworth added. "You'd have more control steering a piece of shit down a toilet."

"Yeah," I grunted, still astonished by the size of the barges.

The U.A. battleship was long and narrow like a flying dagger. The barge could have held four of those ships easily and possibly even a fifth. It was that big.

More barges followed in a series of flashes. They floated out of the broadcast zone like boxes on an assembly line.

"It's getting pretty close to zero hour. Why are you going down to the planet now?" Hollingsworth asked.

I gave him a one-word answer, hoping to brush off the question. "Reconnaissance."

"Are you coming back to the *ad-Din* to watch the attack?" Hollingsworth asked.

"I'm staying on the planet," I said.

He paused, grinned at me, and finally said, "I'm just curious. Does your martyr complex ever get in your way?"

"What did you say?" I asked, though I'd heard him perfectly well. If he'd yelled or raised his voice, I would have been certain he was trying insult me, but he sounded calm and sincere.

Alone on the observation deck, we stood side by side, staring out the viewport.

"You assigned yourself to point position when we fought the aliens on Terraneau."

"I led a team—"

"You were the commanding officer, not some specking platoon leader. You were supposed to observe and direct."

"I thought I could do a better job if I was on the field with my men," I said.

"You got stuck in a basement. You got trapped in a specking basement with half the specking Avatari Army swarming around you."

"You don't think I did that on purpose?"

"No, but it shouldn't have happened."

"We won the battle," I pointed out.

"Thomer told me you led the team that went into the Avatari mines on New Copenhagen." Thomer was Kelly Thomer, my second-in-command until he died on Terraneau. He was a good Marine and a great human being, even if he was synthetic.

"He went in right beside me," I said. "Maybe he was a martyr, too."

"He's a dead martyr. You're a living martyr. People respect dead martyrs. The living ones are just a pain in the ass."

I did not say anything. We'd both been friends with Thomer.

"I heard you led the attack on the Mogat home world."

I saw no point in responding.

Outside the ship, a line of ten enormous barges paraded past us. The barges were beige and marked with flashing lights to help transport pilots find landing pads.

"I won't go down after you," Hollingsworth said. "If you get in trouble, you will be on your own."

"I wouldn't ask you to," I said.

"I won't send men down after you, either."

"What's your point?" I asked.

"I just . . . Damn it, Harris, you're so specking self-righteous. No, it's not even that. You're not self-righteous; you're the goddamned real thing. You're righteous. I don't know how that happened, how you became right, and I became wrong."

"I'm not so righteous," I said, feeling truly offended.

"Sooner or later, you'll be a martyr, you're just counting the days," Hollingsworth said. "Just passing time until you meet your specking maker."

"I'm a clone, I've already met my makers, and I don't like them," I said.

"So why go down to Olympus Kri? You say there's going to be an apocalypse, fine, I believe you. What do you think you will accomplish by riding it out down there? Do you think they're going to make you a saint or something? Saint Harris, guardian saint of clones and Marines."

He did not sound angry, but he did sound frustrated. He'd stood by quietly when Warshaw announced the airlift; but now that we were alone, he spoke his mind.

"I don't think I'm a saint, but I sure as hell am not cut out to be a general," I said. "I don't like giving orders, and I don't like watching battles from a safe distance."

"Look, Harris, I admire you. You're the best goddamn—"

Rather than suffer through another eulogy, I interrupted him. "You didn't like me much on Terraneau."

"That's 'cause I thought you were wrong about everything. Turns out you were right about everything."

"I thought it was about Ava," I said. "I thought you were mad about my hiding a girl in my quarters while everyone else was confined to the ship."

Hollingsworth's face flushed. "Yeah, well, that was more envy than anger. I would have done the same thing if I had a shot at Ava Gardner. Any man would."

His honesty stunned me.

"You don't really want to kill yourself, do you?" Hollingsworth asked.

"Kill myself?" I laughed. "I tried that once. It didn't work. Liberators can't kill themselves; it goes against our programming."

I wasn't lying. Part of my programming gave me a survival instinct. Even if I wanted to, I lacked the ability to pull the trigger—or the pin. The time I did try to commit suicide, my weapon of choice was a grenade.

"It's not a question of suicide; it's a question of needing to be in the middle of the action. It's in my DNA. I can't kill myself, and I can't sit out the fight."

"So you're screwed," Hollingsworth said.

An impressive array of ships now filled the space above Olympus Kri. Warshaw sent six additional fighter carriers to watch out for the empire's interests during the evacuation. They floated in seeming stasis beside enemy battleships. If the Avatari suddenly began traveling in spaceships and appeared in range, I thought they might find themselves in the fight of their lives.

Of course, the Avatari did not travel in ships. They had no time for such primitive contrivances as traveling at the speed of light. In fact, they did not travel at all. We called them the "Avatari" because the army they sent to our galaxy was made of avatars instead of living beings.

They'd used some new weapon during their latest assault on New Copenhagen, and we had no hope of making a stand against them until we knew what they had. That meant having men on the ground as well as eyes in the air. Our satellites would record the destruction from outside the atmosphere while I experienced it firsthand down below. Maybe I would see things or hear things or just feel things hiding underground that we would miss from above.

And if I died? I had a bunch of patriotic and macho responses; but they were all for show. The truth was that I had survived too much already. I was ready to go.

Checking my watch, I saw that I would probably arrive ahead of schedule, but I felt the urge to get started. I could stand around up here, safe and sound on the *Salah ad-Din*, or I could stand around down there, on the planet. Down there I would be in place, ready to react if something went wrong.

Hollingsworth stayed on the observation deck as I went to my quarters and swapped my service uniform for combat armor. "Nickel" Hill had offered to loan me shielded armor; but I turned him down. What a laugh. With shielding from head to toe, the only weapon you could carry was a dart gun that ran along the outside of the right arm. It fired fléchettes made of depleted uranium, good for killing people, but I doubted it would have much effect on the Avatari.

My mood turned dark as I fastened my armor. Hill said that the Avatari we faced on New Copenhagen were just the janitors and that this time we would face the A-team. When I asked the ghost of Sweetwater about it, he said, "Not so much janitors. We think they were more like scarecrows, mostly harmless and designed to scare away pests."

I had answered him with one word, "Bullshit."

But it hadn't been bullshit, and I accepted that now as I prepared to fly down to Olympus Kri. Alone, in my billet, I owned up to the truth.

My armor included a rebreather, temperature-controlling bodysuit, and protection against radiation, yet it only weighed a couple of pounds. My portable arsenal, on the other hand, registered seventy-three pounds and thirteen ounces. My go-pack contained six disposable grenade launchers, six hand-held rockets, a particle-beam pistol, a particle-beam cannon, and a handheld laser. Facing anyone but the Avatari, that would have been overkill.

I wondered what weapon the Avatari would use when they attacked and realized that while I was down there, my fate was entirely in their hands. Handing over the controls always made me nervous. No Marine expects to live forever, but we all hope to see the day through.

"Wheel, are you there?" I asked, testing the special inter-Link connection Hill had given me so that I could contact the virtual version of the Arthur C. Clarke Wheel.

Arthur Breeze answered. "Are you heading down to the planet?"

"That I am," I said.

"Sweetwater is asleep," said Breeze.

The virtual versions of Sweetwater and Breeze ate, slept, passed gas, and shat. Whoever designed them had to give them foibles along with strengths to prevent them from figuring out that they lived in a computer. Along with mapping and scanning their brains, the engineers had mapped and scanned their bodies. Nothing was left to chance.

The digital ghosts of Arthur Breeze and William Sweetwater spent their time playing with digital replicas of the finest scientific equipment in their little virtual laboratory on a computer model of the Clarke space station. When interactive Breeze ran atoms in his virtual collider, did he control real equipment accelerating real particles and getting real results? When he peered through his spectroscope, did he examine real samples with virtual eyes? Even now, he was watching the real me through eyes that only existed in a computer. Did the digital program that emulated his brain hear the digital protocol that simulated his voice?

If I allowed myself to play with these questions long enough, I could have driven myself insane. A lab assistant worked at a desk behind Breeze. I wondered if the avatar was attached to a real man and if that man currently stood in a real-world lab working with real-world equipment.

Breeze was a physicist who had published volumes on

particles. He was probably a better scientist than Sweetwater, but his lack of confidence was an Achilles' heel. He stuttered during briefings and used so much jargon that he could never communicate his ideas clearly. Sweetwater, whose expertise extended into chemistry as well as physics, had no shortage of confidence.

"You're sure fifty feet down will be enough?" I asked.

"Based on my best calculations, ten feet might be enough," Breeze said. He pulled off his thick glasses, polished them, and replaced them on his face. The grease and dandruff were still there, now wiped into a spiral pattern.

"The combustion on New Copenhagen was strictly a surface event. Sweetwater sent a drone down to take soil samples. The heat penetration was only a few feet."

"So if someone was in a basement apartment on New Copenhagen, they might have survived," I said, thinking not so much about survivors on New Copenhagen as civilians on Terraneau.

"It's not likely," Breeze said. "Concrete calcifies at two thousand degrees. At three thousand, soil melts."

"Not all of the buildings melted on New Copenhagen," I said.

"The surface of the planet retained heat longer than the atmosphere," Breeze said. "The soil and air samples show that the atmosphere reached temperatures of nine thousand degrees before the heat subsided. If you were in a building with any kind of ventilation system, you'd be incinerated."

"Good to know," I said.

"Harris, you might want to consider flying down to the planet's surface after the event. Any structure exposed to those kind of temperatures is going to sustain fundamental damage. You could survive the event and still find yourself buried alive."

I thanked Breeze and signed off. *Buried alive, Hell's lobby.* I thought about the Unified Authority Marines I buried in that underground garage on Terraneau. If I died the very same way, the irony would not be lost on Hollingsworth.

# CHAPTER
# FORTY-NINE

As my shuttle exited the *ad-Din*, Lieutenant Nobles offered to stay on Olympus Kri for the mission.

Ahead of us, swarms of transports clambered in and out of the Olympus Kri atmosphere. The planet looked normal and healthy, just another green-and-blue marble no different than Terraneau, or St. Augustine, or Earth for that matter, only this one had a death sentence hanging over it.

"Are you out of your specking mind?" I asked.

"I don't understand, sir. I heard you were going to stay down there," he said.

Interesting point.

Here in the cockpit, this shuttle was no more comfortable than a transport. The ceiling was lower. I sat in the copilot's chair and considered the instrumentation, which was more like the controls in my old Johnston Starliner than the controls in a transport. *I might be able to teach myself how to fly this bird in a pinch,* I told myself.

I started to say, "I fight, you fly," but that sounded dismissive. Instead, I asked, "Do you know about any underground runway systems?"

"Not offhand," he said.

"Then we wouldn't have anyplace safe to store the shuttle."

"Oh, yeah. I didn't think about that," he said

"See if you can get your hands on a transport for the return trip. If things go wrong, I may need to get off this rock in a hurry." Unlike transports, which had skids instead of wheels, the shuttle needed a runway. I would have flown down to the planet in a transport as well, but I did not want to risk some other officer commandeering my luxury ride.

As we reached the atmosphere, a convoy of transports rose

past us. They looked awkward and overburdened by their own weight. There had to be a better way of emptying the planet than evacuating its population one hundred people at a time; but when I tried to think of an alternative, I came up empty.

Because transports take off vertically, the evacuation was not limited to airports. Sports stadiums, shopping malls, schools, train stations, anyplace with room for processing masses of passengers and an open field for landing became an evacuation center.

Crossing Odessa, I saw hundred of transports flying in wing formations like flocks of geese. Below us, the streets were choked with cars.

"I've got your friend's signal," Nobles said. "He's by an airstrip on the edge of town."

A call came in from Sweetwater, his gravelly voice sounding anxious and excited. "We just got back the results from our atmospheric test," he said, the "we" meaning him. "The Tachyon D concentration is rising quickly."

"Are they forming an ion curtain?" I asked.

"Breeze doesn't think so. He says these new tachyons act differently than the tachyons in the curtain. Their energy levels are off the charts." Tachyons were subatomic particles traveling at sublight speeds. How Breeze could measure their activity and energy levels was a mystery; but I did not ask about it.

"How much time do I have?" I asked.

"Before the event?" he asked. The *event*, now there was a euphemism for the ages. Not the *cataclysm*, or the *holocaust*, or even the *big bang*; the *event*? It sounded so specking benign.

"Yeah, how much time before the *event*?" I asked.

"We have no frame of reference, General. Your guess is as good as ours."

We were coming in for a landing, flying just a couple of hundred feet off the ground, slowing, dropping altitude. Freeman's signal had led us to a private airstrip. Whoever owned the property had apparently abandoned it. No planes sat on the runway.

"We can tell you that the Tachyon D concentration on Olympus Kri has increased significantly over the last hour, perhaps by a factor of four."

"Does that mean something is about to happen?" I asked as we touched down.

"It may mean several things, General; but we do not have sufficient information to make any predictions," Sweetwater said.

Nobles taxied. There was a three-story control tower at the far end of the runway. Freeman stood beside the tower, dressed in custom-fitted Marine combat armor. He might well have been listening in on this conversation, Sweetwater had contacted me on an open frequency. If Freeman wasn't listening, it meant he and Sweetwater had already had this conversation.

"If we have drawn correct conclusions from New Copenhagen, the tachyon particles the Avatari are using for this attack won't be recycled like the ones they used in their first wave of attacks," Sweetwater said.

"What does that mean?" I asked.

Nobles slowed the shuttle as we approached the tower.

"In their first invasion, the Avatari kept recycling the same base of particles. They bonded them together to form soldiers and guns. When we destroyed the soldiers, the tachyons returned to the atmosphere, where they recharged. We believe these new particles vanish once their energy is expended."

"I don't like the sound of that," I said. Images of atomic explosions danced in my head.

Nobles stopped the shuttle, and the fuselage lowered, but I remained in my seat.

"That is the bad news. The good news is that the Avatari appear to want the planet in one piece."

"Do they have other options?" I asked.

"General, with the kind of energy those tachyons produce, the aliens could demolish Olympus Kri. They could reduce it to a floating cinder or make it explode into atom-sized fragments. Our analysis of the attack on New Copenhagen leads us to believe that the aliens plan to annihilate any opposition on the planet without destroying the planet itself."

"That's the good news?" I asked.

"We do feel a little better knowing that they do not want to destroy the planet, yes," Sweetwater said. I could not tell if the cocky little bastard was joking or not.

"Breeze says we'll be safe if we're fifty feet underground."

There was a pause.

Normally, I let these pauses work themselves out. This time I asked. "What am I missing here?"

"We've looked at Arthur's calculations," Sweetwater hedged.

"You don't agree with them?" I asked.

"Arthur's calculations always add up perfectly," he said, still not sounding confident. "In fact, we think you would be safe fifteen feet underground. It's the intangibles that have us worried."

"The intangibles?" I asked.

"With the kind of power the Avatari have in those Tachyon D particles, they could destroy the entire planet. That is clearly not what they plan to do; but our question is, how much damage will they be willing to inflict on the planet if they know you are on it?"

## CHAPTER
# FIFTY

"Why is your fleet landing men?" Freeman asked me, as we watched the shuttle streak across the runway. I felt like a passenger on the deck of the *Titanic* watching the last of the lifeboats rowing away.

"Are you sure they're ours? Maybe the Unifieds are landing troops," I said, sensing another betrayal.

Freeman shook his head, and said, "No, these men are clones, and they are riding in on E.M.N. transports."

"Shit," I said, realizing who those clones would be. They were leaving the Double Ys behind. *What do you do with seventeen thousand unwanted prisoners?* I asked myself, and I knew the answer. If you considered them an inferior form of humanity, you sent them to burn.

"They're killing the Double Y clones," I said.

I felt no urge to prevent the genocide. I could not stop it if I wanted to; but deep down, I did not want to stop it. The Double Ys were volatile, as unstable as primed grenades, and potentially more dangerous. The universe would be a safer place without them.

"Are they in Odessa?" I asked, halfheartedly wondering if perhaps there might be some way to lead them to safety. I would not put my life on the line to save the pathetic bastards, but I might warn them to go underground.

"Jerome, it's on the other side of the planet," Freeman said. Jerome was the second largest city on Olympus Kri.

"So it's out of our hands," I said.

Freeman said nothing.

Our conversation had hit a stalemate that Sweetwater broke when he contacted us over the interLink. "Gentlemen, you should be aware that the temperature on Olympus Kri has risen by six degrees over the last fifteen minutes."

*Six degrees,* I thought, putting the Double Ys out of my mind completely. "That doesn't sound so out of the ordinary," I said. It was late in the morning . . .

"Was that change global?" Freeman asked.

"Global," said Sweetwater.

"So at this rate, we'll hit nine thousand degrees in another six months," I said.

"The surface temperature is unstable; but for what it's worth, we don't believe this change is a preamble to the event," Sweetwater said. "Still, you might want to get to safety as quickly as possible."

"Have you notified the fleet?" Freeman asked. He meant the Unified Authority Fleet. The Enlisted Man's Fleet had supposedly come to oversee the evacuation; the Unified Authority had come to conduct it.

"Yes, sir," Sweetwater said. "They are on the last stages of the evacuation as we speak."

There were so many transports climbing through the skies over Odessa, they looked like a swarm of flies. How long would it take to lift seventeen million people? At one hundred people per transport, it would take 170,000 trips. *How in God's name did we ever get ourselves into this speck-up?*

I asked myself. I knew the answer. We didn't. This one was thrust upon us.

Sweetwater said a quick good-bye and signed off.

Freeman had an all-terrain armored truck waiting just off the airstrip. Without saying a word, he headed toward that truck, knowing that I would follow. And I did.

I walked to the truck and climbed in on the passenger's side, pausing for one last glance at the metropolis that had been zoned for extinction. The air was still and quiet. The sky was crisp and blue and clear, with frothy clouds floating across it. Twenty miles away, downtown Odessa loomed like a vertical shadow, like a butte that filled the horizon. The thousands of smoke trails rising above the city looked no more substantial than the filaments of a cobweb. They rose in odd angles and twisted into the sky.

"I used to know a girl from Olympus Kri," I told Freeman. "I met her when I was on leave."

"So she was scrub," he said.

"She was my first," I said, feeling nostalgic. I could not remember her name, but I remembered her smile and her laugh. The truck's engine growled like some kind of prehistoric beast, and I sat back and closed the door and wondered if the girl had made it off the planet alive. I wondered if she remembered me.

We did not have far to drive. Freeman, as always, considered every contingency when he made plans. We cut across an empty suburb. I had seen many abandoned suburbs in the last few years, but I still got a haunted feeling when I saw them. Driving down avenues in which houses sat empty, the doors of some homes left open, I wondered if I would ever drive down neighborhood streets in which children still played.

Freeman veered toward the mountains, and I saw our destination. We would ride out the *event* in a power station that had been built into the side of a cliff.

Only the façade of the administrative offices was visible from the street. It was a three-story pillbox made of concrete and steel, with no effort given to ornamentation.

The land in front of the building was parklike, with sprawling hills, a manicured lawn, and a footbridge spanning a man-made river. Freeman drove us across this jade-and-sapphire

setting and into a concrete alley that opened to a parking lot
in which a fleet of heavy equipment sat unguarded—ladder
trucks and cranes and bulldozers. Across the lot, the open maw
of a subterranean bunker gaped from the side of a mountain.

"Picturesque," I said to Freeman, who only grunted. He
stopped the truck just inside the bunker, climbed out, and
worked some buttons, causing a thick metal curtain to close
behind us. Lights bloomed along the ramp leading down deep
below.

"Think we'll be able to exit the same way that we came?"
I asked.

"There's a back door if we need it," he said as he climbed
back in the truck. He had to work to wedge himself in behind
the steering wheel. I would have offered to drive, but he would
not have accepted the offer. Comfortable or not, he preferred
to drive.

We drove down the spiraling ramp, passing floors with
twenty-foot ceilings. The walls of the ramp were foot-thick
cement. The subterranean structure housed massive turbines
and generators. We had entered a shadowy underworld of
concrete and steel, driving three floors down beneath the foot
of a mountain.

"It doesn't get much safer than this," I said. I kept my
armor on but took my helmet off. The air in the power station
was cold and slightly moist. Once Freeman killed the engine
on the truck, I listened for the whir of turbines; but I heard
nothing.

Freeman placed his little two-way on the dash of the truck
and tapped the button. A moment later, Sweetwater and
Breeze appeared.

"I know they're almost done, but they're still cutting it too
close," Breeze said without looking into the screen. I got the
feeling he was talking to Sweetwater. "The temperature on
the planet is fluctuating wildly."

Hearing this, I envisioned hundred-degree swings with
snow falling on burning desert sands and melting into steam,
but I knew better. We had just come from the surface.

Sweetwater put the fluctuations in perspective. He turned
toward the camera, and said, "We're seeing ten-degree temperature swings."

*So much for icebergs melting and oceans boiling,* I thought.

"Have you told General Hill?" Freeman asked.

"He says they're going as fast as they can," answered Sweetwater.

"Oh my," said Breeze. "They just had a twelve-degree fluctuation." Shaking his head with decision, he looked into the camera, "It could happen any moment." He grimaced. His looked like they were meant for chewing hay.

As it turned out, Breeze was wrong, the *event* did not occur for a long time. One hour passed, then another. Sweetwater and Breeze gave us hourly reports informing us that surface temperatures had stabilized more or less. Strangely, stabilized temperatures panicked Breeze just as much as fluctuations.

Three hours after we sealed ourselves in, Sweetwater called to tell us that the Tachyon D count had doubled over the last hour.

Between calls, I had nothing to do but sit and wait. I explored the power station, examining enormous turbines that reached to the ceiling. At one point, I went looking for something to eat. I found a refrigerator in the employee lounge and stole people's lunches. Some of them were old, with withered apples and petrified bananas.

Despite the temptation to hoard food for myself, I brought the lunches back to the truck and shared them with Freeman. He chose a plate with several pieces of chicken. I took a sandwich.

"What if the building collapses?" I asked Freeman. "How are we going to dig our way out?"

He took a bite from a drumstick that looked like it might have come off a parakeet in his big hands. He bit off a mouthful of meat and pointed toward a distant wall, where an emergency exit sign glowed.

"Stairs?" I asked. "That's your answer if the building comes down around us? We can just take the stairs."

"The rest of the station will collapse before that stairwell," he said.

We continued divvying the food. Freeman chose meats first. I went with fruits and snacks. By the time we got to the salads, we'd both lost interest.

Another hour passed. I thought about the Double Y clones. Did they know they were in danger?

Breeze called in to tell us that the last of the transports had docked with the barges. He guessed that a few looters might be left on the planet, but not many. He didn't know that Warshaw was dumping prisoners to be killed. I wondered how he would have reacted to the news.

As Freeman chatted with Sweetwater and Breeze, I found a comfortable curve on the back of the truck and fell asleep against it.

Apparently, I slept right through the event.

# PART V

# AFTERMATH

# FIFTY-ONE

"It's over."

Freeman woke me from a light sleep. I opened my eyes, got my bearings, and slid off my spot in the back of the truck.

The air down at the bottom of the station was cool. An odd pattern of emergency lights showed from the ceilings. I looked around the shadowy chamber and thought to myself, *It couldn't have been much of an explosion if I slept through it.*

I was still reviewing that thought when an explosion occurred. As cataclysms go, it was not much. The ground did not shake, and the walls did not crumble. An audible thud rang through the underground power station, and that was that. *Shit. If that little thud is all that we get, Warshaw's going to ride my ass forever,* I thought to myself. The underground station seemed to have survived the *event* without so much as a crack.

Putting on his helmet to seal his armor, Freeman started walking up the ramp. I donned my helmet and followed, scanning for radiation as I went. I used the night-for-day lens in my visor so I could see clearly in the dark.

The top level of the station seemed unaffected by whatever had happened. The structure looked sound, no breaks in the walls, no toppled equipment. As we rounded a turn and started toward the exit, I noticed something on the ground. In the blue-gray graphics of my night-for-day lens, the stuff looked like ice. It had an organic look, like a thick liquid that had spilled on the ground and frozen in place.

I switched the lens in my visor to heat vision. Through this lens, frozen objects appeared blue and humans gave off an orange signature. The stuff on the concrete near my feet was white. Had I stepped on it, my armored boot would have melted.

I started to ask Freeman what it was, but when I looked up the ramp, I had my answer. I saw the night sky. The heavy metal shutter Freeman had lowered to block the entrance had melted soft, then imploded. Its soggy cardboardlike remains still blocked the bottom third of the doorway, but some of the metal had melted to liquid and run down the ramp.

"We might as well blow the rest of it right off its tracks," I said.

"Once it cools down," Freeman said.

I examined the magmalike liquid using heat vision. It no longer gave off a glowing white signature; in just those few seconds, it had cooled to the color of butter. The concrete around the entrance glowed a dark yellow. Freeman stood fifty feet back from the entrance; the walls around him barely registered on my visor.

"What the speck happened here?" I asked.

Freeman did not answer.

I asked, "Have you checked with Sweetwater and Breeze?"

"Communications are out."

If a nuke went off outside this station, the shock wave would have sent the door flying, but it wouldn't have specking melted it. Not a thick metal door like this one. I looked back at the remains, noting the way the top curled in like a badly hung curtain. Above the wilting metal, the night sky looked almost ablaze, the lower clouds glowing an eerie orange.

A moment passed before I realized that I wasn't looking at clouds; I was looking at a sky filled with steam. The re-breather in my armor would protect me if I stepped out; but without it, that air would have poached my lungs.

Whatever had struck Olympus Kri, it wasn't just powerful, it was cataclysmic. Did it land on the planet or simply strike from space? The Avatari's new weapon of destruction had an almost velvet touch. The ground had not shook. Hell, I slept through the entire event.

For now, Freeman and I were trapped in the underground station, not buried alive, but trapped. We could not leave the ramp, there was too much molten metal on the ground, and the concrete around the entrance was burning hot, heated to crystal.

Not daring to step any closer, I stared out through the

ruined entrance and into the sky. I saw clouds of steam that smoldered against a dirty black sky. With its roiling orange clouds and its layers of steam and smoke, the horizon looked like it was made of embers.

"What do we do now?" I asked.

"We wait," Freeman answered.

"How long?" I asked.

"Till the planet cools off."

Had one of my Marines said that, I would have busted the sarcastic prick in the nose. From Freeman, I smiled and ignored it. He wasn't capable of sarcasm . . . and I wasn't capable of busting him in the nose.

So we walked back down the ramp and I found my place on the truck and tried to sleep. I closed my eyes and pretended to drift off, but it was all pretend. The image of a planet burning like a lump of coal in a furnace filled my mind. I thought about Terraneau reduced to a cinder and Ava caught in the blaze.

If I made it off this planet, I would go to Terraneau. I would beg Doctorow to evacuate the planet. I would beg Ava to leave with me. At some point, I slipped into that frenetic state between sleep and consciousness in which I could never tell the difference between dreams and reality. I imagined myself walking through the ashes of Norristown, looking for Ava.

In my dream, the streets had vanished, and all of the buildings had vanished, all but the three towers that Doctorow used as dormitories. The three skyscrapers in the center of town still stood, but they had melted. Their straight edges had melted and they now had curves and convolutions and I realized that they looked like skeletal fingers sticking out of the ground. They were black, like the color of charred bone, and they reached up to the ashen sky, and I recognized them. The finger on the left belonged to Ellery Doctorow and the finger on the right belonged to Scott Mars; and though I desperately tried to deny it, I knew that the finger in the center was Ava.

"Ava!" I shouted. In my sleep, the name came out so slowly that it sounded like a wind that could blow apart rocks.

Freeman woke me from the dream. He tapped on my helmet until I sat up, then he said, "We can get out." As I stood and stretched my arms, he climbed into the truck and started the engine.

Sweetwater greeted me on both the interLink and the little two-way as I slipped into the passenger's seat. "Glad to see you made it," he said, sounding unnaturally cheerful.

"What happened out there?" I asked.

"We were just telling Raymond," Sweetwater said.

Breeze came on as well. He must have been sitting and Sweetwater standing, or maybe Sweetwater was on a ladder. They looked to be about the same size on the little screen of the two-way.

"I've never seen anything like this," Breeze said. "We had satellites all around the planet looking for an explosion. From all we observed, it was a spontaneous event."

Excited by a discovery that seemed to ignore the laws of physics, Breeze no longer stuttered. "The temperature over Odessa rose from seventy-two degrees to nine thousand degrees so quickly that our instruments recorded it as instantaneous. The same thing happened all around the planet—a spontaneous and uniform change in temperature to nine thousand degrees."

"Which also explains why the Tachyon D levels dropped," Sweetwater said. "The little devils consumed themselves. They burned themselves up like gas in a fire. Do you have any idea how much energy it would take to generate that much heat?"

The dwarf scientist squared his shoulders, and said, "Here. Here are some of the satellite images. You can see for yourself."

Sweetwater and Breeze disappeared from the screen, replaced by the image of a city at night. Streetlights shone, but no cars roved the streets. Without lights shining in their windows, the buildings of Odessa hid in the darkness.

Then it happened. The *event* did not start on one side of the screen and move to the other like an explosion; it happened everywhere all at once. The very air seemed to catch on fire.

"Nine thousand degrees," Sweetwater said. "It's nearly as hot as the surface of the sun." Sweetwater, the communicator, used analogies. Breeze, the scientist, spouted them.

The satellite footage showed a car parked along the side of the street. The paint dulled, metal sagged, and the car exploded. It flipped through the air, landing on its roof. It looked like a turtle turned on its shell. Moments later, its tires burst into flames.

Grass, trees, cloth awnings, and signs burst into flames. Steam rose up around an iron lid covering a manhole, then the cover launched and spun through the air like a tossed coin. By the time it hit the ground, the street had melted, and it sank into the tar.

Thick fog rose from the flaming wreckage of a grassy park. The steel cables along a suspension bridge stretched and drooped like melting plastic, finally giving way and dropping the bridge into the river below. The cloud of steam coming off the river was thick as linen.

*You can't fight this,* I thought, as I watched the scene with grim fascination.

I saw cars and trucks sinking into the street below them and thin coils of steam rising from cement sidewalks. I saw concrete shelters collapse in on themselves. Explosions occurred everywhere. A fire hydrant burst, sending a column of steam into the air. The camera focused on a skyscraper, the windows along the bottom of the building melting in their casings.

A counter appeared in the top right corner of the screen. It ticked off seconds and hundredths of seconds.

"Now this is curious," Sweetwater said, the excitement obvious in his gravelly voice.

The camera panned back, showing more of the street. The windows of several buildings along an avenue exploded, spitting out shotgun bursts of glittering glass shrapnel that turned a fiery orange and melted in the air.

Sweetwater continued to narrate. "You see how the windows are bursting outward? We think it is because the atmosphere is rising. That means the pressure from the air trapped inside the buildings is not being matched by air pressure on the outside of the building. It's all guesswork, of course, no one has ever seen anything like this before; but we think heat is causing the atmosphere to rise like a hot-air balloon, so the pressure on the outside of the buildings is dropping. Here, look at this!"

The camera moved in on a skyscraper. The building coughed glass out of its windows floor by floor, the damage rising quickly. Not all of the windows shattered. Some had already melted.

The image changed to show a forest, and the timer in the corner returned to zero. At five seconds, the trees in the forest lit up like match heads in a book that had been set ablaze. The trees did not ignite one here and one there, they all lit up at once, flaring into a brilliant orange.

The image changed again, this time showing a vast body of water, maybe an ocean or maybe a great lake. Then the heat started. Twenty seconds in, steam began to rise off the water.

"We estimate the heat penetrated no more than five feet deep," Sweetwater said. "Any fish swimming close to shore would have been poached."

To this point, the video feed did not show anything that might have caused the explosion I had heard when I awoke. Nor had it shown anything that would have caused the shutter at the top of the power station to burst inward.

On the screen, the timer showed eighty-three seconds and froze.

"It lasted precisely eighty-three seconds," Sweetwater said, the former excitement missing from his voice. "At eighty-three seconds, the heat stopped, and the air temperature dropped sharply."

The timer started counting. It reached ninety-six seconds, and there was the explosion. Nothing big or fiery, but something powerful enough to make weakened buildings collapse as it flushed enormous clouds of ash and soot into the air.

"What was that?" asked Freeman.

"The heat from the event lifted the atmosphere. We estimate that the atmosphere rose approximately 550 feet from ground level because of the heat. After the event ended, the atmosphere dropped back into place," said Sweetwater.

Freeman said nothing. He sat silent and unmoving, his helmet hiding his expression. I whispered a constant stream of expletives to myself as I watched the destruction.

The video feed stopped, and the scientists again appeared on the screen. Breeze stared into a monitor on his desk instead of the camera. Sweetwater stared into the camera as if watching us.

Breeze looked up from his monitor and turned to face us.

"I've reviewed the data again, and I still cannot find evidence of an initial explosion, not even a transfer of energy that might have set this off."

"The only anomaly is the tachyons," Sweetwater agreed.

"Does the atmosphere look stable?" Freeman asked.

"Completely stable," said Breeze.

"Raymond, you want to be careful out there," Sweetwater said. "We're tracking movement on the planet."

"You mean survivors?" I asked, thinking of the Double Y clones and wondering how any of those bastards could have survived.

"Whatever it is, it's so fast it barely registers on our instruments," Sweetwater said.

"It's behaving like an electrical current in circuit," Breeze said, trying to be helpful but unable to divest himself of scientific jargon that meant nothing to us military types.

"We think it's traveling a set path, but we only pick it up in certain locations," Sweetwater said by way of explanation. "We can't tell if there is a single current streaming around the planet or several separate currents traveling in vectors, but our instruments keep registering it in the same key locations."

Until that moment, I had taken it as a given that the *event* had ended—the Avatari had come, they'd toasted the planet, and now they were gone. But maybe my assumptions were wrong. Maybe after toasting the planet, they left something behind to finish off survivors.

"What about the tachyon levels?" Freeman asked, sounding more like a scientist than a mercenary.

"Oh, now that is interesting," Sweetwater said. "Ninety-nine percent of the Tachyon D concentration was spent during the conflagration. The rest is diminishing quickly."

"Will the current disappear when the tachyons run out?" Freeman asked.

"Excellent question, Raymond. That is our guess," said Sweetwater. "Only time will tell if our hypothesis is correct. Of course, we still found a residue of Tachyon D on New Copenhagen, so the assumptions may not be valid."

"How long before it's safe out there?" I asked. By this time, I had fished five grenade launchers out of my go-pack.

"At this rate, fifteen minutes," Sweetwater said. "Perhaps

you should stay where you are and wait until the currents runs down."

The truck was already moving before he finished the suggestion. Freeman asked, "Do you have a fix on our location." When Sweetwater nodded, he said, "It's time to run the tests."

Freeman stepped on the gas, and the truck lurched ahead, growling like a mongrel dog, tearing around corners and speeding up the ramp. As we approached the entrance, I expected him to fire a rocket at the remnant of that steel door, but he didn't. He pulled to a stop about twenty feet from the top.

"What are you doing?" I asked.

"I'm going to set a charge," he said.

I laughed and handed him a grenade launcher. He didn't need my weapons, the truck had rockets and a chain gun mounted on its front fender.

Freeman ignored me. He placed charges beside both ends of the door, then came back to the truck. His charges produced tiny explosions, and the door tipped over and fell out of its track.

Using charges instead of rockets struck me as prissy, but it probably saved our lives.

# FIFTY-TWO

Freeman's charges exploded, and the remains of the metal shutter toppled backward in a drunken twist, revealing an altered world. The parking lot had not changed much, but the fleet of heavy equipment was no longer parked in neat rows. A steamroller had simply sunk into the street. Cranes lay on their sides, and a few of the trucks now lay upside down.

"What the hell?" I hissed as I surveyed the wreckage. Having seen the video feed, I should have known what to expect; but I still was not prepared for it. The feed showed me places I had never seen, but I had just driven through this parking lot a few hours earlier.

Stolid as ever, Freeman said nothing.

"Gentlemen, you will want to keep your helmets on," Sweetwater said.

"If you mean it's hot out there, I can see that," I said. Sitting in the truck, eyeing the devastation, I felt overwhelmed.

I looked to my right and saw the remains of a Dumpster. The thin sheet metal of its walls had simply wilted in the heat.

"The temperature outside the tunnel is 126 degrees," Sweetwater said. "That qualifies as toasty. But the reason you'll want your helmets is to breathe. You're in the middle of a fire zone, the oxygen is thin."

"How thin?" I asked. I thought about lessons I had learned in science growing up in the orphanage. "Does oxygen burn at nine thousand degrees?"

"Oxygen doesn't burn," Sweetwater said.

As Sweetwater spoke, Freeman returned to the top of the ramp, where he attached some kind of panel to the wall. A large white light at the top of the panel winked sporadically, and smaller diodes flashed red, blue, yellow, green in no discernible order along the bottom.

"What is that?" I asked.

"Raymond, it is essential we get the meter up right away," Sweetwater said.

"It's up," Freeman said.

"What is that?" I repeated.

"Harris, this little invention just may save your life. It detects tachyon activity. If the tachyons flood into your hidey-hole, we should be able to detect them."

"I thought tachyons were too small and too fast to track," I said.

"The meter tracks energy fluctuations along a defined plain," Breeze explained.

"Does that answer your question?" Sweetwater asked, mostly because he knew that it had not. I decided to move on rather than risk more scientific gibberish.

As I watched the lights on the panel, Freeman walked around the truck and pulled out a black case that looked about the right size to carry a spare set of armor. It did not carry armor, however. When he opened it, I recognized the contents. I had seen him use one of these before.

The head of the robot was a radio-controlled drone with a propeller and wings. The body was a twelve-foot-long train made of a heat-resistant silver material. It reflected the ember-and-smoke sky like a mirror. He removed the "flying snake" from its case, stretched it out, then used his remote to launch it in the air behind the truck.

The snake took off from the ground and swirled through the air like a Chinese dragon. The last time I saw Freeman use one of these remote-controlled robots, he had deployed it like a lightning rod, sending it out to distract motion-tracking robots called "trackers."

The drone's terephthalate ruffles fluttered as it sped off, making a noise like a flag in a strong wind. The robot flew out of the underground power station and into the parking lot. It managed an aerobatic loop, then burst into flames. The spontaneous combustion lasted only a second and left nothing in its wake, not even smoke.

"Did you get that?" asked Freeman.

Damn straight I saw it, and I started to say so, then I realized he wasn't speaking to me.

"Localized ignition," Breeze said. "Of course, it happened so quickly I can only speculate."

"Raymond, can you launch the second drone?" Sweetwater asked.

Freeman set off to prepare a second drone without responding.

I eavesdropped as Sweetwater and Breeze spoke privately between themselves, their voices carrying over an open mike as if they were real. They traded scientific jargon, but they could have been speaking some long-extinct language for all I understood of it.

Meanwhile, Freeman returned with another black case. A few moments later, a second silver dragon soared up the ramp, its reflective train wagging behind it. It flew over the top of the truck and into the parking lot, where it burst into flames.

"It appears the tachyons are drawn to movement," Breeze said.

"Should I run the shield test? Freeman asked.

"Yes, we better move along. The tachyon level is dropping faster than we expected," said Sweetwater.

Freeman's next toy was a little robot car, which he placed on the ground beside the truck. He fiddled with a remote, and a bright yellow glow formed around the car. I knew that glow. I'd seen it around Unified Authority ships. It hung like an aura over the new U.A. combat armor. It stopped bullets and particle beams.

Using a remote to guide the car up the ramp, Freeman asked, "Are you ready?"

"Go ahead, Raymond," said Sweetwater.

Those shields might have been able to stop bullets or absorb lasers, but they didn't do shit against tachyons. As the car wound its way into the yard, it burst into flames.

Seeing this, I felt hollow inside. "Could they do the same thing to our ships?" I asked anyone who might answer.

Sweetwater fielded the question like a politician. "We don't see any reason why they would bother attacking a ship."

Breeze took a more honest approach. He simply said, "Yes."

We were running out of time. When Freeman asked, "Should I try the weapons?" Sweetwater said, "By all means."

Freeman pulled a sniper rifle from the back of the truck. He was the finest marksman I had ever known, but in this case it wouldn't matter. All he had to do was fire a bullet through a thirty-foot-wide doorway at the top of the ramp. He pointed the gun in the right direction and pulled the trigger. A split second later, with the sound of the shot still echoing off the walls, a tiny flicker of flame ignited just outside the entrance to the tunnel. The bullet had combusted, just like the toy car, just like the drone dragon. It disappeared so quickly, I barely saw it.

"Six feet," said Breeze.

"Six feet?" I asked.

"The bullet traveled six feet out of the station before it caught fire," Sweetwater said.

Breezed corrected him. "It might have caught fire the moment it entered open air, but it traveled six feet before it disintegrated."

Freeman removed a particle-beam cannon and started toward the top of the ramp.

"Are you sure you want to do that?" I asked, knowing that if its ray superheated, the gun would explode.

He did not answer. As he moved up the ramp, I watched the light on the sensor. It stayed mostly white, with an occasional flick of yellow. As Freeman got closer, the light turned yellow. The tachyon activity had shot up; they might even have homed in on him.

"Ray, stop!" I yelled.

He saw it, too, and froze, but the light remained yellow.

"What do I do?" I asked Sweetwater and Breeze.

"Raymond, stay perfectly still," Sweetwater ordered.

Sounding calm as ever, Freeman asked, "Should I run the test?"

Sweetwater did not even consider the question. "Stay still. According to our latest readings, the tachyon concentration will drop to a safe level in two minutes."

Freeman chose that moment to do something that was absolutely insane. Instead of concentrating on standing as still as possible, he fired the cannon. The glittering green beam of the particle beam traveled in a perfectly straight line the rest of the way out of the power station and out, into the yard.

My eyes switched from the particle beam to the meter warning panel and back. I had already slipped into the driver's seat of the truck and started the engine. If the meter turned orange or green or black or any color other than white, I would launch the truck up the ramp to try to distract the tachyons.

Unlike the bullet, the shielded robotic car, and the drones, the beam seemed not to interest the tachyons. The meter flashed orange for a millisecond, and I stomped down on the gas, stayed behind the wheel just long enough to guide the truck around Freeman, then jumped from the cab. Trying to run straight up a spiral path, the truck bumped one wall and skidded across the ramp, a shower of sparks trailing behind it. Armored or not, the truck burst into flames the moment it entered into the yard. The explosion that followed launched the truck fifteen feet in the air. It spun like a corkscrew as it flew ass first, then landed nose down, three-foot flames dancing on its engine and all four wheels.

Freeman said nothing. His silence was icy.

"Sweetwater," I said. "How much longer?"

Nothing.

"Breeze?"

Nothing.

"They're gone," Freeman said. "We were linked to them through the two-way communicator."

"The one in the truck?" I asked.

Freeman did not answer.

"Does that mean they're dead?" I asked, wondering if I had somehow destroyed the computer world in which they existed.

Freeman responded with a rare show of humor. He said, "Not any deader than they were before."

# CHAPTER
## FIFTY-THREE

Without Sweetwater and Breeze guiding our next steps, Freeman and I ended up sitting on the ramp for twenty minutes before deciding to take our chances on the street. I still had a go-pack filled with weapons, so I piped a grenade into the parking lot. When it lasted long enough to explode, I hurled the empty launcher after it. The six-inch chrome cylinder clanked when it hit the cement, rolled in a circle, and came to a stop.

"Looks safe," I said. Freeman climbed to his feet and started hiking toward the entrance without responding.

As we stepped out, I took a temperature reading using the atmospheric thermometer built into my visor. The air temperature had dropped to a mere ninety-three degrees—about one percent of what it had been earlier that evening. I took a Geiger reading and found that the radiation levels were normal, possibly even low.

I looked at what had once been a brick-lined planting bed with large bushes. There was no sign of the bushes or the soil below them. Instead of dirt, the ground was covered with a combination of soot and coal-like crystals that sparkled like fool's gold.

Wispy spirals of steam rose from the ground below our feet, but our boots did not sink into the ash-covered concrete. Ripples of heat rose from a crane lying on its side a few feet ahead of us.

My brain numbed by the devastation on every side of me, I followed Freeman around the administration building and out to the street. Newly formed air pockets in the sidewalk caved in under my feet as I walked along the road; crystalline glass and ash crunched under my boots when we walked on the soil.

Using my commandLink, I signaled for Nobles to come and get us. When he asked if he should come in a transport or the shuttle, I told him to bring the shuttle. Soft seats and a carpeted cabin sounded good at the moment.

A few minutes later, the sleek bird appeared in the sky, winding its way down to us so quickly it looked like it might crash. Nobles touched down on an empty stretch of highway, his wheels sinking two inches into the crumbling ground.

We flew to the *ad-Din* through almost vacant space. The barges had long since left. So had most of our ships. With Olympus Kri evacuated and burned, there was no reason to maintain a fleet in the area. What remained was a small coven of six E.M.N. cruisers, which included the *Kamehameha*. That meant that Warshaw had called yet another summit, which I hoped to avoid. Now that Warshaw was grooming Hollingsworth to replace me, I thought he would go as the token Marine.

My ship, the *Salah ad-Din*, hovered by itself several miles from the others. So did a Unified Authority cruiser. It looked so small beside our fighter carriers. Seeing the U.A. ship, I realized this might be more than an Enlisted Man's summit. That cruiser had probably ferried some high-level U.A. negotiator.

As we approached the *ad-Din*, I received a message from Captain Villanueva directing me to the *Kamehameha*. I acknowledged the transmission and cursed under my breath.

"Do you have any interest in attending an Enlisted Man's summit?" I asked Freeman.

He shook his head. He looked down on politicians and general officers every bit as much as they looked down on him. "I have a plane waiting on that cruiser," he said.

"What are you going to do next?" I asked.

"Same as you, I'm getting ready for Terraneau," he said.

I laughed, and said, "It sounds like you're out to save humanity."

He did not answer.

I went to the little stateroom at the back of the shuttle and changed out of my armor before meeting with Warshaw. I showered, shaved, and put on a fresh uniform. By the time I came out, Freeman was long gone.

No one came to greet me as I came off the shuttle. I left the landing bay and found my way to the fleet deck; only with Warshaw in charge, it was more than a fleet deck—it was the seat of an empire.

One of Warshaw's lieutenants interrupted the summit to let him know that I had arrived. About thirty minutes later, having called a brief recess, Warshaw and his entourage came out to greet me.

"General Harris, the man of the hour," Warshaw said, giving me a rare salute. "A lot of people are still alive because of you."

He looked tired. His eyes were red, and dark blotches showed on his cheeks. His broad shoulders were tight and as straight across as a board.

I tried to despise Warshaw for the genocide of the Double Y clones, but in my heart I doubted myself. I had mixed feelings. He had disposed of them in a way that was heartless, logical, and efficient. I would not have disposed of them that way; and the Enlisted Man's Empire would have paid the price for my inability to act. In this instance, Warshaw was not my moral inferior; he was simply more courageous than me.

He guided me into the meeting room. Admirals came and shook my hand. The greetings were cordial, but the smiles did not last long.

"We need to get back to the negotiations," Warshaw said.

"What negotiations?" I asked.

"I would have thought that was obvious," he said, a frigid edge in his voice. "You saw what happened down there."

The tiny drops of sweat on his shaved head reflected light like a coat of wax. He tried to wipe them away, but the perspiration was too fine. He wore his dress whites, with all of its stars and medals and epaulets. Even tired and frustrated, he cut an impressive figure, his bodybuilder's physique stressing every inch of his stiff white uniform.

"Life as we know it just ended," he said. "The Unifieds are talking about resurrecting the old Cousteau undersea cities programs. They think we might be able to survive this storm if we go underwater."

I vaguely remembered learning about the Cousteau program. When the United States and its allies began colonizing space, the old French government turned its eyes toward deep-sea exploration. The program lasted a couple of years before the French gave up and signed on with the Americans.

"Rebuilding those cities could take years, maybe decades," I said.

"You got any better ideas?" Warshaw asked.

I wasn't challenging him, but he crushed me just the same. I felt rage spreading through me, then I realized it was embarrassment. I did not have any better ideas. I stood there wishing I could fade away.

"Looks like we're rejoining the Unified Authority. Earth is the only planet that never got invaded. The aliens will go there last; hopefully, we can get everyone underwater by then.

"Welcome to the future, Harris; it's just like the goddamned past."

I stood there, silent and frustrated.

Warshaw studied my expression, and finally said, "This is a negotiation, not a war council. I can't bring you in, I just wanted to thank you for what you did on Olympus Kri. You gave us a fighting chance, but it's over now."

The words stung because I knew he was right.

"I need to get to Terraneau," I said.

"You're going to warn them?" Warshaw asked.

"They're next," I said.

"I hear you had a girl on that rock," Warshaw said. "Hollingsworth says you hooked up with Ava Gardner."

"Yeah, something like that," I said, already anxious to leave.

"How are you going to get there?" he asked. "I can't give you the *ad-Din* if you're traveling into neutral space. The Unifieds might see that as an act of bad faith."

He was right, of course. None of the reactivated broadcast stations were programmed to send me out to Terraneau. I would need a self-broadcasting ship. "I'll find a way," I said.

Warshaw smiled and shook his head. "You're on your own with Terraneau. It's not part of our empire." Then he signaled for an aide to join our conversation. "McGraw, the general needs a broadcast key."

The aide was an old man. He gave me a surprised glance, then said, "Aye, aye, sir."

"A broadcast key?" I asked.

"You're going to need a key if you're going to get that shuttle you're flying to Terraneau," Warshaw said. He started to leave, then turned back, and added, "You be careful with that key, Harris. I only issue them to fleet commanders . . . and now to you. God knows you've earned it."

"Thank you, sir," I said. The man was a prick. The man was a bastard. The man was a savior.

Warshaw gave me a weak salute, and said, "Good luck." With that, I seemed to dematerialize before him. He turned away as if I weren't there and began speaking with the officers in his entourage.

"General, perhaps we should get going, sir," the petty officer said. He was an older man, a veteran sailor with white hair to show for decades of service.

I nodded.

We took a lift down into Engineering. From there, we wound our way into the arcane maze of high-tech specialists, where sailors who worked on weapons systems, communications, and life-support systems maintained their offices. The door to Broadcast Engineering stood out; that was the door with armed guards on either side of it. Warshaw's aide showed the guards his badge, and they let us through.

We entered, and the petty officer went to a computer and filled out the requisition protocol. It took twenty minutes.

Broadcast Engineering looked like a mediaLink repair shop. A workbench littered with parts and tools ran along one of the walls. The lights were so bright they dried my eyes. A half dozen men worked here, all of them sitting on tall stools and gazing through magnifying lenses as they tinkered with circuit boards. Everyone in the room, of course, was a clone.

When McGraw finished typing out the request, he hit the SEND button, then called across the room, "Baxter, I just sent you a high-priority requisition."

"Got it," Baxter yelled back.

They were joking around. They were sitting less than thirty feet apart and could have whispered to each other. Once Baxter saw the requisition, however, he became serious. He climbed from his stool and walked over to McGraw. "Why in the world would Warshaw issue a broadcast key to a Marine? Does this guy even have clearance to be up here?"

"All I can say is that Magilla gave me the order," the petty officer said.

"Shit. You're kidding."

The old petty officer shook his head.

I don't know what I expected a broadcast key to look like, maybe a torpedo or some other projectile that I would fire into the broadcast zone. When the sailor returned, he handed me a palm-sized box no bigger than a candy bar.

"And a book," McGraw told Baxter.

The sailor sighed and went to fetch the book.

The key was a tiny touch screen, an unimpressive trinket that would fit in your pocket without making a bulge. The book was three inches thick and lined in black leather. The petty officer took the book, handed it to me, and said, "General, sir, you now hold the key to the empire."

McGraw traded salutes with Baxter, and we left Broadcast Engineering.

As we waited for the lift, I examined the key, and said, "It's a lot less impressive than I expected."

McGraw laughed. "It's a transmitter. Transmits old-fashioned frequency-modulated radio waves. Warshaw set up the hot zones to disassemble anything that enters them, but the zones don't disassemble signals from the key."

"And the Unifieds haven't figured that out?"

"No, sir. I mean, these are FM signals, it's old, old technology. The Unifieds aren't watching for ancient technology, it's like we're controlling the stations with smoke signals, it's that old."

"And the book?" I asked

"It's an index of established broadcast coordinates. It's the same book the Mogats used on their self-broadcasting fleet . . . same codes and everything. We stole the books along with the broadcast equipment off their wrecks."

Back in the days when the Unified Authority counted the entire galaxy as its territory, the Republic established 180 colonies. The coordinates for the colonized worlds all fit on the inside flap, the rest of the volume held coordinates for scientific research sites, satellites, and rendezvous spots.

Seeing McGraw tap the lift button several times, I asked, "Are you in a hurry?"

He apologized, and said, "I'm nervous about the negotiations, sir. I don't trust the Unifieds."

The elevator arrived, and we rode it to the fleet deck. Still carrying the key and book, I followed McGraw into a small side room in which most of Warshaw's remoras sat watching the negotiations on a large monitor.

*I'm not entirely sure such a partnership would be in our best interest.* I did not recognize the man who said that, but he spoke in the same imperious tone as Tobias Andropov. The screen showed a nearly empty conference room in which Warshaw sat flanked by three admirals on one side of the table, the man representing the Unified Authority sat with two male secretaries on the other.

"Who is that?" I whispered to McGraw.

"His name's Martin Traynor. He's the U.A. minister of expansion; but I get the feeling he thinks he's God."

*We have more people than you. We have more planets than you do. We have more ships than you do. What do you mean the partnership isn't in your interest? We control the broadcast network,* Warshaw said. I expected to see him flexing the various muscles in his arms as he spoke, but he did not do that in this negotiation. He sat hunched in his chair, looking like a man kept alive by coffee and prayers.

*Unless you do something quick, you will be out of planets and civilians in three more months,* Traynor said. He looked like the quintessential bureaucrat, perfectly coiffed, manicured, dressed in wool and silk. Satisfied that he had just laid down an unbeatable hand, he leaned back in his chair and smirked.

Warshaw responded by drawing a line in the sand and daring the U.A. minister to cross it. *So you're going to wait for those people to die?*

His bluff was called, and the smirk vanished. Traynor said, *Obviously, we want to save as many lives as possible. The only reason we're holding these negotiations is to save lives.*

There was a moment of silence, then Warshaw said, *I must have misheard you. A moment ago I thought you said you didn't mind if they all died.*

The players might have kept their cool in the conference room, but the men watching the negotiation wore their emotions on their sleeves. The man next to me said, "Specking Traynor. Specking Unified Authority. Specking . . ." His rant lasted more than a minute, and he said "specking" every other word.

Seeing Warshaw put Traynor in his place, McGraw slammed his palm on the table, and yelled, "Right! Damn right!"

Watching the negotiation, it was clear that neither side trusted the other. I thought that was a good sign. Having found himself abandoned in the Scutum-Crux Arm, then used for a target in a military game, Warshaw had little reason to trust the Unifieds.

*Maybe the smartest course of action would be to evacuate the people from your planets and leave you and your superior military to handle the aliens,* Traynor suggested.

*Excellent idea,* Warshaw said. *Do you think you can fit that many people in your hypothetical underwater cities?*

McGraw and several other viewers shouted their approval. On the screen, one of the admirals sitting beside Warshaw gave him an approving nod.

Traynor coughed. He poured himself a glass of water, but still seemed to be choking. His right hand in front of his mouth, he excused himself and asked for a five-minute break.

The tension in the viewing room relaxed as soon as Traynor stepped out of the picture. We watched Warshaw conferring with his admirals. Across the table, Traynor's secretaries silently reviewed their notes.

While I enjoyed watching the fireworks, I needed to get to Terraneau. I thanked McGraw for the broadcast key and signaled Nobles to get the shuttle ready.

As I stepped out of the viewing room, I saw something that struck me as odd. Walking like a man who is late for a meeting, Martin Traynor stomped past me and continued down the hall. Our shoulders brushed, but he did not look back as he hurried away.

"Where do you think you are going?" I asked in a whisper as I watched him rush past the head. He didn't even give the door a second glance.

Temporarily shelving my concern for Terraneau, I followed the son of a bitch.

Maybe he heard my steps, maybe he only sensed me behind him, but Traynor picked up speed. His legs pumping quickly, he rounded a corner and headed for the elevators. I jogged to gain ground on him.

By the time I reached the corner, I could see him running to the lifts. He stabbed a button with his forefinger, then held the button down in an impatient bid to speed things up. As I came toward him, one of the elevators opened, and he leaped in. I ran to catch up, but the doors shut before I arrived.

I hit the button, calling for another elevator, trying to sort out the scene as I waited. Traynor fleeing the negotiations made no sense to me. Even if the negotiations fell through, Warshaw would not arrest him, he was an ambassador. Had he forgotten something on his shuttle? *A bomb, maybe?* I thought; but he wasn't a saboteur. If anything, he struck me as a stiff.

My lift opened. I pressed the button for the bottom deck, the deck with the landing bays. If I ran into Traynor, I would follow him. If I did not see him, I would board my shuttle and ride to Terraneau. I doubted I would see Traynor, though, and I tried to put him out of my mind.

The doors of the elevator slid open, and there he was, walking down the hall. Hearing my lift open, he turned to look back and saw me. Our eyes met for just a moment and I did not like what I saw. In his eyes I saw abject terror, then he looked down and started speed-walking away.

He scampered down the hall, and I followed. I wanted to yell after him, but I had no idea what I should or should not say . . . what I could or could not say. I could not arrest him. If I made the wrong move, the negotiations might collapse.

Traynor looked back, saw me following him, and ran. The rule book went out the window the moment he picked up his pace. If I'd had a gun on me, I might have shot him in the leg just to stop him; but he was short and domesticated, and if it came to a chase, I would overtake him in a couple of seconds. I was gaining on him, then I passed an observation window, stopped, and forgot all about the minister of expansion. In that moment, he became the furthest thing from my mind.

Staring out that observation wall, I saw white holes in the blackness of space. The anomalies appeared so far away that their brightness only created spots before my eyes. At first, only five or six appeared, then a dozen followed, then still more. As I watched the scene, Klaxons began to sound.

Hatches opened along the hall, and sailors flooded out, rushing this way and that, headed for their battle stations. I forced my way against the current, fighting to get to the landing bay.

Even as I cut through, something struck the *Kamehameha*, rocking the ship. When a big ship shakes, the people inside it become as insubstantial as snowflakes in a blizzard. The force struck the *Kamehameha*, throwing all of us against the walls and the deck. Barely noticing that I had fallen to my knees, I gathered my balance and tried to press forward to the landing bay.

I was almost there when we took the first real hit. Something had penetrated our defenses and struck the ship. At the far end of the hall, the outer shell of the ship gave way. Lights flashed off and on, men screamed, the force of the suction nearly lifted me off my feet in the split second that our atmosphere bled through the breach, then emergency bulkheads slammed into place, dividing the corridor into airtight sections.

The lights came back online, revealing men strewn on the floor, some bleeding, and some writhing in pain. We would remain trapped between the massive bulkheads until the atmospheric pressure stabilized. This was the naval equivalent of an amputation. Parts of the ship that were too badly damaged were sealed off in order to save the whole.

Bulkheads blocked the hall on either side of me. I could not run to the landing bay or return to the elevators. All I could do was wait and wonder if the hull would crack, and I'd be flushed into space.

The bastards hit us again, and I was helpless. How many men had we lost? What part of the ship would the next laser or torpedo hit? How much damage had we taken? How much more could we sustain? If the ship broke into pieces, would my little section of hull float into space with me sealed inside like a bird in a cage? Like a body in a coffin. How many ships had the Unified Authority sent through the broadcast zone?

What if the attack on Olympus Kri had all been a hoax? I knew it wasn't. I knew it wasn't, but Andropov had used it as an opportunity to get the upper hand. All that bullshit about the Liberators never losing a battle . . . With the unintended help of the Avatari, Andropov would succeed where his Double Y clones had failed, the bastard.

The lights went off-line again. In the darkness, men screamed and pounded the atmospheric bulkheads with their fists.

*Two birds with one stone,* I thought. With our cooperation, Andropov had built a temporary broadcast station by Mars, and now he was using that broadcast station to send battleships and destroyers.

Our broadcast station was programmed to send ships to Mars; they'd just sent their specking barges through it. They could hit us and return home, and there wasn't a specking thing we could do to stop them. Now that they had their own sending station and a way to broadcast their ships home, we were at their mercy . . . as if the Unified Authority had ever had mercy.

They hit us again. There, in the darkness, I fell as the ship shuddered around me. I listened to the screams, the calls for help, the prayers. I made my way to my feet, and felt my way ahead until I reached the cold smooth surface of the emergency bulkhead. I wondered what I would find on the other side if it ever opened.

Moments passed, then the bulkhead slid open. The lights remained out; so, groping the wall for balance, I pushed forward, tripping over men I could not see in the darkness. The only light shone from panels and signs along the walls.

More shots hit the ship, but these felt like glancing blows. Perhaps the shields were up, perhaps they came from weaker weapons. I knew so little about naval combat. The floor shook. People toppled. Whatever damage was going to be done to the *Kamehameha* might already be done.

Moving ahead slowly, taking faltering steps and reaching out with my to feel my way ahead, I reached the landing bay. The hatch slid open, revealing emergency lights and the glow of fire. Crews hosed down a blaze under the control booth. Across the deck, fountains of sparks shot out of a row of panels.

Lieutenant Nobles waited for me just inside the door. He pulled at my arm, and yelled, "They're going to let us through, but they can't protect us once we're out!"

We ran into the shuttle and started rolling toward the launch tube. The nose of the shuttle veered right and left, as if Nobles were steering like a drunk, he, all the while, shouting into the microphone, "Open the first lock. Open the first lock!"

I could hear commotion over the radio. Several seconds passed before we got an answer. "You're cleared. God help you."

The first of the atmospheric locks slowly ground open just far enough for us to fit through and began closing even before we cleared it. The men controlling the flight deck were not taking any chances. They handled the second and third atmospheric gates the same way, just giving us enough room to pass and closing it quickly behind us.

A wave of relief washed over me as we launched. I had not really believed we would make it off the ship; but there we were, trading the tight confines of the launch tube for the endless expanse of space.

Huge fighter carriers loomed before us. Fighters sped around us, ignoring us, approaching us and ducking away. Tiny fireballs erupted from the side of the *Kamehameha*. They flared out of the ship and evaporated into nothing. The ship's shields were down and the antennae that projected those shields were destroyed. It was only a matter of time until the ship went dark; large portions already had.

Beside the *Kamehameha* hung the *ad-Din*, looking stronger, but still wounded. Villanueva had sent all of her fighters to circle the ship. They formed a protective screen around the big carrier, but what did it matter?

Using the radio, I hailed the *Salah ad-Din*. I identified myself and asked for Captain Villanueva, but I only got as far as one of his lieutenants.

"General, where are you?" he asked. "We can try to—"

"I'm on a shuttle. If you scan, you'll find us. We're headed to the broadcast zone," I said.

"Now listen, I have a broadcast key aboard the shuttle. I am about to broadcast to Terraneau. Tell Villanueva to try and enter the zone. The Unifieds won't follow you; they'll think it's a trap."

"Aye, aye."

"Pass the message. Tell any ship that can to follow us."

"Aye, sir."

I signed off, knowing that if any ship's captain could possibly break free, it was probably Villanueva. Maybe we would salvage a few ships.

Glancing back at the damaged fighter carriers, six of them—one representing each of the six galactic arms—I saw immediately that the outlook was bleak. Layers of U.A. ships had clustered around the E.M.N. fighter carriers. The Unifieds had sent old ships and new ones as well. It looked like the entire Earth Fleet had joined in on the attack. Seeing four battleships advance on the *Kamehameha*, I realized that this was not so much a battle as it was a lynching.

I took one last glance at that proud old ship, then I opened the front cover of the book and found the forty-two-digit code for Terraneau. The new generation ships that the Unifieds had sent had broadcast engines, they would be able to return to Earth. Most of the ships involved in this ambush were older ships, however. They were not self-broadcasting. The plan was to send them back to the Sol System using our broadcast station, which was currently set for Mars. By programming a new code into the key, I would strand some of those Earth ships in Olympus Kri space. Their only escape would be to follow me to Terraneau; but, fearing a trap, they would be slow to come after me.

# FIFTY-FOUR

Earthdate: November 17, A.D. 2517
Location: Terraneau
Galactic Position: Scutum-Crux Arm

"They're not going to make it out of there, are they?" Nobles asked, as we emerged from the anomaly.

"Some of them might," I said. "If Villanueva reaches the
broadcast zone, he's home free. The Unifieds won't follow
him."

Nobles changed the subject. "Why did they attack us?"
The words came out in a groan. He looked miserable, somewhere between tears and insanity. A wild look of fear and
anger showed in his brown eyes, and his lips quivered as he
spoke. "Why the hell did they attack us?"

I looked out into the calm corner of space we had just entered. Stars shone around us. Terraneau, a planet with lakes
and rivers and oceans, sparkled like a rare gem.

"They attacked because they can't afford an open war," I
said in a quiet, subdued voice, the voice of defeat.

Nobles turned to me. His eyes tightened, and he asked,
"What?" in a hardened angry voice.

"We showed them how to rebuild their empire. The planets, the broadcast network, the Navy . . . they want to take it
all back in one piece," I said.

*The clone assassins failed, so they lured Gary Warshaw
and his top admirals into a negotiation, then they massacred
the whole lot of them. Now they want to round the rest of the
clones up like sheep,* I thought. *They will round us up like*

*sheep, and send us out like slaves . . . like eunuchs, the guardians of the republic that massacred their empire.*

The Romans manned their legions by filling them with conquered soldiers; why shouldn't the Unifieds do the same? And then they would . . . What would they do? Would they hide under the sea in watertight cities while aliens charbroiled the galaxy? They would not need clones for that. Now that they had a broadcast network, if they managed to capture the network, they could send us out to find the Avatari. We'd be the second wave. They would send us out the same way they sent out the Boyd Clones and the Japanese Fleet; only the Japanese Fleet had self-broadcasting ships. They could return from the mission; we would be stuck wherever they sent us.

"The aliens were real, right?" Nobles asked. "The attack on Olympus Kri was real." He needed assurance. He knew the attack was real; but at times like this, are you ever sure about anything?

"It was real," I said.

"Then why?"

I thought I finally understood. Andropov wanted to send out a second wave. After winning the battle for New Copenhagen, the Unified Authority sent out the Japanese Fleet, but that was only four ships, four lowly self-broadcasting battleships. The brass hedged their bets by manning them with a special line of SEAL clones instead of Marines, but still only had four ships tracking an alien signal across an entire galaxy.

If they managed to ingest the Enlisted Man's Navy, the Unifieds would gain thirteen fleets, over one hundred fighter carriers, hundreds of battleships, millions of clones. And they could broadcast their *disposable* new fleet into space to search for the alien world, never to return. Kill the chain of command, orphan the ships and the crews . . . it finally made sense. Maybe Andropov even wanted to send a token Liberator out on the mission to bring it luck; after all, the Clone Empire had gone undefeated in open war. Bastard.

I left the cockpit and went to my little stateroom, where I spent the rest of the flight in silence, brooding over how much I hated my creators.

Nobles alerted me when we neared the planet. We entered an atmosphere with clouds instead of smoke. We crossed over snowcapped mountains and frost-dusted forests that would soon be burned to ash. I took in the beauty, knowing that nothing could be done to protect it. No weapon existed that could defend this planet, and humanity had no bargaining chip that could turn the attackers away. The most I could hope for was to save a few people. *Ava*.

Far ahead of us, Norristown shimmered in the afternoon sun, a city healed from most of its wounds. The wreckage had been cleared, and an extensive patchwork of parks and open markets now filled the void.

We received a message from the spaceport asking us to identify ourselves. When Nobles answered that we were an unarmed envoy from the Enlisted Man's Fleet, the control tower cleared us to land.

Judging by the lines of military trucks and police cars waiting along the runway as we began our approach, I got the feeling that the locals did not want guests.

"I don't think they're happy to see us," Nobles said.

If understatement were a form of humor, Christian Nobles would have been the funniest man alive.

Police cars closed in behind us as we rolled forward down the runway, moving toward the line of armored trucks and the militiamen with guns. Doctorow did not want Marines on his planet, but that did not stop him from using his militia. Judging by the tanks and transports, he'd helped himself to the weapons we left behind.

We rolled to within twenty feet of the trucks and stopped. The shuttle's struts compressed, and the fuselage dropped. Men with anxious, angry faces and government-issue M27s stared in at us.

With Nobles following behind me, I opened the shuttle door. Guns pointed directly at us. I could see that much through the glare, but I stopped and had to place a hand over my eyes to block the sun. Somebody yelled for us to step out, so I held my hands above my head and stepped out into the sunlight. Men with guns intercepted me as I stepped to the ground. Dozens of militiamen formed a circle around me. One of them shoved me from behind to get me clear of the shuttle, but most of the militiamen looked scared. They had the numbers and the guns; but I got the feeling that they were more scared of me than I was of them.

For a split second, we all stood there in silence in the cool evening breeze, then a militiaman asked, "Are you carrying weapons?"

I said, "Not on me."

Nobles shook his head.

A captain in the militia stepped up to me, gave me an embarrassed grin, and asked, "Do you mind if we search your ship?"

*Nice of him to ask,* I thought. I told him, "We came empty-handed, but feel free."

The standoff continued as three men in soft-shelled engineering armor carrying an array of detection equipment entered the shuttle. A couple of minutes ticked away as we waited for them to conclude the obvious, that two men traveling in an unarmed shuttle did not pose much of a threat.

There was no point in trying to explain why we had come, not to these men. They were just the foot soldiers. I needed to take my story to the top. I needed to explain everything to the president himself. No one under Doctorow would have the authority to react even if they believed me. In the meantime, every second wasted here on the runway felt like a crime. Had the planet already seen temperature fluctuations? Maybe we would be cooked as we stood on the airfield waiting for locals to search our unarmed ship.

"Any weapons?" the militia leader asked.

I turned and saw one of the men waving the go-pack I had taken to Olympus Kri. He held up the pack, and said, "He's got combat armor, a couple of grenade launchers, a particle-beam pistol, and a cannon."

"Was that a particle-beam cannon?" asked the captain. He turned back to me, and said, "I thought you said you came unarmed?"

"I forgot they were there," I said.

"Anything else you forgot, Harris?" the captain asked. I did not recognize him, but apparently he recognized me. I had spent a lot of time on this planet and made a lot of enemies.

# FIFTY-FIVE

They did not place us in handcuffs. They led me and Nobles into the back of an armored truck along with a dozen guards, and they drove to town. Jeeps and trucks followed behind us.

Our escort delivered us to a police station, where a platoon of militiamen led us down two flights of stairs and into a basement. The militiamen hauled Nobles away. I watched them lead him down a hall with a sinking feeling.

I ended up locked in an interrogation room, and there I sat and waited. A team of armed guards stood outside the door. I would not have known they were there except that they looked in on me every few minutes. For all I knew, an entire firing squad waited for me just outside that door.

I sat alone in that little room with its soundproofed walls and wondered what happened to all of the big talk about utopian ideals. In Ellery Doctorow's new order, the terms "police," "military," and "militia" seemed nearly interchangeable. From my perspective, *liberated* Norristown operated like any other police state.

Precious time slipped irretrievably away as I sat alone in that room.

I tried to piece together how much time passed between the attacks on New Copenhagen and Olympus Kri. Had it been a week? Five days? It was possible that nobody knew. The only video Sweetwater had of the attack on New Copenhagen was of the aftermath. The planet might have been a scorched wreck for a week before anyone noticed.

Only a day had passed since I left Olympus Kri. Time might have been running out, but I did not think we had reached the midnight hour just yet.

The door opened. "Okay, Harris, so why did you come

back?" the man asked as he stepped into the interrogation room. He was a natural-born, of course, a tall man with a slender build, his black hair combed back and oiled.

He could have been a hard-living twenty-year-old or a well-preserved quadragenarian. He had a trace of stubble across his cheeks, chin, and throat, and he projected confidence with his cold gaze. I looked at him, sized him up as someone of minimal importance, and dismissed him all in an instant.

*How long would it take the Avatari to reach Terraneau?* I wondered. *A week?* I had time, but I wanted to be out of this jail and off the planet when they came. I was in a basement, but it wasn't very deep. If the attack occurred while I was down here, my cell would turn into a crematorium.

"I asked you a question," he said, demanding my attention. He had the demeanor of a gangster; but, of course, now he was an idealist working for Ellery Doctorow. Gangster, militant, pacifist; chameleons like this guy presented themselves as true believers in any cause that kept them in power.

I glared back at him and said nothing.

"I asked you why you came back to Terraneau," he said.

"A mission of mercy," I said. "I came to save you."

"To save us from what?"

"From an invasion," I said. "Look, I'm sure you're a very big man around here; but I need to see Doctorow." That was my best attempt at being polite. I had no idea how I might act on my next approach.

"Maybe he's already listening," the man said. He pointed to a little glass window built into the wall. The window was a square inch of bulletproof glass with a tiny surveillance camera peering out behind it. "Tell me what you got, and maybe we'll both hear it at the same time."

"He's not watching," I said. I knew assholes like this guy. They'd do anything to increase their sphere of influence, the unscrupulous specks. The problem is, by the time this fool figured out that he was in over his head, it might be too late. "He's not watching, and this situation is out of your pay grade."

"What makes you so sure?" the man asked.

I ignored the question and delivered the punch line. "The aliens have attacked Olympus Kri and New Copenhagen. They'll come here next."

"Aliens?" He looked back over his shoulder, giving the camera a nervous glance.

"Are you lying to me, Harris?" the man asked.

I did not answer.

"Are they the same aliens as before?" He did not sound like he believed me. He sounded like he was humoring me, allowing me a chance to pitch my shit, so to speak.

"Yes," I said, though, come to think of it, that was only an assumption. We didn't really know if the Avatari were behind the last attacks.

"Think you can beat them?" he asked.

"Beat them?" I repeated, stunned that I had not anticipated such an obvious question. "I just want to outrun them."

Silence. I was not sure if my message was getting through. I watched him cycle through several emotions—suspicion, doubt, fear, then more suspicion. When he finally spoke, he asked, "Why would they come here?"

"Look, we really don't have a lot of time," I said.

"Then start answering my questions," the man demanded.

"They're taking back planets," I said, stating the obvious.

Apparently, that was enough for him. He moved to the next question. "Got any proof?"

I knew that question was coming; and the answer was no. Without virtual Sweetwater and his video feed of the destruction, I had nothing to show. Because I had not prepared for one obvious question, every last person on Terraneau might die, and that included me.

"Maybe I should leave," I said.

"What?" he asked.

"I don't have any proof," I said. "The mission's a bust, and I might as well head home."

The man laughed. "An act like this doesn't get you in with Doctorow."

"You're right," I said, throwing up my hands. "You are exactly right. The problem is, I don't have anything more to give you. I shouldn't have bothered you, I'll just leave."

"You're not going anywhere."

"So I'm a prisoner," I said.

Looking exasperated, the interrogator sat and stared at me,

slowly shaking his head. After a few seconds, he said, "We're all friends here. I'm trying to help you."

"So why do you need the guards?"

"What?"

"Why do you need armed guards if you are trying to help me?"

"You're a dangerous man, Harris. We all know that."

"Look, you're out of your depth," I said.

I did not mean to offend the bastard, but obviously I had. He yelled at me, but I didn't listen. He ranted, and spit flew from his lips. If I had been an average prisoner, he might have turned off the camera and had his guards beat me; but I was a prisoner who came with an implicit threat. For all he knew, I had an armada circling the planet.

Not knowing what else to do, the man simply stormed out, and my interrogation room once again became a prison cell. Time passed slowly. I sat in my metal chair and glared up at the camera in the ceiling, occasionally giving it a one-finger salute.

At some point I climbed out of the chair and stretched out on the table. Since there was nothing else to do, I caught up on my sleep.

The sound of the door woke me from my nap, but I remained on my back on the table, my fingers laced together over my chest. My shoulders and neck felt stiff.

"You're awfully calm for a harbinger bringing tidings to a doomed planet," Doctorow said.

Like the revitalized city in which he lived, Ellery Doctorow had a new face. Gone were the long hair and beard, replaced by a square-cut coif in which the white hairs had been dyed coal black. He wore a navy blue suit, tailored to make his shoulders look wide and his waist look small. He'd been dressed in a suit the last time I saw him as well. Gone were the days of fatigues and ponytails.

Doctorow entered the interrogation room alone. He might have had a dozen bodyguards outside the door, but he entered the interrogation room alone.

"Have a seat, and I will tell you about the end of the world," I said.

The comment earned me an enigmatic smirk.

As I climbed off the table and returned to my seat, Doctorow pulled a chair close. He sat there, stroking his chin while staring at me, apparently deep in thought. Finally, he said, "You say you're here because the aliens attacked two other planets."

"New Copenhagen and Olympus Kri," I said.

"Both planets in the Orion Arm," Doctorow noted.

"Liberated planets," I said.

"Yes, yes, you defeated the aliens on New Copenhagen. I'm guessing that you rescued Olympus Kri the same way you rescued Terraneau. That much of your story makes sense to me."

"They're coming here next," I said.

"So you say," Doctorow said. "Why would they come here? Olympus Kri and New Copenhagen are in the Orion Arm. Why jump from the Orion Arm all the way to a planet in the Scutum-Crux Arm? Wouldn't Earth be the logical next stop?"

"Olympus Kri was the first planet we liberated after the war," I said.

"I thought you came here first," Doctorow said.

"I wasn't involved. Olympus Kri was already in the works before they transferred me here."

Doctorow nodded to show that he accepted the explanation. "So we're the third planet in line . . . if their advance is chronological." He spoke in a flat tone that would veil both belief and skepticism equally. He sat very still, his hands on his lap, his eyes meeting mine.

"Did you come here to organize an army?" he asked.

I shook my head. "An evacuation."

"An evacuation?"

"There's no point even trying to fight," I said, and I told him what had happened on Olympus Kri. I explained about the destruction and how Freeman and I had hidden in an underground power station during the attack.

Doctorow listened to my story, his face a mask hiding whatever emotion he felt. When I finished, he summed it up by stating, "So you propose we evacuate the planet."

"We'd need to contact Andropov and—"

"Andropov? Are you here in concert with the Unified Authority?" he asked, sounding suspicious. "I thought you were at war with them."

"They declared war on us," I said.

"You stole their ships," Doctorow said.

"They sent us out here for target practice. This is ancient history; we don't have time . . ."

"Absurd. Everything you have said is preposterous," Doctorow said.

"I see, then your only other choice is to take your people underground."

"I will need some time to think it over," Doctorow said. Though he tried to hide it, I could tell that he had already made up his mind. "Do you have any evidence to prove what you are saying?"

"No," I said.

"So I have to trust you. I have to take your word on blind faith?"

"That just about sums it up." I had never lied to him, at least no times that I could think of on the spot.

He responded with an elegant laugh. "Walk by faith," he said, a vestige from the religious life he had abandoned. "Here's my theory. I think New Copenhagen and Olympus Kri are just fine. The Unified Authority may have taken those planets away from you, but I suspect the people are safe.

"What happened, Harris? Did the Earth Fleet crush you again?"

I had told him the truth, and he called me a liar. Maybe the truth was on both his side and mine. The Earth Fleet had indeed just served us a bloody defeat. Had any of our ships survived the attack at Olympus Kri?

"You've got it wrong," I said, though perhaps he didn't.

"You want us to evacuate our cities and send everyone underground," Doctorow continued. "Wasn't that how you won the last one; you invited the U.A. Marines into an underground garage, then you buried them?"

"Bullshit," I said.

I expected Doctorow to tell me to watch my language; but now that the Right Reverend was president, bad language no longer seemed to concern him. "Interesting strategy you have there, Harris, persuade your enemies to go underground and bury them—"

"You're not listening," I said.

"Then you start the invasion while we're digging ourselves out."

"Invasion? What kind of invasion? I came in an unarmed shuttle."

"We know about the other ship," Doctorow said. "We picked up the anomaly when your fighter carrier broadcasted in. We've been tracking it for the last hour."

*So the* ad-Din *made it out,* I thought. That ship might have been the only reason I was still breathing. Doctorow was scared of her, and that made him scared of me.

"I'm trying to save lives," I said.

"By flying a warship into neutral territory?" Doctorow glared at me, and added, "I'm not afraid of you, Harris. I'm not afraid of you or your clones or your ships."

He delivered the lines well, but I could tell that I frightened him. I could see it in his forced expression. I could hear it in his voice.

"I'm not the one you should be scared of," I said.

That ended the meeting. He stood up and left the room without saying another word.

I did not want to die in this police station. I did not want to die saving this worthless planet. I imagined what would happen to this room when the heat hit nine grand, how the glass would melt, and the walls would turn a glowing orange.

Looking at the camera, I let my thoughts drift, rewinding my interview with Doctorow. I replayed my story and his response. What I hated most about his explanation was that it sounded more plausible than mine. How ironic, his fabrication sounded more reasonable than the truth.

On this planet, I was the boogeyman, and I would die because no one trusted me, even when I told the truth. Doctorow had his ideal society, all right. He'd created a fleeting utopia; and now that he'd built it, his citizens would burn.

# CHAPTER
# FIFTY-SIX

Nobles and I spent the night in an underground cell, a small cage about ten feet long and ten feet wide with bunk beds, a sink, and a little chrome toilet that rose out of the floor like a tree stump. I'd stayed as a guest in worse accommodations. I'd stayed as a prisoner in better.

An ever-present camera, sitting like a bird on a perch, watched over us from outside our cell. I had no idea who was on the other side of the camera, but the winking red diode on its base told me it was live.

I lay on the top bunk, and Nobles took the bottom. We seldom spoke if ever. He never told me his thoughts. I had Ava on my mind. I needed to find her. I needed to get out of this prison. Thinking of that, I asked myself, *How many prisoners fried in their cages on New Copenhagen?* And that reminded me of the Double Y clones we left on Olympus Kri.

Time continued to pass slowly by.

The hall was empty but brightly lit. Lying on my bunk, I covered my eyes with my right forearm and tried to sleep. The light did not keep me awake, but my thoughts did. For that reason, I was awake when the visitor arrived.

He appeared in the corridor that ran along the outside of the cells. As he reached our cage, the door slid open.

The visitor was a clone with no unique scars to distinguish him, but I recognized him just the same. It was the way he carried himself, I think. Maybe it was his cheerful expression. "Mars, what are you doing here?" I asked, remembering that he had chosen to stay on Terraneau.

"I came to help," he said. He stopped just outside the door and watched me, possibly made nervous by my hostile tone.

"I thought you were a loyal citizen of Terraneau," I said. Not sure if I should trust a man who had chosen Doctorow and his utopia over the Enlisted Man's Empire, I decided to rake Mars over the coals. If he took it too easily, I'd know he was a spy.

Still standing outside my cell, Mars said, "Half the planet would come if you asked them now. Anyone who's got any sense is more scared of Doctorow than they ever were of you."

I heard him, but thought I must have misunderstood. Something was wrong with a world in which a retired priest scared people more than a Liberator clone.

"Don't you like living in a utopian society?" I asked.

"Don't know; I haven't seen any utopias lately," Mars said. "Once you left, Doctorow decided that his society could only work if everybody participated, so he armed his militia and moved them into Fort Sebastian. That's when things got bad.

"When people disagree with his government, Doctorow sees it as a threat to his perfect world. The man keeps lists of agitators. Many of them have disappeared."

Muttering some sort of "Hail Mary," Mars stepped into our cage, and said, "I'm just glad we got to you before he stashed you away in Outer Bliss." Outer Bliss was a relocation camp on the other side of the planet. It was an entire town surrounded by razor wire and guard towers.

"That would have been bad," I said, thinking that an apartment or maybe a house in Outer Bliss would have come with windows and a private toilet.

As Mars passed under a lamp, I noticed the flat sheen of his hair. I started to ask him about it, then I noticed that his irises were no longer brown, they were black. "What's with your eyes?" I asked.

He looked up and down the hall as if making sure that no one could see him, then he held up a bunched-up washcloth covered with oily brown stains. He tried to give this to Nobles, but Nobles only stared at it.

"What's that?" Nobles asked, not reaching for it.

"It's a disguise to make you look like a clone," Mars said. "If someone comes into the building, we'll pass you off as one of my men."

Hesitating before accepting the grimy bundle, Nobles opened the cloth. Inside, he found a small tube, and looked at Mars questioningly.

"Hair dye to make your hair brown like a clone's."

"This?" Nobles asked, holding up a tiny bottle.

"Colored eye-drops that turn your irises brown."

"Oh, to make me look like a clone," Nobles said. "Brilliant." He squeezed the tube onto his left palm, rubbed the brown spew between his hands, then ran it through his hair. The dye gave Noble's hair the same muted shine as Mars's.

Once he worked the dye into his hair, Nobles wiped his hands on the cloth. Next, he squeezed a couple of drops of iris dye into his eyes, changing their color from dirt brown to very nearly black.

"Perfect," Mars said, feigning surprise. "You could walk into any base in the galaxy, and they wouldn't spot you."

And he did look like one clone, at least. He looked exactly like Lieutenant Mars.

"What about the guards?" I asked, pointing toward the camera. "Aren't they watching us?"

"Sure they are, but they work for me," said Mars. He walked right up to Nobles and checked the coloring in his eyes like a doctor examining a patient, then said, "Head out that door and up the stairs. My boys will take care of you."

"Thank you," said Nobles. He left in a hurry, jogging up the corridor and out the door.

As soon as Nobles was out of earshot, Mars said, "Sort of a waste of time putting brown hair dye and colored eyedrops on a clone; but with that whole death-reflex thing . . . you just can't take any chances." He sounded apologetic.

So that was what had happened. Thinking he had blond hair and blue eyes, Mars had used the same disguise.

"The regulars won't roll in until 06:00," Mars said. "That gives us three hours."

"We have bigger things to worry about than guards," I said, and I gave him a brief description of the Avatari attacks on New Copenhagen and Olympus Kri. I also told him how the Unified Authority ambushed Warshaw. I thought it would take a long time, but the whole sorry tale took less than ten minutes.

"Why would they do that?" he asked. "It doesn't make sense."

"It makes sense from their point of view," I said. "They

want a disposable Navy to send out after the Avatari. By assassinating our command structure, they stand to inherit disposable ships, disposable crews, even a broadcast network for sending them into space."

"But they'd be marooned. They'd be stranded . . ." He did not bother finishing the thought.

I finished for him. "Just like we were left stranded out here."

"What do we do?" Mars said.

I told him about Tachyon D concentrations and temperature fluctuations, and said, "I think we probably have a few more days, but we want to be long gone before the temperatures start changing."

"How can we check for tachyons?" he asked.

"I don't know. The U.A. had a couple of dead scientists figure it out."

He didn't know who or what I meant, not that it mattered.

"I can have my men check the weather reports," he said. "Tracking temperature changes shouldn't be a problem."

"Good place to start," I said.

"What do we do about Doctorow?" Mars asked. "Do you think you can get him to see the light?" He must have already known the answer even as he asked the question. Doctorow would not listen to us, never in a million years.

I shook my head. "How do you make an *enlightened* man see the light?" I asked, amazed by my own pessimism. "He doesn't trust me, and there is nothing I can do about it. Maybe it's for the best. I'm going to have enough trouble getting you and your thousand engineers off the planet."

As I said this, I remembered what Doctorow said about tracking a fighter carrier. "Do you know anything about a carrier circling the planet?" I asked.

Mars nodded. "It's the *Churchill*. She's hiding up in the graveyard."

"What about the *Salah ad-Din*?"

He shook his head. "The only ship we've seen is the *Churchill*."

"Good thing she's there; we can use her to get off the planet," I said. "Now for the next problem, I need to get a message to Ava."

"Your girlfriend?" Mars asked.

"Ex-girlfriend. Do you think she knows I'm here?" Though the question was more for me than for Mars, I asked it out loud.

"She probably doesn't. Doctorow is trying to keep the whole thing quiet."

By this time, a couple of hours had passed, and Nobles appeared at the door of the cell. His hair still had that matted sheen and his irises were black as wet rock. The door slid open, and he stepped in. He and Mars traded places. Nobles went to the sink and began rinsing the gunk out of his hair and eyes.

"Are you sure you can trust her?" Mars asked as he left the cell. "If she's not with you anymore, I mean—"

I put up a hand to stop him. "We could always kidnap her," I said. I was joking.

Mars smiled, and said, "Now there's an interesting option," and he left our jail cell a free man. Nobles and I spent the rest of the night locked behind bars.

# CHAPTER
# FIFTY-SEVEN

The inquisition began again at 07:00.

Armed guards ushered Nobles and me out of our cell. I wasn't asleep when they came, but I was awfully tired from the long night.

As they had the day before, the guards placed Nobles in one room and me in the next. The waiting game began again. I sat in the soundproofed room, staring into the coin-sized camera lens that watched me from behind a bulletproof window, wondering when and how I would make my next move.

I was still slumped in that chair, fighting exhaustion but fully awake, when my new interrogator entered the room. He did not arrive alone. He came with a matched set of three guards in Marine combat armor. The man was tall and thin, with a gray handlebar mustache that extended well past the corners of his mouth. He had a familiar face. I could not dredge up the memory of where I had seen him before, so I dismissed him as just another militiaman.

"Well, well, Wayson Harris, I always expected you to end up in here," the man said. Clearly he knew me, and I got the feeling he bore a grudge.

His guards planted themselves on either side of the door, where they stood as still as statues. The armed guards weren't necessary. I would not try to escape, not yet. I would wait for Mars.

"Tell me about your plans to recapture Terraneau," the interrogator asked as he sat down in the chair on the side of the table. He spoke in an easy, informal way.

"I have no interest in retaking this planet," I said.

"Oh, right. I heard about that. You came here to warn us. Wayson Harris the Liberator messiah.

"We spotted two more fighter carriers this morning."

"Now there are three of them," I muttered to myself. Things were looking up.

"What's with all that firepower if you are here to rescue us?"

I locked eyes with him. He was one of those guys who meets your stare and doesn't blink and doesn't look away because he thinks it's some sort of macho challenge. I played along for a second, winked and smiled and had a look around the room. Metal chairs, wall-mounted camera, armed guards, locked door . . . yup, I was in prison.

I wondered which carriers had made it out. The *ad-Din* had almost certainly survived. *Could the* Kamehameha *have made it to the zone?* The thought left me elated.

"I didn't actually bring them with me," I said. "It's more of a rendezvous." For some reason, I felt fidgety. I caught myself tapping my fingers on the table and dropped my hands to my thighs. Alarms sounded in my head, and it wasn't fear. Something was about to happen, I could feel it.

Like animals sometimes do, I sensed a coming storm, but I did not know the nature of that storm.

"Are there more ships on the way?" the interrogator asked.

"I sure hope so," I said, thinking of the U.A. barges.

"Where is the rest of your fleet?" he asked.

I sighed. "That depends what you mean by my 'fleet.' If you mean the Scutum-Crux Fleet, most of it is in the Cygnus Arm. If you mean the Enlisted Man's Fleet, that's all over the galaxy."

Doctorow, his high-minded ideals now mingled with paranoia, would probably object to my being tortured; but that did not mean he wouldn't have me executed. He'd happily leave me locked up until he was sure I posed no threat.

I could wait this out. Mars needed time to make the arrangements. I knew he needed time, but I couldn't get past the feeling that something was about to happen. A bomb was about to explode, or a gun was about to go off, or a planet was about to go up in flames. Or was it just a case of nerves?

"I'm going to ask you again. How many ships do you have in your fleet?" The man sounded like he had run out of patience.

"I really don't know," I said, not thinking about what I was saying. "It depends how many ships survived the ambush."

"What ambush?" he asked.

I saw no reason to hide the whole truth, not anymore. "I told Doctorow that we helped evacuate Olympus Kri. What I did not tell him was that the Unified Authority attacked us after the evacuation. They caught us napping, and we lost some of our ships."

"So you came here looking for asylum?"

"I came here hoping to pull your worthless asses out of a fire," I said. Not the most politic response, but at least it was honest.

"That's what you told President Doctorow. He didn't believe you either," he said, picking up a clipboard, presumably looking over notes from the previous interrogations. "You told him that aliens have attacked two other planets, and they are coming here to kill us."

"I wouldn't worry about it," I said.

"You wouldn't?"

"You've got your head so far up your ass, the aliens might not notice you," I said.

He looked up from his clipboard and gave me a plastic

smile. He wanted to hit me, I could see it in his eyes. He stood, squared his shoulders, placed the clipboard on the table. "So you came here to warn us? To be honest with you, Harris, I always thought you were a coward. I still do.

"We lost every man and vehicle we sent out with you when you took on the aliens . . . every last man. Everybody died but you. You came waltzing out of it without a scratch."

Behind the interrogator, one of the guards moved his right hand along the grip of his gun. You need to be a very good shot to cover a target in a fistfight; otherwise, you're just as likely to shoot the man you are trying to protect.

"Are you saying I hid during the fight?" I asked, on the verge of laughing in the man's face.

"A lot of good men died trying to help you," the interrogator said. "One of them was my brother."

"O'Doul," I said, finally putting a name with the guy's face. "Your brother died saving me."

"What a mistake that was," he said.

I started to respond, then stopped. "If you don't want me on your planet, just say the word. I'll take my pilot and my shuttle and head home."

"It's too late for that, Harris. You should not have returned in the first place."

"Doctorow wants me off the planet, but he's not going to let me leave. Is that how things work on Terraneau now? Is he planning to kill me or just bury me in a jail cell?" I wondered how far Doctorow and his friends would go to protect their utopian society.

"Kill you?" the interrogator asked, sounding both shocked and amused. "Why would we kill you? You came to save us."

Another moment passed, then the battle began.

It started with an explosion that shook the building. The soundproof walls of the interrogation room muffled the blast, but the walls vibrated just the same. Alarms went off, but they sounded like they were a million miles away.

"What the speck?" the interrogator said. Now his guards drew their M27s. One of them aimed his gun at me while the other watched the door.

The electricity went out. I remembered the police station that the Double Y clone attacked on St. Augustine. This attack seemed to go by the same numbers. The lights went out, then emergency lights kicked in, casting their pale white glow. Through all of this, I remained in my chair. I did not know if this was the work of the Corps of Engineers or the last surviving Double Ys, but I did not want to give the guards a reason to shoot me.

The clock on the wall had frozen at 07:45.

I sat on the far side of the table, facing the door and the two armed guards. Had the table been loose, I might have kicked it toward them, but the table was bolted to the floor. I thought about leaping over it and trying to grab O'Doul, but what would it get me? In the end, I had no choice but to trust Mars and his engineers.

Thirty seconds after that initial explosion, the door of the interrogation room burst open, and in walked a giant of a man wearing custom-fitted combat armor, its green camouflage coloring looking taupe in the emergency lighting.

The screaming alarms tore into my thoughts. With the guards occupied, I shot over the table, knocking O'Doul out of his seat, and tackled the guard hiding behind the door. His armor protected him from punches, not grappling. I slammed into his chest, and we both hit the floor, me on the top and him on the bottom. I pinned his right hand down as he tried to raise his gun.

The giant in the specially fitted combat armor, he could only have been Ray Freeman, lifted the other guard in the air, slammed him against the wall so hard it must have knocked the fellow senseless, and slung him at O'Doul as if he were a sack of laundry. The guard and the interrogator lay there on the floor as Freeman drew his M27 and shot them both. Their blood looked black as oil in the dim light.

"You didn't need to kill them," I said, ignoring the fact that I had already snapped the second guard's neck. So there we were, Ray Freeman, the homicidal humanitarian, and me, killing the very people I had come to save. Was it murder? With the Avatari on the way, everyone on the planet was as good as dead.

"You're early," I said.

"The temperatures started jumping yesterday afternoon," Freeman answered.

"That's not supposed to happen yet," I said, taking the dead guard's M27 and following Freeman out of the room.

Water rained from burst mains along the ceiling. Inch-deep puddles had formed on the corridor floor. Light fixtures dangled from wires, and in the middle of the entropy, three guards lay dead where Freeman had shot them. Smoke or maybe steam or possibly exhaust wafted out of the vents along the wall. The air had a burned and dusty smell to it.

Someone peered from around a corner down the hall. In the brief glimpse I had, I saw that he was natural-born; so when he peered around the corner for a second glance, I shot him in the face. He fell to the ground, and his M27 clattered across the floor.

"What about Nobles?" I asked, as Freeman led the way.

"Who's that?"

Freeman was ruthless that way. The Marines lived by the code that no man gets left behind, but Ray Freeman was no Marine. He was a mercenary, his loyalty was selective.

"My pilot," I said as I turned and headed down the hall. A guard stepped out through an open door. I would have shot him, but Freeman got him first—three shots in the chest, and the man flew against the wall, then slumped to the floor; the water sprinkling from the ceiling washed some of his blood from the wall.

The locals must have dismissed Nobles as unimportant. I found him alone in his interrogation room, the door locked from the outside. I opened the door, and Nobles followed me out. Freeman led us out a back door and into an alley, where two Jackals waited. Freeman and I climbed in the first vehicle, and Nobles rode in the second. No one fired at us as we pulled away from the station. No one followed us.

The man driving the Jackal removed his helmet and turned to look at me. "How in God's good name can you stand this armor?" asked Mars. I recognized him by his badly dyed hair. "If these thigh plates dug any deeper in my crotch, I might end up a eunuch."

Freeman, sitting in the backseat with his feet behind my seat and his body behind Mars, removed his helmet as well.

The streets around us were still semisilent. I expected police cars and sirens, but the streets were almost empty of cars, and I saw very few pedestrians.

"Where is everybody?" I asked.

"The militia is busy stopping the invasion," Mars said.

"What invasion?" I asked, wondering if perhaps Doctorow had taken me seriously after all.

"The Enlisted Man's Navy just landed fifty transports outside Scott Card Park on the east side of town. Doctorow is evacuating Norristown."

"Why the hell would fifty transports land outside Scott Card Park?" I asked. The park was nothing but an open field.

Mars gave me a patient smile, and said, "They're ghosts, General. It's a fake. I hacked into the Terraneau tracking system last night. The transports are fakes, just like the additional fighter carriers."

"There's only one fighter carrier?" I asked, my spirits suddenly dropping.

Mars didn't notice. "Just the *Churchill*." He sounded cheerful as he pounded another coffin nail into my soul.

We sped over a viaduct, toward the southern edge of town; and again, I was struck by the emptiness of the road around us. Doctorow had risen to power during the Avatari occupation. If there was one skill the people had learned under his leadership, it was how to evacuate town efficiently. My real warning of an alien threat did not impress Doctorow enough to call for an evacuation, but Mars's phantom clones did the trick.

"What happens when they get to the park and find out it's empty?" I asked.

"That could take a while," he said.

"Why's that?" I asked.

"I left trackers," he said. "That park has never been so heavily guarded."

I had to laugh. He'd left the park in the hands of robots that consisted of nothing more than a motion-tracking sensor and an automated trigger finger.

But Mars was more of an engineer than he was a military strategist. Scott Card Park was a flat grassy field with a stream and a few shade trees. We would not have much time before the militia figured out that the invasion was a hoax.

We were halfway across town, and the second Jackal lagged a few hundred yards behind us. As it drove down the ramp at the end of the viaduct, I glanced back and wondered how long it would take Doctorow to figure out that Mars had outsmarted him.

As the second Jackal reached the bottom of the ramp, Mars said something softly into the radio. I did not catch what he said.

The voice on the other end gave a one-word response, "Clear."

Mars gave me a wicked smile, and asked, "Do you believe in burning bridges behind you?"

I turned in time to see the horizon go up in flames. At first I thought the crazy bastard had detonated the entire city, then I saw that he'd just blown up the bridge. He'd destroyed the viaduct that ran from the north end of town to the south. An enormous, twisting curtain of smoke, dust, and debris rose from the spot where the ten-mile-long bridge once stood.

"You just cut Norristown in half," I said.

"No one's hurt, no one's killed, and no one's going to follow us," Mars said. "Praise Jesus, God is good."

*And so are well-placed explosives,* I thought.

The cloud of smoke and dust settled, revealing sections of bridge that hung like severed limbs over battered city blocks.

"Mars, you missed your calling," I said. "You should have been in demolitions."

"Yeah, I know," he said, sounding extraordinarily cheery about his act of benevolent terrorism. "It's much more fun to bust them than to build them, but the Corps of Engineers giveth, and the Corps of Engineers taketh away." He laughed, and I could not help but smile. Freeman, on the other hand, kept his rifle out and his finger on the trigger.

I turned to him, and said, "Why the speck did you come here, Freeman?"

He didn't answer, but Mars did. "He was the one that got you out of jail."

"Stay out of this," I told Mars. "Freeman and I have a few issues we need straightened out."

I asked Freeman, "Whose specking side are you on? Are you working for the Unified Authority this time, or are you just out for yourself?"

Had my mind sped up or had time just slowed down? We

were in the Jackal driving through Norristown, but everything seemed silent and slow. The world around me seemed to disappear so that there was nothing left except for me and Ray Freeman. Even Mars had vanished.

"Somebody has to survive," Freeman said.

I saw agony in his generally emotionless face and understood. "Marianne?" I asked.

Ray shook his head.

"Caleb?"

Freeman did not answer, and by not doing so, he made the answer even more clear. Marianne was Ray's sister. Caleb was her son. They had lived in a Baptist colony on the edge of the Milky Way. As the Avatari began their invasion, the Navy moved the colony to New Copenhagen. They were still on New Copenhagen when the Avatari returned.

"Hill didn't tell me he was going to attack your ships," Freeman said. He did not say this by way of apology, just explanation. Millions of people were about to die; he did not have time to grieve over a few dead clones.

## CHAPTER
# FIFTY-EIGHT

"The temperature's been playing roulette for the last fourteen hours," Mars said, as we drove the slalom course leading to the Norris Lake tunnels.

Mars and his engineers had placed cars, trucks, Dumpsters, and heavy equipment along the road. Our sporty little Jackals had no problem threading the gaps between the barriers, but larger vehicles like tanks and troop carriers would need to go slow to get through. Once we made it through the obstacle course, Mars set off a pyrotechnical display that left the trucks, cars, and Dumpsters in flames. His engineers had rigged a masterful barrier.

Ahead of us, the twin tunnels rose from the waters of Lake Norris like a double-barreled shotgun. Mars drove the Jackal right up to the tunnel for northbound traffic, then came to a stop.

I climbed out. To my left was Lake Norris, an endless stretch of sparkling water. A bright sun hung high into the sky. Like Olympus Kri, Terraneau would have a radiant final day. Perhaps the tachyons caused clear weather; perhaps they needed clear weather to perform their work of death. All I knew was that the sky was clear, and a chilled, crisp breeze blew off Lake Norris. The wind cooled one side of my face, and the heat from the fires warmed the other. The breeze put a crease in the column of greasy black smoke that rose from the flames. Heat ripples hovered over the wreckage, and the flames looked especially orange.

I climbed back into the Jackal and powered up the radarscope. Mars, a sailor and engineer who had never seen ground fighting, asked, "What's that?"

"It's radar," I said.

On the scope, swarms of dots appeared. Some represented the burning barriers, some were in the air.

I looked back at Freeman, and said, "The home team's coming in at six o'clock." The militia would not need to drive across town to get to us; as long as they had pilots, they could fly here in transports. I'd left a small fleet of transports behind when I evacuated Fort Sebastian.

Transports were big and bulky, but unarmed. Had we left fighters behind, Tomcats or Harriers, they could have fired rockets at us from the air. They could, of course, ferry tanks and troops in those transports, but they would not be able to attack from the air.

Freeman pushed his way out of the Jackal, bringing with him his rifle and gear. He surveyed the three-lane entrance of the tunnel. The way his mind worked, he instantly spotted tactical advantages that most men would miss. He was clever and cunning; and though he had come to save lives, he would kill without mercy. With Doctorow in charge, the only lives that could be saved on Terraneau belonged to me and Mars and the Corps of Engineers.

The first transports appeared above the barriers. They flew

so slowly they looked like they would fall, hovering like bees as they passed over the fiery obstacle course. Mars watched them and chuckled, then asked, "Where do they think they're going to land?"

The only road leading to the front of the tunnels was blocked; and the tunnels rose out of the lake. There was no place to land behind them.

A transport passed over our heads, circled us in the air, then returned the way that it had come. Several more transports followed. I counted eight, but there might have been more. Each of those transports could carry one hundred troops, but they could also carry a tank or a combination of men and machinery.

I walked up beside Freeman as he geared up, attaching grenades to his armor and checking the clip in his rifle. "How long do you think we have?" I asked. "How long before the planet burns?"

Freeman shrugged his shoulders and continued loading bullets and grenades.

"Care to guess?" I asked.

"Maybe ten minutes, maybe ten hours," he said. Freeman was an agent of action who left prophecies and predictions to the likes of Arthur Breeze and William Sweetwater.

"I don't suppose you brought Sweetwater with you," I said.

"They're in a U.A. computer. The only way to talk to them is to have a capital ship nearby."

"But you had them with you when I met you on Olympus Kri . . ." I stopped myself in midsentence. Another piece suddenly fitted into the puzzle. "Their self-broadcasting spy ships . . . they had a cloaked ship orbiting Olympus Kri."

Freeman, of course, did not comment. Instead, he said, "We need to get into the tunnel. We can't get pinned down out here." As I left him, he was carrying equipment into the tunnel and preparing for a fight.

The differences between men. Freeman stood silent and subdued, all of his attention focused on the road as he waited for the militia to attack. I found Mars gabbing with a knot of about thirty engineers. They were in the tunnel, but no more than fifty feet from the entrance.

"Where are the rest of your men?" I asked. When I left Terraneau, Mars had one thousand engineers in his corps.

"In there, waiting for us." Mars pointed down the tunnel as he spoke.

"Do you have men guarding both tunnels?" I asked.

Mars shook his head. "We flooded the southbound tube."

I nodded, and said, "You better tuck your men in; the fighting is about to begin."

"What about the aliens?" he asked.

"One battle at a time," I said. "Freeman and I will slow the militia while you and your men dig in. After that, we'll work on the blast doors."

"Hear that, guys. It's time," Mars said. He sounded so damn cheerful that I thought he must have misunderstood me. His engineers scattered. Two of them climbed into a freight truck that was parked along one wall of the tunnel. As they started up the engine, Mars and a few of his engineers hopped into a Jackal.

The big truck headed out the tunnel, then cut a wide U-turn and squealed to a stop. It was so large it blocked out most of the sunlight. It also completely clogged two of the three lanes leading in from the city.

The engineers hopped out of the truck unscathed.

Moments later, huge metal doors pivoted out from the shadows along the walls and shut out the rest of the sunlight. The doors were perfectly fitted for the entrance. They were tall and thick, and they slid along rails, making no more noise than a bicycle riding on a flat paved road until they connected together with an earsplitting clang.

With the doors shut, the tunnel went as dark a closet. Just a narrow seam of daylight shone in around the edges of the doors. I turned and looked into the darkness. Far away, a Jackal moved slowly through the darkness, its racks of lights casting a blinding glare. And then the tunnel lights came on, shining down on the spider's web of scaffolding that ran along the walls.

When I did not see him immediately, I worried that we might have sealed Freeman outside the tunnel, but my worries proved unfounded. I spotted him working under the scaffolding, probably setting charges or some other defense.

One of the Jackals rolled up beside me, and Nobles hopped out. I said to him, "That flimsy door isn't going to keep anyone out," though I thought it might protect us from the pressure shift of a falling atmosphere.

"It's just supposed to slow them down," Mars said.

I kept my eyes on Freeman, watching him walk around the piping. He moved slowly, deliberately. I could not tell what he was doing.

*How ironic,* I thought. *Ray Freeman, out to save the universe.*

The first grenade exploded. The force of the explosion did not destroy the iron door, but the sound of the blast echoed inside the tunnel.

One of the engineers came to me, and shouted, "Your armor is in the back of the Jackal."

"No shit," I said. They'd brought me armor, I was touched.

A rocket struck the door, nearly blasting it off its rails. The deafening sound was followed by the sharp *tak tak* of bullets striking unyielding metal.

"It's in the turret," the man said.

I nodded and jogged to the back of the Jackal. The militia would break through in another moment. I needed armor and firepower. When I opened the door of the turret, I saw that Mars had used the space to stow a lot more than a set of armor and a handful of weapons. Two figures lay huddled on the floor, tied up and gagged.

I stared in at Ava, and she stared back at me. Her hands were bound behind her back, and someone had taped her mouth. Seeing me, she struggled and shifted her weight, mumbling incoherently all the while.

"Ava," I said. "I'm glad you're safe."

She mumbled something, twisting and turning and struggling to get free. I might have untied her, but I did not have time. The next rocket knocked one of the huge metal doors out of its tracks. With a deafening yawn, it fell, kicking up a blast of air that smelled of dust, oil, sulfur, and iron.

The man lying beside Ava screamed and struggled. There was no mistaking the look of terror in his eyes. In Ava's green eyes, I saw nothing but fury. As I grabbed my rucksack, Ava began babbling all the louder. She thrashed to get my attention as I removed the various sections of my armor from the bag. After laying out the armor, I gazed at the assortment of weapons Mars had brought me.

I leaned in, and said, "Well, Ava, nice seeing you again."

She brought up a foot and tried to stomp it on my face; but she was slow, and she telegraphed the kick. I dodged her foot, and said, "That wasn't very polite." As I closed the door to the turret, I could hear her kicking and shouting.

Freeman must have captured them, Ava and her new lover. Maybe it was Mars. I did not have time to think about it; but if I survived Terraneau, I would have a debt to repay.

It took me under a minute to strip out of my service uniform and step into my bodysuit. In another thirty seconds, my armor was in place.

"Mars, are you on?" I asked over the interLink.

"Sounds like it's getting hot out there," he said. That was an understatement. By that time, the other half of the door had caved in. A fusillade of militia bullets struck the jackknifed truck and dug into the walls and ceiling. Sunlight and bullets and the sound of explosions poured in through the tunnel entrance.

Retreating deep into the tunnel and hiding behind whatever protection the engineers had installed would be easy, the trick would be stalling the militia so that they did not have time to kick in the doors. We would not fight them, per se, so much as slow them down; but even that had to be timed just right. If we stalled too long, we might get ourselves cooked in the bargain.

"Get your men in deep," I told Mars. "Get settled in and get the doors ready."

Someone fired a grenade into the scaffolding where I had last seen Freeman. The grenade burst, sending smoke and flames and twisted pipes in every direction. My helmet deadened the sound, and my armor absorbed the percussion, giving the explosion a dreamlike feeling, and I felt no fear and realized that my combat reflex had already begun.

The militia fired automatic weapons along the walls, their bullets kicking up sparks as they struck steel pipes. "Freeman, where are you?" I asked over the interLink. As I checked for Freeman, I saw Lieutenant Nobles climb behind the wheel of the Jackal that carried Ava and her lover. He drove away.

Freeman answered my query with action instead of words. Three men tried to sprint from the entrance of the tunnel. Using his sniper rifle, Freeman picked them off.

I spotted him by following the angle of his rifle fire. He had taken cover behind a crane. "The engineers built a steel barrier a quarter mile in," he said in his low, ineffable voice. "We need to get back there."

A few of Mars's men tried to come back and help us; but they were engineers, not combat Marines. They crawled along the walls and froze when the gunfire erupted, and I told them to get back into the tunnel and guard the door. "Fall back," I shouted over the interLink on a frequency that every man could hear. They did not need to be told a second time.

Several guns opened fire. Shooting blindly into the tunnel, the militia leaders hoped to keep us pinned while some of their men tried to flank us. They made a mistake. They over-estimated our numbers. They must have thought there were dozens of us instead of two men hiding in the shadows along the wall. They fired toward the center of the tunnel, then they sent out six men who ducked low and sprinted for cover. Free-man picked them off, starting with the man in the rear and working his way forward. He hit them so quickly that the first four went down before last ones noticed.

A grenadier spotted Freeman. As he stepped out to fire an RPG, I picked him off with my M27.

"Where are you?" I asked Mars over a frequency that only he and Freeman would hear.

"We're dug in behind the next blast wall, about a quarter mile in," he said.

"Okay, we're going to try and work our way back to you."

"Your girlfriend escaped," Mars said.

"Shoot her if she gives you any trouble," I said. I wasn't joking.

The sound of a large engine caught my attention. The growl of the engine seemed to fill the tunnel, drowning out the gunfire. It became louder, then vanished under the thunder of a shell striking the jackknifed truck. The blast sent the truck skidding along the street, kicking up a trail of sparks as large as dandelions. A Targ Tank had entered the tunnel. Low to the ground and very fast-moving, Targ Tanks were the Jackal killers and troop displacers of the battlefield.

The tank fired a second shell into the truck, sending it into a slow roll. It crashed into a concrete barrier and smashed it to rubble. Still rolling, the truck rammed into a scaffolding platform and crushed it like a house of twigs. The tank headed toward a dark corner in which Freeman knelt behind a bulldozer.

I pulled my first grenade launcher, flipped the safety, and fired. Before the pill even hit, I'd chucked the first tube and pulled out a second. The first grenade hit home, striking the turret just behind its guns. The second shot caused the tank to skid sideways, crumpling the turret and bending the cannon so that it hung askew.

By that time, I had found a new hiding place. Rocket-propelled grenades were great for killing tanks, but they left a trail of fine smoke that stretched from your target to your front door. I had barely dug into my new spot, semisafe behind a concrete barrier, when Freeman said, "Harris, we're out of time. We have to get behind the wall."

Knowing that the militia would spot me the moment I left my new hiding place, I sprang from behind my barricade. I caught a quick glimpse of men pouring into the tunnel, then I began my sprint, thinking I might just survive this action. The militia would shoot at me, but they would not fire missiles. If they fired missiles, they might rupture the walls of the tunnel, and lake water would flood in.

"Mars, close the gates," I shouted over an open frequency. I knew Freeman would be listening.

"Where are you?"

"We're on our way," I said. By the time I said that, it was already a lie. We were both pinned down. The militia had spotted me. Bullets rang out and chipped at the ceiling and the walls of the tunnel.

Freeman fired off the charges I had seen him placing by the front of the tunnel and something amazing happened. Instead of triggering a massive explosion, the charges burst into a wall of flames that filled the tunnel from roof to floor in a solid sheet of fire. He triggered a second of those explosions, then a third.

The militia fired bullets through those flames, shooting blindly, not compensating for the downhill grade. Running just ahead of me, Freeman spun and set off one last explosion. I did not stop to watch the fireworks. I dashed ahead, making my way through the tunnel until I reached the front metal doors, where I did not so much stop as fall. Panting for air, I skidded behind a crane, then slid for cover. Freeman ran in beside me.

Mars and another engineer watched us from behind the door. I could see them; but I could not see if there was concern on their faces.

Bullets struck the heavy metal door; but this was shielded metal, and they might as well have been shooting spit wads for all the damage their bullets would do. The sound of the bullets was faint, a dull thud, then that stopped.

And then the event began.

A quarter of a mile deep in the tunnel, I did not hear or feel a thing; but when I looked back up the tunnel, I caught a brief glimpse of the glowing red sky, the color of lava or maybe molten metal. Anyone near the front of the tunnel was already ash; but this far in, with the lake distributing the heat, we were safe. There was plenty of cool air in the tunnel; and as long as we stayed behind the metal door, we'd be safe from the back-lash when the superheated atmosphere came down. Freeman and I dashed the last few yards and ducked behind the door. By that time, though, the shooting had stopped.

The last thing I saw as the engineers rammed the doors in place was a passel of militiamen lined up like stones in a cemetery. They stood facing toward the mouth of the tunnel, their backs bathed in shadow. Beyond them, I could see just a sliver of open sky in which the colors were all wrong, and the air itself seemed to have caught on fire.

They must have all seen what I saw before they sealed the doors. Ava, her courage spent and her strength gone, sat on the ground crying like a child. When her boyfriend tried to comfort her, she pushed him away. Mars's army of engineers stood silent. I lost track of Freeman.

It was crowded in the tunnel, Mars had a thousand men in his Corps of Engineers; but I think every soul in that tunnel went through the next dark hours feeling alone. Mars came to me and said something about Noah closing the doors of his ark. I heard the words, but I wasn't listening. I did not respond.

It would be like this all across the galaxy—running, warning, hiding, waiting. The Enlisted Man's Empire still had twenty-two planets. The thought of trying to rescue so many planets left me exhausted. The thought of failing left me hollow.

I needed to sleep.

I had come to rescue people, and now I wanted to escape from the few people I had actually managed to save. No one paid attention to me as I pushed through the ranks of engineers, slowly walking deeper into the tunnel. I removed my helmet. The air was still and cool. It was musty and smelled of iron. I tasted ash in the air, but that might have been my imagination. I could not tell.

Deep in the tunnel I spotted the shuttle, parked under a flickering light that only illuminated its nose. Nobles sat inside the cockpit doing what he always did when he was nervous, checking instruments, running tests, distracting himself. I watched him, not really paying attention as I stared in his direction.

I had no idea how much time passed.

Ava found me. She planted herself in front of me and stared into my eyes until I looked back at her, then she pressed herself against me. I think she wanted me to hold her, but I felt nothing for her at that moment. I had come all this way because I loved her. There was a time when every man, woman, and child on the planet could have died, and I would have considered my mission a success because I had rescued Ava. Now she stood before me, wanting me to make her feel safe, and I would not even wrap my armor-plated arms around her.

"They're all dead?" she asked.

I said nothing.

"Could you have stopped this?"

"No," I said.

"Hold me," she said, and she pressed the side of her face against the cold and hardened plate that covered my heart. She locked her arms around me the way a frightened little girl might lock her arms around her father. I let her hold me, but I did not put my arms around her. After a moment, I stepped away.

"Don't leave me, Wayson," she said; but she was too late, I already had.

Later, I had no idea how much later, we heard the thud of the atmosphere crashing back into place. Some men moaned, and other men shouted, but the impact was not especially loud.

Freeman found me, and said in a soft voice, "We're going to open the shield." He stood behind me. I could not see him, but I could feel his presence.

As I followed him toward the shield, I saw Ava begin to sob. I watched her fall to her knees, and I felt no desire to comfort her.

I placed my helmet over my head as I followed Freeman toward the front of the tunnel. Holding our guns ready, we waited as the engineers pulled back the doors, revealing a scene I'd seen too many times before—the aftermath.

The tunnel was intact, but its contents were in tatters. Men lay like puzzle pieces across the concrete. The heat had not penetrated that far into the tunnel, but the pressure from the atmosphere had. There was blood on the ground and on the walls. Two overturned jeeps sat in a pile. I took my first tentative steps from behind the steel doors and stopped.

Not all of the men were dead. A half dozen militiamen sat huddled along one wall of the tunnel. They had blood on their faces and bloodstained clothes and blood in their hair, and they looked stunned as they sat and moaned. I stepped over a body and saw blood running out the man's ear.

"Maybe the medics on the *Churchill* can save them," Freeman said.

The *Churchill* was a fighter carrier, it would certainly have beds and medicine. "Do you mean *save* them or *fix* them?" I asked.

Freeman said nothing.

Walking just outside the door, I found two more pockets of survivors. Three men sat beside each other, they were silent and still. As I approached them, one looked up into my visor, and asked, "Is it over?" He yelled the words. The heat hadn't reached these men; when the atmosphere dropped back in place, the pressure it created obliterated their eardrums.

But it wasn't physical pain that left them numb. They had lost everything and everyone that meant anything to them.

"Harris, come here," Mars called over the interLink.

He stood in a little clearing. I went to join him.

Not far from Mars, a single body rested against a wall. The Right Reverend Colonel Ellery Doctorow, president of Terraneau, sat with his finger still around the trigger of the gun he had used to kill himself. His head had shattered like a melon tossed from a tall building, but I recognized his tailored suit just the same. The jolt of recognition did not include sympathy; I felt nothing but disgust for this man whose high ideals and sense of self-importance had cremated an entire population. How many millions had he killed with his visions of moral superiority simply because he did not trust any authority other than his own?

I came up beside Mars, who was dressed in his engineering armor. He stared down at Doctorow. I had no idea what he felt; but I thought his feelings toward Doctorow might not be any kinder than my own.

"General, should we take your shuttle out?" he asked after several seconds passed. They really were magicians, Lieutenant Mars and his engineers. They saved ships, built bridges, dug tunnels, and resurrected the left-for-dead.

"Give it a few more minutes," I said, remembering the tests Freeman had run on Olympus Kri. "Let's let the dust settle."

Outside the tunnel, the sky would be filled with soot and steam and smoke. The final dregs of Tachyon D would still be dangerous as they traveled their circuits like angels of death.

Mars did not leave. He stood there, beside me, staring down at Doctorow's lifeless remains. He did not speak for several seconds. I could not see his face through his helmet, but I could imagine his expression. He was new to this kind of war. The first time you see the bodies and the blood and the waste, the muscles in your face go numb and your mind goes numb and you feel as if you are no more alive than the men lying on the ground.

"What about the other planets?" Mars asked. "Is it going to be like this? Can we save them?"

I took a deep breath, held it in my lungs until I felt them searing; and even then, I still did not exhale. I thought about the Unified Authority, its leaders waiting for another chance to betray us, and the Avatari traveling from planet to planet, burning entire worlds.

"We can't save them all," I said, but I would try just the same. Staring down at Doctorow, I realized that the only time I appreciated the value of life was when I saw it spent and wasted.

Earthdate: November 17, A.D. 2517
Location: Solar System A-361
Astronomic Position: Bode's Galaxy (M81)

"Takahashi-san, what are we doing out here?" asked Yokoi
Shigeru, the least Japanese of the four ship's captains.

Takahashi Hironobu, captain of the self-broadcasting battleship *Sakura*, took the question at face value and dismissed
it as the kind of stupid talk men make after too much sake.
"We're here to track down the aliens and to protect our home
planet," he said. Even as he said it, he knew it was more slogan
than answer.

Takeda Gumpei, the captain of the *Yamato*, accepted the
patriotic answer as an excuse to toss another bowl of sake.
*"Kanpai!"* he yelled, then he flipped the inch-round bowl
with so much force that the well-aimed rice wine sailed over
his tongue and down his throat.

*"Kanpai."* The rest of the ship's captains echoed his toast
with limited enthusiasm. Takeda could keep drinking long
after most men would pass out on the floor.

"No, Takahashi-san," Yokoi said, "you misunderstand me.
I asked what we are doing, not what we came to do. We came
to kill the alien invaders. We have been here a long time. In
another few months, we will have been on this mission for
three years. Have we killed any aliens? Have we seen any
aliens?"

As Yokoi spoke, a waitress in a pink-and-white kimono
came to the table to deliver another bottle of sake. The waitress's kimono, the tiny finger bowls from which they drank,

the knee-high table, and the tatami mats on which the four captains sat were neither practical nor comfortable, but they were tradition. So much of what they did in the Japanese Fleet was based on the ancient traditions that defined the Japanese. Even in Bode's Galaxy, eleven million light-years from Earth, they sat on the floor and drank rice wine from cups shaped like mustard bowls because their ancestors had sat on tatami mats, made wine out of rice which they drank from tiny ceramic cups.

Takahashi could tell that Yokoi was drunk. His words came out in a mishmash of Japanese and English. It was time for him to return to his ship and sober up, but telling him so would go against tradition. Japanese men did not criticize each other for getting drunk.

"It's a big galaxy," Takahashi said. "Who knows where the aliens are hiding."

For Takeda, the size of the galaxy was yet another reason for a toast. He yelled, *"Kanpai!"* and the rest of the captains had to follow. They murmured, *"Kanpai,"* and Takeda tossed his drink back and swallowed it in one fluid motion. The others brought their cups to their mouths, not sure if they would drink or drown.

By that time, Yokoi, the youngest and smallest officer of the four, was so drunk he could no longer support himself. He rested his chest and head on the table. His right arm was extended beyond his head, bent at the elbow, so he could hold his sake cup above his head. The next time he drank, he would raise his mouth to the cup instead of the other way around.

The waitress came with another bottle of sake, gave the captains a polite bow, and backed away.

"Three years? Has it really been three years?" asked Miyamoto Genyo, the captain of the *Onoda*. The oldest and most stoic of the officers, Miyamoto allowed the others to drink and chat while he watched with a disapproving scowl.

Yokoi, not bothering to lift his head off the table, swiveled around so that he faced Miyamoto, and said, "We left in February 2515."

"So we did," said Miyamoto. He was not drunk. He sat with his back straight and his head held high. He had white hair around his ears and temples, and he packed a few extra pounds; but Miyamoto Genyo was a prime example of the aging generation. He lived the codes of loyalty, honor, and tradition.

"Perhaps we are wasting our time," he conceded. Coming from an old warrior like Miyamoto, that comment was tantamount to mutiny. Men of his generation endured any inconvenience in stony silence when it involved the honor the fleet.

*Did I stop at seven bowls or eight?* Takahashi asked himself when the call came in the next morning. It came at 06:00, and he was still lying facedown on his futon.

"Takahashi," he said, trying to sound more alert than he felt.

"Captain, sir, one of the SEALs is waiting for you outside your office."

Hearing this, Takahashi groaned. His head hurt, he felt tired, and he did not want to see a SEAL clone, not when he was already feeling sick. "On my way," he said.

"Should I tell him you may be a minute?"

"Let him wait," Takahashi said, and signed off.

He remained on the futon, facedown, for another minute, then climbed out of bed, stretched, and washed his face. He moved slowly, hating Captain Takeda for making all of those toasts and hating himself for not leaving early.

In truth, Takahashi saw no reason to stay sober. On this mission, every day was just like the one before. They had been out nearly three years, but to him it seemed more like three decades.

He put on his uniform and tried to walk upright as he made his way to the bridge.

Even after three years, his crew still flinched when the SEALs entered the bridge. The SEALs never threatened anyone. They conducted themselves in a manner befitting officers; but they were so damnably ugly, just the sight of them hurt Takahashi's head.

Before leaving on this mission, Takahashi had met with Admiral Brocius of the Unified Authority to warn him that the SEAL clones would never fit in on a Japanese ship. "They are too strange, too different. They do not belong among the Shin Nippon."

Brocius listened to everything he had to say, and answered, "You're going to need them."

Now, three years into the mission, the SEALs were useless cargo, and everybody knew it—twelve thousand trained killers with no one to kill.

The leader of the SEALs was Master Chief Petty Officer Emerson Illych. Like the rest of his men, he stood a scant five feet and two inches tall and weighed less than 150 pounds. His physique reminded Takahashi of the twelve-year-old son he had left back on Earth.

Everyone was scared of the SEALs even though they behaved themselves. Captain Miyamoto described Illych as having "the heart of a Samurai and the face of a Chinese dragon."

The description fit. Illych's nose turned up so far that it looked like a snout. His head was completely bald, devoid of whiskers and eyebrows. The bony ridge that ran above his tiny dark eyes was thick and sharp. And his skin . . . his skin was leathery with a dark gray tint. It did not look like it belonged on a living human.

Illych stood at ease just outside Takahashi's office door, as if stationed there to guard it. When he saw the captain cross the bridge, he snapped to attention.

Takahashi returned the SEAL's salute without looking at him. Along with revulsion, Takahashi felt a stab of pity for the SEAL and his facial deformity.

"What can I do for you, Master Chief?" Takahashi asked, holding the office door for him to enter.

"Captain, I received orders to report to your office," he said in English. Japanese sailors spoke English and Japanese, the SEALs only spoke English.

"I didn't send for you," Takahashi said, not wanting to admit that he had still been asleep until a few minutes earlier.

Several messages flashed on his computer screen, including an urgent message from Admiral Yoshi Yamashiro, the highest-ranking officer in the Japanese Fleet.

Takahashi opened the message and read it.

"Well, it appears we are about to receive some important guests," he told Illych. "Admiral Yamashiro is coming."

And so they waited for the other officers to arrive.

Yokoi Shigeru, captain of the *Kyoto*, arrived first, looking pale and stiff, and sickly. He handled hangovers about as well as he handled being drunk. He managed to croak out a question, "Why are you holding a meeting at 06:30?"

"You're going to need to ask Admiral Yamashiro," Takahashi said.

"Oh," said the freshly sobered Yokoi.

He did not even notice Master Chief Illych until after he sat down. He dropped into a chair, looked over, and started. "Master Chief, I am so sorry. I did not notice you when I came in."

Illych smiled and said nothing.

The three of them sat in silence for several minutes. Finally, Yokoi returned to his rant from the night before. He leaned toward the SEAL clone, and said, "It's been three years, Master Chief, do you ever worry that we will not find the aliens?"

"No, sir," Illych said. It was part of the SEAL persona. They never initiated conversations with outsiders. When outsiders asked them questions, they kept their answers brief.

"You never feel discouraged?" Yokoi asked.

"No, sir," said Illych.

Yokoi turned to Takahashi and spoke in Japanese. He asked, "Do you think they like women?"

Takahashi responded in Japanese, "With a face like his, perhaps he likes bats."

Illych sat content, staring straight ahead and ignoring the conversation. He sat with his legs crossed, his talonlike fingers clasped over one of his knees.

"Maybe the Unified Authority has a program for cloning blind prostitutes," Yokoi said.

Both officers laughed.

Austere old Miyamoto Genyo was the next officer to arrive. He stepped in the door, and the joking came to an end.

Miyamoto was the captain of the *Onoda*. When asked to christen his ship, Miyamoto named it after the final hero of the Second World War—Second Lieutenant Hiroo Onoda, who spent twenty-nine years hiding in a jungle because he refused to believe that Japan had surrendered. He would have remained in hiding until he died, but the government sent his former commanding officer into the jungle to tell him to go home.

Around the fleet, many people believed that the story would have been different had it been Miyamoto Genyo hiding in that jungle. Miyamoto would have hidden for twenty-nine years, just like Onoda; but when the retired commanding officer came to tell him the war was over, Miyamoto would have shot him for treason.

Last to arrive at the meeting were Takeda Gumpei, captain of the *Yamato*, and Admiral Yamashiro himself. They arrived together, talking like old friends. The hard-drinking, life-loving Takeda was Admiral Yamashiro's favorite, and the other captains loathed him for it.

Admiral Yamashiro only gave these briefings when he had particularly bad news. For the last three years, all of the news had been bad.

Bode's Galaxy had millions if not billions of solar systems. The fleet was prepared to search each system for the aliens. Every time they traveled to a new solar system, they discovered it was dark, "dark" meaning the sun had been expanded and killed. "Dark" meaning one of the planets in the solar system had been mined by the aliens and that there was no life left on that planet.

"We have located a new solar system," Yamashiro began. "It has a living sun.

"Gentlemen, our invasion is about to begin."

Penning my author's notes is one of my favorite parts of the book-writing process because it gives me a chance to create a snapshot of my work. Snapshots are interesting anomalies. They do not explain the past or give a hint of what lies ahead; they simply describe the moment. Look at a photograph of John F. Kennedy stepping off the plane in Dallas, and you see a young, handsome politician with a promising future. There is nothing to indicate that tragedy looms ahead.

Today is Thursday, March 25, 2010. I have just completed the first round of revisions of *The Clone Empire*. You, looking backward in time, are holding the book that from my perspective must still undergo another round of revisions.

I finished my rewrite at 7:23 P.M. and plan to go to sleep early this evening as I will begin work on a young-adult novel early tomorrow morning. I am also nearly halfway through the first draft of *The Clone Redemption*, book seven in the Wayson Harris saga.

And there is more good news. Chris and Ed, two of my closest friends, are getting married in a few days. I am traveling to attend their wedding. Two days after I come home from the wedding, I will fly to Hawaii to teach at a college. I will return home in June, just in time for my daughter's high-school graduation.

Needless to say, it's been a long time since we've seen so much excitement around the Kent household.

So, a few words about the writing of *The Clone Empire*, the novel I am just now putting to bed.

It is fitting that the first Double Y clone to speak in this book bears the name Kit Lewis, because in a very real way, the Double Y clones were his idea. The real Kit Lewis is one of the regulars on my Sad Sam's Palace website. As I was writing *The Clone Betrayal*, he wrote in to ask if perhaps the reason Wayson Harris was so tough was because the scientists who created Liberators used two Y chromosomes instead of an X and a Y.

The idea had never occurred to me, but I liked it. And so, as my way of saying thank you, I had Harris beat Kit's literary effigy to mush, then I had Ray Freeman shoot him in the head, then I had him frozen, stripped, and autopsied.

Thanks, Kit. No good deed goes unpunished, eh.

I have other people I need to thank as well. As always, the lovely and talented Anne at Ace made all the difference with this book. When I first submitted *The Clone Empire*, I wrote the epilogue from the point of view of Captain Hironobu Takahashi. All of my test readers loved the concept once I explained it to them; but that was only after they asked, "Why is Harris going by the name Takahashi?"

Since the rest of the book was told from Wayson's perspective, switching heads created confusion. Anne found a solution, of course. Tell the epilogue from the third-person perspective. Duh!

The lovely and talented Rachel Johnson also helped with this novel. She always does; and, as always, I appreciate her help.

As of this snapshot, this will be the penultimate installment in the Harris saga. I am eternally grateful to the kind folks at Ace Books for publishing my novels; and I am equally grateful to you for reading them.

Steven L. Kent